"In *A Darkly Hidden Truth*, Donna Fletcher Crow creates a world in which the events of past centuries echo down present-day hallways—a world in which saintliness and devotion compete with the noise of traffic, a world in which a thoroughly 21st-century young woman can be drawn to the timeless and luminous peace of the convent—and then, on the surface of this world, she engraves murder, violence, and theft. I came away from the book feeling as though I'd been someplace both ancient and new, and had learned a great deal there. Donna Fletcher Crow gives us, in three extremely persuasive dimensions, the world that Dan Brown merely sketches."

– **Timothy Hallinan**, Edgar-nominated author of *The Queen of Patpong*

"Donna Fletcher Crow's novel, *A Darkly Hidden Truth* is a character-rich contemporary mystery based on English church history that made me want to turn every page, and spend a year in England."

– **Sally Wright**, author of the *Ben Reese Mysteries*

"A gripping modern mystery enriched by liturgy, iconography, and medieval history."

– **Donn Taylor**, author of *Rhapsody in Red*, *The Lazarus File*, etc.

"The intrepid Felicity and lovable Anthony have their noses to the trail of more dark and sinister goings-on. As they investigate, a tale wonderfully rich in history and spirituality unfolds."

– **Penelope Wilcock**, author of *The Hawk and the Dove*

"Donna Fletcher Crow's Monastery Murders series gets better and better. In a book notable for its meticulous research, Felicity is at a crossroads in her life. She has a vocation to the religious life, but where does that leave Antony, who has come to love the young, engaging American? Matters are further complicated when Felicity's mother, Cynthia, fresh from the break-up of her marriage to Felicity's much-loved father, arrives in England, attempting to forge new bonds with the daughter she never really knew. Matters come to a head when a valuable icon is stolen and a student murdered.

"A sound grasp of Christian history informs this contemporary thriller as Felicity, Anthony and Cynthia are plunged headlong into the dangerous hunt for the stolen icon."

– **Dolores Gordon-Smith**, author of the *Jack Haldean Mysteries*

"Readers who enjoyed *A Very Private Grave*, the first in Donna Fletcher Crow's Monastery Murders, will be delighted with the second in the series. With this book, Crow establishes herself as the leading practitioner of modern mystery entwined with historical fiction … Her descriptions of the English characters read like an updated and edgy version of Barbara Pym. *A Darkly Hidden Truth* weaves ancient puzzles and modern murder with a savvy but sometimes unwary protagonist into a seamless story. You won't need a bookmark – you'll read it in a single sitting."

– **Mike Orenduff**, author of *The Pot Thief Who Studied Pythagoras*

A DARKLY
HIDDEN TRUTH

THE MONASTERY MURDERS 2

Donna Fletcher Crow

MONARCH
BOOKS
Oxford, UK, & Grand Rapids, Michigan, USA

First published in the UK in 2011 by Monarch Books
(a publishing imprint of Lion Hudson plc)
Wilkinson House, Jordan Hill Road, Oxford OX2 8DR, England
Tel: +44 (0)1865 302750 Fax: +44 (0)1865 302757
Email: monarch@lionhudson.com
www.lionhudson.com

ISBN 978 0 85721 050 0 (print)
ISBN 978 0 85721 052 4 (epub)
ISBN 978 0 85721 051 7 (Kindle)
ISBN 978 0 85721 209 2 (PDF)

Distributed by:
UK: Marston Book Services, PO Box 269, Abingdon, Oxon, OX14 4YN
USA: Kregel Publications, PO Box 2607, Grand Rapids, Michigan 49501

The text paper used in this book has been made from wood independently certified as having come from sustainable forests.

British Library Cataloguing Data
A catalogue record for this book is available from the British Library.

Printed and bound in the UK by MPG Books.

God of compassion,
Whose Son Jesus Christ, the child of Mary,
shared the life of a home in Nazareth
and on the cross drew the whole human family to himself:
strengthen us in our daily living
that in joy and sorrow
we may know the power of your presence
to bind together and to heal;
through Jesus Christ your Son our Lord
who is alive and reigns with you,
in the unity of the Holy Spirit,
one God now and for ever

BOOK OF COMMON PRAYER, COLLECT FOR MOTHERING SUNDAY

With endless gratitude
To my gracious editor
Jan Greenough

Acknowledgments

The question I am asked most often is, "How much of it is true?" Since I try never to write about any place I haven't visited, or describe any experience I haven't had—except the murders and other nefarious doings, of course—it's all as true as I can make it. As far as things have been recorded. Where the history books end, the novelist's job starts. Dame Julian's words are almost all her own, as are Margery Kempe's. Robert Spryngold was, indeed, Margery's confessor, but if his successor wrote his memoirs the manuscript is still lying concealed in a cupboard somewhere.

One of my goals as a writer is to give my readers a "you are there" experience by making every scene in my books as accurate as I possibly can. To that end I am enormously grateful to everyone who hosted me and helped with my research endeavors: Hazel Flavell and Nancy Sawyer, my friends and helpers in England through twenty-five years of researching and writing; Father Lee Kenyon for his unending patience in sharing his detailed, in-depth knowledge of all things liturgical; Sir Richard Temple of the Temple Gallery; Father Philip North, Priest Administrator of the Shrine of Our Lady of Walsingham; Sister Mary Luke Wise, Mother Superior, Community of the Holy Cross, Rempstone; Sister Pamela, All Hallows House, Norwich; Sister Anita, Mother Superior, Community of the Sisters of the Church, Ham Common, London; All of the brethren at the Community of the Resurrection, Mirfield, Yorkshire.

You can see pictures from my research trips at: http://www.donnafletchercrow.com/joinTheJourney.php

TIME LINE

AD

1023 Knights Hospitaller formed

1061 Shrine of Our Lady of Walsingham established

1119 Templars formed

1307 Templars disbanded

1375 Julian of Norwich enclosed

1417 Margery Kempe visits Julian

1698 Peter the Great visits England

1931 Walsingham shrine re-established

Glossary

Alb: A vestment of white linen, reaching to the feet and enveloping the person.

Anchoress: One who renounces the world and secludes herself for religious reasons.

***Ancren Riwle*:** Manual for anchoresses written in the early thirteenth century.

Baldacchino: A structure in the form of a canopy above an altar.

Caesura: A metrical break, commonly near the middle of the line.

Cassock: A garment resembling a long frock coat worn by traditional clergy as an outer garment.

Ciborium: The coffer in which the host is kept.

Cope: An ecclesiastical vestment or cloak, semicircular in form, reaching from the shoulders nearly to the feet, open in front except for a band or clasp, worn in processions and on other liturgical occasions.

Exultet: An ancient hymn blessing the Paschal candle sung at the Easter Vigil.

Humeral veil: A long, narrow scarf worn round the shoulders by the officiating priest used to protect the sacred vessels from contact with the hands.

Mensa: Top surface of an altar, usually stone.

Muniment room: Room where documents such as deeds and charters are kept.

Novice: One who enters a religious house as a probationer.

Ordinand: One studying for ordination.

Parament: Ornamental hanging, such as altar cloth.

Parapet: A low wall serving to protect the edge of a platform or roof.

Paschal candle: Large, white decorated candle blessed and newly lit every year at the Easter Vigil.

Postulant: A candidate for membership in a religious order.

Precentor: A leader of a choir, spoken or sung; one who leads first in antiphonal reading.

Reredos: A shelf or partition behind an altar, usually holding candles, cross, or flowers.

Rood screen: a screen, between the choir and the body of the church, over which the rood (crucifix) was placed.

Sacramentary: An ancient book giving the rites for Mass, the sacraments and other ceremonies.

Sacristan: One who has the care of the utensils, vestments and movables of the church.

Sacristy: A room in a church where the sacred vessels, vestments, etc. are kept.

Thurible: A metal censer for burning incense, held suspended by chains.

Thurifer: A server who carries a thurible.

Triduum: The three Great Days leading up to Easter.

Votary: One devoted, consecrated, or engaged by a vow or promise.

Prologue

C. the year of our Lord 1375
Church of St Julian the Hospitaller, Norwich

"Veni sanctificator, omnipotens aeterne Deus..." *The words of the Mass of the Dead echoed from the flint walls of the old church. Dorcas clenched her fists. St Julian's Church. The church where her daughter would be "buried". The church which would become her daughter's tomb. And her daughter's name.*

The bishop, sprinkling ashes in her wake, attended "Julian" to her immurement. "Do not weep for the dead, do not mourn them with tears. For if we believe that Jesus died and rose again, God will bring forth with him all who have fallen asleep believing in him."

The serene young woman stood at the altar in only her shift. Two black-robed Benedictine nuns from the Community at Carrow Abbey, about half a mile down the road, clothed her in a grey gown and white veil.

How many times could a mother die? Dorcas felt her heart constrict, saw the darkness closing in around her. And yet it was not herself, but her daughter there at the front of the church in the pale grey gown. It was her dearest Gillian over whom the priest prayed. But Gillian was not dead. Dorcas had never seen her daughter more alive.

Following the processional cross carried by an acolyte, and accompanied by chanted psalms and litanies, the procession moved out of the chancel and around the church to a small apartment built against the side of the building. The cell was blessed, the newly professed woman sprinkled with holy water and censed, and then the bishop invited her to enter her tomb. Her face aglow, "Julian" kissed her mother, embraced her sister, and entered. Dead to the world. Alive only to God.

"Let them block up the entrance to the house," the bishop declared. The stonemasons began their work.

It had all happened once before. Once before her daughter had been pronounced dead. But that time she had returned to life. This time she would not return.

So what was left for Dorcas? Why couldn't she die, too? She fought against the hardness in her heart. Once she had been totally yielded to the divine will. At least she had believed she was. When Gillian lay dying, Dorcas had prayed first for her daughter's life, then for the eternal repose of her soul, for it's eventual glorious entry into heaven.

Now, when Gilly would be living, by her own choice, within the same city walls, why was this yielding so much harder? Why could Dorcas not even pray to be made willing to be willing?

As the grating of the stonemason's trowel ground in her ears, everyone around Dorcas turned to her with their congratulations. "What a fine thing for Norwich." "How proud you must be of your daughter." "Such a privilege to be the mother of an anchoress." Her daughter would live the rest of her life sealed in this tiny structure built onto the side of the church, and she was expected to celebrate? "A great day for your family." "A great day for all of us."

The rejoicing continued. Why wouldn't it? Of course it was a great thing for Norwich. It was a matter of much prestige for a town to have their own anchoress. People traveled from all over England — even from the continent— to visit such famous holy men and women. It was a fine thing for the innkeepers, merchants, and the churches. But did anyone ever think of a mother who was required to stand by and see her beloved child so sealed?

"Holy Mary, Mother of God, pray for me." And as Dorcas spoke those words, the understanding came. Simeon had warned Mary that a sword would pierce through her own soul. Now Dorcas knew: that warning was not just for Mary. It was for all mothers. It wasn't possible to love as intensely as a mother loves without experiencing that sword in her own heart. Dorcas pressed a hand to her breast to still the sharpness of the ache.

Chapter 1

Felicity could hear her heart thudding in her ears as Father Oswin smiled in his slow, thoughtful way and steepled his fingers into a Gothic arch. "And how long have you been feeling this drawing to become a nun?"

Felicity's swallow was more of a gulp. It all sounded so audacious. It was so unlike her. Fighting a sudden impulse to run from the room, she managed to squeak out in a small voice, "Well, for several weeks now." *Was almost two "several"?*

Father Oswin nodded slowly and thoughtfully, as he did everything. At least he didn't burst out laughing. "I see."

"But the thing is," Felicity was quite certain he *didn't* see. "The thing is, it's so intense. I can't eat. I can't sleep. It's been growing and growing." She placed her hand over her heart in the region of the growing feeling—compulsion, she might even say.

"Yes."

Was there ever a more infuriating spiritual director than Father Oswin? Felicity felt so full of exuberance, of desire for action, of nervous tension, it was all she could do to make herself stay seated in her chair while the man sitting across from her in the small confessional room sat so deep in meditation he could be in danger of drifting off to sleep. *What should I do?* she wanted to yell at him.

"Yes. I see." At long last the monk opened his hands and raised his head. "Yes." He nodded slowly, giving the word at least three syllables. "Then you must test the Spirit."

"Great! Er—how do I do that?" Ever since she had come

to study in the theological college run by the Community of the Transfiguration on its remote hillside in Yorkshire many months ago Felicity had experienced almost constant friction between their slow, understated pace of life and her out-to-conquer-the-world American energies, but she had never felt the conflict so sharply before. Nor had her urgency for action been so great. "What do I *do*?" She pulled out a notebook to jot down his instructions.

"How much time have you spent in a convent?"

"Um, well, I was at Whitby—Order of the Holy Paraclete—when Father Antony and I were looking for Dominic's murderer... When Sister Elspeth..." Felicity stopped with a shudder.

"Yes, terrible business that. Tragic loss." Father Oswin shook his head. "Hardly a good time for testing a vocation, I would say."

The tiny room fell silent as Felicity's mind replayed those all-too-recent events of chasing and being chased across half of northern England with her Church History lecturer, of how her own rashness had led her so far astray, of the penitence she felt for her guilt in the tragic events. And yet, surely good could come even from that. If she were to become a nun herself, perhaps even in some small way fill the enormous gap left by Sister Elspeth's energy and scholarship and holiness...

"Perhaps you should revisit the sisters there? Or perhaps look around a bit: Rempstone near Nottingham, All Hallows House in Norwich..." Walsingham, Oxford, Burford, the list went on. Who would have thought there were so many convents in England? "The sisters in Ham Common do a wonderful work among the poor, but London might be a bit far afield." Felicity scribbled as he rattled off the unfamiliar names. "Select two or three for a mini retreat. That should give you some perspective as to what you might be undertaking if you were to pursue a discernment process."

Discernment process? Couldn't she just go off to a convent and take the veil? That's what women did in books. Maid Marian, in Robin Hood, for example. Yes, Marian's convent was supposed to be around here somewhere. The Nun, a pub on the main road behind the Community, was said to mark the spot.

"Of course, you understand, it can take years to test a vocation," Father Oswin's steady voice brought her back. "It's very important not to rush. Let the Spirit lead you one step at a time. Stay in constant tune with him through prayer."

Felicity sighed. She should have known.

"No snap decisions," he added.

Felicity nodded, even as she argued internally. *But that's how I make all my decisions,* she almost blurted it out. And it was the truth—for better or for worse—that was how she always made her decisions. Fast! Just a year ago she had been teaching Latin in a C of E school in London, and hating it. When Rebecca, the vicar of the church sponsoring the school, reminded her that the church was one place Latin was still used and told her about the College of the Transfiguration, it immediately fired her imagination, and here she was—just like that— living through the most momentous year of her life.

Well, OK, not just like that. There was a lot more to it than that. Although her family was far from devout, she had always loved the services she was taken to at Christmas and Easter: the prayers, the music, the altar cloths shimmering in candlelight, the banks of flowers, and then, working with Antony in the past weeks—seeing true dedication up close and personal—after she got over her irritation with him, that is…

Father Oswin brought her back to the present. "I don't know what your class schedule is like just now. Perhaps you have some time off before Easter, if you're thinking of starting right away?"

Felicity nodded. So he did sense her urgency.

"You won't be likely to find space in any of the houses during Holy Week and, of course, you'll want to be here then anyway."

Holy Week. Yes, just over two weeks away. How she looked forward to that. Time to spend immersed in silence, in worship, in holy contemplation. She smiled at herself. If it hadn't been for Father Oswin's presence, she would have laughed out loud. If she had been told a month ago she would have had such thoughts, she would have declared that the speaker had taken leave of his senses. Now perhaps she was the one who had gone bonkers. Felicity Howard, the all-American girl, sure of herself, goal-driven, out to set the world on fire, to right all wrong—after all, that was what the priesthood was all about, wasn't it? Especially for a woman priest.

And then, in the space of a few life-threatening—and life-changing—days, she had encountered true faithfulness in the man she had thought capable of murder. Now she must rethink her whole life. It still galled. She had been *so sure*.

"Don't rush it. Give the Spirit time to reveal his ways to you." Father Oswin's words recalled her once more.

"What? Oh, yes. Yes, thank you, Father. Yes, Holy Week. I am looking forward to that. Everyone says it's an amazing experience." In the tumult of her mercurial emotions she smiled at herself once more. Fifty-some services in one week, most of it spent in silence—and she was looking forward to *that*? She truly must have gone round the twist, as the old Felicity would certainly have told her.

"Was there anything else you wanted to talk about?"

The length of her pause was telltale, but Father Oswin wouldn't probe even if he knew she was holding back. How could she discuss something she couldn't even put into words to herself? And what if she was wrong? After all, it wasn't really her problem until—*if*—Antony actually said something. Was it?

And besides, he had said he was considering becoming a monk. It was all very well having notions about an Anglican priest who happened to lecture on church history in a theological college—not that she was willing to admit to any such feelings, of course. But if she did have any and then he chose the religious life…

"No, nothing else. I've already taken too much of your time. Thank you, Father." She rose and hurried out. Should she have asked him to bless her? Would he have been expecting her to make her confession? She wished she knew more of the forms of this Alice Through The Looking Glass world she had entered almost by accident.

As she made her way through the tangled passageways of the monastery back toward the college, the lengthy skirt of her black cassock—regulation student wear—wrapped itself around her long legs, impeding the speed of her stride, but she still managed to move fast enough to make her golden hair in its characteristic braid bump against her back. Thoughts tumbled through her mind. She had been so certain Father Oswin could help her. Their little talks always helped. And he had given fairly concrete advice—as concrete as he ever did. So why was she even more confused than when she started?

Perhaps, a little voice niggled at the back of her mind, *because you didn't discuss the whole picture. But how could I? There isn't anything to discuss. And I would look such a fool if I'm wrong.* She shut the door on that train of thought.

What about Father Oswin's suggestion that she take a sort of mini personal pilgrimage? She had heard others talking about making Lenten retreats. It seemed to be part of the system— the accepted thing. Why shouldn't she? Visit some convents. Get some practical idea of what she was really contemplating for her future. She had vaguely thought that the past seven months she had spent essentially living in a monastery as a student would have been preparation enough, but perhaps she did need to see a wider picture.

It made such excellent sense, really. So why did she feel reluctant to undertake what should be a very pleasant break? A few days in each convent, just getting the feel of the place. Meet a few nuns—the sort of women she would be living with. As Father Oswin said, it wouldn't be a real discernment process, but enough to get the lie of the land, so to speak.

She would have to get permission to miss two lectures, but if she said it was at the advice of her spiritual director, it would surely be allowed. She had intended to finish her essay on the early sacramentaries and get started on her Old Testament paper, but they weren't really due yet. That wasn't the problem. Why was she who was always ready to go and to do suddenly reluctant to leave Kirkthorpe?

Still without an answer, she headed toward the common room where her fellow ordinands would be gathering before evening prayers, reading tattered copies of *The Church Times* or *The Church of England Newspaper*, depending upon their churchmanship, and sharing the latest gossip or debating the latest controversy in the church. But first, she would just stop by her pigeonhole and check her mail—or post, as she was becoming accustomed to saying.

The usual notices: cantor tryouts for Holy Week services, workers needed for the weekly youth night at the St James centre in town, sign up for day out to Rievaulx Abbey... And a letter. A real, written-on-paper, put-in-an-envelope letter. With a stamp bearing an American flag. Must be from her father, Andrew Howard, a soft-spoken man who worked for the state of Idaho as an employment counselor, but whose main role had always been to keep the family ticking along while his lawyer wife worked an eighty-hour minimum week.

Just holding this tangible contact from home gave her a sensation of warmth. She started to rip it open when the bell sounded for evening prayers. She stuck it in her pocket with the wry thought that delaying pleasure was good for the soul, and made her way into the early April evening. Swathes of brilliant daffodils at her feet and birds chirping in the overhanging branches cheered her every step up the hill to the church as the bell continued to peal from the tower.

Oh, yes, yes, yes. Peace and beauty. This was what she loved. This was what she wanted for the rest of her life. She would obey and undertake the obligatory discernment, but there was really no need. She *knew*.

Inside the cool stone arches of the Community church, the ever-lingering scent of incense greeted her and the ancient quiet enfolded her. She turned to the side aisle to make her reverence to the icon of Our Lady of the Transfiguration, as was customary.

Her eyes were still adjusting to the dim light as she bowed her head and crossed herself, then raised her eyes to look into the gentle face she knew so well: the Madonna with her head tilted gently toward her infant Son, whose hand was raised in blessing and pointing to the background scene of Christ on the mountain top with Moses and Elijah. Felicity always loved the way the candlelight on the glowing gold background seemed to propel the dark-veiled Virgin and Child toward the votary, and the flickering light could seem to make the Transfigured Lord shimmer as he must have done to the astounded disciples seeing him in his transformed glory.

But no tender scene of Mother and Son met her uplifted eyes. This time only the bare stone column stared back at her. The votive candle on the small shelf was cold. Only a smudge of smoke on the stone attested that it had ever been lit.

Puzzled and disappointed, Felicity turned to her seat in choir and opened her prayer book. As every Friday in Lent, the evening Psalm was 22, "My God, my God, why has thou forsaken me:" the precentor set the first line of chant. As if taking a deep breath, the entire Community paused for the caesura, then Felicity joined the response "and art so far from my cry?"

But her mind only half-followed the familiar words and rhythms. It was almost three weeks yet until the Maundy Thursday ritual stripping of the church as if preparing a body for burial, followed by the Holy Saturday church cleaning when she had been told every student turned out to clean every dark corner, polish every crucifix and candlestick, and dust every carved crevice as an important part of the ancient pattern of Holy Week. And, wasn't it the week before that—the week they called Passiontide—when all statues and images would be removed or veiled? Felicity was new to all this high church ritual she had taken to so suddenly and so wholeheartedly, but she was quite sure she had the information right. Why, then, was the icon gone now? Perhaps they had removed it early to be sent away for professional cleaning? Or perhaps she needed repair, although Felicity hadn't noticed any damage on the vibrant image.

Bowing, kneeling and chanting with the collected college and Community, Felicity was soon swept upward with the echoing prayers and wafting incense until, offering a final bow to the altar cross, she left her seat, walking beside Neville Mortara, the friend and ordinand who sat next to her. Neville turned aside to reverence the icon, but Felicity stopped him. "Don't bother," she whispered. "She's gone."

"Gone?" Neville's blue eyes startled beneath his gold-rimmed glasses, "Gone where?"

Felicity shrugged. "Cleaning, I suppose."

Neville shook his head. "She didn't need cleaning." He spoke with the authority of one who knew his field. Neville had achieved considerable success as an artist before coming to CT, as the College of the Transfiguration was familiarly known to its members, to study for the priesthood.

At the door Neville dipped a long, white finger into the

holy water stoop and offered his hand to share it with Felicity. The gold of his signet ring glowed dully as Felicity extended her hand. Together they crossed themselves and went out into the April evening.

Felicity smiled and looked up to continue chatting with Neville as they walked back down the hill to the refectory. It was unusual for Felicity, who stood slightly over five foot ten inches in her stockinged feet, to be obliged to crane her neck for a conversation. The breeze whipped at their long black cassocks, and Felicity had the impression of the reed-like Neville swaying with the branches around them.

But it wasn't the gust of wind that disturbed Felicity's comfort. Neville, whose generous friendship made him the easiest person she knew to chat with, seemed oddly distracted today. "Is something wrong, Neville?"

He looked startled. "Why do you say that? What should be wrong?" His brow furrowed under his pale fringe.

Before Felicity could answer they were joined by Neville's friend Maurice Paykel, waving the latest issue of *Inclusive*. "Nev, Have you *seen* this? A big rally at Manchester Cathedral—" The stocky redhead bore Felicity's companion away and she at last had a moment to open her father's letter.

The breeze riffled the page as she pulled it from the envelope. Then she stopped dead in the middle of the stone path. "Oh, sorry," she said to the group behind her, and stepped aside. Blinking, she looked back at the paper in her hand. *Not* from her father. Her *mother* had written her a letter. On paper. By hand. When was the last time her mother had done such a thing? Birthday cards "to our darling Felicity, love, Mother and Dad" had always been written by her father. "Have a happy day, Muffin" notes in her school lunch box had always been from her father. Forms for summer camp to be filled out and signed by parent were signed in Andrew Howard's neat script. What on earth could have spurred the fast-moving, high-tech Cynthia to put pen to paper? An email would have been shocking, but believable. Just. A letter was frightening.

And Felicity was right to be alarmed. Her stomach tightened and her breathing stopped as she read. Cynthia's law firm had joined one of the new international firms. She had a choice of joining the firm in Los Angeles or in London. "Of course, I could stay in Boise, but there seems little point in that with Jeff's consultancy job taking him to Asia all the time and Charlie and Judy settled in the Silicone Valley and your father and I getting a divorce…"

Felicity gave an audible gasp as she backed into a tree for support. Had she read that right? She smoothed the crumpled paper and looked again. Yes, there was no mistaking. That was what it said.

"Oh, how typical! Can you believe it?" She exploded with disgusted anger to no one in particular.

"Believe what?"

She turned to the rich tenor voice behind her. "Oh, Antony." She thrust the crumpled sheet at Antony with an angry growl as if he had written it. "My mother! How could she? How could she be so—so—oh, I don't know." *Stupid. Uncaring. Pigheaded. Impulsive. Rash. Selfish.* Words whirled through her head too fast to enunciate.

Antony looked up from a quick perusal of the sheet. "Your parents are divorcing?"

"You noticed? My father doesn't bother to write at all and my mother finally gets around to mentioning it as an aside. A postscript after discussing *her* job and what's a convenient place for *her* to live. I mean, no one pretended it was an ideal marriage. But they're *my parents.* They live together. At home. What is she thinking?"

"And she's coming to see you."

"*What?*" Felicity stepped forward and snatched the paper back. She hadn't read the concluding paragraph. "'… Sunday, week after next, so we can have a nice visit before I look over the London office.'" Felicity shook her head. "A 'nice visit.' When did we ever have *a nice visit*? Why should we start now?"

"Um, Felicity," Antony ran his fingers upward through his thick dark hair, then flattened it again with a downward stroke. "Did you see the date on this?" He held out the envelope. "It took this two weeks to get here. She'll be here tomorrow."

Felicity threw her hands in the air. "I can't believe she didn't have the sense to ring or email. But fine. She can come whenever she wants to. It's a free country and all that. But I won't be here." If she had had any doubts about leaving, this settled the matter.

When Antony didn't reply, she continued, "I'm going on retreat. Rempstone. To test my vocation. Father Oswin's orders. Oh, and I'll be missing your church history lecture on Monday."

A far corner of Felicity's mind registered the fact that all color drained from Antony's face when she mentioned testing her vocation. She supposed she could have broken it to him more gently, but now it was out. Just as well. She certainly didn't need another complication to her life.

"We need to talk, Felicity." Anthony spoke in a tight voice.

"I don't want to talk about it. Not now." *Maybe never.*

He gave a jerky nod. "All right. But what I meant was that I need to talk to you. I've just come from Father Anselm's office."

Hearing the name of the Father Superior of the Community immediately took Felicity back to that day just a few weeks ago that now seemed like another world when she had so blithely started out with Antony to solve Father Dominic's murder. Little could she have foreseen then what a different person she would be now.

"He's asked me to undertake another investigation,"

Antony said.

"Not another murder?" Felicity blanched and her voice rose in alarm.

"No, no. Nothing so dramatic. Our Lady of the Transfiguration has disappeared."

"Oh, I noticed she was gone. I thought she'd been sent out for cleaning or something."

"Sadly, nothing that easily explained, I'm afraid."

"Why don't they call the police?"

"Father Anselm suspects—well, shall we say an inside job? He'd rather have it handled quietly."

"He wouldn't suspect one of the brethren. That must mean a student. I don't believe it. Not even as a prank, surely."

"I suppose a prank is a possibility. But I think he had something more specific in mind. A well-known artist and collector who might have reason to—well, er, borrow her for closer study?"

Felicity was outraged. "You mean Neville. What an absurd accusation! We were talking about it just a minute ago. I'm the one who told him the icon was missing. I'm certain he didn't know anything about it. Besides, he's one of the most honest people I know."

Antony shrugged. "Well, I have to follow up. If it's returned quietly that will be the end of it."

"Why doesn't the superior ask around himself?"

"He wants the whole business kept low-key. The thing is, a representative of the Patriarch of Moscow is coming for the Triduum."

"To Kirkthorpe? For Holy Week? Oh, is that part of your ecumenical thingy?"

"In a way. Our icon was Russian—said to have been brought to England by Peter the Great on his Great Embassy in the seventeenth century. The Russian Orthodox Church has made enquiries about our loaning it for a special celebration this year. Some anniversary of the Christianizing of Russia or something. Anyway, it seemed like a great opportunity to build bridges between our churches."

"Oh, I get it. And so this emissary of his holiness shows up here in less than three weeks and we've mislaid the icon. Not good for ecumenical relations, to say the least."

"That's it exactly. And Father Anselm said that I—we—did so well last time, he was hoping…"

Felicity shook her head. "Sorry. My plate is more than full. But good luck and all that." She turned and started walking rapidly toward the dining hall, no matter how little she fancied the Friday night Lenten vegetarian fare that would be awaiting her. Then she paused. "I mean it. Really. Good luck."

Just before the path curved downhill she hesitated once more. "I'm off for Rempstone on the first train in the morning." She flung it over her shoulder, telling herself she didn't care whether he heard her or not. But when she allowed herself a brief backward glimpse she was struck by his bruised look.

Chapter 2

Later that Evening

Antony shut his eyes against the pain. Vocation? Did he hear rightly? Felicity was going to a convent to test her vocation? Felicity wanted to be a nun?

What a bitter irony. Just when he had concluded that he wasn't called to be a monk. Oh, the stories of St Francis offering refuge and spiritual counseling to St Clare and their lifelong friendship, each forming religious orders and supported by their correspondence, were inspiring reading, but not at all how he had pictured what he had come to hope would be his life with this brilliant, impulsive, stunning, infuriating young woman who had turned his world upside down.

He had been aware of her deepening maturity since they returned to Kirkthorpe from their recent harrowing adventure, but he had no idea... Antony berated himself. What was he thinking? He should be thrilled for her. That someone who had been so new to spiritual things could have been drawn so deeply into the faith that quickly...

And yet, the other side of his mind argued that this had to be another one of Felicity's hare-brained, impulsive leaps. Or was that wishful—selfishly wishful—thinking on his part?

He only knew he couldn't leave it at that. He would make one more attempt to talk to her tonight after supper, before the Greater Silence began. He had to get through to her. Instead of continuing on toward the dining hall he turned back to the quiet of the church.

Two hours later he found her just leaving the common room after coffee hour. She made no objection as he fell into step beside her. They walked down the hall in silence but once outside in the cold, damp evening air, Antony cleared his throat, praying he could get this right.

"Felicity, there's no reason you should do this for me, but Father Anselm specifically asked, and he did seem so worried."

She shook her head. "I don't know anything about icons. Get Neville to help you. He's always ready to help everybody and what better way to investigate him? And doesn't he have an uncle who works for the Victoria and Albert or something?"

Antony nodded. "Right. Fine. I'll check that out. See, you've been a help already." He tried to force a casual smile.

Of course he was failing miserably at any attempt to seem offhand. He knew he was always too intense. He could almost feel Felicity gritting her teeth at the implication that she should continue helping—confirmation that he was botching the whole thing—but he went on, "Right. Forget the icon. But really, Felicity, the far more serious matter is your mother—"

"Whoa!" Felicity held up her hand. "Don't. You don't know anything about it. It's none of your business."

"No, I don't know anything about your situation. But I do know something about being without a mother." The last thing he wanted was to get sentimental, but he couldn't help remembering the dark night in a rain-whipped bus kiosk in Northumbria when he had told her about the death of his parents in a sailing accident and his dreary, isolated childhood.

Apparently Felicity was recalling the same scene because she took a breath of air as if she would speak, but no words came. He sensed a momentary softening in her. It was enough to give him courage to press on. "Felicity, the day after tomorrow is Mothering Sunday. Couldn't you…."

Whatever he was about to suggest, and he wasn't at all sure what it was, was cut off by her vigorous head-shaking. "I said, don't go there. You want a mother—you can have her. She was never a mother to me, and now she's leaving my father and

I'm supposed to change my life for her because she suddenly decides maybe she needs me?"

Antony threw out his hands in a helpless gesture. "All right. I get it. You're hurt and angry and you dislike your mother—"

"Dislike her? I don't dislike her. I don't know her well enough to have an opinion. I'm indifferent."

"Did she mistreat you?"

"No. She was never there enough to mistreat us."

"Hmm, so I wonder why she had children."

Antony spoke without thinking, but he could see that his words stunned Felicity.

After a long silence she said, "I have no idea. I never thought about it." And that was the end of the subject.

Antony could think of nothing more to say, so in the end he fell back on the practical. He offered to meet her mother's train which was scheduled to arrive several hours after Felicity had embarked for the Community of the Holy Cross outside a tiny village in Nottinghamshire.

The incongruity of Felicity joining an enclosed community of sisters that still wore traditional habits and spent their days in prayer left him speechless. He stood rooted as Felicity strode down the path and out of the high, black iron gate to her apartment. Would he ever see her again? Of course he would. But whatever change was about to take place in their lives, he knew things would never be the same again.

Chapter 3

Saturday, Fourth in Lent

"We've saved lunch for you. Reverend Mother asked that you be served and she'll join you in the refectory." The Guest Sister who answered the door with a welcoming smile took Felicity's bag and led the way across the polished dark wood of what had once been the hall of an elegant eighteenth-century home. Felicity, her head whirling, followed obediently behind the nun dressed in full black habit.

"I didn't expect a meal." In spite of being genuinely hungry she felt she should protest. "When the bus was late in Loughborough—"

"Oh, but of course you must eat." Sister Mary Gabriel opened the door on a room with long, scrubbed tables facing French windows looking out over an extensive rolling lawn and flower beds bursting with spring bulbs.

"It's beautiful." Felicity sank into the chair in front of the single table setting. A plump, smiling young woman in black habit and a white veil that distinguished her as a novice bustled in from the kitchen with a cheesy pasta dish that smelled wonderful to Felicity, who hadn't eaten since breakfast.

"If you'll forgive me for leaving you on your own, I'll just slip out to the guest house to make certain your room is ready for you." It wasn't necessary for the sister to add that she had had little warning to prepare for their guest's arrival. "We are always so busy during Lent. So many requests for retreats, you know, and we only have the two rooms plus the hermitage. Fortunately, we had an unexpected cancellation." With a final welcoming smile the Guest Sister left the room.

In spite of the pungent scent of herbs and cheese rising from her plate, Felicity found that she could only swallow two bites. Now that she was here—now that she had made her escape from Antony, from Father Anselm's request, from her mother—she was feeling anything but the peace she should have found in this serene setting.

It had been a two-hour train journey involving three changes, then an extended wait for a local bus which had deposited her alongside a busy road across from a gate set in a high hedge. She had arrived at the red-brick, white-pillared house hidden behind the shielding shrubbery in none too good a mood. And her mood refused to improve in spite of the Guest Sister's warm welcome, the tasty food set before her, and the lovely view from her table.

Felicity simply couldn't make herself quit replaying that last conversation with Antony and—she had to admit it—her unreasonable response. Something in the back of Felicity's mind told her that her flippant responses had made her sound like a brat.

And as usual, Antony's almost off-the-cuff question had gone to the heart of the matter. Why had Cynthia had children?

"I've never thought about it," was her honest response. And now that she did, the question left her speechless. Why had the career-driven Cynthia bothered with a motherhood that obviously didn't mean anything to her? If it had simply been a matter of Andrew wanting a son, well—Jeff and Charlie were born before she was. The idea of Cynthia caring about having a daughter seemed laughable.

Felicity blinked at the mystery of her own existence. She felt almost curious enough to want to see her mother so she could ask her. Almost, but not quite.

And why had her replies to Antony been so bitter? She had

had no idea she felt so strongly about her mother. In the past, when anyone would ask her about her family she would give an indifferent shrug and a noncommittal answer about supposing her childhood was as happy as anyone else's. And she would have thought she was telling the truth. Well, maybe Cynthia would find something helpful at Kirkthorpe. She probably had a better chance of that on her own than if Felicity had been there confronting her with recriminations.

Fortunately, Felicity was spared going over the whole scene again by the entrance of the Mother Superior. "I'm Mary Mark," she introduced herself. Felicity blinked. Were they all called Mary? Must be a custom of this house. "We're so glad you could join us. Sister Mary Gabriel said you had some questions for me, and as we have another booking for tonight this might be our only chance for a chat. I do hope you don't mind talking while you eat?" She glanced at Felicity's barely touched plate. "Oh, could we bring you something else? Perhaps some cheese and salad?"

"No. Thank you, Mother. I'm just not very hungry." Actually she was starving, but her throat simply felt too tight to swallow.

"Some tea, perhaps?"

"That would be lovely."

Mother Mary Mark glided to the door that led to the kitchen and spoke a few words to the novice there. Even in that brief introduction, Felicity had the impression of an intelligent, efficient woman of great beauty. The bulky black habit couldn't hide her trim figure, and the severe veil only served to frame her delicate features.

When the tea arrived, she was giving Felicity a brief history of their order. "We were founded in 1857 by Elizabeth Neale, a sister of John Mason Neale, the hymn-writer." She paused and Felicity nodded as if she knew the names, since it seemed to be expected. "He had founded the Sisters of St Margaret and when

Elizabeth felt a call to the religious life she, probably quite wisely, founded her own order rather than joining her brother's."

The Reverend Mother smiled, then went on more seriously. "Actually, her call was quite specific—to work among the fallen women and destitute children in the East End of London. At first there were riots organized by the publicans and brothel keepers because their trade was being threatened by the sisters. But when the area was hit with a cholera epidemic, the sisters worked unceasingly among its victims and they won the confidence of the people.

"But the Sisters were never just glorified social workers. From the earliest years the liturgy has been the most important part of our day. It would have been impossible for the sisters to do the heroic work they did without the strength and grace given to them through their time of prayer and worship.

"During the war, the convent was turned into a war emergency hospital with the sisters sleeping on bunks in the cellars. The day after the hospital closed, the Community changed from being an active community into an enclosed one. We moved up here in 1979, just before I joined the order. Prayer and work for Christian unity have become increasingly the central purpose of our existence."

Ah, here was something Felicity could relate to. "Oh, are you a member of the Council for Christian Unity that Father Antony chairs?"

"Yes, indeed, I and three of our sisters were at the conference just a couple of weeks ago. Father Antony will make a fine new chairman."

Felicity nodded, remembering how their recent investigative adventure had been driven by the need to clear Antony's name so he could take up that post, and the fear that he might actually be in prison at the time.

"For years we have distributed leaflets to encourage awareness of the scandal of Christian disunity and have dedicated

ourselves to prayer so that it might be redressed." Mother Mary
Mark paused as the novice arranged the tea things on the table.
"Thank you, Bernadette." Then the Reverend Mother turned
back to Felicity. "Forgive me for going on so long, my dear. I've
just been preparing for a meeting of ROOT—that's Religious
of Orthodox Tradition—so I had it on my mind. You've rather
served as a sounding board for my speech, I'm afraid. Now, let
me hear your questions."

Felicity took a long drink of tea to get her thoughts
together, but they still didn't seem to come out in a very orderly
fashion. "Yes, I think—that is, I do—want to become a nun.
Father Oswin said I should visit convents to discern. I'm afraid I
don't know very much…" Her voice trailed off. It was obvious
she didn't even know enough to ask an intelligent question.

Felicity set her cup down with an air of calm she was far
from feeling. "What do you look for in a prospective nun?" She
actually wanted to ask *would you take me?* But that seemed too
direct even for her.

"You should be talking to our Novice Mistress, but since
she is on retreat today and since she and I confer on all such
decisions, I'll attempt to speak for her. The most important
thing of all is to be sure that the person who comes to us is
truly seeking God. Secondly, is she fervent in the work of God?
Here our work is the Divine Office, our sevenfold daily office
of prayers, Scripture and meditation."

Felicity gulped. It sounded so simple. Love God and pray.
Seven times a day, plus your private prayers. Yet she had a feeling
that could be the hardest work in the world.

"We would, of course, contact the applicant's priest—find
out is this person serious? Is she emotionally stable?" Once again
Mother Superior smiled. "We always say that even if you have
no emotional problems when you come—you will eventually.

"Seriously, though, the first step is to come and stay here.
Get to know the Community. Live alongside us for a fortnight

or longer. If that looks good, then we expect a candidate to spend several months in the postulancy. After that, if she desires to be clothed as a novice the postulant, the Novice Mistress, myself and our warden would confer. The clothing itself can be hard. Some women find wearing a skirt hard. The veil can be impossible."

Her voice trailed off, giving Felicity time to think. Fortunately she had possessed the forethought to wear a plain black, knee-length skirt, dark tights and a black turtleneck, so skirts were obviously no problem for her. With a subconscious gesture she tossed her head, making her heavy blond hair, as long as the Mother Superior's veil, swish across her back in its heavy braid. Before she could decide how she would feel about covering it with a veil, Mary Mark went on. "Of course, the matter of giving up is different for every person. With a widow or a divorcee, it's a matter of putting the Community ahead of her children. This can be hard on both sides.

"A candidate must think of her relationship with her own family before she takes on a new one. Is her calling intense enough to counteract the pain and distress she might cause in her own family?" She looked at Felicity. "How will your own mother react, for example?"

Felicity almost choked on her tea, thinking she had been asked a direct question, then relaxed when Mother Mary Mark continued and she realized the questions, again, had been rhetorical.

"There is a cost no matter what your circumstances. If someone comes in young they give their life—blossom and all; if they come in older they give only the fruit. If they have never had sex, they wonder what they're giving up. If they have had a sexual relationship they wonder, can I live without it?"

Felicity blinked at Mother Mary Mark's straightforwardness. She hoped that was a general reference as well. Surely even this wise, perceptive woman couldn't have an inkling of the unanswered questions in Felicity's life.

When Felicity didn't respond, the Mother Superior went on. "We look for signs of seriousness about worship and devotion. Does this person have a thirst for the Eucharist? Do they say an office?" Felicity blushed at her recent irritation with Antony for his own keeping of the office. Could she have changed so much in such a short time? Mary Mark's light voice went on in her perfect accent that marked her as well-educated upper middle class. "If a postulant asks, 'What if I don't *feel* like praying?' My reply is simply, 'Sorry, dear.' The postulancy is about learning to live not by feelings and emotions, but about living by the will.

"Can the person take correction? Everybody does things wrong; you can't help it. Don't feel rejected, we're trying to help you learn the life. The hardest thing for me was being taught how to make a bed. I was a *nurse*, for goodness' sake. Then there was the fifty-year-old mother of five who had to submit to being taught our way of peeling potatoes."

Felicity shifted on her seat. She would have to think about this obedience issue. She had hoped to hear more about peace and beauty, not about making beds and peeling potatoes.

Mother Superior continued as if she had read Felicity's mind. "Thomas Merton lived by the Dominican vows of poverty, chastity and obedience. He said, 'Poverty is a cinch; chastity you can get used to; obedience is the bugger.' But above all, we ask, is there a true attraction to self-giving to God, or is she simply seeking to distance herself from life?" Mary Mark smiled. "Another way to say it is, does the postulant have a sound call or is she romanticizing? Remember, God will use your own characteristics to guide you."

Ah, Felicity liked that last bit. After all, she loved Latin. Her Classics major had been one of the things that had led her to priestly studies in the first place. She knew this traditional Community still prayed in Latin a lot. And, thanks to Antony's coaching, she totally agreed with what Mother Superior had said about prayer for Christian unity.

"Then, if all goes well for the aspirant and two-thirds of the Community agree, she spends two or three years as a novice. At the end of that time she enters into temporary vows for three years before being professed in life vows."

Good grief. Felicity had lost count. "So that's what? Five years? Six?"

The Mother Superior smiled. "Yes, that should be long enough to discern the will of God. Don't you agree?"

Felicity felt dazed. Mother Mary Mark paused, inviting her to ask a question, but she couldn't form any. "Perhaps the thing to ask yourself is, what kind of life do you feel drawn to? Here we are very traditional, contemplative, enclosed. The Sisters at Ham Common in London, on the other hand, are very active, very modern. The Sisters of St Margaret at Walsingham have a very specific work helping the pilgrims at the shrine. The Sisters of the Love of God in Oxford have an influential publishing ministry. And there are many others. Take your time and explore." She handed Felicity a small book. *"The Rule of St Benedict,* we live by this, as have all Benedictines for a millennium and a half. Look it over and we can talk in more depth tomorrow afternoon." She rose to her feet

"Now, if you've finished your tea, I'll show you around. The chapel and the refectory are the two poles of our communal existence—where we worship and eat." She led the way back into the central hall and to the chapel beyond into what Felicity guessed must have been a grand salon in the eighteenth century. The paneled walls were painted a pale yellow and the pews and altar were of a golden oak, reflecting the spring sunshine filtering through the floor-to-ceiling windows which opened onto more extensive grounds. The scent of incense lingered in the hushed air.

"Now, let me show you our garden." The Mother Superior led the way out the back into the April afternoon. "I'm afraid you've missed our snowdrops. They are quite amazing in February. Then the daffodils come on." A wave of her arm directed Felicity's gaze toward the distant oak wood where the ground under the giant trees was more golden than green. "The bluebells will be coming into bloom soon. Then there's the lily pond, the herb garden, the orchard..." Again, her arm swept the landscape.

"And beyond all that, the Charnwood Hills. I so often gaze at this scene and think, 'God's in his heaven, all's right with the world.' Even when I know that in human terms it isn't." And then, indicating a majestic oak at the foot of the rolling lawn, "When I'm inclined to think everything is ghastly I look at that tree and think, 'That's been here for 200 years.' It gives one perspective."

But the Reverend Mother's words were lost on Felicity as a movement at the edge of the distant garden caught her eye. A group, led by a nun—probably Sister Mary Gabriel—was emerging from behind the tall, neatly trimmed hedge. Felicity blinked to be sure. Then gaped. There was no mistaking the tall, willowy form of Neville Mortara and the familiar figure of Father Antony. With their black cassocks blowing in the spring breeze they looked completely at home with the Sister. But the tall, slender lady in the assertive pinstripe suit with the sun glinting off her sleek golden hair couldn't have looked more out of place as she struggled to keep her three-inch spike heels from sinking in the turf with every step.

"Mother." Felicity didn't even attempt to keep the groan out of her voice.

Chapter 4

Saturday, Fourth in Lent, Evening

Felicity strode across the lawn, her softly gored skirt and flat shoes giving her complete freedom of motion. Barely glancing at her mother, she didn't slow her momentum until she was practically nose-to-nose with Antony. "And what is the meaning of *this?*"

"Neville and I are on our way to Norwich. This is a convenient midway stop."

Hardly an adequate explanation. "Norwich?"

"Actually, it was your idea. To involve Neville in the investigation, that is. You were absolutely right. He knew that a valuable icon had been stolen from St Julian's Shrine there a year or so ago. Father Anselm wants us to see if there's any connection."

With Mother Superior's shepherding the group moved up the lawn toward the wide, classically pillared verandah of the convent, Felicity and Antony following at the back. Felicity's voice was tight with anger. "And you brought *her* because—?"

"What else was I to do? Her train came in just before ours left. I could hardly leave her standing at the station. And besides, she did come to see you, Felicity."

Felicity took a deep breath. *Live by the will, not by feelings and emotions*, Mother Superior had said. Being rude to her own mother in front of Mother Mary Mark would be like exhibiting bad manners in front of the Queen. Giving a curt nod to Antony, she quickened her pace to catch up with Cynthia.

"Hello, Mother. This is quite a surprise."

As Cynthia turned to her, Felicity saw her mother's

shoulders relax and a tightness leave her features. Felicity was afraid she might engulf her in a hug, but thankfully, Cynthia just reached out and squeezed her daughter's hand. "Oh, my dear, it's so good to see you. Father Antony explained about my letter arriving late and your plans already being set. I am sorry my arrival has been so awkward."

It was impossible to imagine her mother making an arrival that wouldn't be awkward. Felicity forced a stiff smile. "Well, can't be helped. You're here now."

Fortunately she was spared having to make further conversation as the bell began ringing for the early evening Vespers service. They filed into the chapel, Felicity sitting beside her mother in the back pew, as the nuns took their seats in the choir. It was a short service of prayers and readings, none of which made the slightest impression on Felicity. She felt entirely overwhelmed by the events of the last twenty-four hours. How could things have gotten so completely out of control?

She mouthed the Our Father automatically and managed to take in a few lines of the closing prayer: "… fill our hearts with your love and keep us faithful to the gospel of Christ. Give us the grace to rise above our human weakness…"

After a brief period of silence, the nuns filed out. Felicity, who wanted to flee, managed to remain still until she could walk out behind Antony. She was so intent on escape that she almost walked into Neville who was standing stock still just outside the chapel door, staring at an icon resting on a heavy brass stand on a shelf. "The Virgin of the Passion." His voice was hushed with reverence and awe.

"Yes." The Reverend Mother's head barely came up to his shoulder. "You've spotted our greatest treasure. It was a gift to us from the Sisters of the Holy Paraclete for the 150th anniversary of our foundation."

Neville leaned closer. "It's very fine. What an unusual representation." The Virgin draped in deep blue with a large golden corona, held her empty hands folded before her breast, her head inclined sadly toward the cross with the crucified Christ in the background. Even with as little knowledge as she had of the matter, Felicity was sure that the patina of the gold and the depth of the colors indicated a very old work of art. She moved closer to get a better look. Was Neville's interest only aesthetic, or could he be thinking this could be connected somehow to the missing Virgin of the Transfiguration?

"You're quite right." Mother Superior nodded to Neville. "I've never seen another one like it. As you can imagine, as the Community of the Holy Cross, this representation has special meaning to us."

"Er—may I?" Neville reached both hands toward the icon as if to pick it up.

"Yes, certainly you may examine her. Of course, we put her on the altar for all the Marian feast day masses, so she is moved about quite a bit."

"I'm not an expert, but this looks very old. Even medieval, perhaps. You realize that would make it very rare?" Neville gazed intently at the image for several moments, then turned it over. If Felicity had been standing at any other spot she would never have seen the mark stamped into the corner, but being just to Neville's right as she was, she glimpsed what looked like a sunburst or a spikey star with a black, multi-pointed cross in the center of a ring of leaves. Where had she seen an emblem like that before? What did it mean? She couldn't remember, but somehow it looked vaguely familiar.

Just then they were interrupted by a jangling of the front door bell. Neville hastily replaced the icon and the Guest Sister hurried off to greet the newcomer. A moment later they heard a low murmur of voices moving across the hall and toward the side door.

"Our new guest will be staying in the hermitage, so you may not be seeing him, but his arrival reminds me that we must get you all settled. We can manage accommodations for the night," she turned to Felicity, "if you ladies don't mind sharing a room."

Cynthia spoke up. "Oh, that would be delightful. Thank you so much, Reverend Mother." Felicity gave a reluctant nod.

"Thank you, Mother," Antony said. "Neville and I will be off after mass tomorrow morning, so we won't put you out long." Felicity noticed he didn't say when Cynthia was leaving.

Felicity was thankful that at least Cynthia was quiet as they settled into the spare but comfortable room in the guest house beside the convent—even if her mother's reticence was caused by the wall of bristly silence Felicity couldn't help exuding. Felicity knew she should apologize, or at least say something like, "It's nice to see you, Mom." But she couldn't bring herself to do more than ask which bed Cynthia preferred.

Felicity had never been more thankful for a rule of eating in silence than she was at dinner that night. She couldn't repress a smile for wondering how many monks and nuns through the centuries had been equally thankful for the requirement when they were finding their brothers or sisters particularly irritating at the moment. And yet, quite without warning, a memory of family dinners around the large oak table in their dining room at home flooded over her. Her brothers, bolting their food and talking nonstop about their activities; her father, who had more often than not prepared the meal, asking her about her day. And, when asked, her mother, if she happened to be home for dinner, telling about her most pressing case. A less than perfect family, to be sure, but her family. And the fact that such an occasion would never come again left Felicity with a hollow ache inside.

Back in their room after Compline, Felicity slipped into her pajamas, then sat stiffly in her bed, waiting for her mother to start. After all, Cynthia was the one who had called this meeting.

"Felicity, darling, I know you're furious with me. But I

don't know what to do about it. I've already apologized for arriving at such an inopportune time. I should have called you, I know. But I didn't have your number."

"No, that's it, isn't it? You've never known anything about me. Because you never bothered to find out. You did have my email address though. At least, there's a computer in the house."

"But that's so cold, isn't it? So businesslike. I wanted something more personal."

The illogic left Felicity all but speechless. "So why didn't Dad call me? You always left all the nurturing to him. And now you tell me you're leaving him, too. Well, fine. So go if that's what suits you. But why run to me?"

"Felicity, you don't understand."

"I expect I understand quite a bit. But try me." Felicity folded her arms and leaned back against her headboard awaiting a spiel about how hard Cynthia had worked for this once-in-a-lifetime career opportunity, and how Andrew simply didn't understand her.

"It doesn't suit me. I don't want a divorce. Your father…" She dropped her head and continued in a low voice. "Andrew asked me to,,, He.. " To Felicity's horrified amazement her mother burst into tears. "He has found someone else," she finished through her sobs. "That's why he hasn't contacted you. He's left us all."

In all her life Felicity had never seen her mother in anything but perfect control. Oh, in a rush, almost always, and frequently worried about a case, but never out of control. Torn between an instinct to take her mother in her arms and comfort her, and a desire to tell her it was her own fault for not spending enough time with her husband, Felicity sat frozen.

At last Cynthia's sobs subsided with two final hiccups. As if reading Felicity's mind she said, "I suppose you're thinking it's my own fault. You don't have to say anything. You couldn't possibly say anything I haven't already berated myself with. Spent too much time at the office, not enough at home; paid too much attention to my clients, not enough to my husband; expected too much of him, didn't show enough appreciation…"

Felicity was afraid her mother would begin crying again, but after the echo of one more sniff died away, the room became silent. Felicity would never have believed her mother capable of looking so miserable. The silence had begun echoing unbearably before she spoke. Questions, accusations, emotions fought for expression.

If they started now on endless recriminations they would be up all night. Perhaps she should even offer some word of comfort to her mother. But she simply couldn't imagine what to say. She couldn't cope with any of it. The silence lengthened.

In the end, fatigue won. "Matins is at daybreak in the morning. Let's get some sleep."

"Well, slip out quietly. I intend to sleep in." That was the last Felicity heard from the other bed. It was clear that after her brief show of vulnerability Cynthia's shields were back in place. This was the mother Felicity had always known.

She turned out her light and snuggled in her duvet, but sleep was far from coming. Her father with another woman? It was unthinkable. And yet she could hardly discount Cynthia's distress. She hadn't even asked who the other woman was. Was it someone she knew?

But she still didn't understand why her mother had come to her. What could Felicity do about it? Why hadn't Cynthia gone to one of Felicity's brothers? Cynthia had always paid more attention to Jeffrey and Charles than she had to her daughter. Besides, they were men. If her mother wanted one of her children to speak to their father on her behalf surely it was the sons' place to do that.

And what about her own feelings? How was she supposed to feel? She had been so angry at her mother. Should she be angry with her father now? And in the end, to what purpose? What good did anger do anyway?

And if she were as holy as she thought she wanted to be—holy enough to become a nun—shouldn't she be praying? Ah, if she were a nun, professed in an enclosed order, then she would be protected from this, wouldn't she? But then, putting the Atlantic Ocean between herself and her family hadn't kept out the conflict. Why should she think a convent wall would?

Besides, they were in a convent at the moment.

Chapter 5

Fourth Sunday in Lent, Commonly called Mothering Sunday

The first notes of the dawn chorus woke Felicity from a light doze. Why did she have a headache? Going to bed with a headache sometimes happened. Waking up with one was unfair. And then she remembered. It was Sunday. Mothering Sunday. The English Mother's Day, with the added bit of honoring Mother Church and Mary the Mother of God. Oh, great. No pressure. She could hardly keep the day by honoring the church and Mary and rejecting her own mother.

Suppressing a groan she pushed her duvet aside and padded across the room to splash water on her face. In keeping with Cynthia's request—demand, really—she dressed quietly and hastily and slipped from the room without disturbing her mother. It would be easier all round if Cynthia simply stayed asleep. And fortunately the deep, rhythmic breathing from across the room indicated that Felicity would be spared the need for any forced brightness before sunrise.

The chapel was dim and cold as she slipped into a seat beside Antony. Apparently Neville was sleeping in, too, so the silent nuns, sitting with bowed heads and folded hands in their stalls were the only other occupants of the room. Matins, the first prayers of the morning, was followed, after only a brief pause for silent meditation, by Lauds, traditionally the sunrise service of praise. Somewhere along the way, the harmonious rhythms of the antiphonally chanted psalms echoing from side to side in the tranquil room began soothing Felicity's pounding head. She felt the tension leave her shoulders. Her breathing slowed and steadied. A pale pink glow slowly filled the floor-to-ceiling windows on either side of the eastward-facing altar and Felicity felt herself able to pray, and think, for the first time since the arrival of her mother's letter.

Gradually the words of the office began to penetrate the buzz that had been in her head. Even with their emphasis on giving thanks for our mothers and all they do for us Felicity found she was able to enter into the prayers for more love to be expressed in families. The prayer that fractured families be reunited was acutely appropriate:"Oh, Christ, who on the cross drew the whole human family to yourself, strengthen us in our daily living that in joy and sorrow we may know the power of your presence to bind together and to heal..." OK, she would make an effort. She would give her mother a chance.

By the time she had finished breakfast, where she and Antony were the only guests present, she was feeling almost excited to tell her mother. Once Felicity made up her mind to do something it wasn't in her to do it half-heartedly. She would tell Cynthia... Well, she wasn't sure what she would tell her. But as soon as the Greater Silence ended, right after Terce, a brief service of prayers before Mass, she would say something. Something welcoming. As warm as she could make it.

Felicity, lingering in the refectory after most of the others had left, remembered Mothering Sunday last year when she was teaching school in London. At the end of the service, all the children in the congregation were invited to come forward to receive a handful of bright yellow daffodils to take to their mothers. Suddenly Felicity wished she had a handful of daffodils to give to Cynthia, if only to see how surprised she was. Of course, there had always been the dutifully made cards, overseen by her father or a teacher, when she was a child, but this would be her first spontaneous gesture.

She was still musing on whether or not she could slip out to the oak wood after Terce and cut a clump of golden daffodils before mass started, when a loud crash and piercing scream propelled her to her feet so fast she added to the mayhem by knocking over her own chair. She threw open the refectory door and raced across the main hall toward the chapel at the same time as several people emerged from other doors and rushed in the same direction.

Felicity reached the chapel first. And there she froze. A black-robed nun lay before the altar in a pool of red. Felicity couldn't stop the cry that tore from her own throat. As she staggered backward, the scene of finding the battered body of her beloved Father Dominic in a pool of his own blood only a few short weeks ago replayed in her mind. "No!" she cried and felt her knees going weak.

A pair of firm arms steadied her. "It's all right, Felicity. It's only wine." Antony's voice held off the darkness that threatened to engulf her.

"Wine?"

"I know what you're thinking—what you're seeing. I thought the same. But come on, look." He pushed her to her feet and turned her shoulders toward the scene at the altar.

Yes. She nodded. Wine. It wasn't really blood-red. It was the replaying of the earlier experience that had made it so vivid. And yet— "But, is—is she…"

Mother Superior knelt over the still, silent form, feeling for a pulse. The entire room held its breath. Felicity recalled the Reverend Mother's reference to her former life as a nurse. She certainly seemed completely professional as she removed the sister's veil and continued her examination. Without looking up Mother announced, "She is breathing. Thanks be to God." All the nuns crossed themselves and murmured thanksgivings as Mother Mary Mark continued her examination In another moment she stood. "Sister Mary Julian, will you please ring for an ambulance. Sister Mary Perpetua has fallen and been injured." Several sisters gasped when they saw the blood on the Mother's hands that had been examining Mary Perpetua's head.

Had she merely slipped on the polished wood floor and hit her head as she fell? Perhaps on the edge of the altar? Or had a blow to her head caused her to fall? Almost against her will, Felicity glanced around the room for a blunt instrument. The heavy candlesticks were all in place.

The novice who had made Felicity's tea the day before burst into tears. "Will she be all right?"

"I trust so, but I ask you now to please return to your cells and pray for her. Mass will be delayed." Mother Superior rose to her feet as she directed her house in her calm, efficient way.

Felicity started to file from the room with the others when she felt Antony's hand on her arm holding her back.

When the room was empty except for them and the Mother Superior, Antony stepped forward. He had apparently also been considering that the fall had not been a simple accident, and now he offered his services, explaining briefly about their recent investigative experiences.

"Yes, I know, of course, about our dear Father Dominic. Such a tragic business." Mother Mary Mark shook her head. "I pray our matter won't come to anything so grave. But it is difficult to see how Sister Mary Perpetua could have struck her head like that by accident." She ran her hand over the corner of the altar as she spoke. The pure white fair linen was undisturbed.

Antony pointed to what he had apparently not noticed earlier: the heavy brass stand that yesterday had held the icon of Our Lady of the Passion now lay askew on the altar—without the icon. "It certainly couldn't have been an accident if that is what struck her on the head." At his words, Mother Superior started to reach for the stand. "No! Don't touch it."

He drew her back from the altar. "I think perhaps you should call the police. The icon seems to be missing."

"Robbery?" Even the unflappable Mother Superior appeared to be fighting to keep her composure. "Surely not."

"What was she doing in here?" Felicity asked.

"Mary Perpetua is our sacristan. She would have placed the icon on the altar before mass—for Mothering Sunday. She must have just been preparing to fill the cruet with wine." She gestured toward the side table where a small glass vessel stood empty beside its twin filled with water. An empty wine bottle lay on its side under the table. "There simply must be an explanation. Thank you for your advice, Father Antony. Father Bernard, our warden, will be arriving any minute to say mass. I'll confer with him."

Just then the wail of a siren sounded in the distance. Seeming much louder in the small chapel, however, was the welcome sound of Mary Perpetua groaning and stirring. Mother Superior knelt at her side again instantly. "Don't get up, my dear. You've had an accident. Help will be here in a moment."

"My head. I—I can't remember—"

"It's all right. Just lie still."

In spite of the Mother Superior's urging, however, Mary Perpetua reached out and clutched the corner of the long rose frontal with which she had draped the altar for the fourth Sunday in Lent. Felicity was the first to spot it. She darted forward with a cry. "The icon! Under the cloth!"

Sister Mary Perpetua muttered something incoherent, then sank back into Mother Superior's arms. A moment later the chapel was filled with the efficient confusion of the arrival of the medics. Mary Perpetua was lifted onto a stretcher and carried to the waiting vehicle. "I must go with her," Mother Superior said to Antony. "Sister Mary Julian, my assistant, and Father Bernard will see to things here." Then she turned to Felicity. "I'm so sorry. I know we had planned to spend more time together this afternoon."

"No, No," Felicity hurried to reassure her. "You've been so helpful. You don't need to be worrying about guests now. I'll just ring the sisters at Ham Common and see if they can take me early. I'd planned to go there next anyway."

The fact of the matter was that her retreat had ended the moment her mother had appeared yesterday.

Just as Mary Mark had said, Father Bernard, the warden, arrived and immediately took charge with the help of the Assistant Superior even before the ambulance left. Felicity looked out of the window of the parlor just as the white vehicle with green and yellow stripes disappeared through the hedge.

Felicity stood blinking for a moment. Why did that picture seem out of synch? What had she expected to see? The rise and fall of the siren died in the distance and then she remembered. "Antony, the ambulance. It didn't look right."

"What do you mean?"

She wasn't sure. What possible difference could it make how the ambulance was painted? Then she saw one of the nuns reverently replacing the icon on its stand and she realized what she had expected to see. "Last year, in London, I took some students to a gymnastics exhibition at Earl's Court. There was an ambulance there. I suddenly remembered—it had a cross thing on it—a big black cross with points. What does it mean?"

"Must have been St John Ambulance—rather like the Red Cross. They attend big public gatherings. This one was NHS. Why?"

"That's the emblem. That's what I saw on the back of the icon when Neville examined it yesterday."

"Are you sure?"

"Yes, and I've seen it somewhere else before. Just like that." She closed her eyes to focus on the mental image. "A pointy cross, with a design around it. I can't remember…"

Behind them in the chapel Father Bernard and Sister Mary Julian were busily cleaning up the chapel, setting all to rights for mass to be celebrated. Apparently they hadn't chosen to call in the authorities. Any forensic evidence—should there have been any—would have been destroyed by the Assistant

Superior's vigorous scrubbing anyway. Antony walked to the altar, picked up the icon and turned it over. Felicity pointed to the small mark engraved in the lower right hand corner. "Yes, I see. Clever of you to spot it."

"What do you think it means?"

Antony considered. "It's definitely the Maltese Cross in the middle. Symbol of the Knights of St John. Not sure what the leaves and nine-pointed star around it is. I wonder why it's on the icon."

"Could it be a kind of signature? Maybe someone is stealing works of this iconographer? Maybe something has been discovered to make them suddenly valuable to a collector."

Antony furrowed his brow. "A very esoteric collector that would be."

"And unethical," Felicity added.

"Beyond unethical. Criminal, you mean."

They were still examining the mark when the clatter of high heels on the polished wooden floor made Felicity look up. Cynthia entered the chapel and peered at the icon. "What is going on here? It seems I missed some excitement." Her well-groomed appearance and clearly enunciated speech would easily have been at home in a courtroom. "And where is Neville? I've looked everywhere for him. He seems to have disappeared."

Chapter 6

Fourth Sunday in Lent, Afternoon

"**J**ulian of Norwich. I keep hearing that name, but who was she?" Felicity asked the question more out of desperation than any real desire for knowledge. If she couldn't stop her mind from going over and over the events of the past two hours and coming up with the same unthinkable solution every time, she would be driven to banging her head against the train window.

Felicity's call to St Michael's Convent at Ham Common had not met with the invitation to come right on down that she had expected. They were so sorry to hear about the disturbance in a sister Community and were, indeed, looking forward to welcoming her next Tuesday, but could not accommodate her before then as they were hosting a large parish group. The Guest Sister was terribly polite and most apologetic, but there it was. And Felicity really could not impose on the Rempstone sisters' gracious hospitality any longer when they were in distress over Sister Mary Perpetua.

Cynthia suggested they should go to London together and get a hotel room. "Wouldn't that be fun, dear? We could see some shows, go shopping at Harrods, have tea at the Ritz." Felicity still felt exhausted by the effort it had taken her not to snap at her mother.

In the end there had seemed to be no other solution than that they all go on to Norwich. They could stay at the All Hallows Guest House that served pilgrims to St Julian's shrine, and Cynthia could make arrangements to meet her London host from the law firm and then easily catch a Norwich to London train any time that turned out to be convenient. That seemed a quite perfect solution for Felicity because it would give her the opportunity to get acquainted with the Community of All Hallows as well as helping Antony with his enquiries. She shook her head. No matter how many times she said *no*, it seemed she wound up involved in this investigation.

And no matter how much time she spent trying not to think about it, it was all she could think about. An extensive search of the convent and grounds had assured them that Neville was no longer at the Community of the Holy Cross.

Neither she nor Antony had voiced the obvious scenario. It had taken Cynthia to blurt it out in front of three of the sisters as well. (Felicity was beginning to see where her own rashness had come from, and how it must affect those around her.) "Goodness, who would have thought it? Neville was such a quiet, polite boy. Who could have imagined him capable of hitting a nun over the head in an attempt to steal an icon? I suppose he got frightened when she screamed and ran off without it. Do you suppose she maintained consciousness long enough to hide it under the altar cloth herself? What amazing presence of mind."

When Cynthia's accusations went unanswered by her stunned listeners she continued, "I suppose he was just lifting the icon off the altar when she caught him. She must have placed the icon on the altar first, then gone for the wine. That seems the only explanation for her to be carrying a bottle of uncorked wine. Do you think they struggled over the icon—"

"Mother, please," Felicity had pleaded, hoping her own anguish would silence Cynthia. Neville was a friend. It looked bad, she admitted that, but surely as a lawyer, Cynthia should understand innocent until proven guilty.

"Please, what, Felicity? It's only common sense. I'm sorry, I know he was your friend. And everyone else here is far too polite to say what everybody must be thinking. You don't have to have a trained legal mind to see that it's just pure logic."

Felicity had grabbed her mother's arm and bundled her off to their room where they packed in less than three minutes. And now, with every click of the train over the rails, her mother's courtroom voice rang in her ears. "It's only logic." Logic, common sense, obvious; but wrong, wrong, wrong. And she had to sit through a three hour train ride that included eleven stops before they could find anything to disprove Cynthia's theory.

"She was a fifteenth century mystic who had marvelous showings of God's love in a near-death experience, and spent the rest of her life living in a cell attached to the Church of St Julian in Norwich writing her *Revelations* and giving spiritual counsel to those who visited her." Antony's words came to her in a vacuum as if from another planet.

"What? What are you talking about?"

"Julian of Norwich. You asked."

"Oh, yes." Felicity had gone back so intently to the problem at hand she had forgotten she had attempted a ploy to distract herself. "Yes. Now I remember. *Revelations of Divine Love.* They have the book in the Community book store."

"You'll find it in just about every book store, I should think. It's amazingly popular."

"And she wrote it after a near death experience?"

Antony nodded. Apparently he welcomed a distraction as well, because he continued with animation. "On the 8th May 1373, when she was thirty years old, Julian suffered a severe illness from which she almost died. During that illness she received a series of visions of the Passion of Christ and the love of God.

"When she recovered, she became an anchoress and wrote down what she had seen, consequently becoming the first woman to write a book in English. She lived enclosed in her cell for the rest of her life, giving spiritual counsel to those who sought her wisdom, writing two versions of her *Revelations of*

Divine Love and dying at the considerable age of eighty-seven. Scholars disagree about everything else. We don't even know her name."

"I thought it was Julian."

"I mean her name before she became Julian. She was named for the church, dedicated to St Julian the Hospitaller, not the church for her. I like to call her Gillian. Somehow it seems a good name for her, and it's not a far reach from there to Julian."

"So was she a nun?"

"Again, no one knows. Some think it likely that she had taken vows before her visions, some think she had married and borne children but that her family had died in the plague which raged at that time, but I prefer to think of her living quietly at home with her mother and perhaps a sister. Probably of the merchant class. A cheerful, devout woman going about her daily tasks. It seems certain, though, that whatever her status at the time of her visions she had been nurtured by a careful, loving mother because her understanding of God as a loving, nurturing Mother is so clear."

Motherhood again. Felicity felt too drained to bristle at the reference, even as she glanced at her own mother sleeping in a rather uncomfortable-looking position on the seat across from her. She even managed to muster some sympathy for the jetlag Cynthia was undoubtedly suffering. Not that her mother wasn't capable of being perfectly impossible without jetlag, of course. Felicity shut the door on that unhelpful line of thought. "OK, tell me about it—about her visions." What might it have been like, for Julian and her family, that day in the springtime of 1373?

At her invitation Antony began his narrative in the spell-weaving style that had made him the most popular church history lecturer the College of the Transfiguration had ever known. It became hard to tell where his voice left off and the pictures in Felicity's mind began:

The last of the daffodils had faded from the green hills around Norwich, but the wallflowers still shone a vibrant gold. The fresh, May-time beauty of land and air called to the young woman who had always so delighted in them. Always, with an abandon that belied her thirty years, she would run barefoot through the tall grasses, arms outstretched and face lifted to the warmth of the sun. Always she would raise her voice in a merry trill of joy with the robins and wrens. But not today.

Today Gillian was dying.

For three days Gilly had lain helpless on her bed. For three days her mother had left her side for only the briefest of respites while Clarice, her elder sister, had taken a turn at the nursing and the brewing of possets. But their best efforts had produced no effect. Clarice swabbed Gillian's temples and wrists with minted vinegar water in an attempt to relieve the fever. When she paused to wipe her own streaming eyes, her mother shook her head. "Rest from your labors, my dear. It is no use."

Clarice embraced Dorcas with a sob. "No. It cannot be. Gilly is our sunshine. What will we do without her?"

The grey-gowned mother adjusted the white wimple framing her face, then leaned forward to trace the deep furrows in her beloved Gillian's broad, white forehead. "Her physical suffering is great, but I fear her spiritual suffering is far greater."

"But why should she suffer spiritually? Gilly was so good. She was never headstrong, or frivolous, or..."

As if to prove the correctness of the mother's understanding, the unconscious Gillian ground her teeth and tensed her whole body as if resisting an attack of demons. Deep cries tore at the cords far down in her throat before they burst from her lips with an anguish that was awful to hear.

"What can we do, Mother?"

"We can pray. I have sent for the priest. Pray that he gets here in time to speed her soul upward with the holy sacrament."

Before Clarice had time to form the prayer, they heard the door open. "Oh, please, do hasten, Father. Don't let Gilly die without comfort."

"I'll do my best, my child." Father Thomas Whiting, who had the Cure of Souls at St Julian's Church, pulled a wrinkled stole from the basket he carried, kissed it and hung it, lopsided, over his black robe. As he began arranging items on the small bedside table Gillian gave a strangled cry. "But I fear there is little I can do. None but the Lord can do aught now."

The women slipped to their knees as the priest began, "In nomine Patris et Filii et Spiritus sancti..." In the name of the Father and the Son and the Holy Spirit...

"Kyrie eleison..." Lord have mercy. Clarice's unstifled sobs accompanied the priest's words. "We beseech thee to have mercy upon this thy servant visited with thine hand..." A shuddering sigh racked Gillian's body. ".... and whensoever her soul shall depart from the body, may it be without spot presented unto thee; through Jesus Christ our Lord."

All joined in the "Amen."

The service proceeded to the Viaticum. Father Whiting held up the bread. "Jesus Christ is the food for our journey; he calls us to the heavenly table." The priest partook, then turned to the still form on the bed and placed a crumb on her tongue.

Father Whiting removed his stole and repacked his basket, then bent to embrace the still kneeling, weeping Dorcas. "It is in God's hands."

Gillian lingered for two more days and two more nights. It seemed she grew weaker with every shallow breath she drew, but no longer was her body racked with fearful sobs and cries, no longer did she tremble and writhe as if in torment of soul. A great peace had descended on her. So great that at times she seemed almost to float above her bed as if an angel enfolded her in wings of tranquility.

On the third night Clarice stood long by the bed, gazing at the smooth, ivory oval of her sister's face. Each breath was so light she was certain it must be the last. And yet, at length, another would follow. Not enough, surely, to sustain life. Clarice took Dorcas's hand and pressed it to her own cheek, wiping away her tears. "You must prepare yourself, Mother. She will not last the night."

"I know, my dear. I am yielded. God's will be done."

And yet Gillian still lingered when the first rays of dawn struck the window and the candle guttered.

"Help me sit up."

The words were the more startling for their very faintness. Had Gillian spoken? Or had they heard the rush of air as her spirit departed her body?"

Gillian's voice was weak, but distinct. "I am dead from the waist downwards. Yet I would sit up."

Clarice placed a fat goose down bolster behind the thin back and tugged to raise the inert form. Dorcas shook her head. "Alas, my dear. It can be but the lightening-before-death. After this last effort her soul will haste to depart."

Gillian's lips made the slightest movement. "I surrender my will wholeheartedly."

"Does she speak?"

"Yes, dear. To God. She hasn't strength to make us hear, but he who is closer than mother and sister can hear her."

The blue lips moved again. "I would be completely at your disposal. I would think of nothing but you while my life lasts."

Father Whiting returned, and they moved aside to make room for him. "Daughter, I have brought you the image of your Maker and Saviour." He held a cross before her face. "Look at it, and be strengthened."

Gillian's eyelids fluttered. With great strength of will she held them open enough to gaze on the face of the crucified Christ. "Your face, my Lord, I fix my eyes on your face. I thought that what I was doing was good enough, for my eyes were fixed heavenward where by the mercy of God I trust to go. But I will gaze on you as long as I have strength.

"Oh, but the room grows dark. Is it night again just after the dawn? All is dark except the cross. Your face, Lord, my eyes cling to you.

"Now the death creeps upward. I feel nothing. My breath comes shorter. Shorter. This it is to die. My God, my God. Your face. Your face."

And then, in the space of a breath, the pain dissolved.

Antony's narrative had carried them past Peterborough. All the way the land had become increasingly flatter and flatter until now the level Cambridgeshire fens stretched in every direction, dissected by rivers and drains. But the landscape held only the periphery of Felicity's attention. "She died?" What a letdown. "No, wait a minute. She wrote a book. She recovered and was enclosed."

The slowing train drew Felicity's attention to her surroundings again. They were pulling into Ely. Felicity gazed out the window at the flat, treeless fields stretching on every side of them. And from the town ahead of them, the tower and lantern of the cathedral rose like a magnificent ship sailing across the flat landscape.

No sooner had the image formed in Felicity's mind than Antony pointed. "Ely Cathedral—they call it 'the ship of the fens'."

"It's amazing. And so is your story about Julian." They left Ely and its cathedral behind. Three more stops before Norwich. "So that's when she became a nun?"

"Perhaps, we don't know. It's all conjecture—except the words. They are as she wrote them later."

"Oh, yeah, I remember you said."

"Her cell, which was lived in before and after her, was

under the control of the Benedictine nuns of Carrow Abbey, about half a mile down the road. Apparently the nuns referred to her as Mother Julian, but that could have been merely a term of respect. It was quite possible for one to become an anchoress without being a nun. Whatever the case about that, however, she was probably enclosed about two years after her showings. That would have been the normal waiting period for anyone who had asked to embrace the solitary life of an anchoress."

As Antony resumed his story Felicity found herself irresistibly drawn back in time, to the merchant's home in Norwich before Gilly left everything to become Julian.

"Two years? Just going on living quietly at home after all she had been through?" Felicity couldn't get used to the idea of all that waiting. She thought perhaps hearing Julian/Gillian's story would help her sort out some of the confusion she felt over her own call.

It must have taken considerable time even for Gillian to sort out what had happened. Perhaps Gillian tried to explain the experience to her family, sitting on a summer evening while Dorcas slid the soft woolen fibers through her fingers to wind on her twirling spindle, just as Julian recounted it later in her book

"How was it so, Gilly? One breath was your last, the next your rebirth?"

"I do not know how it was. I am more amazed than you. It must be a special miracle of God."

In that time since her recovery not one day had passed without Gillian feeling more serenely certain of God's hand on her life. She could feel it now with the warmth of the sun on her head while she sat in the lengthening shadows of a summer evening, the stripes of deep gold and shade stretching out from the fruit trees behind their house. Although they preferred to make their own gowns from the fine wool their father secured for them from the markets he frequented, no woman of their class would choose to sit idle for long, so Clarice carded a basket of wool from the spring shearing, while Dorcas, pausing to wind a length of spun thread on her spindle, then running it up her leg to set it spinning again, worked with easy rhythm. Gillian, as always, sat reading.

"And did you truly ask to suffer so, Gilly?" Clarice stopped mid-brush in her smooth stroke with the long-toothed comb that straightened the wooly fibers, staring wide-eyed at her sister.

Gillian set her book aside and looked up with a soft smile. "Yes, truly. I wanted to be ill to the point of dying. To the point of receiving Last Rites."

"But why?"

"I wanted to know more of the mercy of God so I might live more worthily of him. I wanted to know true sorrow for my sins so I could have more love for God."

"But I don't understand."

"Sister, surely you knew always of my devotion to the passion of our Lord. As was the devotion of our dear St Francis who was granted so great a grace as to receive the stigmata. I would not dare to ask for so great a grace, but I was granted the grace that our Lord himself directed to me a divine impulse to pray for the second wound. Indeed, I had so long desired it—for fifteen years or more—that I had all but forgot. But our Lord did not forget, and so he granted me the fulfillment of my longing for such union with him in this life.

"I cannot tell you the wonder and perplexity which filled me. I was convinced that I was going to die, and yet the purpose of the whole revelation was not merely to comfort me in the moment of death, but was revealed to this lowly servant for those who would go on living."

"In truth, did you want to die? To leave us?"

"Never that I loved any of you less—especially my dear mother—but that I loved God more. And truly, I thought it would be a great pity to die, as I am still young. But the truth is, I wanted to live not because of anything on earth I wished to live *for of itself, but because were I to live I might come to love God more and better in this life, and so ultimately to know and love him more in the bliss of heaven."*

"But you suffered so. It was awful." A shudder shook Clarice's shoulders.

"My dearest, I do beg forgiveness for any pain I caused you or our mother. But I could not stop my longing to experience in my own body and understand in my own mind the blessed passion of our Lord. I wanted his pain to be my pain. I desired to suffer with him."

Gillian's hands rested palm upward in her lap; a distant look of deep serenity spread over her face. "Our Lord showed me how intimately he loves us. I saw that he is everything that we know to be good and helpful. Everything owes its existence to the love of God. And I saw that by his grace it is truly pleasing to him that we should pray with confidence and cling to him with real understanding and unshakable love."

"And what will you now?"

Gillian shook her head slowly. "I will think long on these mysteries our Lord has granted me. This great goodness of his. He will show me what he wills that I do with his gifts." The lowering sun struck the gold of her hair, making a halo around her head. The very beauty of the scene struck terror to Dorcas's heart. All this time she had been sitting a little apart observing the serenity of her most-beloved daughter. My daughter prayed to share Christ's suffering. Am I so weak, so pale, so cowardly that I cannot contemplate suffering the pain of Mary, his mother?

But scolding herself was useless. It brought no yielding to her heart and no lessening of the fear. For Gillian had not spoken the words, yet Dorcas knew what the end result of such a profound experience as Gillian's must be. One day, no doubt soon, Gillian would say the words Dorcas would blot from her mind if she could. Gillian would surely become a nun.

Hadn't Dorcas been fearing exactly that for years? Where had she failed? Had she not been a good enough mother?

Is my reluctance—horror, even—to see Gilly become a nun a matter of sin in myself? *Dorcas wondered, not for the first time.* Shouldn't I be so totally committed to his will that I say whatever you want, Lord—take all of me—all of my family? Is not my reluctance to give him my daughter selfishness and lack of commitment on my part?

Felicity blinked, coming out from the spell Antony's words had woven for her. And echoing with Antony's words were those of Mother Mary Mark, "A candidate must think of her relationship with her own family before she takes on a new one. Is her calling intense enough to counteract the pain and distress she might cause in her own family?"

Felicity had refused to make a personal application of those words at that time but now, having spent twenty-four hours in close company with her own mother, having witnessed her grief over the breakup of their family and having heard the albeit fictional account of Julian's mother, perhaps it was only fair that she consider her mother's feelings as well. Now that she realized her mother *had* feelings.

Pushing these more difficult topics from her mind, she turned to Antony. "And to think that her cell is still there. That boggles the mind!"

"Well, don't be too boggled. Yes, it is an amazing story, no matter how much you allow for my embroidery, but the cell that's there is a reconstruction. A church has stood on that site tucked away in St Julian's Alley since the year 950 and has been destroyed and rebuilt many times. Most recently it was rebuilt in 1953 from the rubble of a 1942 air raid. Dame Julian's hermitage, which had been pulled down at the Reformation, was reconstructed on its original foundations with that rebuilding."

Reconstruction or not, Felicity was now glad to be making

her way to Norwich. Surely on the site of such ancient holiness she would be able to find answers to some of the questions plaguing her. Was it too much to hope she might find the peace and love Julian found?

Just over an hour later the three of them stood at the door of All Hallows House. Felicity rang the bell with some trepidation. Sister Johanna, the nun who ran the retreat centre, had assured Antony she could accommodate them, but what sort of reception they would receive on such short notice?

Felicity had barely formed the question in her mind, however, when the door flew open to the accompaniment of enthusiastic barking from a golden brown, long-haired terrier, and a tall, slim nun with a long, floral apron over her tidy dove grey habit engulfed her in a hug.

"Felicity? Do come in." Cynthia and Antony were greeted with equal enthusiasm. "Don't mind the mess." She shoved garbage bags aside with her foot. "I have the decorators in. Let me show you what we're doing."

She whisked them through the guest house at a breathless pace, the cavorting terrier she introduced as Barnaby, bounding at her heels. "This is the only way forward. As Julian said, 'Love is the way.' Showing love, caring for people—there are so many needy people out there. It's a grass roots thing. Jesus worked with ordinary people. Julian had the ordinary people on the street. To *be available*, that's the thing. That's why I want to get this house homely so people will feel loved and cherished, and will unfold. So many people are like little tight rosebuds. They need to unfold in the light of Christ. People want to hear the message, experience the love."

The images of love shown in homeliness flashed by as they zipped through the rooms: the kitchen in charming French provincial print: "I found that beautiful white oak table under some awful yellow vinyl covering"; the sitting room with chintz covers over the tired brown furniture: "This was a dirty peachy color. I'm making it sunny yellow—I want to brighten the place up"; The arbor newly planted with honeysuckle and jasmine; the dining room with beautiful woods, woven rattan floor cover, candles on table, rich burgundy paper on two walls.

"Sister Johanna, you're a whirlwind!" Felicity managed to gasp.

"Well, I have been called the flying nun." Her bright eyes flashed.

They sat in the parlor with welcoming cups of tea while Barnaby snuggled against the skirts of Sister Johanna's habit, and she continued in her breathless manner telling them about her work. It was clear that she was anything but the enclosed anchorite Dame Julian had been. She told of her experiences in Peru walking the Inca Trail to raise money for children, and of her travels in Europe. "Father Antony, I have been so pleased to read your newsletters on church unity. You are absolutely right. Everywhere people are coming together. We are finding our underlying unity in prayer and the sacraments—a *lot* of prayer and sacraments. I was a sacristan at Lambeth. We had Eucharist every morning, Bible study and prayer every day, worship every evening—four and a half hours of worship and prayer a day. 'You're trying to make us all monks,' I told the archbishop."

They chuckled at the idea of a nun protesting over too much prayer, and Antony explained to Cynthia that Lambeth was the once-every-ten-years conference of worldwide Anglicanism. Then Sister Johanna turned to Antony. "But do forgive me for going on so. You said on the phone that you are making enquiries. How can I help?"

As Antony explained briefly about the apparent attempted robbery at the Community of the Holy Cross, Sister Johanna became more and more intent, leaning forward in her chair, her forehead furrowed. "Oh, but that's terrible! Sister Mary Perpetua will be all right, won't she?"

They all expressed their fervent hope and belief that she

would be. "Even before that happened, Sister, I was on my way here." Antony explained about the theft of the icon from the Community of the Transfiguration and his information that an icon had been stolen from the Julian Shrine some time ago.

"Yes, it was. You're quite right. But we have kept the matter very quiet. I believe our bishop has asked the archdeacon to look into the matter. Perhaps wrongly, one hesitates to call the police where objects of worship are involved. I wonder how you knew?"

"A student at the College of the Transfiguration knew of it, I believe through his uncle who is a curator for some London museum. As a matter of fact, I was rather hoping you might have heard from him, Sister. He was coming here with me, but disappeared from the house at Rempstone. You've not had a call from Neville Mortara, have you?"

Barnaby's sharp yip as the contents of sister Johanna's teacup baptized his head was followed by the clatter of china as her cup fell to the floor.

Chapter 7

Evening of Mothering Sunday

"Oh, I'm sorry. So silly of me." Johanna picked up her cup and dabbed at the spilled tea with the apron she had removed earlier. "I was just so surprised at the name. Neville Mortara. Yes, he has made one or two retreats here. But that was some time ago."

Felicity was musing over the unlikelihood of someone as self-possessed as Sister Johanna so overreacting at hearing an unexpected name, when Johanna continued. "Disappeared, did you say?" She paused. "No, your call was the only one we've had today. Of course, it's unusual to have any calls on a Sunday, but I am glad I happened to be near the office, since your circumstances were rather urgent. When I'm out, calls are switched to Angela St Claire in the visitors' center."

"Do you have this Angela's phone number?" Antony asked. "Perhaps Neville contacted her directly if he's been here before."

"Possible, I suppose, but unlikely. She's not my employee. The visitors' center maintains an archive service for which Angela serves as researcher. It's all quite separate from the retreat house. I don't know her number. I don't think she lives in Norwich. I have the impression her home is somewhere out in the Broads. But she will be in tomorrow. The visitors' center opens at 10:00 in the morning." Before Felicity could voice her frustration at the prospect of more delay, Sister Johanna looked at her watch. "Oh, it's almost 6:30. Solemn Evensong and Benediction at St Julian's. I can give you a light supper afterwards."

"That would be perfect, thank you, Sister. I think we would

all appreciate an early night tonight." Cynthia's yawn evidenced her agreement with Antony's words.

A few hours later, though, in spite of the appealing idea of curling up in her tiny, cozy room to read the copy of *Revelations of Divine Love* offered on her bedside table, Felicity's restlessness would not let her settle. And, in spite of her insistence that she was not participating in this investigation, her mind wouldn't quit running over the disturbing events of the past days. At last she gave up, threw her duvet aside, and pulled on a pair of jeans and a turtleneck. She padded down the silent hall, hoping she remembered which door was Antony's.

His immediate response to her light knock showed he wasn't making a success of the early night idea, either. Together they slipped quietly to the kitchen and closed the door. All Hallows didn't make an issue about keeping silence, but they wouldn't want to disturb Sister Johanna or Cynthia. Antony put on the kettle, and Felicity made toast.

"So, I think we can scrap the idea of Our Lady of the Transfiguration simply being borrowed for devotional purposes." Antony settled himself at the large, scrubbed oak table and poured two mugs of tea. "It seems obvious that there's a larger pattern going on here."

"But I still can't accept the idea that Neville might have done it." Felicity added milk to her mug. "I know it looks awfully suspicious. He has connection to all three incidents." She still couldn't bring herself to say thefts.

"Connections? Having made a retreat or two here hardly counts as a 'connection'."

Suddenly Felicity brightened. "Maybe Neville saw the attempted theft at Rempstone and followed the would-be thief!"

"A hopeful thought, indeed. Except for the fact that Neville hasn't got in touch with us."

"Well, we have been traveling."

Antony shook his head. "Mobiles."

"Oh, yeah." Felicity, who seldom used hers, looked sheepish. "So you mean that if he *did* try, perhaps the thief turned on him?"

"Possibly. One could put more unpleasant interpretations on it."

"I find that thought plenty unpleasant." Felicity shook her head. Unable to find any obvious solutions, she decided to put the puzzle of Neville's role in all this to one side for the moment. "OK, tell me more about this cross thing. Did you see it on the welcome folders at Evensong tonight? What was it doing there?"

"The Maltese cross is the symbol of the Knights of St John or the Knights Hospitaller."

"Oh, and St Julian's Church was dedicated to St Julian the Hospitaller. Was he a knight?"

"No, he probably lived centuries before the knights were founded, although his legend was extremely popular in the Middle Ages and his example of providing hospitality and care for travelers was undoubtedly an inspiration to many of the knights. Hospitals are still occasionally dedicated to him.

"The nearer connection here is the church of St John the Baptist, Timberhill." He continued before Felicity could express her confusion. "St John's is the main Anglo-Catholic church of Norwich and is the parish church for St Julian's. They display the Maltese cross because it is the emblem of St John the Baptist, for whom the Knights of St John were named."

Felicity was silent for several moments, sipping her tea thoughtfully. "So, it's all logical and all coincidental. The emblem isn't a clue to anything?"

"Well, don't put too much weight on it, but I wouldn't dismiss it that quickly, either. After all, you did see it on the icon."

"Which Neville was looking at. And Neville has

disappeared." Felicity brought the conversation back to the most immediate, most disturbing point. Finally she broke the long silence that ensued. "Why do you think Sister Johanna overreacted so at hearing Neville's name? You don't suppose she suspected him, too?"

"I don't know, but I hope we can learn something from this Angela in the morning."

"Right." Felicity gave a resigned sigh. "I guess there really isn't anything we can do until she comes in tomorrow."

"I think I'll slip up to St John's for morning prayers and have a chat with the vicar afterwards. I suppose it's just possible he might know something about the emblem on the icon," Antony said as he tidied away the tea things.

"I wish we knew whether or not it was on Our Lady of the Transfiguration." Felicity followed him from the kitchen.

"I'll ring Father Anselm tomorrow and see what I can learn."

"Yes, and ring Mother Mary Mark, too. See how Sister Mary Perpetua is. And ask about that hermit they have staying there—maybe he saw or heard something."

They continued on in silence until a floorboard creaking under their feet made them jump and forced them to suppress their giggles. Felicity turned suddenly sober at a new thought. "Antony," her loud whisper echoed in the empty hallway. "Why didn't I ask before? You *have* tried ringing Neville?"

His slow, slightly crooked smile gave her heart a little twist she refused to acknowledge. "Oh, yes. Several times." He didn't even say, *Of course,* or *How stupid do you think I am?* How could anyone be so unfailingly courteous?

"No answer?"

He shook his head, that lock of dark hair falling over his fine, high forehead. He really was the most strikingly handsome man. It tended to catch her unawares when she really looked at him. Unfair in a priest.

Antony paused at the door to his room. "Felicity—"

The intent look on his face made her take a step backward. Had he read her thoughts? Or sensed the weakening she felt?

"Thank you. I appreciate your help more than you can know." He silently shut his door.

Chapter 8

Monday, Fifth in Lent

Antony strode up the hill, taking deep breaths of the fresh morning air in hopes it would invigorate his muzzy head. Despite the late hour, when he finally got to bed last night he hadn't slept well. His attempts to focus on solving the puzzles of the missing icon and their missing friend always ended in the same place—with focusing on the question that truly shadowed him; the question over which he had no control, the question he didn't even dare voice—the question of Felicity's future. And the more staunchly he told himself he had no right to dream of taking her in his arms, the more he dreamed of doing so.

Determined to focus on matters at hand, he walked through the gate in the iron-railed fence and entered the silent church. Although the door stood open the priest wasn't present and no time was posted for morning prayers, so Antony crossed to the Lady Chapel filled with pale morning sun from the east window, taking a prayer book and Bible from the rack.

A few minutes later, his office completed, he was disappointed that the rector still hadn't appeared, so he wandered around the beautifully appointed church. Clutter in a church drove him to distraction. The house of God should be clean, orderly and beautiful. As this one was. And the two icons he found were equally lovely: appropriately, one of the Baptism of Christ and one of the Mother and Child—both affixed tightly to the wall with no possibility of his checking for cryptic markings on the back. His efforts were as useless as he felt.

Back outside he noticed subliminally a young homeless

man sitting on the stone bench beside the church wall, his shoulders slumped, the hood of his sweater covering his face, a small box at his feet with no more than a few small coins. With a sense of sharing the young man's dejection, Antony pulled a few coins from his pocket. They made a satisfying clink as they landed in the box. At least he had been able to do some small bit of good on his wasted task.

And he did feel better. All the way back down the hill he told himself that the lift to his spirits was due to having helped the rough sleeper, not to the fact that he would soon see Felicity. However it was Cynthia, not her daughter he encountered when he entered the hall of the guest house.

"Good morning, Antony, you're out bright and early, aren't you, in spite of your late night?"

If Antony had been given to blushing he would have. He knew the hallway creaked. What must she imagine? "You're off to London, then, are you?" He indicated her bag by the doorway.

"Yes, Johanna said there's a train every half hour, so I've called a cab. I don't want to be any more trouble."

Felicity came around the corner from the parlor but hung back from her mother. Cynthia turned to her. "Darling, I do wish we could have talked more." She paused, but Felicity was unresponsive. "In spite of everything, it has been truly lovely to see you." Felicity stood rooted. Cynthia reached out and just brushed her shoulder. "I do love you, you know. And I hope you can forgive me. Some day."

The arriving taxi crunched on the gravel driveway outside. Cynthia turned to pick up her handbag. And Antony could read the turmoil on Felicity's face. He held his breath. No matter how hard this was for Felicity, he was certain she would never forgive herself if she didn't do something.

Felicity took a tiny step forward. "Goodbye, Mother." She gave Cynthia a stiff little hug. "Travel safely." Antony smiled and picked up Cynthia's suitcase to follow her to the taxi.

"Oh, I almost forgot." Cynthia turned back, rummaging in her purse. "Here, the firm's number. You will call me when you get to London? You're visiting some convent or something there, aren't you?"

"Yes." The answer left it indefinite which of Cynthia's questions Felicity was answering.

When Antony returned, Felicity was still standing ramrod stiff watching the departing taxi. When it was out of sight she turned to him. "Did you learn anything?"

He shook his head. "Beautiful church. Two icons; neither one them look particularly old or valuable."

"Waste of time, then?" Her words stung, and Antony could not find a response.

Just then Angela arrived a few minutes early to open the visitors' center. They waited while she unlocked the door, then walked along the path to introduce themselves. The researcher was a stunning redhead dressed in shades of turquoise and gold that suited her perfectly.

"Neville Mortara?" She rolled the name around on her carmine lips, apparently thinking hard. "If he booked a retreat here I suppose there might be some details on the computer, but Sister Johanna should have had them." She tossed her cloud of red hair and led the way into the center. The large room, which served for both hospitality and research, was lined with shelves of books. Several long work tables invited serious study or casual browsing.

It took a few moments for her to boot her computer. She began clicking through files. "When did you say he was here last?"

"I'm not sure, but I got the idea it might have been a couple of years ago."

"Hmm." She scrolled through several listings. "Oh, here we are. Apparently he gave a cousin as a contact person. Simon

Mortara. Do you want his mobile?"

Antony wrote down the number, and he and Felicity stepped back outside for him to place the call on his phone. He put it on speaker so Felicity could hear, too. It was answered after only a few rings. "Simon here."

Antony identified himself and explained his concern for their missing companion.

"What, Cousin Nevvie's gone missing?"

Antony tried to explain about the attempted robbery.

Simon gave a shout of laughter. "So that's why you want to get in touch with Nev! You suspect him of pilfering! I must say I never could understand how he supported himself in London as an artist, but I never imagined that."

"No!" Antony hoped his protest wasn't too vehement. "We're worried about him. About his safety. Not his honesty."

"Oh, I expect our Nevvie can take care of himself."

"So you haven't heard from your cousin for some time?"

"Not much communication since he went off to study with a bunch of monks. I thought that would keep him out of mischief. But then, maybe that was precisely the problem for Neville, the dear boy. Of course, today it's all perfectly PC and all that, but I'm afraid Aunt Sheila just couldn't see it that way. Very traditional, she is. Desperate to have grandchildren, and Neville her only child."

As the monologue continued, Angela turned the Closed sign to Open, and rolled out the book cart. She gave Antony a brilliant smile, ignoring Felicity before ducking back inside.

"Well, so that's the scoop on the family," his informant continued. "Probably more than you wanted to know. What else can I help you with?"

"When did you last see your cousin?"

Simon thought for a moment. "That would have been Christmas. The usual family do at Riddlington."

"Riddlington?" Antony asked.

"The family pile. You said you're calling from Norwich? It's not far from you—out past Wroxham, in the really boggy bit of the Broads. Family's been there for yonks, and undoubtedly will be until it subsides into the ooze."

Antony thanked the garrulous Simon and disconnected, shaking his head.

"What do you make of that?" Felicity asked.

"More than I wanted to know about his cousin's attitudes." Antony sighed. "Nothing very useful about Neville. Unless he might have gone to his family home in the Broads, I suppose."

Felicity wrinkled her forehead. "That's the second time I've heard that term. What's the Broads?"

"The Norfolk Broads," Antony began explaining as he led the way back inside. "A very unique corner of our little island. A vast area of wetlands that were used for peat excavation from Roman times. Sometime in the late Middle Ages or so the sea levels rose and the pits filled with water. It formed seven rivers and sixty-odd wide, shallow broads that were used for transportation for centuries and recreation now."

"It sounds like a very interesting place to live," Felicity said.

Angela looked up from her desk and shrugged "If you're a waterfowl. Great place for birdwatchers, boaters, fishermen—ramblers, too, I suppose, if you wear your wellies." She turned to her desk. "If you plan to spend some time in the area I can supply you with maps, boat rental information…" She held out a selection of pamphlets. "Tours, woodland and water gardens, stately homes. Let me know if you need anything else."

Felicity took them. "Thank you. I don't think we'll be staying long, but I'd love to learn more about the area."

Antony stepped forward. "Actually, we wanted to ask you about the icon that was stolen from the shrine."

"Yes?" Antony wondered if Angela's body stiffened ever so slightly. Her smile, however, did not waver.

"You see," Antony continued, "one was stolen last week from the Community of the Transfiguration, so of course, we're interested in anything that might indicate a lead to finding it."

"Yes, of course. Glad to help in any way I can." If the subject had made her uneasy she had certainly made a quick recovery.

"So what can you tell us about your icon?"

"Well, it was a milk-nourishing icon. You're familiar with those?" She looked at Antony.

He nodded. "Yes. It depicts the Virgin nursing. I believe icons of this type are known from as early as the sixth century in Egypt. The need for Christ to be fed exemplifies the incarnation while also alluding to his future passion."

"That's right. It was so especially appropriate for Julian's shrine because of her emphasis on Christ as our Mother." She picked up a book of favorite quotations of Julian of Norwich, turned a few pages and held it out to Antony. "I expect you're familiar with the quotation."

He perused it quickly. "Yes: *he needs to feed us ... it is an obligation of his dear, motherly, love. The human mother will suckle her child with her own milk, but our beloved Mother, Jesus, feeds us with himself, and, with the most tender courtesy, does it by means of the Blessed Sacrament, the precious food of all true life. ... The human mother may put her child tenderly to her breast, but our tender Mother Jesus simply leads us into his blessed breast through his open side, and there gives us a glimpse of the Godhead and heavenly joy...*"

"Oh, that's beautiful!" Felicity's eyes were shining. "May I buy that? Is it for sale?"

"Take it. It's yours" Angela said with a wave of her hand that served to show off an exquisite pearl and aquamarine ring.

"How long had the shrine had the icon?" Antony asked.

"Forever, as far as anyone knew. I searched all our archives—" She gestured at the file cabinets behind her desk. "No actual records have survived. There were legends, though. My favorite was that it was given to the church by a grateful pilgrim. It was quite *de rigeur* for pilgrims to bring valuable gifts, of course. That compensated a church for keeping an anchoress or anchorite. The problem is that the proponents of the theory have no explanation of how it later survived the Reformation or Cromwell's despoilers."

"Or how such a pilgrim came to possess it?" Antony asked.

"Well, pilgrimage was a big business in medieval times, as tourism is now. It is fun to think of a devout traveler picking up something like that in Rome or the Holy Land and then giving it to Julian for her wise advice."

Felicity broke in with a note of irritation in her voice. "But that's all speculation. What we really need to know is if there was a special mark on the back of the icon. A fancied-up Maltese cross?"

A shadow seemed to cross Angela's face, but it could have been a shift in the morning light. "What? Why would you ask that?" If there was a sharpness in her voice she recovered instantly with a small laugh. "Sorry. Our motto is that there is no such thing as a silly question, but I've never heard that one before. I don't know that I ever examined the back.

"The thief was very clever, you see. The icon was kept on a high shelf in the church and another milk-nourishing image was substituted in its place."

"So you don't really know how long the original had been gone?"

"No, Sister Johanna was the first to notice that something was different. A lack of subtlety in the colors, the gold lacked depth—something."

"How did you confirm it?" Antony asked.

"I'm no expert, so I sent it to an authority in London. His name was Mortara, too. Perhaps a relative of your friend? He confirmed that our icon was very new and not very good. We have left it on the shelf, though, since it's all we have."

She rose and extended her hand to Antony. "Well, it's been lovely to meet you. You'll let me know if there's anything else I can help you with, won't you?" She ushered them to the door. "Do enjoy your stay in Norwich. Be sure to visit the cathedral. They give excellent tours."

Back outside in the spring sunshine Felicity laughed. "'Oh, please don't rush. Here's the door.'"

"Yes, she did seem anxious to get rid of us."

"Am I paranoid? Or did we startle her?"

"I couldn't say." He paused and grinned. "On either point."

Felicity ignored the bait. "What now?"

Antony shook his head. "I wish I knew. I'll try ringing a few people, I guess."

"Good. I think I'll go see the fake icon and visit Julian's cell."

Antony watched her stride away, her long braid swinging as she walked. No matter how perverse she could be, he couldn't deny that just being with her raised his spirits.

Chapter 9

Monday, Fifth in Lent

Felicity walked around the visitors' center to a tiny flint church. She knew it was a restoration, but it certainly looked medieval to her. The heavy wooden door was unlocked. She pushed it open into a small sanctuary, cool and quiet. The white stucco walls held deeply recessed, leaded, arched windows. Stone-flagged pillars separated the small nave from the chancel where a single sanctuary lamp hung over the purple-fronted high altar standing against a reredos holding six tall candles. It was spare and a little cold.

To her left a leaded and traceried window portrayed a golden chalice with the host above it. On a small shelf beside the window was the icon of the Virgin nursing the Holy Child. Even knowing as she did that it was a replica, Felicity felt the appeal of the representation of the Virgin nourishing the infant that would nourish the world with himself. It was a touching picture: The Virgin so young, the Infant so tiny with his hand on his mother's round, smooth breast.

So what, she wondered, made this icon a fake? Of course it was a copy of the much older one. But there were many modern icons that were "real." What divided real from fake? Other than the flat look, the use of gold leaf and the fact that they were painted on wood, what was the difference between an icon and a painting, she wondered? She looked around, but there was no one and nothing to enlighten her, so she moved on.

Turning toward Julian's cell she crossed the dark wooden floor, entered the zigzag carved round arch in the far wall, and stepped into the fourteenth century.

For a moment she stood transfixed. What was she doing here? Felicity asked herself. What did she hope to accomplish? She felt guilty that she wasn't concentrating on solving the mystery of the icon and their missing friend, and yet she was mesmerized by the peace of the tiny room.

She wandered aimlessly around the small cell, trying to recall the woman Antony had conjured so vividly yesterday. Felicity read the sign on the wall: "Lady Julian was called to serve God in the solitary life. From her anchorhold—on the site of this chapel—she enriched the world by her writings."

And carved under a stone crucifix:

> *Here Dwelt Mother Julian*
> *Anchoress of Norwich 1342–1430*
> *"Thou art enough to me"*

Thou art enough. Felicity couldn't imagine it. Would she ever be able to say such a thing? She who wanted it all? But then, what *was* all? She turned to sit on a small bench against the wall. Golden sun, dappled by the leaded glass, fell on a crucifix on the wall to her left. It was a pleasant enough room, light, with a high, steep-pitched wooden ceiling. But for this to circumscribe all of one's universe? She tried to put herself in Julian's time, imagine what it would have been like in Julian's day. How would it have been furnished? A bed, a table, a stool, perhaps a bench similar to the one she sat on—only narrower? But the window was so high, considerably above street level. How did Julian give counsel through that? Felicity vowed to find out.

A door led to the outside. So the anchoress could walk in a walled garden? Surely she would have become ill without fresh air. And a door to the church. For her servant to bring in food? The window to the church overlooking the altar was obviously so she could receive the sacrament. Flowers brightened the windowsill and candles flickered on the table that now served as an altar. Surely in Julian's day it would have been covered with writing instruments.

There was no fireplace. Gratefully Felicity pulled the cord to switch on the electric heater mounted on the wall. Could anyone have really survived in this damp cold with no fire? She made another mental note to find out. But for now she sat, listening to the silence, feeling the stillness.

She had seen all that she came to see, yet Felicity felt anything but ready to leave. The cell enclosed her in a womb of hushed holiness as if it had something to give her or tell her.

Felicity realized she was still carrying the book of quotations Angela had given her. She opened it to the "Christ is our Mother" section from which Antony had read. Such an arresting image—beautiful and disturbing at the same time.

> *"Our Saviour himself is our Mother for we are for ever being born of him ... Jesus is the true Mother of our nature, for he made us. He is our Mother, too, by grace, because he took our created nature upon himself. All the lovely deeds and tender services that beloved motherhood implies are appropriate to Him .... A Mother's is the most intimate, willing, and dependable of all services, because it is the truest of all. None has been able to fulfill it properly but Christ, and he alone can.*
>
> *"This fine and lovely word Mother is so sweet and so much its own that it cannot properly be used of any but him ... In essence motherhood means love and kindness, wisdom, knowledge, goodness."*

She put the book aside, unwilling to delve further into Julian's theology or to continue the fight to suppress the little voice that kept telling her she should be applying this to her own life. If Julian was right, should she be more forgiving toward her own mother, or did she have even more right to be angry over Cynthia's shortcomings as a nurturer? And what about the saintly Julian? The way Antony told the story her decision was difficult for her own mother. Felicity couldn't help wondering whatever became of the imaginary Dorcas.

She looked around the room. Julian lived sealed in here for—what—some forty years? Until she was about eighty-seven? And what was happening to her family all that time? Felicity was struck with an irreverent thought: What if Julian's desire for enclosure was spurred by a wish to escape difficulties in her family life? As if directing her thoughts, a shaft of light coming through the uneven panes of the leaded window fell on the sign on the wall: "In this holy place we can almost hear her saying, 'God said not "Thou shalt not be afflicted," but "Thou shalt not be overcome."'" Ah, so whatever the facts of her life, Julian did know affliction—maybe more than the physical affliction for which she was famous. Maybe Felicity could learn something from this woman.

Back in the center among the rows of books, cards and candles for sale, Felicity spotted a shelf of icons. All modern, surely, although a couple at the back looked rather old. What better place to hide a stolen one—like Edgar Allen Poe's *Purloined Letter*? Fanciful, surely, but it made her recall her desire to learn more about icons.

She selected a small, inexpensive one with a particularly appealing pose of the Mother and Child with their heads bent cheek-to-cheek and the child caressing his mother's face. She would put it over her desk when she got back to college.

"Oh, that's my favorite, too," the volunteer at the counter said as she rang up the small purchase. "One of the Tenderness type, they call it. There are even some that depict the Christ Child with both arms around his mother's neck. One can almost feel his embrace."

"Mmm," Felicity paused. "I'm afraid I don't know much about icons. Do you have a booklet or something?"

The lady offered a leaflet titled *A Discourse on Iconography*, written by someone called Sir Robert Tennant. "Perhaps this will help."

Felicity skimmed the first few paragraphs: "An icon is part

painting, part symbol, its purpose is to remind people of the spiritual aspect of the saint depicted. It is a physical representation of a spiritual essence.

"An icon is an image which leads us to a holy, God-pleasing person or raises us up to heaven, or evokes a feeling of repentance or prayer. The value of an icon lies in the fact that, when we approach it, we want to pray before it…"

She was still perusing the leaflet as she entered the guest house and almost walked straight into Sister Johanna emerging from the parlor, Barnaby trotting at her heels.

"Oh, Sister, the very person I wanted to talk to."

"Come into the kitchen. Let's have a cup of tea."

Johanna bustled about the kitchen as Felicity seated herself at the scrubbed oak table. "I've just been looking at the icon in the church. Of course, I'm a total novice on the subject, but I couldn't see anything really wrong with it. Angela said you spotted the fact that a copy had been substituted for the original. How did you know?"

"I suppose there are lots of technical clues, the patina of the gold, the type of wood and pigments used. Things our expert would have looked for. But I just *knew*." She poured boiling water on the tea bags and sat across the table from Felicity, the steeping pot between them. "A genuine icon is a work of prayer. Every brush stroke is a prayer. Everyone who approaches it in truth should be drawn to prayer."

"So, that's how you knew? You weren't drawn to prayer?"

"Yes, no matter how fine an artist might have painted a work, no matter how beautiful it might be, if it is devoid of sanctity it is not an icon."

More questions were forming in Felicity's mind when Antony joined them. He glumly poured himself a cup of tea in silence, adding more sugar than he normally took.

"No luck, then, Antony?" Felicity ventured.

He sat at the end of the table with a sigh. "Father Anselm

had no idea whether or not the Community icon had a Maltese cross on the back, or any other kind of signature or mark of ownership that could be a clue to who might have taken it. He will ask Brother Stephen, the sacristan, on the chance he might have noticed. But unlike the Community of the Holy Cross, the Community of the Transfiguration never moves their icon. It would have been veiled for Passiontide, but not even removed for church cleaning on Holy Saturday. It has probably been years since anyone looked at the back of it."

"And your friend Neville?" Sister Johanna asked.

Again Antony shook his head. "No one has heard anything. I'm afraid the fact that Neville and the icon have both disappeared looks bad."

"But he wouldn't—" Sister Johanna coughed on a swallow of tea. "That is, surely an ordinand wouldn't have had anything to do with a robbery."

Antony sat silent, staring into his cup.

"Er, tell me about him. How was he in the monastery? Was he devout?" the nun asked.

"I'm sure you know about his successful art career, then his seemingly sudden decision to give it up and take holy orders?"

Sister Johanna lowered her grey eyes. "I never quiz our retreatants. Then when suddenly it's too late…"

Felicity sighed. "So essentially we don't know anything more than we did two days ago. I might as well get on to London tomorrow. I told the sisters at Ham Common I'd try to be there in time for evening prayers." Antony nodded without comment. He was clearly even more discouraged than she was. Nothing to do but get on with her plan.

Chapter 10

Monday, Fifth in Lent, Night

That night, in the silence of his room, Antony felt far too restless to go to bed. He picked up a book, but was unable to concentrate. The gentle tapping that told him Felicity wanted to talk sent him to his door with a bound.

"Yes? You haven't been to bed yet, either? You have an idea?" His voice lightened in anticipation as he stepped out into the hall, tying the belt of his dressing gown.

"No, I can't settle. Didn't even try. But no ideas, just questions." She looked over her shoulder as if someone might be listening to their conversation in the silent house. "Um, we can't talk here." She led the way to the lounge and took her time snuggling deep in an overstuffed chair before she drew a long breath and began, "What do you know about Sister Johanna? Do you trust her?"

Antony sank into a chair, the twin of Felicity's, with a small table between them. "Trust her? Of course I do. Is there any reason I shouldn't?"

"No, not really. I mean, I like her a lot. But I don't know anything about her. And, of course, I would have said I trusted Brother Matthew—that is, I did trust him until..." There was no need for her to go into the calamitous results of her earlier naïve reliance.

"No, you're quite right. Until we know what is going on we can't really trust anyone." He thought for a moment. "I don't know much about Sister Johanna. I think she was a sister at the mother house of their order in Suffolk until their Mother Superior asked her to take over as warden here."

"And you don't know anything about her background—education or family or anything?"

Antony was flabbergasted. "How odd. One never thinks of nuns as having a background, a prior life. Oh, no pun intended." He grinned. "But, really, one just thinks of them as nuns. Obviously a failing because they are as human as you or I."

When the words were out their irony struck him. It was impossible to remember that Felicity was thinking of becoming a nun herself. Impossibly painful for him.

"What do you know about her order?"

"The Community of All Hallows is very active."

Felicity giggled. "Can you possibly imagine 'the Flying Nun' in an order that wasn't active?"

"True." Antony pushed his dull ache aside and managed a stiff smile. "They have three guest houses and two retreat and conference centers, I believe. All the sisters are involved in hospitality, spiritual direction and conducting retreats. And then they run a day nursery for infants and a nursing home for the elderly and a hospice for the terminally ill. I think they especially focus on AIDS care."

"So in other words, the whole order is as hyperactive as Sister Johanna."

Now Antony was able to join Felicity's laughter. When that faded they sat in silence for a few moments, the quiet drawing around them, making Antony feel uncomfortably close to his companion, even though they sat in wide chairs separated by a table.

Felicity broke the silence before it became awkward. "Actually, that isn't really what I came about, although Johanna does intrigue me. I can't seem to figure her out. But really, I've come for a bedtime story. I was wondering today in the cell—tell me more about Julian and her mother."

Antony started to run his fingers backward through his hair, then stopped abruptly. A childish gesture of anxiety and indecision. He must break himself of the habit. At least, a story would take his mind off his present anxieties for a time.

"Would you accept a fairy tale? That's as close as anyone can come to reconstructing anything of Julian's life beyond her own writings. I like to imagine her mother still living after her enclosure because the whole motherhood imagery is so central to Julian's writing. But it's entirely conjecture, you understand."

"Pure romance is fine with me." Felicity grinned. "Romance in the old-fashioned sense of an adventure story, I mean, of course." She closed her eyes as his voice filled the cozy room.

"We do know a few facts. For example, Julian lived by the *Ancren Riwle*, so she could have had a cat to keep down mice, hence the white cat pictured in the Julian window in the cathedral, but no cow—because it might get loose and she would have to leave her cell to chase it. She had a servant and, oddly enough, we know the servant's name—Sara—because later in life she became an anchoress herself."

"And how did she keep warm? There was no fireplace in there."

"No, no fireplace. She would have had a small brazier."

"Ah. And was the window really that high? How could she have given spiritual guidance through that?"

"Yes, the window was that high, but the floor is about two feet lower than hers was. The room is eighteen foot square, it would have been fourteen in Julian's day because the walls of her cell were two feet thick."

Felicity apparently had no more questions.

"Right then." Antony put his feet up on the footstool in front of his easy chair and folded his hands over his lap. "I like to imagine that months—or perhaps years—after Julian was enclosed, Dorcas herself was one of the visitors to Julian's worldside window:

"Dame Julian, you have a visitor at your window." The anchoress startled at her servant's voice, a small blob of ink falling from the

tip of her quill onto her closely written parchment.

"Thank you, Sara." *Julian suppressed her sigh with difficulty. After so long one would think it would get easier. That was three callers today. It was past time for her afternoon prayers; she had hoped to finish just this one short chapter today.* Forgive me my trespasses, Lord. You have not refused me any request. You never turn anyone away. Help me to serve yet another needy soul in your name. *She crossed herself and left her table appearing far more serene than she felt.*

Her servant stopped her before she reached the window. "I'll go to the market now, Mistress. Farmer Dereham left us a fine cheese and three beautiful brown eggs this morning, but we have no milk."

"Yes, thank you, Sara."

The servant put on her long brown hooded cloak and crossed into the church. Julian turned to her curtained window. She gave a small cry at the sound of her caller's voice. "Oh, my mother! That silly Sara only said I had a visitor. I would not have kept you waiting so long. Are you well?"

"I am well. Clarice takes excellent care of me. And just see what a fine loaf she has sent you." *Dorcas passed a basket through the window. The bread was still warm and filled the tiny cell with its yeasty scent.*

Julian lifted the linen cloth. "Oh, that looks wonderful. Thank my sister for me, and give her my love."

"But what of you, my daughter? Are you well?" *The unspoken thought hung in the air. Perhaps it was not so bad a thing to be shut away from some of the trials of life.*

"I am very well, Mother. I am never sick."

"Ah, that is good. You have never been sick since—"

"Not once, Mother. Is not our Lord gracious beyond all imagining?"

"And this life, it suits you still?"

"What more could I ask than to serve our Lord through his

beloved children who come to me?" Then Julian laughed. "Well, I could ask more time for my writing. I would not that any of his showings which he so graciously vouchsafed to me should be lost."

Dorcas's hesitation to continue the conversation showed that even after all this time her daughter's singular experience and her life that followed it were hard for the mother to accept. "And, ah, do you have new, er—showings?"

"No, no. I could not ask for more. It will take me a lifetime and beyond to understand what has been already revealed to me of his love. That is why I am writing—or struggling to write— another book, to record a fuller revelation of his meaning."

"What of this love, Gilly? That is why I have come. My daughter, I grow old." Julian reached under the curtain and took her mother's hand; whether to comfort her mother or herself, she wasn't sure. She could hear her mother's increased frailty, feel the paper thinness of her skin. "What words of comfort do you have for your mother?"

Julian thought. Strange, it had always been her mother who had given comfort. Now the mother was asking comfort of the daughter. Now Julian was the mother; indeed, many of the young novices of the nearby abbey called her Mother, although she was not professed. "I can give you nothing, my mother, but what you have already given me, for it was you who first showed me him by showing me love.

"He has ransomed us from the evil one by the motherhood of mercy and grace, and brought us back again to that natural condition which was ours originally when we were made through the motherhood of natural love.

"All that you taught me by your love, Mother. Now you must rest in his loving arms."

The tears welling in Dorcas's eyes were reflected in the catch in her voice. "My dear, dear Gilly." She pressed a thin, gnarled finger to her daughter's soft hand and stroked it wordlessly. "My *dear, dear girl. You have always been such a joy to me. In spite of all. Such a joy."*

After a time, Dorcas turned and walked away. Her steps were slow and halting, and yet there seemed to be a lightness about them. Julian turned to her prayers, knowing that she would not see her mother again in this life.

For a moment Felicity sat as if spellbound by the world Antony's words had woven. "Thank you," she said a bit dreamily.

"Felicity— " Antony leaned forward and put his hand out.

But Felicity broke the spell by standing up and moving beyond his reach. "That story was just what I wanted." She yawned luxuriously and padded out of the room.

But Antony sat on, listening to her soft footstep going down the hall. He couldn't help asking himself: How much of his story was a historical reconstruction, and how much simply his trying to deal with the specter of someone he was coming to love more dearly every day being locked away from him beyond reach?

Chapter 11

Tuesday, Fifth in Lent, Morning

Felicity took her backpack with her to breakfast that morning, leaving her room tidy with the bed remade, dirty sheets and towels deposited in the laundry basket at the end of the hall. It would be impossible to say a warm enough "Thank you" to Sister Johanna for her gracious, impromptu hospitality.

She looked around, relieved that Antony wasn't there. She had had the distinct feeling last night that if she had sat longer in the lounge, Antony would have reached out and taken her hand. And then she would have had to decide whether or not to let him hold it. Far better to avoid such scenes altogether.

The thing now was to have a good breakfast and get on to London. She was listening to the rain dashing from oppressively grey clouds as she spread a golden layer of butter on her crisp whole wheat toast followed by a layer of marmalade. She was just taking her first bite when Antony burst into the kitchen.

"Felicity, thank God you haven't gone yet. I just heard from Neville!"

"Oh, that's wonderful. Is he all right?"

"He sounded excited." Antony considered for a moment. "Almost upset. He said he found something."

"Something to do with the icon?"

"Must have been. Something about a manuscript. He started to tell me more, then I think someone came into the room or something because we were cut off. When he rang back he just said to meet him at St Benet's. He would show us something there. The key, he said, but he needed help. He was very insistent."

"Where?"

"A ruined medieval monastery in the Broads."

"Now?"

He looked at her bulging backpack. "You don't have to leave for London just yet, do you?"

She shrugged. "Not really. They aren't expecting me until this evening. And I would love to see Neville. How do we get there?"

"I seem to remember the lovely Angela saying something like 'let me know if you need anything.' I wonder how she would feel about loaning us her car?"

A short time later, Felicity was struggling to make sense of an Ordnance Survey map as Antony headed northeast out of Norwich. "It looks like you turn off the B1140 just ahead— toward a place called Ranworth."

"Oh, yes. Ranworth." Antony turned the car down a narrow road with green fields stretching beyond the hedges. "There's an interesting church there. I wish we had time to stop. St Helen's Ranworth, often called 'The Cathedral of the Broads.' It survived the ravages of Cromwell's vandals because the land around it was so flooded they couldn't get to it to smash its statues and crosses." Appropriately, as he spoke, Antony slowed for a puddle in the narrow road.

Felicity lifted her eyes from her map just in time to see a sign. "Road liable to flooding," she read. "No wonder the iconoclasts couldn't get through here on horseback. We may have the same trouble in a car."

In just a few miles the windows were mud-splattered and Antony's knuckles were white, gripping the steering wheel. Felicity could feel his frustration mounting as he negotiated the narrow lanes. "I hope Neville's all right. We should have been there by now."

"Did he say where he had been?"

"King's Lynn."

"Huh?"

"Town north of here. His uncle's a vicar there."

"Must be a big family. They show up all over the place. But I don't understand why he went there."

"I'm sure he'll explain it all when we see him." Antony took another turning and sped up as much as conditions allowed. They plunged into the wet, nascent green; high hedgerows on each side of them, dripping trees overhead. When the hedgerows ended, the first tightly curled shoots of what promised to be enormous banks of fern lined the road. Felicity looked up from her map to see a pile of dark, threatening clouds looming to her right, a tiny patch of bright blue overhead.

They came to a crossroads. "Which way?" Antony asked.

Felicity shook her head. She was too confused even to answer.

Antony examined the map for a few moments before giving it back to her. He took a right turn and drove on with grim determination. It wasn't long, though, until the combination of poorly marked roads and detour-causing puddles forced him to admit they were thoroughly lost. Antony stopped in the middle of the deserted, narrow road and took the map from Felicity again. "Sorry I'm such a hopeless navigator," she said.

"No, no. Don't apologize. I can't make any sense out of this, either. I think we'll head back to Ranworth. There's a visitors' center there, we should be able to get directions. I just hope this is the way."

"And you'd better ring Neville, let him know what's happening."

"I hope he has his mobile with him."

Felicity laughed. "You must be joking. He's compulsive. Even at CT where no one uses them. He even keeps it in a plastic case so he can use it in the rain. One time— Oh, look!"

Felicity interrupted herself as they turned down a muddy farm track with cows grazing in the fields on both sides. "A sailboat!" She blinked. It couldn't be—and yet—"It's sailing right across that field!"

In spite of his tension, Antony laughed. "Welcome to the Broads. Actually, there's a waterway there, but because everything is so flat you can't see it until you're right on top of it. It does, indeed, look like it's sailing across the field."

A few more turns down unmarked lanes and splashings through muddy puddles brought them back to Ranworth. The visitors' center was open, but unattended. While Antony tried ringing Neville on his mobile, Felicity looked over the books on offer about sailing and waterfowl and stately homes. She found the pictures of the wherries particularly interesting: the historic boats with their distinctive single, high-peaked sail that plied the Broads as cargo ships for hundreds of years. Vast swathes of black, red or white canvas billowed against blue skies. And then she spotted something more to the point—a guidebook to St Benet's Abbey.

She was just wondering how to pay for it in the unattended shop when a trim young woman in tight jeans and oversized sweater rushed in out of the rain. "Oh, sorry." She tossed her short black hair, spraying drops of water like a dog. "I just had to run next door. I'm Heather. What can I do for you?"

Antony explained their dilemma in a few words.

"Oh, yes. I know. It's really a very popular spot for visitors, but almost impossible to find across the fields. Much easier up the river." Heather paused. "Actually, Henry, my husband, will be taking *St Helen* out in a few minutes. He could run you up there."

"St Helen?"

"The center's launch. He's been working on the motor. Said he wanted to give it a test spin." She began leading the way.

"That would work very well, if it isn't too much trouble," Antony said. "We're in rather a hurry, I'm afraid. We're meeting a friend there."

"Did you get hold of Nev?" Felicity asked.

"Left a message."

"Oh, good. Probably means he's still driving, so we aren't all that late."

They were on the concrete landing by the river's edge when the red and white six-passenger motorboat glided up and a stocky man with thick brown curly hair tossed a rope to Heather, who wound it expertly around a piling. The sailor jumped ashore with a jaunty greeting to the visitors. Henry and Heather both seemed to possess the ebullient, welcoming personalities perfectly suited to running a visitors' center. Heather explained the situation.

"Right. No problem. None at all. Just need to take the old girl out to be sure there are no kinks in her engine before we start the regular tourist season. Offer trips every afternoon then." Henry glanced at the leaden sky. "You may get a wetting, but not to worry, we've a cover."

They sat behind Henry at the front in the cabin and Felicity turned around for a full view of the placid, wide grey river and the lowering sky sitting just on the top of the straggling willow branches and waterside trees that in another month would form a long, isolating tunnel. The tourist launch slipped through the water to the accompaniment of the steady engine roar. Just them and their escort of ducks, each of the hens followed by a V of recently-hatched ducklings.

It should have been comforting, gliding along inside a cocoon, but the cold, damp air and glowering grey sky made Felicity shiver. In an attempt to shake the uneasy feeling she dug in her pocket for the guidebook. "Oh, how interesting! This is the only abbey in England that wasn't dissolved by Henry VIII."

"That's right. And before you ask, I'm not his namesake," their host Henry responded with a grin. "The Bishop of Norwich is still the Abbot of St Benet's, continuing right on from medieval times. They have a big service here on the grounds every summer. We usually take a boatload up from the parish church."

"So if it wasn't dissolved, why did it cease operating?"

Henry shrugged. "Times change. It was always a pretty out-of-the-way place and the action was in Norwich. After the Reformation I don't suppose many fancied joining a monastery. The monks just left."

A few moments later he added, "I hope you won't be disappointed. There isn't much to see: The gatehouse with an eighteenth-century drainage mill built into it is rather interesting, and there's a big cross that marks where the high altar was in the abbey—that's where the bishop holds his do every year. A few heaps of stones here and there. That's about the size of it. You'd never guess now that it was once one of the richest abbeys in England."

"What happened to it?" Felicity asked.

"The story is often told that the buildings simply subsided into the marshland after the monks left. A picturesque tale, I must admit, but it was really just a case of decay and demolition. Some of the gatehouse was torn down to allow the sails of the mill to turn."

"The guidebook says it's on an island." Felicity told herself she was just interested—not apprehensive. This was not the North Sea. Tides would not cover this island.

Still, Henry's answer felt comforting. "Technically, yes, but only by virtue of being surrounded by a river and canals. Not what you'd think of as being a real island."

Around the next curve in the river the trees and bushes gave way to tall reeds. The river was entirely theirs. Felicity was just urging herself to relax when a sound like a buzzing mosquito signaled the approach of another boat ahead. Felicity turned forward, but before she could get her bearings the small black craft shot around a bend in the river and seemingly headed straight toward them like an obsidian arrowhead. Water sprayed out on either side, emphasizing its speed and power.

"Hey, watch it!" Henry shouted and jerked the wheel to the right. The launch responded sharply.

The speeding craft missed them by inches. Even in the covered cabin Felicity was drenched with spray as the St. Helen rocked wildly.

"What do you think you're playing at?" Henry shook his fist and shouted at the departing boat, his swearing not entirely under his breath.

The speedboat raced on out of sight, leaving them rocking wildly in its wake. Felicity clutched Antony's arm and Henry held the tiller steady. At length the wake receded and *St Helen* steadied. "Idiot! He could have killed us all." Henry wiped his forehead and settled back. "Sorry about that. Not our usual tourist ride, I promise you. People are normally very courteous on the river."

Maybe it was the near miss, maybe it was the darkling clouds and the damp chill seeping into the boat, maybe it was because she had almost got herself killed the last time she cadged a ride on a boat to be let off on an island, but whatever it was, Felicity could no longer shake off her the apprehension that had niggled at her for hours.

Of course they could trust Neville. Ridiculous to think otherwise. But this place seemed awfully isolated. And if Neville was the thief...

Chapter 12

The land on either side of the river cleared to wide, flat green fields as they swung around a deep loop in the river. The looming pewter sky with rolling clouds reminded Felicity of a painting by a Dutch artist. Ruisdael, maybe, if she remembered her art appreciation course correctly. And then Henry was cutting the motor and pulling to the right bank. "There was a regular landing up there by the gatehouse in medieval times." He gestured toward an odd structure of broken stone arches surrounding something which resembled a giant brick kiln. "Sorry. I warned you there wasn't much to see. That's the monastery gatehouse. The strange bit in the middle is what's left of the drainage mill."

Further beyond in the center of the wide, open green, Felicity could just make out what appeared to be a large wooden cross. She pointed. "That's where the bishop holds his service now?"

"That's right." Henry put the motor in neutral, and the boat rocked gently. A gaggle of honking geese with their straggling goslings greeted their arrival. "Can't get you any closer, I'm afraid. All this conservation work to the riverbank is new— about four or five years ago now. Created a new bank. Very sturdy—those wire cages filled with stones—but prickly to rub up against, even with rubber bumpers on the boat." He held his hand out to Felicity. "You sure you want to get out here?"

Felicity was about to say that it looked awfully deserted when a strange, high-pitched buzzing sound like a giant mosquito seemed to come from the broken mill. "What's that?"

The words were no more than out of her mouth than a group of perhaps fifteen schoolgirls in matching blue and bright turquoise jackets emerged from the far side of the ruin chasing the "mosquito."

Henry laughed. "Now, that's a surprise. Wouldn't expect anyone to be here this time of year. Looks like Girl Guides. Must be doing some project with those model aeroplanes."

Felicity smiled. "Oh, that takes me back a few years. I was forever pestering my brothers to let me fly theirs. I never had the excuse of earning a scouting badge, though." She grasped Henry's hand and jumped ashore.

"I don't much like leaving you here," Henry said. "I'll stop on my way back, shall I?"

"We don't want to put you out—" Antony began.

"Yes, please," Felicity broke in. "We're so late, he might have given up on us."

She waited to wave their host away. But Antony was already striding toward the gatehouse some hundred yards across wet grass as the Girl Guides scampered off toward the site of the ancient abbey church, the mosquito buzz swallowed up in their giggles and chatter.

After clambering over the wooden stile that straddled the fence enclosing the abbey grounds, Felicity consulted the map in her guidebook. "In Victorian times there was a pub along the riverbank." She pointed up the river in the direction Henry had gone. "The Chequers. One gets the feeling this area used to be more populated than it is now."

"Except for Girl Guides." Antony grinned and took her arm to help hurry her across the rough, wet ground. When they were a few feet from the gatehouse he called, "Neville! Hello! You here, Nev?"

There was no answer. They entered the dark, conical cavern of the mill. Felicity craned her neck to look upward at the threatening clouds through the open hole in the center. She shivered. It was dark. And cold. And strange. And deserted. "So where's Neville? It took us so long—you don't think he gave up on us and left, do you?"

Antony shook his head. "Strange. He sounded so insistent about meeting here."

"What could he have needed help with here? It's just all empty space with a few broken stones." Felicity shivered. "Let's get out of this place."

Out in the all-too-fresh air she could breathe again. "That's better. That place was like a tomb." She looked around. "He probably got done with whatever it was and is nice and snug in a pub somewhere."

"Maybe." Antony didn't sound convinced. Felicity started walking slowly around the outside of the gatehouse, looking up at what was left of the architectural details. "This must have been quite wonderful in its day. Look, you can still make out the figures over that arch." She squinted at it. "Hmm. A man holding a spear on the left. Some kind of an animal on the right." Then consulted her guidebook. "'Lion with a double tail, holding a circular object in its raised forepaw,' it says here. Wonder what they meant? Symbols of power? Or an allegory of fighting evil?"

Anthony shrugged. "Your guess is as good as mine. Pity so much has been lost, but on the other hand, I guess it's amazing that anything remains."

"Yes." Felicity was still perusing her book. "Here's a sketch of what it looked like in 1722 before they built that silly mill in the middle." She showed Anthony a series of fine pen and ink drawings showing the gatehouse with two storeys of ornate stonework fairly intact.

"And look at that." Anthony took the book from her hand to look more closely. "'A series of baronial shields. Probably the arms of families who had made important donations to the abbey,'" he read.

Peering over his arm Felicity added, "'And gaps suggest there were originally ten.' Do any of those mean anything to you? Could any of this been what Neville was on about?"

"'Beauchamp, de la Pole, Clare, Valence, Warren and Arundel,'" Antony read. "Powerful families indeed, but I don't make anything out of it."

They walked on around to the side of the gatehouse facing inward toward the monastery grounds. "There were more shields on this side." Felicity turned a page in the guidebook. "One to an unidentified family. That's intriguing, isn't it?" She peered at the rough outline on the shield. "Antony, am I imagining it or is that a Maltese cross?"

He considered, his head cocked to one side. "Hmm. I see what you mean. It could be. With some other carving behind it. Possibly a star? Maybe."

"Like the icon. Is this what Neville wanted to show us?" She put the book in her pocket and moved forward to examine the stones more closely, running her hand over the rough, timeworn surface. "What could you tell us, I wonder? Who were the families? What does it all mean?"

"Well, if this was what Neville wanted to show us we've seen it. But we still need him to interpret." They had walked some distance from the mill over the uneven ground toward the cross, the only bit of the grounds they hadn't yet explored, when Antony pulled out his mobile.

Antony's tension seemed to increase with each ring. "Nev, we're here. Ring me."

Felicity was cold and discouraged, and not sure whether she was more puzzled or worried. Still, there was nothing to do but wait to hear from Neville. "We might ask the Girl Guides if they saw anyone leave. Maybe they know where Nev has gone."

The grass was long, and wet. They had gone less than half of the 400-some yards to the cross before Felicity's Doc Martens were soaked through. The Girl Guides were coming toward them. The buzzing of the plane had stopped, so perhaps their outing was finished for the day.

Antony waved and approached one of the leaders, a plump, middle-aged lady with a cheery smile, and short brown hair under a cap. "Pardon me, but we were to meet a friend here. I don't suppose you saw anyone when you arrived? Tall slim chap, blond hair?"

The leader shook her head. "I didn't see anyone, but we could ask the girls. They're quicker off the mark than some of us. I stayed behind to lock up the minibus." She gave a vague gesture to the left where apparently the van was parked alongside the narrow road leading to the abbey. The road Antony never had found.

"Did you meet any cars driving in?"

Now the leader gave a jolly laugh. "Nothing but cows and waterfowl for miles around, is there? We could have picked a better day for our outing, but the school had a half day, so it worked well for the girls. They're very keen." She looked around. "Nadia, Lucy, come here a minute."

A tall, black girl with a dazzling smile, and a chubby blonde, both probably about eleven years old, ran over. "Yes, Miss Scowthorpe?"

"You girls were some of the first off the van. Was there anyone here when you got to the grounds? These people are looking for a gentleman."

The girls looked at each other, shaking their heads. "No. No one here that we saw," the blonde said.

"No," Nadia added. "Just the man getting into the boat."

"What?" Felicity and Antony spoke together.

"Didn't really see him. He was sort of running toward the river. On the far side of the mill."

Antony described Neville, but both girls shook their heads. "I didn't see anyone," the blonde repeated. "Just heard the boat zoom off, like."

"What color was the boat? Did you see?"

The black girl wrinkled her nose as she thought. "Darkish, maybe. Didn't really notice."

They thanked the girls and their leader. "Good luck with your badges," Felicity called as she and Antony turned back toward the cross. It was a good trek over uneven ground covered by coarse grass, the way marked by low piles of stone that had probably once been monastery walls. They were still a hundred yards or so from their goal when the skies opened.

There was an ominous rumble followed by a single, sharp clap of thunder and the heavy, dark clouds so close over their heads simply dumped on them. Felicity shrieked and ran for the only shelter in view for miles around, the old brick drainage mill. She sprinted through the gatehouse arch into the mill, and flattened herself against the wall where the inward slope gave a semblance of shelter.

Antony followed her closely, likewise hugging the wall next to her. After a few moments of gasping they both caught their breath, although Felicity's heart was still pounding. "I never thought I'd see the day I'd look back on that bus shelter in Beal as being sumptuous." She recalled the refuge they had taken in likewise pouring rain on their way to the Isle of Lindisfarne.

Antony glanced upward at the water sluicing through the roofless round hole that served as a funnel to pour rain on the earthen floor at their feet, the center of the floor illuminated by an almost ghostly light from the orifice above. "As I recall that roof only leaked instead of gushing."

"At least there *was* a roof." And with that they fell silent. So much had happened between them. And yet nothing had happened. And even if Felicity had wanted to talk, the rain pummeling the dirt focused all her attention. She moved her feet back fractionally to avoid the mud being splashed up by the downpour, but it was hopeless. She couldn't really be any wetter or muddier than she already was.

And where *was* Neville? What could he possibly have wanted that could in any way justify all they had gone through? Was this his idea of a joke? If he had learned anything about the icon it certainly couldn't be around here. Some ruined abbeys might present secret caverns or hidden cubbyholes to hold purloined icons, but St Benet's obviously didn't.

Now they would miss their ride back to Ranworth with Henry, too. Unless they could ring the visitors' centre. "Antony, get your phone."

"Who did you want to ring?"

She dug in her pocket and withdrew a sodden slip of paper. "I was thinking of calling the visitors' centre. Their number might be on the receipt for the guidebook, but it's too dark in here to read. I thought we could try to reach Henry."

Antony held his open phone to provide a small glow of light and held his hand over it to shield it from the water. Felicity, likewise protecting the flimsy paper from the wet, peered at it, then shook her head. "Nope."

Antony started to close his phone when Felicity said, "Try Neville again. Maybe we'll be in luck this time."

The ring was faint, but they both jumped. "What was that?" Felicity looked around. The circling walls of the mill acted like an echo chamber. It almost sounded like… But it couldn't have—

Felicity screamed when the muffled ring sounded again. From beneath their feet.

Chapter 13

Tuesday, Fifth in Lent, Afternoon

The thing that held Antony transfixed in horror, though, was not the deadened ring, as if a call from another world, but the scene he knew would haunt his dreams forever. The specter appeared to rise at their feet as the pouring rain washed back the mud to reveal a slim white beringed finger, then hand, then wrist, the receding soil making it seem in that small circle of light inside the blackness that the arm itself was rising from the grave. Reaching upward for light, for air—for them.

Felicity gave another piercing shriek and ran for the doorway.

"Felicity!" Antony's one instinct was to protect her. Whatever horror had risen at their feet, Felicity mustn't be allowed to dash out into the storm alone.

They were some distance beyond the **mill** before he caught her and pulled her into his arms. She clung to him, gasping and shaking. Only when Felicity calmed did Antony realize the rain had slowed to a faint drizzle. "It's all right. We're safe." He wasn't even sure what that meant, but he had to say something to reassure her; to reassure himself. "Steady on. You'll be all right," he repeated.

He felt the shudder go through her body as she gave a faint gasp. "It can't..." Her words were strangled.

"Hold on. I'll get help." His hands were shaking so he could hardly punch the 999 emergency number with a muddy thumb.

"It was Neville, wasn't it? It must have been. His phone...

His hand…" She buried her face against Antony's shoulder. "But it can't be. We were to meet him. You spoke to him…"

Antony looked around frantically for a place for Felicity to sit. The stone base of the cross seemed miles away across the field. The foundation of the gatehouse presented no place to perch. The best he could offer her was the slippery wooden boards of the stile.

They sat on the narrow step, clinging to one another for warmth, for comfort. Emergency services had to come all the way from Norwich. It would be a long, cold wait. But they wouldn't have left if they could have. Their friend was alone in that dark, wet place. "Shouldn't you say a prayer or something?" Felicity said at last.

Antony ducked his head in shame. What was he doing, thinking of his own discomfort? A Christian soul was in need of ministry. He moved toward the mill. Felicity took a step forward.

"Are you all right to go back?" he asked.

"I'd rather. I don't want to sit here alone." He could feel her trembling as she walked close beside him. He longed to put his arm around her, but her head held high on a stiff neck warned him to keep his distance. He had been allowed to soothe her initial panic. Now his indomitable Felicity was back.

"There can't possibly be any forensic evidence to protect after all those Girl Guides and the rain, but you wait here." He laid a hand on Felicity's arm to halt her then hesitantly moved forward. He held his breath, steeling his courage. He had to be sure.

The hand was ice cold. No pulse at the wrist. He rubbed the mud from the ring, placed the hand gently on the ground and went back to Felicity.

The doorway was narrow, but it was a deeper instinct that drew them to stand so close together for several long moments of silence, broken by a short, sharp sniff from Felicity.

"The Lord be with you," he began.

"And with thy spirit." They joined their hearts in prayer.

Antony wished fervently for his prayer book, and darted a quick upward plea for the words to come to him. "Go forth, Christian soul, from this world…" he began, then stopped abruptly. Wrong prayer. The moment of death was well past. His fingertips could still feel the chilled skin they had touched. He racked his brain, praying for the right words.

"Come to the aid of our brother—" Surely it was Neville, but to name him was to abandon hope. He skipped the name and went on, "Ye Saints of God; come to meet him, ye Angels of the Lord, Receiving his soul, Offering it in the sight of the Lord Most High. May Christ receive thee, who hath called thee, and may Angels lead thee to Abraham's bosom.

"Rest eternal grant unto him, O Lord," he paused. Would Felicity know the response?

"And let light perpetual shine upon him." Her choked voice was barely audible.

"Kyrie eleison."

"Christe eleison."

"Kyrie eleison.

"Unto thee, O Lord, we commend the soul of thy servant that being dead to the world he may live to thee … Receive him into the arms of thy mercy, into the blessed rest of everlasting peace, and into the glorious company of the saints in light. Amen."

He made the sign of the cross over the impromptu grave, and together they spoke the most comforting of all prayers, "Our Father, which art in heaven, hallowed be thy name…"

This time Felicity didn't pull away when Antony put his arm around her tentatively. He held her tightly, willing his own body heat to warm her, desiring peace and comfort for her as he felt her heart pounding against his chest.

It could have been three minutes or thirty minutes later

when they heard a familiar voice calling, "Wooee, hello! Needing that ride after all, are you?" Henry strode toward them from the direction of the river. "Sorry to be so long, the rain slowed me down. Thought I'd just walk up to be sure—" He broke off and stopped a few feet from them. "What's the matter? You both look like you've seen a ghost."

"That's exactly what's—"

Antony's explanation was cut short by an hysterical giggle from Felicity. "I'm sorry. It's not funny, but—" And she was shaking again with laughter. High-pitched and uncontrollable.

"She's had a shock," Antony explained.

"What happened?" Without waiting for an answer Henry hurried on. "Never mind. Time enough when we're more comfortable. I've got blankets and good hot tea in *St Helen*— never go out on the river without them."

"We can't leave until the police get here."

"Police?" Henry raised his eyebrows. "We won't go anyplace then, but might as well wait in comfort—such as it is."

The two men propelled Felicity to the riverbank and lifted her into the boat. Her broken giggles changed to sobs which didn't subside until she was well wrapped in blankets and Henry had poured half a mug of hot, sweet tea down her throat. "Wish I had some brandy to lace that with, but this is the best I can do," he said. "Now, tell me."

Antony, clinging to his warming mug of tea as if to a lifeline told him in as few words as possible, not really wanting to talk about it, especially in front of Felicity who had subsided into silence; and yet, in some strange way, finding it a relief to share the horror verbally.

It was a considerable time later when, to the swirling of sirens and the flashing of lights, the silence of the countryside was rent by an ambulance and three police cars making their way as fast as possible down the mud-clogged track behind the abbey grounds.

"You stay here," Antony told Felicity. "I'll go put them in the picture."

A small, dapper man with a mustache, wearing a tweed overcoat, was the first over the stile. He introduced himself as Detective Inspector Marsham. "And this is Sergeant Caister." He indicated a large, rumpled, redheaded man of about Antony's own age. "You're the one who lodged the call?"

"I am, yes." He would have to mention Felicity before he was done, but for the moment she could stay in the relative comfort of the boat.

Sergeant Caister took notes as Antony told them as clearly as he could the events of the day, beginning with Neville's phone call that morning.

"So, what makes you believe this is the body of your friend, Neville Mortara? How do you spell that?"

Antony spelled the name for the sergeant and explained again about the appointment, the ringing mobile and the hand, with Caister interrupting twice more to check his spellings.

"Yes. Quite. And you didn't dig any more?"

Antony suppressed a shiver. "I felt for a pulse. That was enough."

"What makes you so sure it's your friend's hand? Anyone could have been carrying his mobile."

"Yes. You're quite right." Antony would have liked to believe it was some stranger. Perhaps Neville lost his phone and some vagrant picked it up, and... Besides the unlikelihood of that, though, there was something else; something he saw in that fleeting, horror-filled moment that seemed to be distinctly Neville. He closed his eyes, willing himself to see the scene again, but the shock of the moment had wiped any other detail from his mind.

"Well, never mind. We'll know soon enough." The detective inspector waved to two uniformed policemen slogging their way across the field. "Frank, tell the scene-of-crime officers to get to work in the mill. Then you and Alan see if you can find anything on the grounds." He looked around and shook his head. "Not a chance after all that rain. And apparently a clutch of Girl Guides fairly trampled the area. Still—have a look-see."

"Now," he turned back to Antony. "I'd appreciate it if you'd stick around until we get a better picture of things. It'll save us some time if you can give us a definite ID here, rather than meeting in Norwich. Of course, we'll need an official word from the next of kin, but you can do a preliminary. I don't suppose you know his family?"

"He has an uncle in King's Lynn, I believe."

"And there was no one else about when you found the body?"

"Yes—er, that is, my—" what *was* the right word: friend, student, associate? "My colleague, Miss Felicity Howard. We're from the College of the Transfiguration in Kirkthorpe. In Yorkshire." Without waiting to be asked, he spelled Transfiguration and Kirkthorpe for Sergeant Caister. After brief consideration he left him on his own with Yorkshire.

"I'll want to talk to her, too." Marsham looked around.

"She's in the boat." Antony waved toward the riverbank. "The man from the visitors' centre in Ranworth who brought us here returned to pick us up. Miss Howard is understandably upset."

"I'll need you to wait until my team does their thing in there." Marsham nodded toward the mill where Antony could see white-suited figures kneeling just inside the door. "You all might be more comfortable waiting in my car. I'll try not to keep you too long."

As it turned out, it was the better part of an hour before Marsham returned to take statements from Henry and Felicity. Plenty of time for Antony to replay the entire train of events over in his mind several times in detail, and mull over the unexplained questions jostling for preeminence: Exactly what had Neville said about his hasty flight to King's Lynn? Had it, on second, third and fourth look, really made sense? What could Neville possibly have wanted help with here? Was it something worth murdering him for? What did he want to show them? What could all this have to do with the missing icons? Or *did* it have anything to do with them? And who could have killed Neville, and why?

Antony simply had no answers. And he had another worry. Would he—worse, he and Felicity—now be suspects? The alarms and anguish; the doubts and desperation of their previous investigation flooded back upon him. Most especially, the terror he had felt when Felicity was in danger. Could he—could they—go through such a thing again?

They had only started out to locate a missing art object. Correction. He had started out. Felicity had been roped in. By himself. Last time she had volunteered—pushed, even. This time it was on his head. Certainly Father Superior wouldn't ask him to become involved in another murder investigation. As soon as the police were through with them, Felicity could continue her journey of discernment and he could return to the safety of his college. The police would find the murderer even if they didn't find the icon.

But as quickly as he thought it, he knew the answer was unsatisfactory. And he was amazed at the calm the knowledge brought him. Unlike their earlier investigation, he was flooded with questions—but not with doubts. He was fearful for Felicity—but not for himself. He had no desire to run from whatever challenge faced him. This was the first time he had really taken such inventory of himself since the adventures of a few weeks ago. And what he found filled him with strength and comfort. If he could only impart some of that calm assurance to Felicity.

He got out of the car, as did the others, at Detective Inspector Marsham's approach. Now the cool, moist air felt refreshing. It had become rather muggy in the car.

"Not from these parts, are you?" The detective inspector said as soon as Felicity stated her name.

"No, I'm from Yorkshire." She blinked at her own statement. "Oh, I see what you mean. I'm from America." And she explained briefly about her university exchange program, her year of working in London and her decision to study at the College of the Transfiguration.

"Passport?"

"Yes, of course. And a student visa."

Marsham held out his hand.

"Oh. Well, not with me. I left my backpack at the Julian Centre. I'm meant to be in London tonight. I was just going to say hi to Neville and then…" Her lip trembled uncontrollably, and she dashed a hand at the tears spilling from her eyes. "I'm sorry, I…"

"Technically you should have your papers on you at all times, but we won't make an issue of it for the moment. I will need to see them when we all get back to Norwich."

Felicity nodded and dug in her pocket for a handkerchief. After a moment she was able to answer the detective inspector's questions.

The diligent Caister scribbled down her replies, and Marsham listened with a level gaze that indicated a quick, detailed mind. "Right. That should do it for now. I'll need you both to come into the station tomorrow to sign a written report."

After a few questions to Henry, especially about the incident with the speeding boat, Marsham glanced toward the mill where the ambulance crew was just emerging with a covered stretcher. "If you don't mind, Father." He nodded toward Antony.

"Certainly." Antony turned toward the somber tableau with Marsham. As did Felicity.

"No need for you to come, miss. It's not a pretty sight."

"Please. I would like to see him. We were friends."

Perhaps the inspector read more into those words than they merited, but he gave a sharp nod and the three of them squished back across the field. The stretcher-bearers paused, and Marsham pulled down the sheet.

Felicity gasped, and Antony felt the blood drain from his face. It was Neville, just as he expected. But he had not expected the cruel wound on the side of his friend's head that left no doubt as to the cause of death.

Antony had thought himself prepared. But looking death in the face—the face of a friend, a young, talented friend who had only started out on this journey because Antony had asked for his help—was far worse than he could have imagined. He gave a curt nod and made the sign of the cross over the still, cold form caked with mud.

Marsham pulled the sheet back up and started to nod to the bearers.

"Wait." Antony plunged his hand in his pocket and drew out the black and silver rosary he always carried there. "May I, inspector?" He motioned to lay the beads on the body.

"Won't do him any good now, Father."

"It would be a comfort to me. To us." He regarded the pain in Felicity's wide, stricken eyes.

"Go on, then."

Antony lifted the corner of the sheet and slipped the rosary inside, tucking the crucifix into the hand that had been sticking out of the impromptu grave. And then he realized why that first glance had told him it was Neville's hand.

They had turned back toward the car when one of the constables called from the doorway of the mill. "Detective inspector, sir. You'd better come see this."

Marsham turned and strode toward the summons.

"They found another one."

Chapter 14

A nother body? Antony gripped Felicity's arm, whether to comfort her or to reassure himself, he wasn't certain. What had they become embroiled in? Had the world turned upside down?

Automatically they followed the detective inspector. Dreading with each step what they might see at the end, still they moved forward. And no one stopped them.

Now the inside of the mill shone as brilliantly as a hospital operating room with the portable floodlights the SOCOs had set up. A white-suited man with a camera danced around the rim of the wide, empty hole from which Neville's body had been so recently exhumed, snapping pictures in detail. "Right. That should do it. You can touch them now."

A woman, likewise wearing protective clothing that made her look more like an astronaut than a policewoman or a forensic scientist or whatever she was, reached deep into the hole and drew out a badly decayed skull. After a few moments' examination she nodded. "Definitely human."

"Anything else, Dr Streeting?" Marsham barked.

"Most likely male." She pointed to what was left of the bone just above the empty eye sockets. "There's enough of the brow ridge here that we can see that it was prominent," she explained. "And the forehead appears to be fairly sloping—a female would be more rounded, although it's a pity so much of it's gone. It's the wet environment, you see. We're actually lucky to have anything to work with."

"Lucky?" Marsham's furrowed brow and growled response

indicated he didn't see much luck in the event. This discovery undoubtedly presented a major complication to his case, and he clearly was not amused.

"Bones disintegrate fast in wet conditions." She just shook her head at the evidence of water all around her. "We could have been left with a lot less to work with. Perhaps the fact that this was a drainage mill—perhaps it drew the water away. I don't really know how it worked. And then the soil composition—peat is known to act as a preservative."

"Can you tell us anything else?"

She returned to the skull in her hand. "We have the teeth. Teeth last much longer than bone. I would say our man was well off. There are no stress marks on the teeth, so he had a good diet during development." She looked closer. "Oh, and European. He has the Carabellis cusp—an extra bump—on his upper molar." She laid the skull aside. "When I've had some time with them in the lab I can probably give you a rough estimate of our specimen's age—"

"Fascinating," Marsham cut her off. "But what I need to know is, is it forensic or archeological? How long have these bones been here?"

"Well, the unorthodox burial certainly indicates foul play. But you could work that out for yourself. As to how long the bones have been here..." She shook her head as she looked back into the hole. "We'll need to do a careful dig. I have some advanced students at university I might recruit. Then I'll see what I can do with the bits and pieces."

She started to pull back, then leaned forward again. "What's this?" She frowned. "Move that light over here, will you?" Dr. Streeting half-dived into the hole, lying on her stomach and reaching in with full arm and shoulder.

"Careful," Marsham muttered and moved forward to hold her leg. "We've already lost enough forensic evidence today to do us for six cases."

Dr Streeting wriggled backward, grinding the mud into her white coveralls. "Thank you, detective inspector. I appreciate that it was your concern for evidence rather than my well-being, but it was a nice gesture." She held out a small metal disc on a fragment of a decayed chain. "This might tell you something. Judging from its location, it was likely to have been around his neck."

From his unobtrusive position, Antony craned his neck to gain a discreet glance at the medallion. It was much muddied and corroded, so he couldn't be sure; was that a pattern of stars, or was it a multi-pointed star? But certainly the centerpiece was distinctive—a Maltese cross. Like the one Felicity saw on the back of Rempstone's icon, perhaps?

And like the pattern he had seen just moments ago etched on Neville's ring as he tucked his rosary into the cold hand. How many times had he seen it? Always there, so one didn't really think anything about it. Like not noticing glasses on someone who always wore them. He was almost certain that the pattern on the disc was similar to the one on the ring—a star and Maltese cross. The engraving was subtle, but distinctive.

So this was why the mark on the icon had held such interest for Neville. And why their friend had taken such precipitous leave of them to dash across Norfolk? If so, they needed to know more about the meaning of that design. And now he would have to tell the police about the icons. The Superior could no longer keep the police out, internal matter or not. But he would ring Father Anselm first and let him know.

"Detective Inspector? May we go now? It'll be dark on the river soon."

Marsham blinked at Antony's voice as if he had forgotten their presence. "Yes, yes. Go get warm. You'll be at All Hallows House tonight?" Antony and Felicity nodded. "Right then, our county headquarters are based in Wymondham, but if you're in Norwich, just come on down to the station on Bethel Street tomorrow morning and we'll finish up the formalities there."

Back in the security of All Hallows House, Antony led evening prayers at the request of Sister Johanna who was too shocked by their news to lead the service herself. He prayed for their friend's repose, for his family, for the soul of the unknown man who had lain in an unmarked grave for untold time, for the police and for the angry heart of the person who had committed such an outrage against another human being.

He wished with all his heart that the horrors of such darkness could just melt away in the warmth of their cozy surroundings. But he knew they would not. The situation was still truly as dark and as evil as the scene he carried in his mind.

Chapter 15

Wednesday Morning, Fifth in Lent

They started out after a late breakfast the next morning. A welcome sun shone almost warm on their heads and made the clumps of daffodils and other spring bulbs seem to jump to life.

"Oh, what a relief after yesterday's deluge!" Felicity held her face up to the sun. "It's hard to believe this is the same world where yesterday's horrors happened."

Antony, who had wrestled with those horrors much of the night, knew they were still very much with them. Still, there was nothing to be gained by unmitigated gloom, and it was certainly more pleasant to be walking in sunshine than in downpour. A quick glance at the visitors' center told him it remained locked up tight. Closed in respect for their former retreatant? The sudden, violent death of a promising young man was a loss to the whole Community. The shock to Neville's family was unimaginable. "I must call on them," he said aloud.

"Who?" Felicity jumped after his long, abstracted silence.

"Neville's family. Perhaps I could rent a car or something."

Felicity nodded. "Always the priest, huh? That must be one of the hardest parts of the job."

"Calling on the bereaved?" He ran his fingers through his hair. "I suppose it is. It's really no easier for a priest to know what to say at a time like that than it is for anyone else. Still, one seems to muddle through."

"I find it hard to think of you ever muddling."

Antony blinked. If only she knew... "Thank you for that.

Often, the less said, the better."

Antony thought how lovely it would be to put all the specters of death behind them and enjoy this day, this city. But it wasn't possible. They had a duty to do. There were statements to give, bereaved to be comforted. He led the way across Rouen Road and turned up the steep incline of Thorn Lane.

They were passing the colorful stalls of the busy market when he turned to his companion. "Are you all right?"

"Yes. I am."

Her answer sounded hesitant. "I mean, really?" We need to talk, but not if you aren't feeling up to it."

"Talk. It might help take my mind off— off other things."

"That's what we need to talk about. Now that this is no longer just a matter of the theft of an icon I realize how wrong I was to ask you to get involved. I want to apologize and assure you that as soon as we've finished up with the police you can put it all behind you."

Felicity nodded but didn't reply and Antony found the silence from his normally garrulous companion more disturbing than anything she could have said. Had he said entirely the wrong thing? Had she been more traumatized than he realized? He determined to attempt another conversation once they were through with the police.

They walked on wordlessly past the shiny glass front of the Millenium Forum and the huge gothic tower of St. Peter Mancroft and arrived at the severely plain, four-storey, red-brick building on Bethel Street that housed the Norfolk Constabulary. The building was as spare and businesslike inside as out. No decoration, but plenty of efficiency.

They gave their names to a uniformed clerk and after only a few minutes' wait were shown into Marsham's office. "I appreciate your coming so promptly." He offered them chairs and picked up some papers from the desk. "These are the typed notes of your statements yesterday. Please read them carefully, make any corrections you find necessary, and sign and date them at the bottom." He indicated the place on the forms.

While they read, Marsham made a copy of Felicity's passport and visa. A few minutes later, Marsham returned and traded the documents for the signed statements. All a matter of routine. Done. Antony stood to leave.

"If you could give us just a bit more help with our enquiries?" Marsham blocked the door.

"But why? We've told you all we know," Antony protested.

"It won't take long, Father."

Antony sat down abruptly. In spite of the polite form this was clearly an order.

Chapter 16

Felicity was put in a small waiting room in the company of Woman Police Constable Betty Colton, a young woman with soft brown hair framing her face. Felicity couldn't imagine anyone looking less likely to be a policewoman. WPC Colton brought her tea and tried, somewhat uneasily, to chat with her as if they were at a tea party. Felicity found herself wondering if Constable Colton really didn't have any more pressing work. But then, as she responded to questions about life in America with half her mind, she began to worry.

Why were the police keeping them so long? What were they talking to Antony about? Would they let her go to London? "Don't leave town" seemed to be a standard line in most detective shows she had seen.

The Guest Sister at Ham Common had been very solicitous when Felicity rang to tell her briefly what had happened. *Very briefly,* as she had shortened it to "a friend died." But she had been assured of a welcome at St Michael's Convent whenever she could get to London. She should probably have called her mother, too. But she couldn't face that yet.

"We're ready for her now." Felicity jumped at Sergeant Caister's abrupt words. He looked even more rumpled than he had yesterday. Apparently he had worked through much of the night and it hadn't improved his mood or his appearance.

"This way, please. If you don't mind." At least WPC Colton remained her placid self. Felicity followed her down a long hallway. She was shown into a small interview room where Marsham and Caister sat at a table with a cassette recorder to one side. It really was like the scenes she had seen on TV. It gave her an eerie sense of unreality. Almost as if she was watching herself.

The questions were simple enough: How long had she known the victim? What did she know of him? Did she like him? Did he have any enemies, rivals at college? His interests, his connections, his family.... The sum total of it all made her realize how little she really knew her fellow ordinand. And now she wished she could talk to him about the really important things: about his passion for art and his inspiration as an artist; about his sense of calling to the priesthood and his vision for his ministry... Her mind trailed off as she contemplated the loss to herself, to the Community, to society, by the ending of this one dedicated life. She choked and completely lost her train of thought on Marsham's question.

"I'm sorry. I—"

"Close, were you?"

"Not really. That's just it. He had so much to contribute—his art, his ministry, his friendship—and now it's gone and it's too late to get to know him better."

Marsham offered her a box of tissues. "Yes, tell me about his art career."

"I don't know much about it. It's not unusual for ordinands to have had careers before settling on a call to the priesthood. I'm actually rather unusual to have gone to the college more or less right out of university. I know he worked and exhibited in London. He has some relative who is some kind of curator or something there. His family could tell you more, I'm sure."

"So you don't know anything about his art?"

"Well, I've seen a couple of his paintings. He had one in his room at college that was really powerful." How much detail did Marsham want? She paused, then went on. "It was an almost medieval-style crucifixion with the blood and water from Christ's side flowing into a chalice held by a priest with modern communicants lining the altar rail. I loved it because I could place myself in the picture. I often found myself thinking about it when I received communion."

Marsham was still silent, so she went on. "He had exquisite taste as a painter and as a collector. Visiting his room was like going to an art gallery. He had a seventeenth-century Spanish jeweled altar cross, a carved baptismal shell—so delicate you could see light through it, a Georgian silver chalice…"

"Normal, is it, for students to keep fine art in their dormitory rooms?"

"Most have crucifixes and prints for devotional purposes, hardly museum quality. But like I said, Neville had had a career before. And he was a dealer as well as a collector. He sold antique vestments and things, on eBay, you know. So it was sort of a business." She stopped abruptly. Could one sell stolen icons on eBay?

Marsham tried another question or two, but that was essentially all she knew about this man whom she had called a friend. She had enjoyed his company, and she couldn't imagine why anyone would want to kill him. She was engulfed by a sense of vast emptiness. The discussions of art, music and liturgy—as well as the endless wrangles over church politics—that filled so many coffee hours in the common room after dinner before they dispersed to an evening of study would never be the same without Neville's knowledge and wit. Why would anyone do such a thing? She took a deep breath and fought back the desire to burst into tears.

Marsham was silent for several moments then, abruptly, with an attitude of pouncing, asked, "And you were the one who discovered that the icon was missing?"

Thank goodness Antony had brought it up, she hadn't been sure whether or not to mention it. "I wouldn't say I discovered it. It should have been hanging on a pillar in a side chapel. I noticed it wasn't there and mentioned it to Neville, but I expect most of the college would have noticed. It was customary to reverence it after prayers."

"What about special friends at the college?"

"We're a small student body—only about forty of us—so I guess you could say we're all friends. The usual tensions around exam time, the usual disagreements over churchmanship, issues like women bishops, gay marriage—that sort of thing. Made for good discussions. Not violence, if that's what you're suggesting."

"I'm not suggesting anything, just want to get a picture of his life. Girlfriends?"

She smiled. "No, detective inspector."

"Boyfriends?"

"Not in that way, I shouldn't think. Most CT students are celibate. Personal conscience. Maurice Paykel was a good friend."

She thought over what she had said. It was true they weren't close, but Neville was always there with a quiet understanding. Perhaps it was his artistic nature, but it seemed he had so often understood something she was feeling even without her having to say anything.

Perhaps it was because of his chosen celibacy. There was never any innuendo. Never any suggestion that their easy, relaxed relationship should go anywhere else. And she understood that this was not unique to her. Neville was equally available to anyone who came to him with a question, a problem, or simply an observation. Never belittling, never goading, always accepting.

"And an art collector."

A burst of anger abolished any remaining inclination to tears. "I don't know what you're implying, Inspector, but Neville Mortara was good and honest. It is ridiculous to suspect him of wrongdoing."

"Very well, Miss Howard. Thank you for your time."

Marsham brought the interview to a close. She hoped he was as satisfied as he seemed to be. There really wasn't anything else she could tell him. "May I go to London? I've booked a retreat. My mother is there for a few days—"

"I don't see why not. Be sure we have your contact information in case we have any other questions." He thanked her and left WPC Colton to show her back to the lobby where Antony was waiting for her.

The late afternoon sunshine felt wonderful on her head after the drab world of the police station. She felt as if she had been trapped in a black and white movie and had suddenly stepped out into Technicolor. "Oh, I'm so glad to be out of there! It was so claustrophobic. And I wasn't even in a cell. I hate to think what that would be like." She took a deep breath and lifted her face to the sun.

Antony consulted his watch. "I was going to ask if you wanted lunch, but it's too late for that. The John Lewis store here has a good tea room and it's on the way back to All Hallows."

The modern red-brick department store seemed to swoop down the hill and curve around the corner in a continuous curving line, welcoming them in. When they took the escalator to the second floor and entered the light and airy "Place to Eat," Felicity was more than happy to be distracted by mundane thoughts of food. And she knew they needed to finish the conversation Antony had started that morning. It was clear he was trying to sideline her just when she was feeling ready for action.

When her salmon and prawn salad arrived she savored several bites before Antony began, "So you'll be going on to London?"

"Yes. Marsham gave his OK and there doesn't seem to be anything more I can do around here. The police seem to have everything in hand. Inspector Marsham appears to be very efficient."

"Absolutely. I'm sure he has the murder investigation—or perhaps I should say investigations—well under control," Antony agreed.

"What do you make of those old bones? Could there have been a monk's burial ground there at one time?" Felicity hoped he wouldn't refuse to talk about it with her.

But Antony didn't seem in the least reluctant. "No, I think that was always the gatehouse, and from what Dr Streeting said, the bones couldn't have been that old. Not medieval. They wouldn't have lasted that long in the wet ground."

"And the medallion thing with him?" she asked.

Antony nodded. "I'd like to know more about that emblem. The eight-pointed star has to have something to do with the Knights of Malta, although the starburst and leaf design seems to be a unique rendering. Still, it must be tied up in some way with the Knights of Malta, or the Knights of St John, or the Knights Hospitaller—all just different names for the same organization."

"Maybe I can find something in London—in a museum or library or something…"

"No, Felicity. Your retreat has been interrupted enough."

Felicity put on a contrite expression. She had said too much and evoked Antony's protective instincts again. "It hasn't turned out to be much of a withdrawal for discernment, has it? I don't think this is what Father Oswin had in mind at all." She squeezed a few drops of lemon juice on her salmon and savored the last bite. "Still, tell me what I can do."

Antony hesitated. "I don't want you involved."

"I'm already involved. What can I do?"

"Well, I suppose you might try to contact Neville's uncle."

"Offer condolences?"

"Yes—I expect he'd appreciate it from a friend of Nev's."

Felicity smiled. "And since he's some kind of an art expert, he might know about the market for icons."

"Only in general terms, Felicity. Listen to me, Felicity. Nothing that could be dangerous." He paused. "If I hadn't asked Neville to help—"

"At my suggestion—"

Antony's expression became even more severe. "Felicity! Go to the nuns at Ham Common. Go shopping with your mother. Enjoy the museums. Forget all about this. We told the police all we know. I'm sure they'll find the icon."

Felicity gave a little half-laugh. "I'm sure they *won't*. They've got a murder to solve. Maybe two murders. A missing art object in another county isn't going to be high on anyone's list. You just don't want me to get into trouble."

"You're right I don't."

"It's really funny. You know, earlier, I was asking myself if I really could face doing any of that. Now you tell me not to and I realize how much I want to help." She looked down at her empty plate. "We owe it to Nev."

"Felicity, be careful." The intensity in his voice and his eyes made her shiver.

Chapter 17

Thursday, Fifth in Lent

Felicity's head spun as the train hurtled toward London. All the unanswered questions of the past days behind her, all the as yet unasked questions before her. And she was getting such a late start. It was already afternoon. She had meant to catch a train right after morning prayers, but she had had no idea she was so exhausted both physically and emotionally. She had slept until late morning, then made the mistake of choosing to walk to the train station. She got hopelessly entangled in curving, intersecting streets traversed by whizzing traffic.

She was glad Antony had gone on with his plans to contact Neville's uncle in King's Lynn that morning. It made getting on her way easier. It seemed clear to her that the only possible way forward was to ignore Antony's cautions, and focus on getting answers.

And, of course, there were the questions in her personal life, too: Antony, her mother, the convent... Felicity was brought out of her circling reverie by the piercing voice of the lady next to her talking on her mobile: "We must challenge this. It's our job to make money."

"Yes, but we're not making money with that brand."

Felicity smiled. And so turned the world. That was what people called the real world. Where did her world of prayers and icons and convents fit into all the activity around her?

She was still thinking about it two hours later when the train pulled into Liverpool Street station. She stepped out into a sea of commuting humanity and looked at her watch. Should she try to locate Neville's uncle today before going to the convent? She suddenly realized she didn't even know his name. Mortara, she assumed. And *which* museum or gallery was he with? It could be the Tate Britain, the British Museum, the V and A, the National Gallery or one of dozens of smaller galleries. It had sounded so simple. Now she realized what a small needle she was looking for in a vast haystack.

She pulled out of the tide rushing into the station to lean against a pillar as she rummaged in her backpack. She still had her old London A to Z with the underground map on the back. She would start with the Victoria and Albert. She could get on the Central line (red) here, then transfer to the Piccadilly (dark blue) for South Kensington where the museum was. Then she could get on the green District line for Richmond. She traced the route with her finger—from one furthest side of London to the other. She couldn't even count the stops. And rush hour was approaching. There was definitely no time for any investigations this afternoon if she was to make it to St Michael's Convent in time for Evensong as she fully intended to do. After all, her life goal was to be a nun, not a detective.

But even with the best of intentions it wasn't easy. Somehow, in transferring from the Circle line to the District she wound up waiting on the wrong platform. She kept her eyes glued to the electronic listings and counted: six train to Wimbledon, two to Olympia, zero to Richmond. Then she asked an attendant. And there it was on the track behind her. How many trains had she missed? Was there any chance of arriving in time for evening prayers now?

She had less than an hour. She hadn't realized Richmond was so far from central London. So far in time, if not in distance.

Felicity looked at the directions she had written down as the Guest Sister gave them over the phone: Bus number 65 outside Richmond Station (going to Kingston), get off at Ham Gate Avenue, cross over main road… Her heart sank when she stepped out of the station. The bus queue was backed up around the corner. Her only hope was turning to the lavish luxury of a taxi.

Her jolly taxi driver who told her he had worked in the States and had a girlfriend in New Hampshire did his best, but the choked traffic moved at a snail's pace. She looked at her watch again. Less than a quarter of an hour left. She would never make it in time.

Eventually the traffic eased enough for her to enjoy a view of the Thames on her right before they turned into the green spaciousness of Richmond Park.

"Mm, this is beautiful." She felt herself relax as the taxi picked up speed.

"It is, isn't it? Royal hunting ground, it was. Almost 2,500 acres, enclosed by Charles I. It's still a lot like a medieval park—grassland, bog, some oak trees they say are from the Middle Ages."

"Are there still deer here?"

"Oh yes. Herds of them. Roam free, they do." He gestured off toward the center of the park. "You like ballet?"

The *non sequitur* startled her, but she gave a straight answer. "Yes, I do. I thought of becoming a ballerina once. Until I got too tall."

"Ah, well, then, you'll know of White Lodge over there." He pointed to the left where Felicity just glimpsed an impression of a large white building amongst the trees. "Royal Ballet School for the little ones. You have to be seriously good to get in, of course."

Felicity was immediately taken back to the past: all those years of running around in pink tights and leotard with her hair in a bun; the dutiful applause of her brothers who always seemed genuinely proud of her after a recital; the year she was chosen to dance in *The Nutcracker*; the flowers her father brought her after each performance... She turned her eyes abruptly back to the road ahead of her. Her father; the kind, gentle, supportive

Andrew Howard. How could he have turned his back on his family and smashed the security of her childhood?

"Here we are, then." The taxi came to a stop. Felicity looked up to see a high brick wall. "I think it's one of these openings. Not sure which."

"That will be fine. Thank you so much." Felicity scrambled for the door and pulled out her wallet. She was in something of a state of shock at the figure shown on the meter. Evensong was long over. But at least she was here. Late, but here.

She chose the nearest opening in the wall, ducked inside, then stopped to look at the large, ocher brick building, its plainness relieved only by a few red-brick facings, three storeys of tall, white-trimmed windows and a vigorous, soon to be green vine covering much of the south wall. The building was fronted, however, by a large white-framed, glass conservatory, the cross standing on its roof the only identifying mark that this was, indeed, a convent. Felicity crunched her way across the wide gravel drive, forming an apology in her mind. It wasn't enough that she had postponed her arrival, now she had missed evening prayers. What would Mother Superior think of her commitment?

Before she reached the door she saw a tall woman in a floral dress rise from one of the wicker chairs to meet her. Felicity stepped into the fragrant, greenhouse fug of a steamy, heated room filled with bright flowers. "I'm so sorry—" she began her flustered apology.

But the tall, thin woman with long dark hair clasped back from her face who introduced herself as Sister Margaret wasn't the least bit flustered. "Don't worry. It's no matter. None at all." Her voice was calm, her smile welcoming.

Then it hit Felicity—as it always did at Kirkthorpe as well—the peace of it all. Those high brick walls weren't there to keep the nuns or monks in. They were there to keep the noise, the rush, the worry, out.

Pointing out bits of information as she went, Sister Margaret led the way into the interior, through a parlor, where she was introduced to Thomas, the convent cat, down a hall, past several offices, through the refectory, along another hall, up a flight of stairs and back down a hallway. The Guest Sister pointed out a small room where Felicity could fix her own breakfast or tea or coffee anytime she wanted it. "The toilets here. The bath here. Shower in there." Then she opened the door onto a spare, tidy room: neatly made bed with white cover, table, sink, chair. Everything she could need. "Will this be all right?"

"Oh, yes. Perfect. Thank you so much." Quiet. Solitude. Safety. The room engulfed her like a cocoon.

"Dinner will be in an hour." Sister Margaret took her leave with a final shy smile.

Felicity dumped her backpack on the chair and gave her hands a quick wash. An hour. Plenty of time for a walk in the garden, and it was a lovely, sunny evening.

Sister Margaret had shown her the exit to the back garden through the library and given her the number for the keypad to let herself back in. She crossed the wide green lawn bordered with flower beds that would soon be bursting into bloom, and circled various plots carved from the grass. It was already beautiful; she could only imagine what it must be like in the summer. A break in the hedge took her into the orchard. Long shadows cast by fruit trees heavy with blossom; pale pink and white petals drifting onto the green carpet.

She could hear the murmur of distant traffic from the busy road beyond the hedge. Commuters rushing home for their dinners, people rushing out for evening engagements, the bustling world rushing this way and that. And inside the green walls of her little world, spring flowers budded in peace. A peace she was struggling to make her own. It was so amazing, this sheltered haven just several dozen steps from the fighting, snarling traffic she had left behind her, the River Thames only a few teeming blocks away. And here she was, with apple blossoms drifting down on her head.

Turning her back on the orchard, she crunched down a gravel path toward a flower bed encircling a grey stone statue of the Mother of Christ. She stood for a long time gazing at the grave, beautiful face encircled by graceful drapery, the delicate hands crossed over the carved breast as if entreating a blessing. Felicity wanted to pray, but no words came. It was as if she had nothing more to say to God. Could Mary ask her Son for her? For her relationship with her own mother, for guidance for her future, for grace to come to terms with the brutal death of a friend? Perhaps the Mother who had pleaded and questioned and witnessed the suffering of her own dear Son would understand, would know what to ask for.

It would be too much to say Felicity felt peaceful. Yet her mind cleared enough to allow the hush of the garden to enter her. She drifted on toward the Calvary. As before the statue of the Virgin, she stood long, gazing up at the crucified body of Jesus, perhaps as his own mother had done. She had no idea how long she stood. Not praying; not thinking. Just standing and gazing.

At length a tiny shiver told her the day was moving on; evening chill was settling. But still she didn't move. Her gaze circled to the high hedge behind the border and on to the yellow brick walls of the convent itself. She felt so safe. Sheltered. A deep desire arose in Felicity to stay right there on that spot. To shut herself up here. Wall herself in. Wall death out.

Of course it wouldn't work. Sister Mary Perpetua had been attacked in her convent; Father Dominic had been murdered in his monastery. Like Poe's characters attempting to wall out the plague in *The Masque of the Red Death*, it never worked. Yet the impulse remained.

Felicity forced herself to take a deep breath and begin

walking. And even now, after all that quiet reflection, she was aware of how fast her long legs were striding through this place that so invited a leisurely stroll—as if her realization that walling out death wouldn't work had motivated her to try outrunning it. Still, she couldn't slow herself. She had brought the rush in with her because she came in herself. And she didn't want to be late for dinner. So she continued at her long-legged lope, even as she told herself to breathe deeply, to savor the evening, to smell the hyacinth, to listen to the birdsong.

Unlike her first dinner as a guest in a convent—that in Whitby, where she ate with a roomful of noisy retreatants—here she ate in the refectory with the nuns. In silence. She winced at the noise she made as she scraped butter across her crisp toast before spooning scrambled eggs over it. She soon discovered her mistake in topping her potato salad with chunks of equally crisp celery. How had the nuns learned the knack of eating all this noiselessly?

Chewing as discreetly as possible, she looked around her. Of course, many of the nuns were elderly, but she was amazed to find two or three girls who appeared younger than herself among those she assumed were novices. Did girls of sixteen actually join a convent today? The girl with the sweet face and long, blonde hair didn't look as if she could be much over that. Felicity wondered what her story was. Could she manage to talk to her sometime? If one so young had already made such a momentous decision, perhaps her story could help Felicity.

Maybe the fact that this was an active order with houses working among the poor on four continents attracted younger women. Perhaps the fact that they wore modern dress, only donning habit and veil for formal occasions made it easier for today's woman. She recalled Mother Mary Mark's comment about how hard some women found wearing a veil. How would she feel about it? Felicity wondered. Already she could see Father Oswin's wisdom in instructing her to take a look at various orders. The variety was astonishing. But she wasn't sure it would help her decision-making process. All she felt at the moment was confusion.

After the silence of the evening meal, it was almost a shock to enter the cozy parlor filled with easy chairs where the sisters sat chatting and laughing like schoolgirls on holiday. One of the sisters visiting from the Solomon Islands had brought a photo album from her Community there, and several were engaged in pouring over it with myriad questions. Others were chatting in groups of two or three, or engaged in various projects. But even in this time of recreation, Felicity noted that no sister sat idle. Every pair of hands was busy with embroidery, knitting, painting, fashioning beaded jewelry, or some other project that could be sold at the craft table in the foyer to bring in money to help the poor. And one elderly sister was engrossed in brushing Thomas's long gray hair. Felicity smiled a greeting, then backed out the door. Perhaps this could be a moment to seek out Mother Superior regarding her questions.

What advice would the head of the convent give to a seeker such as herself? If she should decide to make this her home what would the process be? She found Mother Lois in her office—a small, energetic lady with short dark hair, wearing corduroy slacks and a green Shetland sweater. She readily lay aside her pen and smiled at Felicity. "We are so happy you were able to make your retreat with us after your difficulties. You must be feeling a great loss for your friend who died."

"Yes, he was an ordinand at the College of the Transfiguration. It's a terrible shock for everyone." Such trite words, Felicity thought. Such a gloss over the actual story. But then, what was the actual story?

"What can I do for you?"

Felicity told her briefly about her discernment journey.

"Yes, if you feel drawn to our order, our way of life, the first step would be to make more frequent, longer retreats here.

Then, if the desire deepens, you might come to us for a few weeks as an alongsider—such as Gabriella. I'm sure you noticed her?"

"The girl with the long blonde hair?"

"That's right." Mother Lois paused. "As far as anything more specific, that's really the province of Sister Katrina, our Novice Mistress. I wouldn't want to encroach on her territory. Unfortunately, she isn't here right now. But you could write to her anytime and she will be glad to answer your questions. Just send it to Discernment on our website."

"Yes, thank you. I will." Felicity couldn't help feeling a bit deflated. She had so wanted answers. Quick, easy answers. Not more of the 'take time to discern, don't rush' variety.

"But in the meantime, enjoy your time here." Mother Lois's smile was warm, making her dark eyes sparkle. "Relax."

Had Mother Superior seen into her need that quickly? Felicity wondered.

The bell rang, summoning them to Compline. Mother Lois rose from her desk and led the way down yet another hall to a large, unornamented chapel. The stalls faced each other in double rows across the room, the plain, modern altar stood to the east in front of a cross hanging on the wall. Sister Margaret scurried over from her seat on the other side of the room to show Felicity to a stall in the back row. She opened the service book to the Order for Compline and pointed out the psalms for the day.

The service couldn't have been more tailor-made to Felicity's needs. The first reading was from the book of Isaiah: "In quietness and trust shall be your strength." The last glow of light faded from the long windows facing onto the garden. The soft coo of a dove joined its voice to that of the sisters: "In the quiet of the evening, now the work of day is done … Father, keep us in your sight."

Fighting the desire to give in to the fatigue she felt and

take refuge in the womb-like comfort her room offered, Felicity knew she should make an attempt to contact Antony. Surely he had accomplished more than she had today, and she wanted to know what he had learned. She rummaged in her backpack and pulled her little-used cell phone from the bottom. She knew she was probably breaking convent rules by making a call after the Greater Silence had begun following Compline. Still, there was no one in any of the rooms around her, so she wouldn't be disturbing anyone. She switched on, although keeping the ring silenced. She couldn't believe it when only one fractional bar appeared in the corner of her screen. What? How could London possibly be out of range for anything? Surely the walls of the convent weren't that thick?

Walking softly, she made her way back along the dim corridors through the silent convent. Was there even anyone else in her entire wing of this great house? She had seen at dinner that she was the only retreatant. Where did the sisters have their cells? Each section of the building was barricaded by heavy fire doors which creaked and echoed as she made her way through them. At last she made it to the library and opened the outside door, reminding herself of the keypad code before she closed it behind her. She really couldn't imagine locking herself out and having to ring the bell. Would anyone even hear her if she did?

Now that the sun was down it was cold in the garden. Wishing she had worn her jacket, Felicity huddled on the back step, hoping she was well away from any nun's cell. At least her phone showed service here. Only two and a half bars, but it should do. Antony's number rang several times. *Don't be switched off. Please. Don't.* It wasn't exactly a prayer, but her longing was fervent. She hadn't realized until the phone started ringing how very much she wanted to talk to him. What had happened to him while she was traveling? What had he learned? What if he had encountered something dangerous?

Come on. Answer. Please.

"Hello?"

"Antony!" She was so relieved she almost shouted. His voice had never sounded more melodious. Sleepy, but melodious. "Did I wake you?"

"I guess so. Sorry. It's been a long day."

"I'm sorry to ring you after Compline, but I did want to talk to you. I wanted to know what you did today. What did you learn? How are you?"

He gave a short laugh, sounding much more awake. "Felicity, it is good to hear you charging ahead as usual. You got to St Michael's all right?"

"Yes." She dithered. Should she tell him about her earlier thoughts in the garden? No. She reminded herself sharply that this this was a business call. "Yes, of course I got here. But what about you? Did you go to see Neville's family? Who did you see? What did you learn? Do you know why Neville—"

Again Antony laughed. "Whoa. Slow down. No. I didn't see any of Neville's family. Insensitive of me, really. I should have thought. After all, there's been a death in the family. I rang, but of course they wouldn't want to see anyone else right now."

"So who did you talk to? Didn't you learn anything?"

"I spoke to the vicar of St Margaret's—Neville's uncle—on the phone. Apparently he was the last one to see Nev at King's Lynn. Neville must have gone straight there from Rempstone."

"Did he know—"

"He didn't know anything. He said he thought Neville had gone back to Rempstone. He had no idea what he would have been doing at St Benet's."

"Did you ask what Neville might have wanted help with? Or wanted to show you?"

"I asked if there was anything Neville showed particular interest in. He said they had lots of musty old books, his words, but he didn't know what his nephew was about. He was pleasant enough, but pretty vague. Again, understandable at a time like this, really."

"And there was nothing about any icon? Nothing with that cross mark on it? Did you ask about that?"

"No. There was no use. I really had a very unproductive day." Antony suddenly sounded tired and depressed. "I'll speak to you tomorrow. Bye."

"Antony—" Felicity wanted to say something heartening. Give him some good news. She wished he were there with her. There to share in the research with her. There to answer her questions. There to comfort her.

"Yes?"

"Goodnight." She rang off.

She was just turning back to the door when she caught a movement from the corner of her eye. By the Calvary. Just a small animal in the bushes, surely. And yet it had seemed larger. The back of her neck tingled. Was someone listening in on her phone call?

Fear changed to anger. How dare anyone violate the peace of this holy place? "Hey! Who's there?" Ignoring the wet grass soaking her flimsy shoes she charged across the lawn. "This is private property!"

The next moment her feet tangled in the soft body and long grey hair of Thomas, the convent cat, and she sprawled her full length on the cold, dank lawn. Thomas let out an angry cry that sounded chillingly human and bounded off toward the orchard. "Thomas!" Scrambling to her feet Felicity started to call after him when her breath caught in her throat. That was definitely a human form scuttling through the gap in the hedge at the foot of the garden.

With that fleeting vision, the discouragement of Antony's phone call dissipated. Was this intruder merely a homeless person looking for shelter, a prowler seeking to do mischief, or was someone worried about their enquiries? That meant there was something they could learn. *Must* learn.

Suppressing the desire to run, she crept back to her room with her mind seething. No use disturbing Mother Lois, even if she had known where to find her. The lurker was long gone.

Felicity didn't even bother turning her light on. She just pulled off her jeans by the ambient light from her partly covered window, pulled on her nighty and slid, shivering, under her covers. But her mind was far too busy for sleep to come. Knowing there was information to be gained was incredibly invigorating. Tomorrow she would find Neville's London uncle. She would learn what that hopeless cousin and uncle in King's Lynn couldn't or wouldn't tell Antony. She would... She startled as a sudden burst of rain splattered against her window.

She pulled the thick folds of her duvet more tightly around her. She must sleep. At first she had to squeeze her eyes to keep them shut as events of the day raced around her head. Then her lids closed of their own weight and she relaxed to the rhythm of the rain spattering against her window.

But as her sleep deepened, so did the rain—. Pounding, pounding, pounding... In her dream mud from the sodden mill floor splashed up on her. Covering her legs, her hands, her face. No, not mud. Blood. And then a long, white hand, unearthed by the pounding rain reached up through the mire. Reached up and grabbed her wrist.

She struggled against the clammy grip as the specter tried to pull her down into its watery grave. She fought the cold, slimy mud, but felt herself sinking. Then she realized, it wasn't trying to entomb her, it was trying to propel her. It was imploring her to action. *Please. Please. Please.*

She watched it all in slow motion, clearly, able to look at every detail. The blackness of the inside of the mill. The circle of light at the top of the funnel. The blue-white streaks of water pouring through the orifice. Like being in the belly of a whale as it gulped in water. And the soil washing away just inches beyond her feet. The earth's abatement making it seem the hand was rising as on the resurrection morning when the graves would give up their dead.

The hand rose, slim and ghostly white, wearing its mysteriously engraved ring, dripping wet as in the narthex of the church at Kirkthorpe, Neville reaching out to offer a drop of holy water from the tip of his extended finger.

The ring. She must learn what that strange insignia meant. It had to be the key to this whole mystery. And she would grasp the key. Grasp it and unlock whatever door was barricading the truth from her.

Chapter 18

Friday, Fifth in Lent, Morning

Felicity bounded from her bed propelled by last night's determination. She gulped a quick breakfast in the tiny cubicle down the hall from her room before finding Sister Margaret to tell her they had an intruder in the garden last night, then started out with a renewed bounce in her step—into drenching rain. But at least she knew the system better now than she had yesterday, and after only one false start at finding the bus stop she was whisked off toward London on the top of a red double-decker bus. She felt she must make good time today. There was so much to be done, and she had accomplished nothing yesterday. Mentally she ran over her list: icons, Knights of Malta… Knights of Malta, icons… icons…

Where did one go? What did one do? Who could she talk to? It had all sounded so easy, just look around a bit, see what she could learn. But London was so vast. Everything anyone could possibly want to know was here—that was the problem. It was a great, surging stew. How could she possibly find anything? She needed an expert to guide her. Right. She would make locating Neville's uncle a priority.

Well, except for one priority she really must deal with first. Reluctantly she pulled her phone out of her bag along with the card her mother had thrust at her before leaving All Hallows. After a few rings Felicity winced at the overly bright voice that answered.

"Hello, Mom."

"Felicity, darling! How nice to hear your voice. Are you in London? Isn't it lovely! Where can we meet?"

No, Mom, it isn't lovely, it's pouring rain and I don't want to meet. "How about the middle of the Thames?"

"What?" Cynthia's laughter was brittle. "Oh, darling, just your little joke."

"I didn't think it would make much difference—it wouldn't be any wetter there than on a street."

"Darling, how lovely. You've been here long enough to develop an English sense of humor. Actually, though," Felicity heard a crinkling of paper that sounded like a map being unfolded and bent around. "I'm so glad you called, I just stepped out of the hotel and was trying to figure out how to get to Harrods. Would you like to meet me there? Your wardrobe really could use an update."

"No. Thanks, Mom. Just take a taxi to Harrods and have a nice morning. I've got work to do. I'll see you later."

"No, wait! Don't hang up. We must meet." Her mother sounded almost desperate. Felicity simply couldn't get her mind around the idea of her mother being clingy. "Honestly. I don't have to go shopping. It was just an idea. I'd much rather be with you. When will you be here?"

Felicity wiped the steam off the window and peered out at the congested Richmond street which had slowed the progress of her bus to a crawl. Surely they must be nearly to the station. She thought back over yesterday's train and underground journey. "A good two hours, I'd say."

"Wonderful! I'll just pop into a museum and then go for a walk." Felicity could hear more crinkling of the map. "There, the Embankment. That looks like a nice place for a stroll."

"Mother, nowhere is nice for a stroll. It's pouring."

"Oh, that won't bother me a bit, darling. Here, I've got it—just as you said—the middle of the Thames, exactly!"

"Mom, what are you talking about?"

"Let's meet in the middle of the, um—Hungerford footbridge."

"Mother, it sounds like you've been watching spy movies. Let's meet at a coffee shop somewhere."

"No, darling. It's exactly what you said—only you were the one watching them. Remember all those English detective shows you used to watch with your brothers? They always walked in places like that."

Felicity blinked. She had had no idea Cynthia paid any attention to what her children watched on TV.

"Besides," Cynthia continued, "Fresh air sounds much nicer. We can go for coffee then, or anything you want."

"You really mean it, don't you? The Hungerford Bridge?" Felicity really couldn't think of anything that sounded a less likely choice for her mother. "Mother, a *bridge*? How about the tea room at Fortnum's?"

But it was all to no avail; Cynthia was set on her romantic notion and nostalgia won the day. Felicity could only think that the stress of the divorce had unhinged her mother.

All the time trundling through the bowels of London on the underground she was hoping desperately that the rain would let up. It would make getting around so much easier. Especially when she didn't know where she needed to get around to. But when she emerged, like a gopher out of a hole, from Embankment station, she saw that if anything, it was raining harder. She looked up at the soaring white cables and inclined steel pylons spanning the river in a series of sky-piercing triangles. Of course, it didn't take so much to pierce the sky today when it was falling down at a great splashing pace to meet one. Felicity sighed and mounted the three flights of steeply ascending steps. Why had she given in to her mother's whim? She looked at her watch. Almost twenty minutes late. She shook her head. Cynthia would get absolutely soaked waiting in her chosen impractical location. Maybe next time she would listen to her daughter.

Even in the deluge, though, the footbridge was being

used. Sporadic clumps of intrepid pedestrians pushed their way determinedly against the elements. People with places to go. Not a day for tourists. Most huddled under big black umbrellas, but a few, like Felicity, preferred the freedom of a trusty rain hat. She stepped to the left to get out of the way and to have a clearer view of the river, away from the Victorian train bridge which ran along the right side. Did Cynthia really mean the middle? There didn't seem to be anyone waiting in the middle of the bridge. She put her head down against falling drops and pressed ahead, looking up occasionally to count the peaked suspension arches as she passed under them. How many were there? Six? Seven? How did she know what was the middle? She made her way toward a black-coated cluster of people, but before she reached them they meandered off. Apparently she was wrong about tourists not being out today. Probably Americans determined not to lose a moment.

This must be the middle, but looking before and behind her she saw nothing that could be the figure of her mother. She paused and gazed across the river. At least the rain had softened to a mist so she could look around without getting splashed in the face.

On the South Bank the great white circle of the London Eye inched its way around its stationary orbit. She remembered the fine spring day almost a year ago when she and Sally, a fellow teacher at St Monica's school, had "done" the South Bank: the London Eye, the Tate Modern, the Globe Theatre. Sally had been as disillusioned with teaching as Felicity was and had gone home to Canada, while Felicity had plunged deeper into her English experience by going off to college in a monastery, of all things. It still shocked her when she thought about it. But it was better than going home. Except now "home" had come to her. She looked again both directions. No mother.

Turning her back on the great wheel she looked up the river. Grey water, grey sky, grey cement Waterloo Bridge, grey skyline of buildings, the dome of St Paul's standing a beacon among the rectangular pillars of city skyscrapers. She shivered as the damp cold seeped in under her padded, waterproof coat.

She glanced over her shoulder again. Then she saw them. Two men seeming to come straight at her, black hulks in their long coats. One staring straight at her in a way that made her take a step backward. Was he the fleeting figure from the night before? Come with reinforcement to silence her before she could learn anything?

She gripped the rail behind her; felt its wet chill against her back. Even as she felt a shrill cry rise in her throat she stifled it. A train rumbling by blocked all other sound. The pair were only a few feet away, exuding menace. She looked wildly to the right and to the left, as did her pursuers, and saw the approaching pedestrians—a clutch of Japanese tourists, chattering animatedly. With only a slight veer in their trajectory the men passed on. Did the one nearest her actually give her a smile?

She turned to the rail in order to grasp the cold steel tube for support, and faced the icy expanse of leaden water below her. Then she saw what she had not noticed before. The side of the bridge was lined by a broad ledge like the wings of an airplane. Or an angel. Even if the men had meant her harm, however unlikely it now seemed, she had been encompassed, girded by wings. A sense of immeasurable comfort flooded her.

And brought her back to the present moment. Where was Cynthia? Felicity felt a renewed irritation with herself for agreeing to the idea of meeting in such a place. She had been a little late, but surely not so late that her mother would have given up. Belatedly she jerked her cell phone from her bag and, trying to protect it from the mist, rang her mother.

When Cynthia failed to answer the repeated rings the frustration was so sharp Felicity all but threw the phone into the river. Jamming her hands deep in her pockets, Felicity turned on her heel and strode back the long, wet way she had come. Head down, eyes on her feet, she almost slammed into the black-coated figure she stepped in front of. "Oh, sorr—Ant—!"

Her cry of delight was cut off when the very proper gentleman, dressed as a banker, not as a cleric, and some years Anthony's senior in spite of the passing resemblance his dark hair and piercing eyes bore to her absent friend, touched the brim of his hat and stepped aside, giving her plenty of room to barge ahead. But the momentary confusion had left her shaken. She had thought of him last night; had wished, fleetingly, for his company; but she had no idea her disappointment could be so sharp, her longing for his presence so intense when the stranger moved on.

Well, nothing to do but carry on with her day. At least her mother couldn't say she hadn't tried. It wasn't Felicity's fault Cynthia hadn't carried through on her own idiotic plan. She marched down the steps, her head high. The Victoria and Albert. She would start there. For some reason it was the museum she most associated with Neville, since her first visit to his room when she felt she had been to a museum of fine design.

"Oh, Felicity! There you are. Thank goodness!" Cynthia stepped out from the sheltered doorway of the station, looking as fresh and dry as the offerings in the flower-seller's stall beside her.

"Mother! What on earth are you doing there? You *said* the middle of the bridge!"

"Well, yes, darling, I know. But I wasn't to know it would be raining so hard, was I? And I knew no sensible person would wait in the middle of the river in this weather. I thought I'd catch you as you came up from the train, but I must have missed you."

"*And* you didn't answer your cell phone!" She flung the accusation.

"Oh," Cynthia pulled the offending instrument out of her pocket and looked at it. "How silly of me. Sorry. I naturally silenced it in the museum. I must have forgotten."

Felicity stuffed down her impulse to a caustic recrimination. It was simply too much work.

"Let's start over." She took a deep, steadying breath. "Hello, Mother. Did you enjoy the museum?" Felicity still couldn't get her head around the idea that this was her mother: the super-efficient, workaholic, never-miss-a-beat machine she had known all her life. Did people really change this much?

"It was absolutely wonderful, darling. Their collection of Old Masters is incredible. And now I'm starving, aren't you? Where shall we have lunch? My treat. Harrods? The Savoy?"

"Mother, I told you I had work to do."

"Well, of course, darling. But you have to eat."

At last they settled for the lunch room at the V and A. From the underground station, they crossed Cromwell Road and pushed through the glass doors of the Grand Entrance of the immense sprawling Victorian architectural concoction. They came to a full stop at the stunning sight of the incredible fantasy of the Chihuly chandelier suspended from the great dome—a dazzling, giant Christmas tree ornament of snaking tendrils and magical bubbles in illuminated aquamarine and saffron blown glass.

Realizing they were standing in the path of traffic, Felicity nudged her mother on and approached the information desk. "Yes?" A young woman in a black dress with dark hair piled high on her head smiled at her from behind dark-rimmed glasses. "Can I help you?"

"Well, I hope so," Felicity floundered. "I was hoping I could make an appointment with one of your curators. That is, I think he works here. I'm not exactly certain."

The young lady pulled the keyboard of a small computer toward her. "And his name?"

"Er, Mortara. I'm afraid I don't know his first name."

"Hmm. Do you spell that M-o-r-t-a-r-a?" She typed as

she spelled.

"Yes, that's right."

"Well, I'm not finding anything here. What is his speciality?"

"Um, art." Felicity was beginning to feel helplessly foolish.

"I wonder if you could be more specific. We work with curators in photography, textiles, architecture, urban planning, childhood, medieval art, oriental art… There's quite a list."

"Yes, I see." She was beginning to.

"Besides, of course, we use many outside consultants. The majority of our curators aren't based here at all. Or even in the UK."

"Oh."

"Of course, you could try the British Museum. They maintain an even more extensive list than we do."

"Yes. I see. Thank you." Felicity was backing away, disappointment clear in her face and her voice.

"I am sorry I couldn't be of more help."

A sense of helpless futility engulfed Felicity, making it hard for her to move. The weight in her throat made it impossible to speak.

"Oh, darling, just look at this. Isn't this interesting!" Cynthia grabbed her arm and pulled her aside, thrusting information pamphlets in front of her. "The Museum of Ornamental Art was established in 1852 by Prince Albert to develop decorative design in British manufacturing by providing models of study, both ancient and modern." Consulting her map, Cynthia propelled Felicity down a long corridor, galleries on either side filled with lavish displays of Renaissance furniture, art and statuary. "Oh, isn't this fabulous. You could spend a lifetime here."

Their way circled around the large enclosed garden to the café at the back. Cynthia, still reading from her brochure, informed her daughter that this was the first museum restaurant in the world and was intended as a showpiece of modern design. Giving it all less than half of her mind, Felicity chose a tomato panini and spinach salad garnished with shavings of parmesan cheese. She had started out with such high determination this morning and she had accomplished less than nothing. What an exercise in futility. She didn't think this entire sprawling vastness of applied arts accumulated over more than a century and a half contained a single icon or reference to the Knights of Malta. She would undoubtedly have been better served to have tried the British Museum. But she just didn't have the spirit to fight her way—and her mother—back across London to face another dead end.

She was pushing a spinach leaf around with her fork, less than half-listening to Cynthia's chatter, when she realized her bag was emitting a strange sound.

"Darling, I think that's your cell phone."

Felicity jumped. She used it so infrequently she almost never left it on, therefore rarely having to charge the battery. In her frustration back on the bridge, though, she must have failed to switch it off again. She rummaged in her bag, pulled the phone out and stepped through the door from the café opening onto the garden. "Hello?"

"Is this Miss Felicity Howard?" A frosty, public-school precise, male voice enquired.

"Yes."

"Cyril Mortara here. A Father Antony Sherwood contacted me through a young lady who had consulted with me from the Julian Centre. He said you are doing some research in London, and asked if I might be able to help."

"Oh!" She blinked. "Yes. Thank you. How amazingly kind."

"He said you are interested in the history of the Knights of St John. As it happens, I have to be at the Temple Church this afternoon. I could meet you there and perhaps sketch in some history."

"Yes. That's wonderful. Very kind," she repeated herself. "Oh, and Mr—er—Dr Mortara, I'm so sorry for your loss."

There was a pause. "Yes. Thank you." He cleared his throat. "I was very fond of Neville."

"We all were." Felicity felt it a lame reply, but what could one say, really?

"Right then. Shall we say 2:00?"

"The Temple Church. Yes. Thank you!"

She returned with a bright smile, wolfed down her lunch and, at her mother's suggestion, followed it with a pot of tea and an apple tart. Now she would get somewhere. Here was the expert guide she had been longing for. So completely hidden beyond her finding out—coming to her.

Chapter 19

"Oo what does this Cyril person look like?"

Felicity was startled by her mother's words. She had been so relieved to have made contact with Neville's uncle, then had concentrated so hard on navigating them back across London in a stifling underground train to Temple station, and was now so perplexed by the puzzling muddle of buildings facing her inside the high wrought iron fence surrounding the Inns of Court that she had given no thought as to how she would recognize the man they had come all this way to meet. "Mother, I haven't a clue."

Which seemed to cover the situation for about any question anyone could ask her. At the top of the stairs from the station they had been greeted by a beautifully laid-out fruit stall: banks of apples, pears, grapes and unseasonably early berries glowed, their vibrant colors lighting the gray day. Felicity turned to the lady at the newsstand next to the fruitier. "The Temple Church?"

"Just walk along here," the lady had motioned with her arm. "Cross over the road, go through the black gate and carry on." People were unfailingly helpful when they heard her American accent. And they always made it sound so easy.

Through the black gate, however, she faced a maze of buildings. "Oh, it's just like *Rumpole of the Bailey*."

For once Felicity was thankful for her mother's effusion. She smiled, recalling the video series they had watched years ago. Something her family had actually done together. Since it involved a lawyer, her mother had taken time to join the family television viewing. "Yes, it is, Mother. But it looked simpler on TV." Rumpole knew his way around.

A casually dressed young man emerged from a building ahead and walked toward them. "The Temple Church?" Felicity approached him.

He offered her a bright smile. "Would you just like to come this way?" He offered as if he had been waiting specifically to direct her.

The thought gave her pause, but she dismissed it instantly. Those men on the bridge had made her paranoid. And their present escort was nothing like them. Besides, it was broad daylight, even the rain had stopped, and they were surrounded by perhaps half of the lawyers—er, uh, barristers, solicitors, whatever—in London. She lost track of the turns and twists along walkways between imposing buildings, but in minutes they crossed a flagged courtyard and were facing a round building of honey-colored stone. "Thank you so much." She shook hands with their escort and, drawn by rich organ peals, entered through the elaborately carved stonework of the arched doorway into the cool gray chamber.

Felicity struggled to take it in: A great circular room, dark marble pillars growing from the stone floor to support the lantern drum high overhead, arched niches ringing the walls, and in the middle of the open space, the effigies of nine knights laid out on the floor, spotlighted irregularly with light falling from the long, leaded windows high on the walls. Beyond, the rectangular chancel lined with golden oak box pews facing either side of a wide center aisle led to the altar at the east end. Perhaps it was the architecture circling around her or the scattered tourists circulating about the effigies that gave Felicity the feeling of being in the center of a panoramic projection. She had no idea where to start.

"I'm just going to find a ladies' room," Cynthia said, and turned to the information desk. Felicity went on into the chancel and sank into the last pew, finding its high stiff back surprisingly comfortable. She simply sat, letting her mind clear of its overload of images and suspicions as people drifted in, wandering around her. Her heart settled to a steady rhythm, aided by the soaring and falling of the organ tones among the high-branched vaults of the ceiling, weaving in and out among the pillars. Behind her, the sun alternately shone and dimmed through the tall windows.

There was no service, no formal prayers, just the organ and the tourists and one very confused young woman. The altar was to her right, backed by stained glass windows whose many-faceted jewel-like pieces of glass reminded her of the kaleidoscopes she had unfailingly delighted in as a child. She would have loved to kneel at the altar to receive—what? Inspiration? A blessing? Some kind of assurance that she was doing the right thing?

But she wasn't here for her own spiritual welfare. She had a job to do, no matter how little idea she had of going about it. Still feeling her heart beating in her throat, she closed her eyes.

"Darling, look who I found!" She startled at her mother's voice coming suddenly just inches from her ear. "Well, really, he found me. Heard my American voice at the enquiries desk and guessed."

"Oh!" Felicity banged her knee on the edge of the pew as she stood.

"Sir Cyril, may I present my daughter?"

"Cyril, please, just Cyril."

Felicity blinked. Yes, this was exactly what Neville would look like in thirty years. Well, would have, if he'd been allowed the time. The man extending a long, slim hand was as tall as his nephew and the years, rather than thickening his figure, had left him even more gaunt, if that were possible. His shock of silver hair was springier than Neville's limp locks, but worn in a similar style just brushing his collar. The tanned skin made his pale blue eyes even more surprising, even if under steel-rimmed spectacles. "Miss Howard? I am so pleased to meet a friend of my nephew's."

"Oh, yes." Felicity grasped his hand warmly. "Oh, I'm so sorry for your loss, Sir—er, Cyril, I can't tell you. But then, I don't have to. You know what a lovely person he was."

Sir Cyril cleared his throat. "Yes. Quite. Thank you." A small pause to mark the passing of the formalities. "Now, how can I help you? Research, I understand."

"Yes. I don't know how much Antony told you?"

"An icon missing from the Church of the Transfiguration, he said. Some possible link to the Knights Hospitaller."

"I know it's awfully vague. We don't even know for sure—"

"Well, shall we start with the present surroundings? I always think it's helpful to put anything in its historical perspective. But then, of course, I'm undoubtedly prejudiced on the subject." His smile was warm and charming, making his blue eyes twinkle. "And plenty of history here." He turned back to the round church. "To Jerusalem!"

"What?" Felicity and Cynthia replied together.

"The order of 'the poor fellow-soldiers of Jesus Christ' was founded in 1119 to safeguard Christian pilgrims to Jerusalem. The most sacred place in the city was the site of Jesus' own burial and rising—the Church of the Holy Sepulcher. The Emperor Constantine had built a shrine over the cave that had entombed Christ's body, and over the shrine, a colossal round church, known as the Church of the Holy Sepulcher. Eventually the Templars, as they came to be known because their headquarters were on the Temple Mount, built round churches throughout Europe—in each one recreating the sanctity of the holy place in Jerusalem. To the medieval mind, to walk into one of these round churches was to walk into Jerusalem." He accompanied his words with a sweeping arm gesture that exhibited the jewel-studded cufflink in the crisp French cuff beneath his well-tailored charcoal pinstripe suit jacket.

Felicity almost gasped when she saw the device. "Oh, nice cufflinks," she managed. "Are you a member of St John Ambulance?"

Cyril followed her gaze to his cufflinks. "Oh, I see, quite. I support them, yes. They do fine work." He dismissed her question and moved forward.

But Felicity didn't move. Yet she must. Now was the time to keep a cool head. And pay close attention to everything Cyril had to tell her. This emblem appeared at every crossroads like a guiding sign—even on Neville's dead hand revealed in the swilling mud of a shallow grave. The memory flashed vividly in Felicity's mind. For a moment her desire to be involved in any of these violent and sinister machinations wavered.

Then she chided herself for feeling shaken. As Cyril said, it was an outstanding charity, just the sort of thing someone in his position would patronize. There was no reason to be startled, nothing fearful about it, and certainly nothing hidden.

Besides, there was no time for being squeamish. Their host was hurrying on with his tale and she had come here looking for information. "The Templars built their first round church about a mile north of here, in Holborn, but by 1160 they had sold their original site to the Bishop of London and moved here. Henry II had moved the center of government from Winchester to Westminster, so London was rapidly becoming the kingdom's capital and the Templars were keen to be in the center of the action." He paused. "Too much detail for you?"

"No, no," Felicity assured him. "It's what we've come to learn." Well, maybe it was. She didn't know what they needed to know.

"These effigies are fascinating," Cynthia looked down at one of the stone knights on the floor. "Is that a dog at this one's feet? Why are their legs in such awkward positions?"

"Yes, the dog at the feet of William Marshall is a quite

common device; thought to be, perhaps, a symbol of fidelity." He turned to Cynthia with almost a bow, answering her questions with accompanying hand gestures, inviting her to follow his every word. "The crossed legs is also a common device; the idea that it meant the knight had been on crusade is now pretty well discredited. I believe it was used to give a sense of action, as if the knight were walking toward the viewer. These knights, you will observe, all have their eyes open and appear to be in their early thirties—the age of Christ at his resurrection and the age medieval believers held that we shall all be when we rise again. Therefore, these knights are not here as symbols of the past, but of the future. They are waiting to hear Christ's summons and spring again to his command at his second coming."

"Oh, my. How, er—interesting."

But Cyril was undaunted by Cynthia's pallid comment. "In the thirteenth century, this would not have been the serene place of meditation and historical contemplation you see today. It was the center of power of a great organization controlling far more wealth than most kings. Perhaps you know that the Templars were the world's first international—multinational, actually—bankers. Their church would have reflected their power and splendor with a riot of color, offering a suitably splendid background to the rich robes of the wealthy and noble who met here. The walls would have been painted with bright lozenges of color and striped with gilt. When the Victorian Richardson carried out his 'restoration' on the effigies in 1841 he found traces of delicate flesh color on the faces. Buckles and spurs had been gilt, and there were crimson and blue traces on the knights' surcoats."

Their guide's restless energy kept him constantly moving as he spoke, pointing to one aspect of the building, then darting to another, moving in close to an object for careful observation, then springing back for a panoramic sweep like a cameraman afraid his battery was about to die. At least that explained his extreme thinness, thought Felicity. It would take a lot of calories to keep moving that fast.

"What it was exactly like, of course, is to some extent conjecture now, because it was all destroyed by a German bomb on the night of 10 May 1941. It's all a reconstruction, you see."

"Um, yes, thank you, Sir—er, Cyril, but what does all this have to do with today?" Somehow Felicity felt they had gotten quite far afield.

He turned to her with a generous smile exhibiting his perfect teeth. "Nothing at all, my dear. Forgive a doddering historian. Somehow I can't seem to quite grasp that not everyone is as fascinated by medieval art and history as I am."

"Oh, but I am!" Felicity blinked at her mother. This was certainly the first she had heard of Cynthia's interest. How very little she knew this woman with whom she had lived for twenty-some years. "I'm fascinated," Cynthia assured him.

"Dear lady, how kind of you. If you will indulge me further, then I shall explain that all the vast power of the Templars came to a crashing halt on the night of Friday 13 October 1307—which ever since has been memorialized in the superstition surrounding Friday the thirteenth." He continued to circle the room as he spoke.

"Oh! Amazing. What happened?"

His words were all for Cynthia now, but Felicity was allowed to listen in. "Philip IV of France, deep in debt and desperately short of gold, had already ravaged the coffers of the Jews and the Lombards—groups dominant in French finance. That left the Templars. The king's agents built a careful case against the order, charging them with a black catalog of corruption, heresies, wickedness—even to blasphemy and occult practices. All backed up, of course, with 'confessions' obtained under threat of torture."

"Was there any truth to it?"

Cyril shrugged his well-tailored shoulders. "Who knows?

A certain amount of corruption in any organization that wealthy and that powerful is quite likely. As to the lewdness and horrors of the specific charges—with which no gentleman would sully a lady's ears, especially in a holy place as this…" He took his eyes from Cynthia long enough to look around them. "I wouldn't deign to comment. But the fact remains that on that fateful night, every Templar house in the kingdom of France was occupied by the king's bailiffs. Their Grand Master burnt alive in Paris. The order extinguished." And now his energetic roving halted.

"And what about other orders? Were the Hospitallers disbanded, too?" Felicity asked.

"No, when Edward II in England disbanded the Templars he allowed the knights to join other orders—except the Knights Hospitaller."

"Too much power for them?"

"Ah, I see you understand the game. He did, however, give the Temple Church to the Hospitallers, after renting it to two colleges of lawyers. It became the lawyers' 'college chapel'—as it has continued to this day."

"Oh, so there *is* a relationship between the Temple Church and the Hospitallers?" Felicity was still trying to find some relevancy to this rambling tale.

"No, none at all. It is the lawyers' church, quite pure and simple. But reeking with history that is anything but." He looked around at the milling tourists. "It would be interesting to know how many of these visitors have been drawn here from reading *The Da Vinci Code*. When a visitor shows up clutching a copy, and asks the warden, 'Have you read the book?' He likes to tease them by pretending to think they mean the Bible."

Right. Nothing to do with the Templars. Nothing to do with the Hospitallers. "Are there any icons here?" Felicity made a desperate attempt to get her day back on track.

"No, no—nothing left of connection to the knights, apart

from the effigies and some tombstones beside the church. We don't exactly know where the bones are, either. That is to say, they're here somewhere all right, but the stones don't necessarily mark the exact spot."

"So what was your work here? Didn't I understand you to say you had found something?"

"Oh, yes. More dry history, I'm afraid." He indicated the effigy of the knight lying below William Marshall, gripping his shield, legs crossed, ready for action at the sound of the last trump.

"'Effigy of a Knight.'" Felicity read the plaque at his feet.

"Hoping to identify him. Found some old documents with some interesting clues that seem to prove…. Well, never mind, but it's fascinating from a scholarly standpoint."

"Oh, wouldn't that be wonderful!" exclaimed Cynthia. "A real plum for you."

Felicity gritted her teeth. Had she ever heard her mother sound so interested in anything Felicity's father undertook? "Why are there nine effigies? It seems an awkward number, having to balance the display as they do with—" Cynthia paused. "Whatever that is."

Cyril laughed. "Very perceptive of you. It's called simply a coped stone. Very ancient. The number nine is interesting. Nine was a sacred number to the Templars. When they started out there were supposedly nine of them in Jerusalem. A pitiful number if they were truly to defend the city, of course."

"So these represent the original nine?"

Cyril gave his characteristic shrug. "Perhaps." Then a smile. "Why not?"

"So are there no ties left to the Knights Hospitaller anywhere?" Felicity hoped her question didn't sound too probing. She needed more information, but she didn't want to go into any detail about the insignia on the back of the missing icon.

"My dear girl, of course there are: The Church of St John, the Grand Priory of England; The Hospital of St John and St Elizabeth; The museum of the Order of St John…"

Felicity rummaged in her pockets for a notebook, then began looking for a pen.

A distinctive click made her look up. Their host held out a gold pen, its tip extended. "Oh, thank you. You've been most helpful." *Perhaps too helpful?* she wondered. This man had a wealth of information, but he made Felicity uneasy.

Felicity scribbled the sites he had listed, then handed the pen back. "We really mustn't take any more of your time." Felicity used the reference for an excuse to glance at her own wrist. Oh, my. There was no way she could make it all the way back to Richmond in time for Evensong.

"But of course." Their host looked inconsolably crestfallen. "Why was I not thinking? Of course you have plans for the evening. Dinner reservations? Theater tickets? And here I was harboring hopes of prolonging the pleasure of your company."

"No, we don't have any plans." Felicity all but blushed for the speed of her mother's reply.

"Ah, then might I suggest a concert at St Martin-in-the-Fields and dinner at my favorite restaurant?" His words ostensibly included them both, but his eyes were all for Cynthia.

"I'm sorry. I really must get back to the convent. They will be expecting me for evening prayers and it takes forever to get across London at rush hour." One really couldn't treat a convent like a hotel. And she *had* undertaken this for discernment purposes, no matter how far she had been distracted.

"Oh, darling, what a shame!"

"But you, dear lady, are under no such constraints?"

"Goodness no, I'm thinking of joining a law firm. Not a convent." Cynthia's laugh sounded so brittle Felicity expected it to crash to the floor and shatter on the stones.

Cynthia gave Cyril the name of her hotel.

"The St James Sofitel? Yes, I know it well." The slight rise to Cyril's eyebrow indicated that he approved of Cynthia's choice.

"The choice was the law firm's, not mine, I'm afraid."

"I'll call for you in an hour. Will that be all right? That will give us time for a cup of tea first. Their Rose Lounge is very pleasant." He bent, and kissed her hand.

Felicity had turned to stomp toward the door when Cynthia caught her arm. "Darling, meet me for breakfast. Please. At the hotel."

Felicity opened her mouth to refuse but the look of pleading in her mother's eyes stopped her. She gave a brief, jerky nod and ran out of the church.

Chapter 20

Friday, Fifth in Lent, Evening

A ll the way out of London Felicity was tense with the internal churning of trying to make the train come sooner, run faster, the traffic disperse, the pedestrians get out of the way. None of which happened. And so she arrived back at the convent, her head ringing with all the unanswered questions of the day, all the frustrations of delay, and with fury at her mother. But then, as before, stepping through the opening in the high brick wall was stepping into a bubble of calm, out of the turmoil of a roaring storm onto a tranquil island.

And, as before, she had missed evening prayers. It seemed that balancing her two lives was an impossible task. But, of course, once she had taken the step to make her convent life permanent she wouldn't have the living-in-two-worlds struggle. Life would be peaceful. Just the thought slowed her breathing and lowered her heart rate.

An hour yet until dinner. Plenty of time to read a bit in the library next to the chapel. If nothing else perhaps it would take her mind off worrying about her mother. What a switch. Mothers were supposed to worry about their daughters. Not the other way around. But what was Cynthia thinking, going off with some man just because he kissed her hand? Well, to be fair, it wasn't quite like that, and Antony had more or less introduced them, but still…

The first book to catch her attention was *Now is the Time: A Brief Survey of the Life and Times of the Community of the Sisters of the Church,* written by one of the sisters. She settled herself in a comfortable chair looking out over the wet garden and turned a few pages idly, then stopped at a page headed "Reflections for the Journey" and was immediately captured by a quotation from Pierre Teilhard de Chardin: "Once again Providence will be found to have led me to a critical point at just the psychological moment." Well, she was certainly at a critical point. Surely the most critical of her life. Whether or not this was the psychological moment—who was to say?

She started to read on, but found her mind drifting away from the printed page, carried by a light, haunting melody floating into the room from some indefinite source. Was someone singing in the garden just beyond her window? Would one of the sisters be playing the radio or listening to a CD? Was it their recreation hour, that brief span of freedom in every nun's day? No, that was after dinner, wasn't it? The beauty of the song shimmered indistinctly, just offstage. And she forced her mind back to her book.

The next quotation was by Moses Mendelssohn, whose words struck her as frustratingly appropriate: "On the dark path on which a person is to walk here on earth just as much light is provided as he wants for him to make the next step. More would only dazzle and every side-light bewilders him." Oh, yes. All too true. But how she hated it. She wanted floodlights. Brightness at noonday. And neon billboards answering her questions and shouting the way. She wasn't rebellious. She would do what God told her to do. But he needed to *tell her.*

And Dietrich Bonhoeffer's offering seemed only depressing. "A day at a time is long enough to sustain one's faith; the next day will have its own cares." This was supposed to be *comforting*?

Finally, a Quaker saying, "Don't outrun the guide." Felicity laughed out loud. How did those Quakers know her so well? All she really wanted was a fully detailed manual with her own name on it in gold letters. Was that too much to ask?

The haunting music continued, winging angelically around the upper reaches of the room as Felicity read on. Two pages over in the book she found the serene charcoal sketch of Emily Ayckbowm, who founded the Community of the Sisters of the Church in 1870. Calm determination seemed to radiate from her slightly downcast eyes and her almost pursed lips. A woman who knew what needed to be done and how to do it. Had Mother Emily ever felt as adrift as Felicity did at that moment? She longed to achieve such serene assurance for her own life.

Well, at least finding Mother Emily's story helped Felicity focus on her primary task which seemed to keep getting sidelined—learning about the various orders she was visiting, and envisioning herself in that Community. Mother Emily founded the Community "to promote the honour and glory of Almighty God and the extension of a life of active charity and mission enterprise." Today that would be called social activism and spiritual renewal, she supposed. She had already noted how different this community of nuns in modern dress was from the fully habited, contemplative Community of the Holy Cross that Mother Mary Mark led.

Mother Emily had seen the degradation and poverty suffered by so many in Victorian England, especially the children, and sought to alleviate their suffering. She opened schools, established orphanages, built convalescent homes for sick children and gave practical and spiritual help to the men building the London Underground. What a lady. Felicity closed her eyes. Yes, she could envision herself doing those things. Well, maybe.

Within thirty years the Community was global, working in Canada, India and Burma, Australia, New York, South Africa and New Zealand. Mother Emily committed her sisters to working "for God amid the din and jar and unrest of modern life." And to carrying the tumult "the calm atmosphere of the sanctuary." If the world needed that in what, in retrospect, seemed such simpler times, think how much more the world needed it today. *Carry the calm of the sanctuary into the tumult.* Felicity knew she could never do that for the world when she didn't have it in her own life.

At last she put the book aside with a sigh and determined to find the source of the puzzling, mystical music. Once in the hall she realized it was definitely inside the building. Coming from behind the closed chapel door, perhaps? She wouldn't have had the temerity to push the heavy door open, but a gray-haired sister who happened to be passing at that moment saw her hesitation and read her desire to enter the chapel. The sister pushed the cumbersome door open with a sharp grating sound on the tile. The music stopped instantly.

Sitting at the piano on the far side of the room where she had been singing to her own accompaniment was the young blonde girl Felicity had wondered about the day before. "Oh, I'm so sorry to interrupt. I was reading next door. Your singing was so lovely. I wanted to find out what it was."

The girl blushed. "My own dabblings, I'm afraid. I guess you could say it's a form of prayer. At least," she ducked her head shyly, her golden hair covering much of her face, "I feel myself addressing God."

"It's Gabriella, isn't it? I'm Felicity, by the way. Should I call you Sister Gabriella?"

"Oh, no, no. That won't be for years and years yet. I'm just here as an alongsider. Here for my Easter hols."

"You're still at school?" Felicity tried to put herself in Gabriella's place at sixteen or seventeen. What had she been doing at that age? Certainly not sitting in a convent chapel composing prayer songs to God. Boys. Pop music. Parties. Clothes. Make-up. Dancing. All the usual—normal—things.

"Yes. One more year of college. Then Mummy says I must go to uni. And Mother Lois agrees. So I have to obey. And then there will be years of being a novice…" She sighed and gathered a handful of her long, flowing skirt into a ball. "It's so hard, though. To have to wait so long to do what I've wanted so desperately to do since I was a tiny girl."

"And you've never doubted that you wanted to be a nun? I mean, there must be boyfriends. And with your talent you could have a professional musical career."

Gabriella's laughter was more magical than her singing. "That's what everyone says. But it just sounds awful to me. All this," she waved her slim white arm in an arc to encompass all of the convent, "is so *right* for me."

"But how did you even know there were such places when you were a child?" Until about a year ago, Felicity had thought all such places had ended with the Reformation.

"I was fascinated by the stories of saints at school and in church. And our family always visited shrines and abbeys and things like that on holiday. Then one summer I went to the youth pilgrimage at Walsingham and I really understood my calling."

"And you've never looked back?"

"Oh, no. The feeling just grows and grows. My friends think I'm insane, of course. My mother says I'll outgrow it. But I *know.* I just have to be patient and show them all that it's real."

There was so much Felicity wanted to ask this girl who must be almost ten years younger than herself, yet projected the centered calm many women several times her age never achieved. But then the bell rang for dinner. "Oh, it's my turn to serve the drinks. Do forgive me." Gabriella said it as if pouring glasses of water and lemonade for a community of nuns was the most delightful treat that could have been offered her, and fairly skipped out of the room.

Felicity followed slowly. Would she ever achieve such calm assurance about anything? Even in her earlier days of headstrong overconfidence, she had the boldness, but not the composure. She was looking inward so intently when she entered the dining room that she picked up her rolled napkin and silverware from the sideboard and took a seat in the far corner of the room without looking up. When the blessing had been pronounced and she did glance up, she almost cried out in surprise at the sight of the handsome, dark-haired priest seated next to Mother Lois.

Felicity caught her breath and staunchly refused to admit to herself how much the sight of Antony's slightly bowed head gladdened her heart. The truth was, her heart so leaped to her throat she could barely eat, and if she could have given in to her impulses she would have run to him, squealing with delight. As it was, she was obliged to sit in prim silence, passing the salt and then the butter and then the sliced cucumbers in response to the pointed gestures of the sisters sitting around her, while all the things she wanted to talk to Antony about buzzed nonstop through her head. And when, at long last, he looked up and swept the room with his steady gaze, she had to all but sit on her hands to keep herself from waving wildly at him. Instead, however, she managed merely to return his circumspect smile. If Mother Lois hadn't risen just at that moment, however, she couldn't have been responsible for her behavior when he winked at her.

After the meal, Felicity made her way from the dining room along the corridor and out to the garden, her enforced restraint made all the harder when she sensed Antony's footstep behind her. Once in the garden she grabbed his hand and propelled him at her long-legged canter across the lawn, through the break in the shrubbery into the orchard. At last they were out of any possibility of being overlooked or overheard.

Then she turned to him, grasping both his hands in hers. "Oh, Antony, I've never been so glad to see anyone in my life! Sir Cyril gave us some interesting background, but then Mother threw herself at him and I ran out of time to ask more, and all there is of the Knights of St John is a museum and a hospital and…"

She stumbled to a halt, looked down to see herself holding Antony's hands, and dropped them shyly, half-turning away. She fumbled in her pocket, drew out the crumpled list she had made at the Temple Church that afternoon, and offered it to him without catching his eye. Antony cleared his throat and perused her list. "Oh, well done. This is exactly what we needed."

"Is it? You mean there's something there we can use? Some sort of clue?"

"Well, I wouldn't go so far as to call it a clue, but a plan of research, certainly. Let's ask Reverend Mother if we can use the computer in her office."

Since Mother Lois had finished work for the day she was happy to turn her office over to the guests. Antony ushered Felicity to the desk chair, indicating that she should take the lead in the search. She looked at him questioningly. "It's your right to do the honors. You did the legwork to produce the list."

She tucked a few strands of long blonde hair behind her ear and opened the search engine. "So, what do you think, 'Knights of St John,' 'Knights of Malta,' 'Knights Hospitalier?' They're all the same, aren't they?"

One of their first searches took them to the hospital of St John and St Elizabeth in St John Wood. "'The Knights of Malta are the world's oldest charitable organization. They originated in a hospital founded by Italian Benedictine monks in 11th Century Jerusalem. After the First Crusade had taken the city in 1099, the hospital broke free from its parent Abbey and in 1113 was recognized by the papacy as an independent Order of the Church, the Order of the Hospital of St. John of Jerusalem.' Shall I keep reading?"

"Yes, please. We need to get the history in perspective."

Felicity laughed. "How did I somehow know you'd say that?"

"You have to know where you've been—"

"I know, I know," Felicity joined in with a broad smile and they finished together, "to know where you're going."

"OK, 'From the first the Hospitallers, as they were called,

proclaimed an original ideal: that the poor, *the holy poor of Jesus Christ* were their lords and they their serfs and slaves, obliged to render them the devotion and reverence which should be given to Christ … They expressed their love of the poor by caring for them when they were sick, and their hospitals influenced all others in the West.'" Her eyes skimmed down the screen.

"'The Hospitallers were monks who provided medical care and protection for pilgrims visiting Jerusalem. The Order gradually took on a military identity and became an Order of Knights. Their headquarters moved to Rhodes in 1312 and to Malta in 1530.'" With a sigh of frustration she flipped back to her search page. "581,000 results. This could be a long night. But what we need is something about England. About *now*."

"Try adding 'England' to your search."

Quiet filled the room as Google assembled a new list, and Felicity clicked on the first listing. "OK, here we go. 'There were English knights of the Hospital from the time of the First Crusade, long before the foundation of the English Langue in the early years of the 14th century.' Um, I know *langue* is French for language, but what does this mean exactly?"

"The word can also mean speech-community. I think it means a branch of the order for English-speakers."

"Right. OK, 'around 1144 a priory was established in England. The superior was the Prior at Clerkenwell.' Clerkenwell?"

"An area of London," Antony supplied.

Felicity nodded. "Sir Cyril said something about a priory. So it's still there?"

"The building is. It's a museum now."

"That's incredible. More than eight hundred years later."

Antony laughed. "I hear a ring of amazement in your voice. If I didn't know better, I would say you're developing a taste for history."

"It's just so mind-boggling that the buildings are still

here, that people are still carrying on an organization from the eleventh century." She scrolled down several pages. "Oh, here's that design that was on the icon." A large black, eight-pointed cross filled the screen. "Well, sort of. It's the same cross, but it doesn't have the leaves or that gold star thingy. I wonder if that makes any difference? 'The Cross of Malta. To the Knights of Malta, its four arms represent the cross on which Jesus suffered, while the eight points symbolize the Beatitudes...'" A wide, face-splitting yawn interrupted her reading.

Antony touched her arm. "Enough for tonight. We need clear minds to work on this."

He started to rise.

"Yes. Sure. Just one more." She blinked to bring the words into focus. "'Today there are some 11,000 knights and dames of the Order of Malta worldwide, 240 of them in Britain.'" She paused. "That's not really very many, is it? But then, if they're really powerful people.... Or really desperate..."

Antony leaned over and took her hand from the mouse, clicking to shut the computer down, then half-lifted her from the chair and guided her toward the door. "You've had a long day." The tenderness in his voice made her look at him. She shrank from what she saw in his eyes. She didn't want to deal with the conflict of her own feelings. And she didn't want to hurt him.

The quicker she got to her room the better. But halfway along the corridor she stopped. "Antony, are we saying that the Knights of Malta are stealing icons? Does that mean that one of them murdered Neville? No, he was wearing their emblem. Maybe he was killed because he was a knight. Could he have been?"

"Felicity, remember," he tightened his grip on her arm and spoke with hushed urgency, "We're not trying to solve a murder. That's police business. We're looking for a missing icon." She knew him well enough to know he meant: *I don't want you anywhere near a murderer*, but that he knew better than to say anything to her that she would interpret as a challenge. Frightening, to have someone understand her so well. It seemed he understood her far better than she understood herself. She really must get alone and think.

They were almost to the stairway leading to the guest rooms when the bell rang from the chapel. "Oh, I forgot about Compline." Even as she spoke another yawn muffled her words.

"You go to bed."

Felicity hesitated, then obeyed. "Thank you." She stopped. In spite of her urgency to be alone and think, she needed to tell him about that other problem she had pushed to the back of her mind all evening. "Antony, I'm so worried about my mother. She went out with Cyril. She had a *date*."

She held her breath. If he laughed or reminded her that her mother was an adult she would want to hit him.

Instead he gave her hand a brief squeeze. "You sleep. I'll pray."

She nodded and stumbled toward her room. But she was still worried.

Chapter 21

Saturday, Fifth in Lent, Morning

"Worried?" Cynthia, looking radiant, smiled at her over her crystal goblet of freshly squeezed orange juice. "Darling, why should you have been worried? I couldn't have been safer with Prince Philip. Or treated more like royalty."

Felicity pushed the Brasserie menu aside. Her stomach was too tight to eat. She might be able to manage tea and dry toast.

"Darling, have the warm Kent asparagus with poached eggs. They put the most wonderful sauce on it." Cynthia smiled at the waiter then leaned toward Felicity. "It was the most amazing evening. I want to tell you all about it. Every detail. Then you'll realize how silly you're being.

"We started in the Rose Lounge with tea, and you'll never guess—Cyril chose the paintings for that room and they're wonderful, so exactly right. He asked me what I thought of them and I felt like such a dunce. Just being with him makes me long to know more about art. I suddenly realize how much I've missed."

Felicity wanted to tell her that art appreciation wasn't all she'd missed by shutting everything but work out of her life, but she held her tongue.

"And then we walked through this charming park—all full of flowers and ducks and children—like a scene in *Mary Poppins*—to a church where they have concerts. Right across from the National Gallery. Do you know it?"

Felicity nodded. "St Martin-in-the Fields."

"Yes, that's it. It was all candlelight and they did this Mozart piece. Well, it was all Mozart, but the 'Ave Verum' was heavenly. Beyond heavenly. It made me feel like I could reach out and touch God."

Felicity blinked. Had her mother just said that? "That's— that's amazing, Mother."

"Yes, that's what I'm trying to tell you. And Cyril told me what it meant about Jesus' body being our food in life and death. I don't understand it, but I know your Antony would and it really helped me understand what you see in all this church business you're so taken with."

Felicity was forming a reply to the substance of her mother's statement, but then was sidetracked. "He's not 'my' Antony, Mother."

"It's obvious he'd like to be. I don't understand you, Felicity. He's very attractive."

Felicity would have liked to ignore that, but it was clear Cynthia wasn't going to let her off. "I suppose so. Clericals seem to do that to a man. Like a dress military uniform. Or a tuxedo."

Cynthia smiled. "Ah, so you have noticed?"

"Mother!"

Cynthia just laughed and then raced on again. "And then we went to this restaurant you wouldn't believe. Rules, it's called. It was the favorite of Edward VII. There's a special room upstairs where he entertained an actress friend of his. And the food! Have you ever tasted crispy duck?

"And all the meat is wild game from their own estates and it made me think of when I was a little girl. Have I ever told you what an avid hunter your grandfather was?"

Felicity shook her head. Her grandfather had died before she was born. She didn't know anything about him. Nothing at all. She realized then how odd that was. But it seemed she was going to learn something now.

"I spent every fall tramping over the fields with him hunting pheasant. It was the one thing we did together. Well, I tramped, my father hunted. And the yearly elk and deer hunts were the pivotal point of the calendar. Not for my mother and myself, but for Father. The work it was, getting everything ready for those male treks into the wilderness area! A two, three weeks' expedition." She stopped abruptly. Just when Felicity was interested.

"Yes, so what then?"

"My mother and I did lovely things together when he was gone—shopping, going out to lunch, visiting her friends." She was quiet for a moment. "But I hated it when they returned. I always ran to the bottom field and hid there. I hated having my cheek rubbed with the bush of a black beard he grew when he went to the mountains. But I could never stay away long enough. Sometimes my cheek would chafe for days." Cynthia gave a little shake of her head. "But that was a long time ago, and it isn't at all what I wanted to tell you."

Felicity pushed her cup of cold tea aside and took a deep breath. What was Cynthia building up to telling her?

"Darling, you'll be so proud of me. This wasn't just an evening of frivolous pleasure, I was working for you."

"Oh, Mother." Felicity had a bad feeling about what would come next.

"I know you feel I've been the most awful drag on your investigation, but Cyril is so knowledgeable and so willing to help. So I told him about the stolen icon—"

"Mother, you didn't! Father Anselm wanted it kept quiet."

"I think Antony might have said something that let him know about it anyway, because he seemed to know. Like I said, he's so knowledgeable. And, of course, he knew all about the one at St Julian's. So I told him about the one at Rempstone—which, of course, he should have been told about anyway, because his own nephew was there. And he was very interested when I told him about the mark on the back."

"How did you know about that?"

"I heard you and Antony talking, of course. You must think I'm the most complete ditz."

"No, Mother, I don't. I just didn't realize you took any interest."

"Well, of course I'm interested. That's what I'm trying to tell you. You're my daughter. I'm interested in everything about your life."

Felicity shook her head wordlessly.

"Now listen, here's the important part. Cyril has a friend, Sir Robert Tennant, who owns an icon gallery. He's the top expert in England—perhaps in the world—Cyril says. And he's going to take me to see him. He'll know if your icon has been offered for sale and may have some really good ideas where to look for it."

Cynthia's monologue continued, but Felicity pushed her chair back. "Mother, I appreciate that you're trying to help but…" What could she say? Cyril's friend might well have helpful information. Surely Felicity was being unfair to react so negatively to Cynthia's friendship with an admittedly attractive man. "Mother, I have to meet Antony."

"Oh, of course, darling. Have a lovely day. I know I will." Cynthia smiled. "Cyril is taking me to lunch at Fortnum's and then to the icon gallery. Anyway, I'm sure we can find out some really useful information for you. Why don't you meet us for tea at this little pastry shop Cyril mentioned near there?"

"Mother, don't…" *Don't say too much. Don't get involved with some strange man…* What was the use? Cynthia wasn't listening.

"I think it's *Maison* something. In Holland Park. I'm sure Antony will know. We'll see you there."

"Mother—"

"Go on. Don't worry."

Felicity grimaced. If people told you not to worry, it meant you should be worrying.

All the way across London the conversation with her mother droned through her mind. Especially the things she hadn't said: *Mother, you're a woman. A married woman. Not a teenager!* She had wanted to yell at her mother, reason with her, beg her to be sensible. But it all seemed so futile. In the end all she had managed was, "Mother, be careful." And she didn't even know what she meant by that.

Chapter 22

Half an hour later, Felicity stood underneath the ancient arch spanning the street leading to the courtyard of the priory of St John, trying to focus on the task before her and thankful for Antony's presence.

"It looks like we stepped out of a time machine. The Tardis, maybe." Over her head was the crypt-like gate which led to the once famous and wealthy priory of the Knights Hospitaller of the Order of St John of Jerusalem. And she was about to enter the premises of the Grand Priory in the British Realm of the Venerable Order of the Hospital of St John of Jerusalem (suppressed by the first Queen Elizabeth and revived by Queen Victoria—if she had her history straight).

She couldn't even recite the titles without taking a deep breath, and she certainly couldn't get her head around the complicated history of this organization shrouded in time and rumor. How could she possibly find something which would help restore stolen icons? It was just all too fanciful. She had seen the pictures of the knights and dames of the order in their long capes and plumed hats, looking as if they were going to a fancy dress ball. Surely all this wasn't to be taken seriously. Something like the Society for Creative Anachronism her brother and his wife enjoyed so much—all innocent fun.

"Come on, the tour is about to begin." Antony's intense look told her he was taking this *very* seriously.

"What are we looking for?" She whispered as a small group formed around a bald man in horn-rimmed glasses standing on the flagged courtyard in front of a wide, arched doorway just inside St John's Gate.

"If we knew, we probably wouldn't need to be here."

The guide was giving a potted history of the knights, beginning with the First Crusade. Felicity let her mind wander; they had read all this on the computer last night, and since the Community's missing icon only went back to the seventeenth century, surely she didn't need to know all this about the Peasants' Revolt in 1381 when the priory was destroyed because the prior had introduced a hated poll tax? She looked around the group of her fellow tourists: a clutch of middle-aged schoolteacherish-looking women; an elderly man leaning on a stick, with a bored-looking young woman in jeans—his granddaughter indulging Gramps?; a family with two school-aged boys— the mother's first question revealed them to be American tourists; and an unshaven young man in wire-rimmed glasses and a gray hooded sweatshirt taking careful notes on the lecture.

Antony nudged her arm at something the guide said. "That's about the time Julian's shrine may have acquired their icon."

"What?" She struggled to get back on track. "Oh, early fifteenth century? OK." So the knights were active in England then. Didn't they already know that? The dates jumbled in her mind. She hoped Antony was getting more out of this than she was.

They moved into the building and up the fine, carved stairway to the council chamber. "This room, where the knights and dames still meet in council, is 500 years old, although the stained glass is late Victorian."

The studious young man paused in his note-taking to ask about a certain piece of furniture. "Oh, I'm sorry. That only goes back to Victoria. But if you'd care to come through here, we have some much older pieces in this room." The guide led the way into another chamber.

"The knights moved their headquarters from Rhodes to

Malta at the Reformation. We call this the Malta Room because everything in this room came through Malta."

One glance around the room left Felicity entirely overwhelmed. The opulence. The symbols of past power. The centuries of prestige reduced to a museum for ambulance drivers. She kept hoping something would start to make a pattern, that some fact or clue would stand out, something they could work from to figure out why anyone would be stealing icons. But the more she saw of the enormous pieces of heavy, ornately carved chests, tables and cabinets, the more hopeless it seemed. *Concentrate*, she told herself. If the icon thefts and attempted theft were connected—and surely they must be—and since one bore an insignia connecting it to the knights it seemed reasonable to think the others must be—then mightn't this be a likely place to hide them? But where?

To her left, the wall was dominated by a mirror whose extravagantly baroque frame loomed at her. She would hate to be under that if it ever fell. She was moving on to peer at the oil painting of the knights' *Castel Sant' Angelo* on Malta when she looked back at the mirror, just in time to catch a darting glance from the weedy hoodie. Had he been observing her? She resisted the impulse to shiver, and moved on quickly to gaze at the black oak floor-to-ceiling cabinet filling the wall.

"I see that our 'Cabinet of Curiosities' has taken your eye," The guide said.

Since it dominated the entire end of the room, one could hardly help notice it, Felicity thought. But she longed to open those shiny black doors, each panel of which was carved with an eight-pointed cross. That cabinet must be filled with secret compartments holding treasures. Stolen icons, perhaps. How could she manage to get a look inside?

She took a step toward the interesting cupboard, then paused. The back of her neck tingled as palpably as if someone had touched her. She was being watched. She spun around, but no one seemed to be staring at her. *Paranoid*, she accused herself, and turned back to the cabinet.

As it turned out, no clever sleuthing was required to see inside the cabinet. The guide turned a key in the lock and opened the doors to display the curiosities within: mostly models of knights. "This cabinet has just been restored to us. About a year ago we had a group of schoolboys visiting. They were just completing their tour of this room when the most remarkable thing happened. The entire cabinet just slowly collapsed and fell to bits before their eyes. You can imagine the chorus of denials of having touched it. I expect every boy in the class thought he was going to be called to account by his master. But actually, the glue holding the cabinet together had simply dried out over the years and it gave way. You are the first tour to see the restored cabinet, as it was returned to us only two days ago."

Felicity turned away. So much for containing stolen icons. But there was that low, carved chest on the other wall. And the massively embellished table in the center of the room. Could that contain hidden drawers under its golden ornamentation? She turned quickly to ask Antony if he had similar ideas. But it wasn't Antony standing so close behind her she could hear him breathing.

Felicity was beginning to feel stalked. *Yah!* Felicity glared at him until he returned his attention to his notes.

Felicity opened her mouth to demand what he thought he was about, but their guide was herding them forward. "Now, if you would just step this way into our library, I have some very interesting documents to show you." She tried lagging back, but the guide's stern eyes behind his horn-rimmed glasses were fixed on her.

A large stone fireplace, decorated with knights' shields, filled one wall of the next room. In the center of the room was a long table covered with manuscript pages, each in a plastic folder. The guide began pointing out interesting royal signatures on charters granting rights to the Venerable Order of the Hospital of St John of Jerusalem, "And here we have the Royal Charter Queen Victoria signed, formally reinstating the order. And here is a charter from the Geneva Conference of 1863 at the founding of the Red Cross. You may not be aware that the Red Cross was originally founded solely to relieve the suffering of wounded soldiers. So the Order of St John said, 'You work in the war zones, we'll look after the people at home.' Today there is a lot of overlap, but that's what we're still doing." He held up another document. "Now, if you'll just look closely at this…"

As everyone bent over the plastic-covered sheets of paper on the table, Felicity edged her way to the back of the group. One final glance at the guide told her he was thoroughly engrossed in his lecture. She ducked around the corner, and almost bumped noses with hoodie. "What do you think you're doing?" she hissed.

"I could ask the same of you." His grin wasn't at all humorous.. "Dropped my notes."

There was nothing to do but return to the library. This time Felicity's attention was taken by a tall escritoire made of a golden, burled wood, its upper cabinet doors faced with heavily beveled mirrors. "Seventeenth century Russian." The guide noted her interest. "Given to the order by Peter the Great when he traveled to Malta and called on the Grand Master. Peter was very interested in the work of the knights, and the Grand Master made him a knight and awarded him a Maltese Cross."

It took all of Felicity's control not to gasp out loud. Peter the Great was a Knight of Malta? And Our Lady of the Transfiguration was said to have been brought to England by Peter. Maybe this all did make sense. Maybe there was a pattern. She caught Antony's eye halfway around the room. Surely he was thinking the same thing she was. She took his little half-nod as a signal.

As the guide moved the party toward the exit, she slipped

back to the table and bent over the manuscripts as if engrossed in them while Antony engaged the guide in a discussion of the reconstruction of the Priory Church after the Peasants' Revolt.

As the footsteps faded, she darted across the floor to the escritoire. The drawers moved easily and opened silently. And were empty. All six of them. She had her hand on the key in the pull-down desktop when a movement across the room made her turn.

"Here, now, what do you think you're doing?" She grabbed the hoodie's wrist and pulled one of the historic charters from between the sheets of his notebook. "Sir!" She summoned the guide from the hallway beyond. "He's stealing."

"I beg your pardon. I was merely studying the document."

"From inside your notebook?" Felicity turned her back on him and left the guide to deal with the impending row.

Outside, bright April sunshine reflected off the pale gold stone of the priory, courtyard and gate, giving the impression of warmth. Antony took her arm and led her apart from their remaining fellow tourists who were all making their way in a group back under St John's Gate and toward the busy Clerkenwell Road to the Priory Church. "What did you make of all that?" he asked.

"I'm not sure. I thought the knights must be stealing, but if that jerk is any example, it looks more like they are being stolen from. Of course I didn't get a chance to look very closely, but it seemed to me, if there was anything stolen in that museum, it would have been done in something like the twelfth century."

"I agree." He took her arm as the light changed and they hurried across the road. "I've been thinking about the fact that icons are sacred objects. Objects of worship that have been venerated for centuries. It seems a much more likely place to find one would be in a church."

As he said that, they were beckoned by one of the schoolteachers to rejoin their group. Since their guide remained at the priory, one of the teachers had taken over the role, reading from a guidebook. "The ancient priory church was burned in 1381 during the Peasants' Revolt. The brass marks in the driveway indicate the area of the original circular nave." Felicity's gaze swept upward from the markers at her feet to the gleaming white church façade in front of her.

"This church was built about 1720, incorporating the choir walls of the ancient church." 1720? How long did Peter the Great reign? His Grand Embassy was in the late 1600s, wasn't it? But still, could something here be connected to his visit? She moved forward to hear more clearly. "In 1930 this again became the priory church of the order and it has been sympathetically restored after its destruction in 1941." Felicity sighed. German bombs. Peasants' Revolt. More destructors to add to her list of Reformers and Cromwellian zealots. Why must people always kill and tear down and demolish? she wondered.

"The crypt, however, is remarkably well-preserved. Three bays date from 1140 and the side chapels from 1185." Their self-appointed guide went on to read about an altarpiece that had been removed at the Dissolution and recovered in 1932, but Felicity was already moving toward the doors. She was just reaching out toward one of the massive lion-head handles when the reader caught up with her. "Those handles were found in the ruins of the original hospice of the order in Jerusalem." Felicity pulled her hand back. She had almost grabbed hundreds of years of history without even noticing what was in her hand. Chastened, she moved forward. The ages were still with us. If only we bothered to notice. Perhaps that was some of what Antony was trying to get through to his students—to her—in his constant nattering on about history. She half-turned and gave him an almost shy smile.

The rest of the group went to the sanctuary above, so Felicity and Antony were alone under the chalky white spanning arches of the crypt. It was well lit by pillar lamps, the coldness of the enclosing stone relieved by red chairs filling the space leading to the altar. Felicity paused to consider the stained glass window behind the altar. Wasn't a crypt under ground? How was the window lighted? But before she had time to discover an answer, Antony led her into a side chapel. She caught her breath. On a marble altar, lit by a circle of flickering votive candles, was an icon of Our Lady. Her red mantle glowed brightly against the vivid green background. Her pensive look invited thoughts of her divine Son.

Felicity trembled. This time she wasn't reaching out to grasp something without thinking of its value. Her hand closed on the icon. She lifted it from its stand and turned it over. "Oh." She was so sure she would find a gleaming black eight-pointed cross, perhaps with entwining leaves, atop a gold star. It seemed as if everything she had seen all morning had been marked with a Maltese Cross. Now, when she expected one, why was the back of the icon a clean expanse of polished wood?

"Why?" She replaced the icon on its stand. "Why isn't there a mark on this one, that we know belongs to the Knights of Malta? Are we completely wrong in thinking the marked icon and the missing ones are connected to the knights?" Her voice faded with disappointment. Were they wrong about the whole thing? Had she only imagined all those connections?

"Maybe that's the point," Antony suggested. "I'm no expert, but this icon looks very modern to me, compared to the others we've seen. Maybe the point is that this icon doesn't have any historic connection to the Knights of Malta."

"But ours did? And Julian's and the one at Rempstone?" Felicity thought. "Maybe that's why the knights are stealing icons—because all their ancient ones have been lost and they want to replace them. And Neville found out somehow and they killed him to keep him quiet." In her excitement, her voice had risen.

Antony's hand closed over her arm tightly and he tugged

her from the chapel, propelling her toward the stairs leading up out of the crypt. His mouth close to her ear, he bit off the words, "That's a lot of speculation, but if there's anything to it, the crypt of the Priory Church of the Knights of St John is the last place you should be proclaiming it."

Chapter 23

I n spite of being back out in the sunshine, Felicity shuddered. What had she said? Had she been overheard? As usual, she had spoken her thoughts before thinking them through. Then, the sound of the splashing water from the fountain in the church garden beyond the gate penetrated her consciousness, sounding like the rainwater splashing down at St Benet's Abbey and she was seeing a white hand emerge from the mud, washed by pounding rain to reveal a symbolically engraved ring.

An even more compulsive shiver shook her body, but was stopped by Antony's firm embrace. "It's all right, Felicity. You're quite safe here."

"Of course I'm all right." She stiffened and shook his arm off. The merest suggestion that she wasn't all right was all she needed to bring her around. "I was just remembering poor Neville. And missing him." She squared her shoulders "I hope you didn't think I was frightened or anything."

Antony gave a rueful grin and shook his head. "Well, I'd be less concerned if you did get frightened once in a while. Please be careful, Felicity."

"Of course I will." She tossed her long hair, worn loose over her shoulders today. "The only thing I'm fearful of at the moment is of starving to death. Do you realize how many hours it's been since breakfast?"

"Yes, and we've gone without one of those luscious midmorning coffee breaks we always got at CT." Antony steered her toward the bus stop.

Just the thought of the thick slabs of fruit cake or jam rolls or lemon bars the cooks at the College of the Transfiguration produced for their "wee lads" every morning made Felicity's mouth water. Never mind that some of their wee lads were now lassies and none were particularly "wee." She was so wrapped up in thoughts of rich pastries she didn't even ask where they were going until the bus lumbered to a stop in front of a large white building.

"Where are we?"

"John and Lizzies."

"A restaurant?"

"Hospital. Hospital of St John and St Elizabeth, to be exact. Run by the Order of Malta. We went on their website last night." As Antony spoke, a white St John Ambulance with its distinctive black cross pulled through the round drive in front of the glass doors.

"But I want food." Antony's devotion to research was admirable, but really, first things first.

"Absolutely top quality food, I promise you." He held the door open for her, then directed her down a flight of stairs to a table by a glass wall overlooking a well-tended garden. "The 'bright and airy Terrace Restaurant' promising 'classic dishes from fully fresh ingredients' according to my Internet research."

Felicity's salmon filet in lemon sauce with sauté of fresh vegetables entirely lived up to their billing, but she shook her head regretfully at the offered fruit tart with pouring cream. "Better not. I promised Mother we'd meet her and Cyril," she simply couldn't say that without gritting her teeth, "at some pastry shop in Holland Park in a couple of hours, so we'd better get on with whatever it is we're supposed to be doing here."

Antony led the way back to the ground floor, past the reception desk to the center of the building. "The Conventual Church of St John of Jerusalem at the Hospital of St John and St Elizabeth," he read the plaque beside the door.

Felicity gasped. If she had thought the priory museum was opulent, she hadn't seen anything. Her eyes were immediately drawn upward to the great blue dome, each of its sections studded with gold Maltese crosses. Below, the marble altar was topped by a white and gold baldacchino supported by four marble pillars, their Corinthian fluting heavily gold-leafed. Against the walls to each side of the high altar were small chapels, their altars all of inlaid marble and gilt. And everywhere she looked, Maltese crosses highlighted the decoration—giant white marble ones at the base of each of the altar columns, white satin ones sewn on the red brocade banner by the side chapel; even the Paschal candle was emblazoned with a Maltese cross studded with heavy gold nails, signifying the wounds of Christ. But for all their profusion, none of the crosses was presented on a golden nine-pointed star surrounded by trailing vines.

"What an amazing place! What is it? It can't be a hospital chapel."

"It is, actually." Antony genuflected to the cross standing high above the altar, flanked by six heavy gold candlesticks, then walked to an information rack and picked up a leaflet giving the history of the church. "'The church is here to be used by the patients and staff of the Hospital and the Hospice, for the Knights and Dames of Malta, for the people of the parish of St. John's Wood and for visitors,'" he read.

"But how did it come to be here? It seems so unlikely to walk right off a London street into some sort of Italian..." Bordello was the word that came to mind, but she was sure that would be sacrilegious.

Antony laughed. "Well done; actually, it says here that the style is Italian baroque." He consulted his pamphlet again. "'The Order, so powerful in Europe in the Middle Ages, had declined almost to the point of extinction after the loss of Malta to Napoleon, but by the 1850s it was once more in the hands of men of vision who were determined to see it flourishing again.' Hmm." His eyes scanned the page. "So they started a hospital run by nuns who had nursed in the Crimea with Florence Nightingale. 'The Hospital had only a temporary chapel so a knight built the present magnificent church at his own expense.'"

Felicity continued to wander around the room as he read, her attention bouncing from one sumptuous object to another. What could be here that could help them in their search? Suddenly she stopped before a side altar holding a large lump of black stone flanked by candles and, on top of the stone, a gold-framed object. "Look! What an odd thing, to have a rock on an altar. And this is the strangest icon I've ever seen. It is an icon, isn't it?"

"Ah, Our Lady of Philermo." Antony produced another leaflet. "'An ancient, sacred icon, painted, according to legend, by Saint Luke. It travelled miraculously across the sea from Jerusalem to Mount Phileremos on the island of Rhodes, where it was kept in a shrine. When the knights of the Order of Saint John conquered Rhodes in 1309, the Philermo Madonna became one of their most treasured possessions. After the loss of Rhodes to the Ottoman Turks in 1524 the icon accompanied the Knights to their new home in Malta.'"

"And this is *it*? I mean, the real thing? Just sitting out here like this?" Felicity looked over her shoulder as if she expected to be bashed on the head as Sister Mary Perpetua had been, and see a thieving hand reach out to seize the icon.

But Antony shook his head. "No, no. A copy. A very meticulous one, judging from the photographs in this leaflet, but the original seems to be in a museum in Montenegro."

"Oh, in a museum. Not in a church? That's sad."

"Yes, but at least she'll be well looked after. According to this, she's had a lot of adventures, even surviving the Russian Revolution."

"How did she get to Russia?"

Antony consulted his brochure. "When the knights were expelled from Malta, the Grand Master took the icon with him. When he abdicated he sent it to Russia, and knights there gave it to Tsar Paul."

"Paul? He was Peter the Great's successor, wasn't he?"

"I think so. It says here that Paul had been 'illegally elected Grand master by a group of rebel knights…' Well, it goes on a bit."

"Hmm, the Russian connection again. But what's all this business around her face? How come we can't see the whole icon?"

"That's called a *risa*. It's like a dress for her."

Felicity regarded the gold plate, the heavily jeweled corona encircling the Virgin's dark face, and the jewel-encrusted neckline of her gown. "What's that sticking out behind her head? Are those supposed to be rays of light?" She pointed to the white spears behind the corona.

Antony grinned. "Look again. Those are the points of a Maltese cross. The cover is there because the face is all that's left of the original icon."

"What a shame." Felicity moved closer to peer at the face of the Virgin. Her first reaction was that the image was—well, ugly. But the more she looked at the sad eyes beneath delicate eyebrows, the long, high-bridged nose, the fine lips, slightly parted, the more she saw the beauty that must have once been there. The beauty that remained in the ravaged image. And the more she looked into those soft brown eyes, the more she felt she knew this woman, had seen her somewhere before. Suddenly it clicked. "Oh, I know. That's the same face as the icon we just saw in the crypt of the church."

"Yes, it says here that a copy was commissioned by Tsar Nicholas I in 1852 for processional use and is kept in the Basilica of S Maria degli Angeli at Assisi." He held out the photograph on the back of his folder.

"Yes, that's it. So the one in the crypt is a copy of a copy."

"Apparently this is the most familiar image of the icon to the modern knights."

Felicity thought for several moments. "So, the order has the original—or, rather, it knows where it is—it has the 'original copy' and it has copies of the original and copies of the copies. And that's their big deal. So why do they need to be stealing icons from monasteries and convents? Are they trying to corner the market, or something?"

"We don't know for sure…" Antony started, but was interrupted by the sound of a heavy object scraping against the marble floor. Antony and Felicity both jumped. They hadn't been aware of anyone else entering the chapel.

Felicity stifled a cry. It was that smarmy young man who kept eyeing her at the museum and tried to steal one of their charters. Apparently they hadn't charged him or anything. He was grasping a large gold object. Was he actually trying to steal a sculpture now? In the broad daylight? The door at the back of the nave did lead directly outside, but to think he could carry that through the streets of London—he must be mad. Or did he think there might be something hidden under it? A stolen icon? Could he be doing the same thing they were? "Hey! What do you think you're doing?" She strode toward him, making full effect of the fact that she was several inches taller than he was.

Apparently he hadn't seen them on the other side of the altar, because he started so violently and turned so pale under his stubble of a beard Felicity thought he might be going to faint.

Instead he uttered a strangled cry, and fled down the nave and out the door.

"What on earth was that all about?" Felicity turned back to Antony, who was examining the object the intruder had managed to move only a few feet. "What is that thing?"

"A model of the chair of St Peter."

"A model of what?"

"St Peter's Chair in the Vatican. A lot of people believe the saint actually sat on it, but later scholarship has proved it isn't that old. Only ninth century or so."

"It doesn't look like a chair."

"Well, all this around it is a sculpture by Bernini, enclosing the actual chair which is really just a wooden bench with a triangular back on it." He pointed to the wooden bit in the center of all the gold, then consulted his information pamphlet. "Interesting. It says that there was originally a statue of the saint on the chair. But it was stolen a few years ago."

"Stolen? Do we have a theme here? I don't get it. Are the knights stealing, or are they being stolen from? And why? It's interesting stuff. And some of it must be amazingly valuable. But where could anyone sell it?"

"Private collectors, I suppose. There's always a market for rarities, if one knows the right channels, I expect."

"So you think it's just a monetary thing?"

"I don't know what to think. I need to know more about these knights and their order."

"Oh, that's comforting." Felicity let her breath out in a sigh of relief. "Do you mean you find all this confusing, too? I thought I was the only one who couldn't make sense out of all these orders and grand masters—all the names sound just alike and seem interchangeable. What a muddle."

"Yes, I think we need to know more about the organizational structure, maybe a bit more Internet research tonight."

"I suppose so, but this is really impossible. We must be barking up the wrong tree. I know thriller novels are full of conspiracy theories about the Masons and Templars and Hospitallers—all that stuff—but these people are so solidly respectable. Oh, there's all the dressing up—like the Shriners at home who wear goofy hats and ride miniature cars in parades, but what they really do is run one of the world's best children's hospitals. And look at this hospital. It's amazing. Surely nobody takes the dressing up stuff seriously? Seriously enough to steal and murder?"

Antony held up his hand.

"Oh, I know. We're not looking for a murderer, still, I'm only saying…"

"I know what you're saying." He paused. "Well, I think I do. Royal charters, cutting edge medical services, the Queen as head of St John Ambulance. Still, something is going on, and I think we need to understand the organizations behind the symbols."

"Yes, and I'd like to know more about the Peter the Great business. The Russian connection seems to link most directly to our icon."

"Right, but now we need to get on to meet your mother."

Felicity groaned. "Mother and *Cyril*. If he kisses my hand I won't be responsible for my actions!"

But when they entered the tiny bakery and tea shop off a leafy road next to the Holland Park underground station, they found Cynthia and Cyril far too engrossed over the pages of a brilliantly colored book to be distracted by anything frivolous such as hand-kissing. When Felicity and Antony approached the table, Sir Cyril stood until Felicity was seated. Her mother leaned over and pecked her on the cheek. "Darling, how lovely to see you. We've had the most marvelous day! Oh, do have one of these raspberry tarts. They're divine. Isn't this just the most charming place—built in 1889 and still has the original décor!"

"Hello, Mother," Felicity inserted when Cynthia paused for breath.

Cyril asked the waiter for a fresh pot of tea and tray of pastries for the newcomers, and Cynthia continued. "Oh, my goodness, Sir Robert was charming, and his gallery is sooo exclusive, and he has written the most gorgeous books about icons—he knows simply *everything*—and he was so very interested when I told him about the little mystery we're involved in. Especially about the cross symbol business on the one at Rempstone. He was so kind as to promise to look into it for us. Wouldn't it be wonderful if he could solve our mystery for us? Oh, and he gave me these incredible catalogs from past exhibits his gallery has done. Just *gave* them to me." She held up a shiny red bag containing several glossy volumes. "I mean, look," she pulled the largest from the bag and flipped open several pages of slick, full-color pictures of icons. "These are framing quality." She turned a few pages more thoughtfully. "I really think that's what I'll do. Have them framed. The only trouble is, I can't imagine how I'll ever decide which ones I want to put up. They're all gorgeous."

"Mother, do I hear you right? Are you saying you want to decorate your walls with religious art?"

"Well, why not? Have you ever seen anything more beautiful?" She held out another catalog for Antony to peruse. "Oh, by the way, guess who we saw leaving the gallery just as we arrived? That nun from St Julian's."

"Sister Johanna?'

"Yes, that's the one. I meant to ask Sir Robert if she had been making enquiries about their missing icon, but then I forgot."

"Mother, please don't…" Felicity wanted to say interfere, but that sounded ungracious, so she bit her tongue.

The conversation continued, with Cynthia actually giving Antony a chance to discuss the meaning of some of the icons depicted in the books on the table, but Felicity was more amazed at her own reaction to the glowing images on the pages before her than she was to her mother's enthusiasm. Felicity realized that she was beginning to develop a real appreciation for icons; icons as art and as sacred objects. The prayer that had surrounded them for ages, their beauty, the power and holiness they portrayed couldn't help but call forth awe and devotion in the viewer.

She turned back to the introductory notes in the catalog she had flipped through and found words expressing what she had been groping toward. "In icons we find a profound sense of being in touch with spiritual practice through the centuries and from a culture so different from our own." Yes, that was it. Intimations of another life—the life of eternity. Icons spoke at a deep, subconscious level. Even to her mother, it seemed.

"Sir Robert said they represent realities our scientific age has largely lost, and yet we continue to feel the longing for authentic spirituality and order." Cynthia smiled at Cyril, obviously proud of herself for remembering the quote.

He returned her smile. "That's it exactly. The echo of these values remain in such works of art. That is precisely why I went into art history myself. It's all about values. Oh, not the crass, monetary level by which our world values everything. The true worth is the incomparable value of birthright, tradition—spiritual heritage."

Felicity was amazed at Cyril's speech. She hadn't thought of him as a religious person. But that must be what was he was alluding to. Maybe she should give him a chance.

But Cynthia was taking the conversation another direction. "Yes, Cyril, it's like you were saying to me last night, isn't it? About families being the building blocks of a sound society."

Cyril smiled. "You must forgive me for climbing up on my hobby horse at every opportunity, my dear. And these youngsters," he looked at Antony and Felicity, "will most certainly say I'm hopelessly antiquated. I believe 'positively medieval' is the term my nieces and nephews are most apt to apply to me. But it will be a sad day when the last of our great traditions falls under the ax of modernism."

Felicity felt the conversation had somehow veered sharply

from the spiritual value of icons. She was still thinking about Cyril and his ideas a short time later as she and Antony walked to the underground station. She could only hope Cyril wasn't the Casanova she had taken him for, because just as they were taking their leave Cynthia had pulled her aside. "Darling, guess what! Cyril has invited me to his country house for a few days. We're driving over this evening—in the Royce."

Felicity had blinked. "*Royce*, Mother?"

"Oh, yes. That's what he calls it. I think Rolls would be too plebeian or something. Anyway, it's the most beautiful car I've ever seen in my life. I didn't know they even made them any more. It's almost entirely hand-crafted. I mean, his *car* is a work of art. I can't even begin to imagine what his house will be like."

Cynthia had paused at Felicity's frown. "Mother..."

"Oh, darling, I know you don't approve. It's very noble of you to be loyal to your father. And, to give him his due, Andrew was a very steady husband and father. Solid and dependable. Well, until that doxy got her hands on him... But never mind. What I'm saying is, please be happy for me. I've worked so hard all my life. I just want to have a little fun."

Felicity was still shaking her head. *And whose decision was it to work eighty hours a week and leave the house and children to your husband? We could have survived on Daddy's salary. We wouldn't have starved. Maybe he just wants to have a little fun now, too.* But she hadn't said any of that to her mother. Who was she to tell her mother how to run her life?

"Oh, bother." Antony's exclamation cut into her reverie. "I left it on the table."

"What?"

"One of those catalogs from the Tennant Gallery. Your mother very kindly gave me one. I was very happy to have it, but I left it behind." He looked at his watch and shook his head. "You go on. No sense in us both missing evening prayers. I'll catch you up as soon as I can, but don't wait for me."

He was already gone before Felicity realized she was alone.

Chapter 24

Saturday, Fifth in Lent, Late Afternoon

Antony had taken no more than a few strides back toward the tea shop when he had second thoughts. Why had he sent Felicity on to battle the crowds alone with rush hour approaching? He would much rather make the journey with her. He started to turn back when his attention was taken by a distinguished, silver-haired figure entering the pastry shop. Surely that was the man whose picture he had seen inside the cover of the icon book. He hurried forward.

The tall, slim man was standing before the enticing case of pastries. "The usual, Sir Robert?" the young man behind the counter asked.

"Yes, the apricot almond tarts, but make it half a dozen. I'm expecting a guest."

While the server was boxing the pastries, Antony plucked up his courage. "Excuse me, but aren't you Sir Robert Tennant?"

Sir Robert turned with a smile and acknowledged his identity.

"It's such an irony to see you here as I just returned to retrieve a book of yours I left behind. You kindly gave a selection of your catalogs to my friends and they loaned me one."

He retrieved the volume from the table where it still lay.

"Ah, Sir Cyril and the American lady?" Sir Robert interrupted himself to receive his box of pastries and pay for them. "Interesting questions they were asking about icons marked with Maltese crosses. The theory that they once belong to the Knights Hospitaller is intriguing, of course, but I can't say I've ever come across such a marking."

Antony's natural reticence gave him pause. But when would he ever have a better opportunity to ask a world famous authority? "Sir Robert, may I speak in confidence? Sir Cyril may have mentioned it—the icon I'm trying to locate is Our Lady of the Transfiguration. She has gone missing from the Community of the Transfiguration and the superior asked me to make enquiries. I don't know whether you know, but the Patriarch of Moscow is coming to the Community next week, so you'll appreciate—"

The troubled look on Sir Robert's face told Antony that, indeed, he did understand. Sir Robert grasped Antony's arm and led him from the shop. "Of course I know. I have had the honor of advising Patriarch Kirill on the collection he is assembling for their Easter Festival. The American lady—Mrs Howard, was it?—did enquire about stolen icons, but I didn't quite follow her drift. Cyril mentioned the one that disappeared from Julian's shrine. I'm afraid the most help I could be was to give him an article I have just written about the travels of icons into England."

They were now standing under the dark blue awning covering the front of the Tennant Gallery. "Perhaps you'd be interested as well?" Sir Robert rang the bell at the door. "It won't go off to my publisher until next week, but I can print you a copy of the draft. You undoubtedly know that the legends surrounding ancient icons are of their traveling on their own, as if of their own will. Lovely stories, but I do like to track down a less mystical provenance when possible." His eyes crinkled at the corners when he smiled.

A smartly dressed young woman with blunt-cut, shoulder-length dark hair opened the door to them. "Sir Robert! Did you forget something?"

"Just bumped into a colleague, Mandy." He indicated Antony. "Glad you haven't left yet. Such a fuss having to cope with the alarm system once it's on. Would you be so kind as to print out a copy of my article for *Art Today* for us?"

"Of course, it won't take a minute." Mandy disappeared through a door at the back of the showroom.

"Do have a look around." Sir Robert swept the well-lighted room with his arm. Antony was immediately mesmerized by the array. "We're just finishing up an exhibition of Byzantine Greek and Cretan Icons."

Antony was drawn to a small panel of shimmering gold leaf behind a knight astride a bright red horse, his lance drawn. "St George?"

"St Demetrios, actually. More obscure than St George, but often paired with him in art. We believe he was martyred in the third century and transformed by popular imagination into a great warrior."

Antony moved next to stand before an image of the Theotokos, the Mother of God in rich, deep purple robes on gold, the Child on her lap holding an orb. "Mediterranean. Perhaps the Ionian Islands," his guide informed him. "And this one of the enthroned Mother of God with archangels and the twelve apostles is dated around 1600, probably from northern Greece. The theme of the Virgin and Child enthroned, accompanied by angels, is of great antiquity. Examples are known from the sixth century.

"Unfortunately, only eight icons of the Virgin survived the mass destruction of the iconoclasts."

Antony nodded his head sadly over the barbarity that followed the edict of Emperor Leo III, outlawing the use of icons in the eighth century. But before he could find words to express his outrage over such wanton destruction, Mandy returned with several printed sheets for him. "Thank you. I'm sorry to have been a bother."

"No trouble at all," Sir Robert and his assistant replied together.

Antony repeated his thanks and hurried from the shop.

Perhaps he could still catch Felicity before she got on a train. He all but ran down the street, and didn't slacken his pace until he reached the escalator. He was halfway down when he saw the crowd gathered around the prostrate figure at the bottom of the steep stairway.

"Felicity!" he cried, and elbowed his way past the man in front of him.

Chapter 25

Passion Sunday

People shouted. Hands reached out to help her. She looked up to see a dark, hooded figure wearing a Maltese cross on a chain around his neck slink backward into the crowd. "Stop him!" she tried to shriek, but only emitted a strangled sound. With that, Felicity came awake enough to be aware of searing pain in her head and ankle. Then she realized she had been dreaming.

The hooded figure was a fantasy, but the pain was real. She opened her eyes, then closed them against the piercing throbs. *Give in to the blackness*, she told herself.

Hours later she came fully awake enough to attempt sorting through the fog. She could remember snatches: She had joined the stream rushing toward the escalator inside the underground station, her thoughts going over and over their day's research. She had stepped onto the escalator in a state of abstraction. There had been people all around her, but it wasn't clogged solid as it would be at peak time.

She groped through her mental darkness, trying to recall. Had she thought of something important? She remembered wondering if it was possible that an organization headed by the royal family could be engaged in nefarious activities. She closed her eyes and saw again the posters lining the stairwell advertising the new musical of *Jack the Ripper*, and thinking about hearing theories that Jack the Ripper had been the Duke of Clarence, in line to be heir to the throne.

Her next sensation was one of flying through the air. She could still hear the cries. Were they hers or those of people around her? Next she felt as if she had fallen on spikes as the sharp metal edges of the electric stairs caught her. Then all went black.

What was dream and what was reality? The pain in her ankle, resting elevated on a pillow at the foot of her bed, packed in ice bags, was real enough. The plunge down the moving escalator all too vividly real. The mysterious, hooded figure? A figment of fevered sleep, surely. One thing seemed clear: If it hadn't been so crowded... If she had fallen all the way to the bottom... Could she remember anything? Had she felt a sharp tug at the front of her ankles—someone pulling her feet out from under her? Or had she been gazing too intently at the theater bills and thinking preposterous thoughts? Was it attempted murder or inattention?

Had she seen anyone? The trouble was, she had seen far too many people. All helpful, concerned faces, close to hers, then backing away. But mostly she saw hands: careful hands holding back the hurrying crowd, hands straightening her clothes, hands feeling her twisted ankle, easing off her shoe...

She must have hit her head, too. Surely she should be able to remember a doctor. She felt carefully, then wished she hadn't when her fingers found the spot just beyond her left eyebrow. Had she been taken in an ambulance? A St John Ambulance? No, Antony said those were just for big events. At least she hadn't wound up in a hospital. She must be all right since she was back in her room in the convent. She was just wondering where everyone was when a soft tap sounded at her door.

"Come in." Sister Gabriella—no, no, just plain Gabriella—looked like a ministering angel with her long blonde hair framing her soft face.

"You're awake, then? Mother said not to waken you, but to bring up some tea and toast just in case you were feeling hungry."

"That's lovely. Can you help me sit up?"

Gabriella set the tray on the table under the window, and expertly plumped pillows behind Felicity's back and rearranged the footrest and ice bags. "How are you feeling? The doctor said you were awfully lucky just to have sprained your ankle. He was most concerned about the bump on your head. Do you have a dreadful headache?"

"Well, it throbs a bit now that I'm sitting up, but a nice cup of tea will help I'm sure."

Gabriella arranged the tray on a chair where Felicity could reach it from her bed. "So you've been in this country long enough to learn that a cup of tea can fix anything?"

Felicity started to nod, but the pain stopped her. "Pretty much, yes. What time is it? Where's Father Antony? What day is it?"

Gabriella poured out the tea and handed Felicity the cup. "It's Sunday. Passion Sunday." She glanced at her watch. "Almost two o'clock. Father Antony should be back soon. He went into town, to All Saints Margaret Street." She gave Felicity a quizzical smile. "He was terribly worried about you. He wouldn't have left, but the doctor said you just needed to sleep." Another pause. "He's awfully nice, isn't he?"

Felicity attempted a smile, but the effort made her head throb again. "Mmm, yes, he is." She handed her teacup back to Gabriella. She knew the girl wanted to hear more, and she was sorry to disappoint her. But she didn't really know what else to say. Protesting they were only friends seemed like too much effort, and she wasn't sure whether it was true or not. "I think I'd better lie down again."

It was nearly dark the next time she woke. Was it night or had someone drawn the curtain? She turned her head carefully, expecting a sharp stab for her effort and was pleasantly surprised to be greeted with only a dull thud. She blinked, trying to make out the identity of the dark form sitting in the chair at the foot of her bed. "Hello?"

"Felicity! I hope I didn't waken you."

This time it didn't hurt to smile. "Antony! What time is it?"

"Just gone five. How do you feel?"

"Better." Actually, she needed to go to the bathroom, but she wasn't about to tell him that. "Er, do you think you could get me something to eat? Gabriella brought me some toast hours ago, but I didn't feel like eating it. Now I do. Oh, and turn on a light."

He hurried away, looking delighted that she felt like eating. Now the test was to see if she could stand up. The ice packs fell away from her ankle when she moved it. As she gingerly moved out of the narrow bed she was relieved to see a pair of crutches leaning against the wall. Someone had been thinking ahead of her needs. She was none too steady and totally uncoordinated, but she managed an upright position and hobbled across the hall. Opening doors was the greatest challenge, but she made it and was comfortably back in her bed by the time Antony returned with a tray of cold roast chicken, fruit, cheese, and bread.

"Oh, a feast! It must at least twenty-four hours since I ate."

Antony placed the tray on her lap, then moved his chair closer beside the bed. He allowed her a few bites before he began quizzing her. "Do you remember anything? Did you see anybody?"

"I think I might have been tripped, but I can't be sure. I was looking at the theater bills and thinking about the Knights of Malta and Jack the Ripper. There were lots of people all around, everyone hurrying. It would have been easy enough for someone rushing for a train to bump me accidentally."

"Or on purpose," Antony added grimly.

"Yes, I suppose so. But I can't imagine why. It isn't as if I'd learned anything that would threaten anyone."

"No. But they wouldn't necessarily know that, would they?"

The room fell silent as Felicity chewed a bite of tender roast chicken. She hadn't realized how hungry she was. Then she thought to ask, "Oh, did you get the book you went back for?"

"Yes, but the best part is, I met Sir Robert. He had stopped in to buy some pastries."

Felicity thought for a moment. "Oh, the icon man!"

"That's right. We got to talking and he took me back to his gallery—it's an amazing place—and gave me a copy of an article he has just written on how some icons traveled to England."

"How nice of him! Did you learn anything?"

Antony gave a rueful smile. "Well, actually I haven't read it yet. Afraid I put it in my pocket and forgot about it. Finding you unconscious did rather take my attention."

"Sorry to have been such a nuisance."

"Felicity…" he grasped her hand with a warm pressure for the space of several heartbeats. Then pushed to his feet. "I'll just go get it now."

He was back in a moment, perusing the manuscript. "Hmm, yes. Sir Robert told me he mentioned Our Lady of the Transfiguration. He gives credence to the belief that Peter the Great could have brought her to England on his Great Embassy. Shall I read that bit to you?"

Felicity nodded, her mouth too full to speak.

"'The Anglican Church interested Peter greatly. He took numerous walks around London and visited several of Wren's parish churches. He visited Thomas Tenison, the Archbishop of Canterbury, at Lambeth Palace. Their discussions included the formulation of the Trinity, the role of the saints and icons.'"

"And Peter gave the archbishop the icon of Our Lady! That's absolutely cool."

"Well, it's a likely possibility."

"But how did it get from Lambeth Palace to the Community of the Transfiguration?"

"Tennant doesn't go into anything like that. His interest is just how icons came to be in England. But Archbishop Thomas Tenison was known for his strenuous opposition to the Church of Rome. Tenison would have been nine years old when Archbishop Laud was beheaded on Tower Hill, so he would have been well acquainted with the unhealthy aspects of appearing too high church."

"So he might have quietly gotten rid of any icons lurking popishly in Lambeth Palace?"

"All we know is that it resurfaced in the nineteenth century when Anglican monasteries and convents were being refounded under the Oxford Movement."

"Right. So does he say anything about Julian's shrine?"

Antony read quietly for several minutes. "Oh, this is interesting. I asked him if he knew of any icons marked with Maltese crosses and he said he didn't. But he goes into a detailed discussion here of pilgrimage routes and of the possibility of pilgrims to places such as the Holy Land and St John Compostela bringing back icons which then might have been presented to popular pilgrimage sites in England."

"Like Julian's anchorage?"

"Yes, possibly, although the shrine of Thomas a Becket at Canterbury and The Holy House of Our Lady of Walsingham were the most popular sites in medieval England."

"Wait a minute—wasn't one of the primary jobs of the Knights Hospitaller to protect pilgrims? Didn't they sort of run inns for pilgrims in the Holy Land? So the idea of a pilgrim bringing back an icon that had belonged to the knights isn't all that far-fetched, is it?"

"Hmmm, interesting." Antony wasn't committing himself.

Something was flitting at the back of Felicity's mind. Hadn't she heard something like that before? Something about a pilgrim to Julian's shrine…She couldn't think and her headache was threatening to return. "I think I'll doze a little, if you don't mind."

Antony turned out the light and closed her door quietly.

It could have been an hour later, or the middle of the night—all she knew was that it was dark when she awoke with a jolt. She knew what she was trying to remember. "Antony!"

She didn't mean to sound so alarmed, but it worked. The cry was hardly out of her mouth before he burst through her door.

"Felicity! Are you all right?"

"Yes. Sorry, I didn't mean to worry you, but I just remembered. Before I stepped on the escalator, on the side coming up—that guy who tried to steal the document at the museum—"

"You saw him?"

"I'm not absolutely certain, but I think maybe. His face came back to me."

"Hmm, I wonder. I hadn't thought of it before, but that morning outside St John Timberhill...I thought it was just a rough sleeper, but it could have been...about the same size, wearing a gray hooded sweater..."

"Pretty circumstantial, you can't walk a block without seeing a smallish young guy in a hoodie, usually gray. Still, as you say, things keep pointing back to Norwich, don't they? And mother said she saw Sister Johanna at the icon gallery. Do you think she was asking about their lost icon? Did Sir Robert say anything?"

"No, but I think I should make another run up to Norwich."

"Why don't you just ring her?"

"I want to see her face when I ask her. You stay here and rest."

Felicity bolted up so fast her head swam, but she held her upright position. "While I what? Don't be ridiculous. I most certainly won't! I'll have you know I already made it to the loo and back under my own steam. I can certainly make it to the train station tomorrow. That is, if you'll be so good as to carry my bag."

"Felicity…!"

Chapter 26

Monday in Passiontide

W ell, he had put up all his best arguments. But in the end, he had to capitulate. As he had known all along he would. And, if he were entirely honest with himself, Antony had to admit he was rather glad. If Felicity continued her pigheaded notion to enter a convent, this might be their last chance to travel together. And, he had to admit that she had done exceedingly well maneuvering herself on crutches, although she did accept the luxury of taking a taxi to the station rather than the bus. And Dr Jagphur did give his consent, as long as she agreed to limit the weight she put on the foot and kept it elevated as much as possible and...

Antony sighed. No matter how many arguments he marshaled in favor of Felicity accompanying him to Norwich, and how many times he told himself he wouldn't let her out of his sight and then he would take her straight back to the safety of the Community of the Transfiguration, he couldn't shake the cloud of apprehension bearing down on him. They had been nowhere that didn't seem safe: Convents, churches, museums, a hospital...And yet Neville had been murdered and Felicity injured. At least she seemed to be resting now, her left foot propped on the seat in front of her, her head leaning against the window, her eyes closed.

To take his mind off his anxieties, Antony picked up the newspaper a previous passenger had left on the seat across the aisle. The headline, in lurid tabloid style, shocked him so much he grabbed Felicity's arm, startling her awake. "Felicity, look! Sir Robert Tennant. Murdered!"

"What?" She leaned over and pulled the newspaper closer to her. "'Sir Robert Tennant, world famous art historian and collector and owner of the prestigious Tennant Gallery, was found shot in his gallery in Holland Park Sunday evening by a cleaner…'" She broke off reading and looked at him wide-eyed. "How terrible! And you were just there. Mother said he was so charming…" Her voice trembled. "I can't believe it."

Antony took the paper from her and scanned the rest of the article. "His assistant said several valuable icons are missing. The police suspect that Sir Robert interrupted a robbery when he returned to the gallery unexpectedly Sunday morning."

"Antony, you don't think he could have been in league with the monastery robberies? No one would be in a better position to profit from them, would they?"

"I don't have any idea, but I'm inclined to think there must be more to this than a simple robbery. The report here doesn't mention a break-in, and the gallery was alarmed. Besides, Sir Robert was expecting someone. He mentioned it when he bought pastries."

"So you think he was killed by someone he knew? Maybe he found out the answer to the missing icons and that's why he was killed? He must have known something."

Antony shook his head. It certainly seemed that the murders and the disappearance of the icons had to be connected in some way. So connected that as soon as they finished talking to Sister Johanna he was determined to get Felicity back to the safety of Kirkthorpe—even if he had to sprain her other ankle to do it.

The only thing he couldn't do was to give up the search himself. If Our Lady of the Transfiguration wasn't recovered before the Patriarch of Moscow and all Russia made his historic visit to the Community of the Transfiguration to venerate Our Lady and borrow her as planned, it was impossible to calculate the harm that would be done to his ecumenical efforts. Bringing some increased cooperation between those of differing churchmanship in the Church of England was difficult enough. Continuing the carefully orchestrated overtures to Roman Catholics and Methodists had been the peak of his ambition as Chair of the Ecumenical Council. This opportunity to reach out to the leader of the Russian Orthodox Church who had made news with his own involvement in the ecumenical movement was far beyond anything Antony had dreamed of. Failure would be all that much more crushing—for him personally, of course, but more importantly, for the future of Christ's church on earth.

Antony was still brooding along those lines when they arrived back at the Julian Centre and were greeted by Angela, today clad in a sunflower yellow dress with copper jewelry that exactly matched her hair.

"Sister Johanna? No, I'm afraid the retreat house is closed for retreats until after Easter week. I'm not sure where she went. Perhaps to the mother house in Suffolk?"

"Do you know if she had an appointment in London with Sir Robert Tennant?"

"Robert Tennant—the icon expert? No, I really don't know anything about where she was going. The study center and the retreat house are really quite separate, for being all of twenty paces away from each other. I suppose she could have gone to London, I really don't know."

"So you hadn't heard about Sir Robert's murder?"

Angela's round green eyes got even wider. "No, how awful! We have several of his books here."

"You hadn't enquired of him about your missing icon?"

"No, I didn't. But I suppose Sister Johanna could have. She needn't have told me about her actions."

Antony described the suspicious young man they had encountered at Clerkenwell: Early twenties, unshaven, wire-rimmed glasses, hooded sweater. "Have you seen anyone like that hanging around here?"

Angela laughed. "A hoodie? Could describe 90 per cent of the dropouts and layabouts in Great Britain."

Felicity was just gathering her crutches when the door burst open. "Darling! Oh, my poor baby, what an awful thing! How are you? Are you in terrible pain?"

Felicity resumed her seat with a sigh. "Mother. What on earth are you doing here?"

"Well, I had to come see how you were. See if I could help you."

"But how did you know?"

"Why, Antony phoned me this morning. Didn't you know?"

Felicity whirled around to glare at Antony. He managed to look abashed. "I knew she would want to know." He really had meant to tell Felicity, but he knew she would object. Then the matter of the new murder put everything else out of his mind.

"Mother, you shouldn't have bothered. Really."

"Oh, it was no bother, darling. Cyril's home is near here anyway, you know." As if on cue, Sir Cyril trailed in after Cynthia. "Aren't the Broads the most fascinating place? And anyway, Cyril wanted to talk to the police—see if there were any new developments about Neville. His responsibility as head of the family." She paused and shook her head. "Such an awful thing." Cynthia gave Cyril's arm a comforting squeeze.

He nodded. "Terrible. I can only hope they find whoever did it soon. Hard on the family. Can't have a funeral. We're just left hanging."

"Are the police making any headway?" Felicity asked Cyril.

"I asked the inspector this morning. Got something about 'following several lines of enquiry.' Which I suppose means they know less than nothing."

"What about the other body?"

Cyril shrugged. "Archeological, not forensic, apparently.

Sent to the university, I believe. Pity to disturb him after all that time."

Felicity spoke into the quiet as the conversation momentarily lapsed. "Did you know Sir Robert Tennant was murdered?"

"What? Impossible. We were just with him Saturday."

Antony produced the newspaper. Cyril read, looking thunderstruck. "I can't take it in. What a terrible loss to the art community. No one else had a fraction of his knowledge in his field. I don't suppose there's any mistake? Could it have been someone else?"

"The news report seemed pretty certain."

"Oh, that charming man. I can't believe it!" Cynthia sank onto a chair next to Felicity. "And he was going to do some research for me. Seemed quite excited about working on our little puzzle. You don't suppose he learned anything, do you? Anything dangerous?"

"The police seem to think it was a straightforward robbery," Antony said, happy to be able to reassure Cynthia, no matter how much he might doubt the theory himself.

"Tell you what," Cyril looked around the room as if addressing a committee. "Seems we're all at a bit of a loose end here. Why don't you two come along with us to King's Lynn?" He turned to Cynthia. "A chance for you to give your daughter a bit of cosseting, my dear."

Antony wondered whether the frown on Felicity's face was for the idea of being coddled by her mother or for Cyril's endearment. "King's Lynn?" she asked.

"Yes. I always like to touch base with the family when I'm close, especially at such a difficult time." He turned to Antony. "My nephew Simon mentioned you were enquiring about their muniments room."

"Well, nothing that formal, actually…"

"Said he wasn't able to help you. Rather a bad time when you rang, of course."

"Yes, it was insensitive of me, really. I regretted it."

"No harm done, but the thing is, they've been having some remodeling done—vicarage is a beautiful Georgian specimen, but going to rack and ruin inside. Fresh paint outside, but rising damp and crumble inside. I don't know what their PCC was thinking of. Criminal, really, historic building like that. Anyway, they finally got around to making some repairs and something quite interesting has turned up in the library. That is, it sounds interesting, anyway. Thought you'd like to have a look."

"What is it?" Antony kept his voice level, but he couldn't prevent a sharp intake of breath. Could this be what Neville found? If only he could recall his words more clearly.

"Well, my brother, Rupert, isn't the scholar in the family." Cyril paused, seemingly to allow his listeners to realize that he was the recognized authority. "But Rupert believes he's found the Book of Margery Kempe."

Antony frowned in confusion. "But I thought that came to light in 1934? Wasn't it the property of an old Catholic family, been in their library since the Reformation?"

"Yes, yes, that's right. Had been in the possession of the Carthusians of Mount Grace Priory, the Bultler-Bowdon family preserved it after the dissolution. But that's the *second* book. Father Antony. Surely you know there was an earlier book?"

Antony nodded. Yes, he did know. Margery Kempe's first attempt at authorship had been to dictate to someone many scholars believed to have been her son. "The first book was almost entirely illegible, but what could be deciphered of it was rewritten by her confessor several years later."

"Yes, right. And then she added the last ten chapters. But that's not to say what happened to that first book. Perhaps it wasn't as illegible as it has always been assumed." Cyril regarded him closely, then gave a crow of laughter. "Ah, ha! Piqued your interest, haven't I? Let's be off, then. Straight across the A47. We'll be there in an hour. Sooner, with luck."

Antony wanted to protest. He didn't like feeling railroaded. And he was determined to get Felicity securely out of harm's way. But then, she would be with her mother and with him. What could be safer?

Chapter 27

Monday in Passiontide, Afternoon

T he flat, green Norfolk countryside whizzed past
her window as Felicity sank into the luxurious pale
wheat leather seats of Sir Cyril's elegant car. After the
clackety-clack of their earlier train journey, the almost complete
silence cocooning them seemed nothing short of miraculous.
Cyril inserted a CD of Haydn's "London" symphony into the
stereo system, leaving her and Antony free to talk or not in the
back seat. She propped her left foot on the deeply padded arm
rest between the front seats and leaned back in comfort.

"So, remind me. Margery Kempe. She had something to
do with Julian of Norwich, but I'm afraid I've forgotten."

Antony gave that little half smile and jerky nod that told
her she could settle in for one of his you-are-there lectures.
She smiled to herself, recalling how she used to resent such
discourses, even when given in response to her questions.

"Margery was one of the most remarkable—not to say
strangest—women of her day; of any day, for that matter. She
was an energetic daughter of the merchant class, her father a
civic leader and Member of Parliament. Her husband, the long-
suffering John Kempe, was also a merchant, but never a successful
one and always debt-ridden.

"After the birth of their first child, Margery recounted that
she went out of her mind and was amazingly disturbed and
tormented with visions of devils 'all alight with burning flames
of fire, as if they would have swallowed her in, sometimes pawing
at her, sometimes pulling at her.' Her torture, she tells us in her
precise way, 'lasted for half a year, eight weeks and odd days.'

"And then she recounts that 'our merciful Lord Christ Jesus—ever to be trusted, never forsaking his servant in time of need' appeared to her 'in the likeness of a man; the most seemly, most beauteous, and most amiable that ever might be seen with man's eye, clad in a mantle of purple silk,' sitting upon her bedside, looking upon her with so blessed a countenance that she was strengthened in all her spirits, and he said to her: 'Daughter, why have you forsaken me, and I never forsook you?'" From that moment Margery Kempe was healed."

Felicity shifted her leg, flexed her knee a few times, and smiled. Antony was taking his time about this. Of course, there was no need for hurry and she was truly interested, but she hoped he would be getting to icons sooner or later. "So she entered a convent then?" she ventured.

"Not a bit of it. She continued her secular lifestyle in her forceful way. Took great delight in following the whims of showy fashion with gold piping on her hoods, her tippets and cloaks fashionably slashed and underlaid with brilliant colors between the slashes to attract popular attention"

"Bit of an extrovert, was she?"

"Oh, yes. And an entrepreneur. She started business ventures all on her own. 'Out of pure covetousness, and in order to maintain her price,' she says, 'she took up brewing and was one of the greatest brewers in the town.' The business failed, however, when her ale, which 'had as fine a head of froth on it as anyone might see, suddenly would go flat.'

"Next she had a horse-mill. She got herself two good horses and a man to grind people's corn, and thus she was confident of making her living. This venture didn't last long, however, for the horses, which had drawn well previously, suddenly refused to turn the mill. Their driver tried everything he could to make them pull together, but his most severe efforts with whips resulted only in the horses drawing backward. A second pair of horses behaved in a similar way."

"So Margery decided God didn't want her to be a businesswoman?"

Antony smiled. "That's about the size of it. She asked God for mercy and forsook her desire for worldly dignity. And God granted her request. She says that one night, as she 'lay in bed with her husband, she heard a melodious sound so sweet and delectable that she thought she had been in paradise.' And immediately she jumped out of bed and said, 'Alas that ever I sinned! It is fully merry in heaven.'

"It so far surpassed all the melody that might be heard in this world that whenever she heard laughter or music on earth, it caused her 'to shed very plentiful and abundant tears of high devotion, with great sobbings and sighings for the bliss of heaven.'"

"Erm, I thought you said she was healed of her mental illness."

"Oh, I didn't say she wasn't strange, but in the medieval world, spiritual ecstasy wasn't mistaken for mental illness."

"OK." Felicity was willing to give Margery the benefit of the doubt, although she wasn't convinced.

"'It is fully merry in heaven!' became her motto. But her next step toward the holy life was less joyful for her husband, for although they had, of her own describing, enjoyed a delectable marriage bed, after this time she never again desired to have intimate relations with him. Not surprisingly, John Kempe didn't agree."

At this point Cynthia turned in her seat to face the back. "Poor man, he hadn't had any beatific visions, had he?"

"None that are recorded," Cyril entered the conversation. "But who knows? After all, Margery did report that they had a jolly good sex life."

Felicity stole a sideways glance to see if Antony was blushing, but he took the discussion entirely straightforward. It never failed to surprise her how worldly monks and priests could be. "You're quite right, and Margery continued to submit to her husband but with 'much weeping and sorrowing because she could not live in chastity.'"

"What a lot of fun *that* must have been!" Cyril indicated his interest in the story by turning the volume down on the stereo.

Antony smiled and continued. "Finally, after the birth of their fourteenth child—"

"Fourteen? She had fourteen children?" Cynthia gave a shout of laughter. "No wonder she felt a call to celibacy. Who wouldn't?"

"—she began to sort out her call by going to visit various places for spiritual health." Anthony finished his sentence, although Cynthia was still laughing. But Felicity wasn't laughing. Margery Kempe sorted out her call by going on pilgrimage? She sat up a fraction straighter. Was history once again providing a pattern to find answers for today's questions?

Antony continued, "John was finally convinced that this was the will of God and consented to go with her to 'such places as she was inclined.'

"On Friday, Midsummer Eve, 23 June 1413, they were walking home from York, only a few miles north of the very road we are now traveling along." He gestured out the window. "The weather was hot. Margery carried a bottle of beer, John had a cake tucked inside his clothes against his chest."

The Rolls seemed to float down the highway. Felicity closed her eyes and leaned deeper into her cushions. She could picture the story as Antony told it:

They had trod many such roads, sometimes dust-choked, sometimes mud-bogged, but always long, dangerous and weary as Margery sought the fulfillment of her vision. But now, amidst the heat, grit and noise, it was hard to recapture the inexpressible sweetness of the moment that had changed the entire direction of her life.

Difficult, but not impossible, for the experience would ever be with her, singing in her heart as it had at that moment. Even with the turmoil around her now, a small smile lifted the corners of Margery's mouth as the sweet strains of heavenly music came back to her. She started at the reality of the sound, then realized that was no angelic choir, but a young shepherd boy piping a tune to his sheep.

And yet even so real had the heavenly melody been. John turned and held his hand out to her with his gentle smile. Margery's feet moved obediently toward him, but her mind stayed fixed on the night of her transformation. Ah, the sweetness of that night. The sweetness of lying beside her husband in their fine, linen-draped poster bed. For twenty years the pleasures of their marriage bed had not faltered. John Kempe had his faults: a poor businessman, always in debt, less well educated than she, of a lower station. But he had never failed to delight her in bed: never boorish or boring, their mutual satisfaction in one another had held through the births of their many children.

No, it was not due to any failing of John's that Margery now entreated him that she might be allowed to live celibate. It was not that physical pleasures had failed, but that she had glimpsed higher ones.

She put her hand in John's strong, broad fist. "Ah, and do you hear that, husband?"

"What, yon shepherd boy playing his pipe? Aye, 'tis a fine melody."

"Oh, John, it's more than that. It's near-to as fine as I heard that night."

"Oh, aye? And would you tell me that it was the piping of a shepherd boy that has brought all this discomfort upon us, as I might at this moment be at home with my feet under my own board and sleep tonight in my own bed rather than in some flea-ridden tavern, except for some rustic lad playing upon a reed pipe outside our bedroom window?"

"John, John, you know better than that. Did not I tell you the moment I sprang from our bed that I heard a melodious sound so sweet and delectable that I thought I had been in paradise?"

"Aye, you did. And had your face not been as shining as an angel of light I would have declared you were dreaming and drawn you back to bed."

"No, it was no dream. For, poor creature that I am, I saw the shame and pity of my sin and the full merriment of heaven."

"The bliss of heaven's a fine thing for some, but I'm not ready to forsake all my pleasures here yet, wife."

Margery sighed. "I know, John, I know." Her husband had been so patient—even with her tearful entreaties to live chaste—and had made only token protest over the cost of hiring yet another nurse to look after their fourteenth child so she could undertake this life of pilgrimage. Master Kempe was patient, but not always fully acquiescent to his wife's pleas.

"John, let us take our noonday rest in the shade of that spinney up ahead." She pointed to a clump of trees, their leaves rustling green and cool in the hot sun.

Margery leaned against the rough bark of a tree and eased the shoes off her feet. "Ahh." With that, she pulled a large stone bottle of cider from her basket.

John reached inside his shirt and pulled out the cake he carried there. When they had both satisfied their hunger and their thirst, Margery renewed her plea.

John shook his head. "Margery, how can you ask? You are no good wife."

"It is because I am a good wife that I do ask. It is because I love your soul more than I love your body. Because I desire your eternal bliss more than your immediate pleasure that I pray you to grant what I ask. I pray you, allow me to make a vow of chastity."

"No. You ask too much."

"I pray that you will consent if it is the will of the Holy

Ghost. If it be not his will, I pray God that you never consent." Margery left her plea in the hands of a higher court.

They gathered the remains of their meal and trod silently on toward the coast where the next day they would board a boat to take them back home to Bishop's Lynn. Never had Margery known such hot weather or such great sorrow or such fear for her sins. The weight of it all was so heavy that, try as she might, she could not pray.

When they were nearing the little seaport town they passed a wayside cross by the edge of the road. John Kempe pulled aside and sat down under it. "Margery, come to me, my wife."

Margery trembled. What would he do? Prove his marriage rights here by the roadside? Beneath the very emblem of our Savior's sacrifice? "John? What would you?"

"I would talk to you. I've been thinking long all this dusty way." She drew out the jug. He drank deeply. "I have a proposal for you. Grant me my desire, and I shall grant you your desire."

"What is your desire, husband?"

"I desire you to eat and drink with me on Fridays as you used to do."

Margery was appalled. She pulled away from him and jumped to her feet. "No, sir! I will never agree to break my Friday fast as long as I live."

"Then I will have my rights."

Margery held out her hands. "Wait. I must think. Does it truly mean so much to you that I eat and drink with you?"

"It does. Margery, Margery, you were ever happy company. My best friend as well as my wife. Do ye not remember our merry times at table? If I'm to have no pleasure in my bed, I ask it at my board."

"Give me time to say my prayers, John."

"Aye." He got up, and strolled on some distance away across the sweet green hayfield.

Margery knelt by the cross. "Blessed Jesus, make your will known to my unworthy self, so that I may afterwards follow and fulfill it with all my might."

Of a sudden her tears stopped and the sweet voice of her Lord filled her mind. Your husband shall have what he desires. For, my beloved daughter, this was the reason why I ordered you to fast, so that you should the sooner obtain your desire, and now it is granted to you. I no longer wish you to fast. In the name of Jesus eat and drink as your husband does.

She ran to John across the evening field, her steps light as the young girl she had been when she first ran to him twenty years before. "John, John, it shall be as you desire. Let us sup merrily together."

He opened his arms and embraced her. "Aye, that's my girl. And may your body be as freely available to God as it has been to me."

Felicity jerked back to full awareness of her surroundings as Cyril braked to allow for traffic entering the highway.

"What a lovely story, Antony," Cynthia said. "So then did she enter a convent?"

"On the contrary. She then began her life of pilgrimage in earnest. That very autumn, she left for the Holy Land. The next year she went to Assisi, then Rome, later to Santiago de Compostela. And she didn't ignore English sites of pilgrimage; she went to Canterbury, Walsingham, sought counsel from Julian in Norwich..."

"Oh!" Felicity cried. Somehow it made Margery seem closer to her, more real, knowing she had been to a place Felicity herself had just visited.

"Yes, John Kempe wasn't her only skeptic. She had a lot of trouble convincing the religious establishment that her call was real. She even questioned it herself. She went first to a vicar in Norwich who was renowned for his scholarship, then to a Carmelite monk. Both encouraged her that her call was from God. Only then did she find the courage to approach Dame Julian, the most famous woman in Norwich. By now Julian was nearing seventy. She had spent almost forty years in her cell meditating on the nature of divine truth and on God's love for humanity.

"Margery recorded only a summary of the historic meeting in her book, but as she spent many days in discussion and counsel at Julian's little window we can be sure that the discourse was much fuller. Margery undoubtedly told her whole life story to Julian as she did to any who would listen.

"And Margery told her about the desire for devotion, the contrition for sin, the compassion for others God had put in her soul, and about her weeping, meditations and visions, asking Julian's advice. Remarkably, Julian's answer has been recorded for posterity. 'The Holy Ghost never urges a thing against charity, for he is all charity. Also he moves a soul to all chasteness, for chaste livers are called the temple of the Holy Ghost. And the Holy Ghost makes a soul stable and steadfast in the right faith and the right belief.'

"Apparently Julian saw fit to encourage Margery to follow her call, but saw her visitor's tendency to instability because she continued, 'A double man in soul is always unstable and unsteadfast. He that is forever doubting is like the wave of the sea which is moved and borne about with the wind, and that man is not likely to receive the gifts of God.'

"Julian's final words were so comforting to Margery that they were still fresh in her mind when she dictated her book some twenty-five years later. 'Holy Writ says that the soul of a righteous man is the seat of God, and so I trust, sister, that you are. I pray God grant you perseverance. Set all your trust in God and do not fear the talk of the world, for the more contempt, shame and reproof that you have in this world, the more is your merit in the sight of God. Patience is necessary for you, for in that shall you keep your soul.'"

Cynthia seemed riveted by the story. "Imagine dictating all that into a book." She turned to Cyril. "And your brother has found an original copy of it? From the fifteenth century? It must be fabulously valuable!"

"Certainly to scholars," Cyril replied. "In the well-known version, Margery is unsparingly honest about her experiences, her fits of holy weeping, her shrieking and 'roaring' that caused her to be abandoned by one company of pilgrims and forced to cross the Alps in a blinding snowstorm with only an aged priest for company. So, if this does prove to be the original and it turns out to be legible, who knows what else we might learn about her?"

"Details she might have failed to repeat the second time through?"

"Precisely."

The main road they were on seemed to take them straight to the heart of the city. "Here we are, the Saturday Market Place, it's called. Heart of the historic town." Cyril pointed ahead to the end of the street. "The river Great Ouse, and beyond that, The Wash, so we're essentially at the seashore. And on your right, the Trinity Guildhall."

Felicity swiveled her head to admire the amazing building patterned with checkered gold stone and black flint. "Margery Kempe's father and husband would both have belonged to that guild," Cyril said.

"And it's still here. And in perfect condition."

"Oh, yes, it's still used. This end is an Elizabethan addition. The Town Hall now."

Cyril swung the car around the corner and came to stop in front of a large yellow and white Georgian house across the street from a magnificent church of cathedral proportions. "And here we are—St Margaret's." Antony waved his hand toward the building.

Felicity boggled. Strange, how quickly one's mind could stereotype places one heard about in history. Felicity had expected Margery Kempe's medieval church to be small and dark, located in some forgotten corner of the town. Nothing could have been further from the truth. Sitting elegantly in the center of a broad green lawn surrounded by pansies and primroses, St Margaret's was an imposing church built of the cleanest, most golden sandstone she could imagine. Either it had just been sandblasted or, which seemed more likely, its daily scrubbing by salt air from The Wash had kept it pristine through the ages.

Cyril sprang from the car and hurried around to open Cynthia's door and extend his hand to help her exit. Anthony likewise helped Felicity, holding her crutches for her and offering his arm for her to balance on. "I think I only need one of those things now," she said, returning one crutch to the back seat. "I can put a little weight on my foot."

"Are you certain? We don't want you overdoing it, darling," Cynthia protested.

"No, Mother. I'm fine. Really."

"Would you two like to go on over and have a look at the church straight away?" Cyril addressed Antony and Felicity. "Cynthia and I can just skip ahead and give Rupert a heads-up. He's not the best organized of hosts."

Her head still full of the stories of the strange, mystical woman who had worshiped at this church more than 500 years ago, Felicity made her way up the wide pavement angling toward the mammoth double towers fronting the church. The arched door stood open under the enormous gothic stained glass window between the towers. Piped organ music—Vivaldi's *Gloria*—wafted out to meet them. "The church is open all day, every day" a sign greeted them. "St Margaret's has been welcoming pilgrims for over 900 years." Felicity wasn't sure she qualified as a pilgrim, but she certainly felt welcomed.

Inside, the music floated among the graceful arches and echoed from the rows of brilliant stained glass windows on each side of the nave. The wooden ceiling gave the church the feeling of a medieval merchant's hall. It all seemed so homely, so comfortable, in spite of the bare starkness of the Passiontide draping. Swathes of sackcloth covered what must have been an ornate reredos under the gothic stained glass window, and the rough brown cloth over the altar somehow seemed natural rather than penitential. Even the intricately patterned tiled floor seemed warmer than the usual stone. She mentioned the fact to Antony who continued to hover close to her, as if he expected her to fall at any moment.

"Yes, I noticed the warmth, too. That would have been a help to Margery; she so often prayed lying prostrate on the floor. Of course, the building has undergone numerous restorations, so I doubt that these are the actual tiles Margery would have lain on."

Felicity continued to wander around with a sense of awe. It was so fresh, so modern-seeming. On the noticeboard she saw a poster for AIDS awareness. What could be more appropriate for a building that had seen repeated outbreaks of the Black Death?

Felicity slid into a seat and Antony sat beside her. "It's all due to Margery's prayers that this church is still here."

"Really?"

"Yes, in 1421 a fire broke out in the Guildhall on a crisp, clear midwinter day and seemed likely to engulf the entire town. Rain or snow was their only hope of rescue, but none was in the offing. Margery records that she cried loudly many times that day, praying for grace and mercy but that the sky remained cloudless.

Now people who had once scorned her for her ecstatic crying and yelling came to her and urged her to yell louder to draw God's attention to their plight. Margery knelt in St Margaret's Church although she could see sparks coming in through the lantern. Margery advised the priest to hold the blessed sacrament before the advancing flames. They formed a procession, under clear blue skies, with Margery behind the priest, praying and weeping loudly. "Send down rain or some weather that may, through thy mercy, quench this fire," she prayed repeatedly.

The procession marched around the town and returned full circle to the church. Sparks flew in with them as they entered. Margery continued to pray with all her might. Suddenly two men rushed in, white flakes clinging to their coats. "Margery, Margery, God has wrought great grace for us and sent us a fair snow to quench the fire!" It was no mere flurry, but a blizzard that smothered the fire and saved the town.

Everyone agreed that the miracle was entirely Margery's doing as the clouds, darkness and great swirling flakes had come too suddenly from a pristine sky to be anything but divine intervention. From then on, no one in Bishop's Lynn questioned Margery Kempe's credentials as a holy woman.

Just as the story ended, they were joined by Cyril and Cynthia. "Hello there. All's fine with Rupert. Knew it would be, but he can be a bit slow on the uptake, so I wanted to make certain he was ready for us."

"Oh, I hope we aren't putting him out," Felicity said.

"Not really. You'll just find my brother more than a little disorganized, I fear." The look on Cyril's face left no doubt of what he thought of such helter-skelter behavior. "Just sorry I had to banish you to the church."

"No, no, it's lovely here. Antony was telling me about how Margery saved the church from fire."

Cynthia then wanted to hear the story, so Antony obliged in a shortened form.

"Oh, so then she finally got to join a convent?"

"No, that's one of the most remarkable aspects of Margery's

life. In spite of her intense devotion and unique mystical experiences, she remained in the world. She seemed to draw much of her spirituality from the everyday world around her. She would burst into tears at the sight of baby boys and beg to be allowed to kiss them because they reminded her of the infant Christ Child, for example. She saw the suffering Christ in suffering humanity.

"She lived out her spiritual life in the noise and movement of ordinary life—not enclosed like Dame Julian. She opted to stay in the world rather than enter the religious life."

Felicity shifted on her seat. She hoped that bit of the lecture wasn't pointed at her. Sure, one could live a life of devotion in the everyday world, but there were others who were called out.

Almost as if he sensed her thoughts, Antony carefully avoided her eyes as he continued. "Hers was a very human spirituality—she saw every human situation as a reflection of the life of Christ. It was a beautiful experience for her." He paused and smiled. "But it wasn't always very beautiful for her contemporaries because she would start wailing.

"In her meditations on Christ, the mother–child relationship is the one she most relates to emotionally. The sheer physicality of the experience of motherhood, with its concern for the physical well-being of the child is, for her, a way of entering into a relationship with God."

"And yet she left her brood to go off on pilgrimage." The barb in Cynthia's voice made Felicity think that her mother was finding the lecture a bit pointed as well. Funny, how the thoughts and actions of a weird woman who lived half a millennium ago could still raise hackles.

Antony chuckled. "Oh, yes, poor Margery, burning with desire for Christ to be her spouse, yet he keeps sending her back to her husband. She had to hold together both love of God and love of neighbor without compromising either. She was called to holiness within the constraints of domestic, married life, and lived with the tensions her vocation involved. When her husband was severely injured falling downstairs, she was required to care for him. She says Christ instructed her to: 'look after him for love of me, as if you were in church saying your prayers.'"

"Yes, well, very instructive." Cynthia didn't bother keeping the barb out of her voice, and for once, Felicity sympathized with her. "But Rupert did say he'd put the kettle on for us, and I'm parched."

Felicity was still fuming as they made their way to the vicarage. What was Antony driving at? Was the subtext to his lecture as blatant as it had seemed to at least some of his hearers? She was certain Cynthia had gotten the "go back to your husband" message which, to be fair, Felicity didn't disagree with. But if all that "serving God while living in the world" stuff was aimed at her… Never mind that it was in response to her questions. She'd show him she could think for herself and make her own decisions, thank you very much.

She tossed her head so vigorously her hair made a tidal wave down her back and her limping stride was vehement enough that her crutch made a resounding thump on the pavement. She was sufficiently caught up in exhibiting her forcefulness that she didn't really take in the gray, sweatered form sitting in the churchyard. It wasn't until that night as she was just drifting off to sleep under a somewhat worn and thoroughly lumpy duvet that she recalled the burning eyes fixed on her from the depths of the hood.

Chapter 28

Tuesday in Passiontide

In spite of Cyril's many peremptory proddings, it was noon the next day before their disorganized host got around to producing the volume they had come all this way to see. Although Rupert was not the least bit unwelcoming it was clear that providing the requirements for overnight guests had taxed him to the limit. Towels and sheets had been slow coming last night, and this morning the corn flakes and burnt toast were served on a dining table littered with bits of old crockery and volumes of absent-mindedly abandoned reading materials.

It was easy to see the source of the conflict between Cyril and Rupert. It would be hard to imagine a more oil-and-water pairing of siblings Felicity secretly suspected Rupert had mislaid the potentially valuable book. If he hadn't, she thought, surveying the piles of books, papers and unwashed teacups covering every flat surface in the house, it must surely be the only object here that hadn't been mislaid. Surprising really, because nothing could have been in sharper contrast to the cleanliness and order the vicar maintained in the church.

"Yes, yes, of course. Don't get your tail in a twist, Cyril. Always were in the most unaccountable hurry, weren't you? Even born five weeks early, you know." The disheveled Rupert gave Felicity a wink. "Just couldn't wait to be getting on with things, our Cyril couldn't. I never could make out what the pother was all about."

Rupert's carpet slippers scuffed against the floorboards as he shuffled his way down the long, dark hall and opened the tall double doors onto what once, Felicity guessed, must have been a magnificent private library. It probably still was, actually, she reflected, if the contents could be unearthed from beneath the dust and littered papers. It all seemed so Victorian, Felicity half-expected Rupert to light a candle with a flint rather than turn on electric light. Miss Havisham would feel right at home here, she thought, remembering the character from Dicken's *Great Expectations*.

"Rupert, this is iniquitous," Cyril barked. "You've got a valuable library here—or you did until the damp got in. Let me send up someone from the British Library to sort out this collection. You really can't go on this way. Have the church wardens seen this? Surely they'll take you in hand."

Rupert shook his head of shaggy grey hair and spoke to Antony and Felicity as if his brother wasn't in the room. "Been at me all his life. He should just make a tape recording and save his breath. 'Rupert, you're a disgrace to the family.' Never mind, he stops in London most of the time."

In spite of his slovenly habits, Felicity couldn't help being drawn to the twinkle in Rupert's eyes. She had the feeling he could be a lot of fun if his older brother weren't riding him so hard to shape up. And he must be good at his job. The church was beautiful. So was the mess in his home his personal rebellion? An act of independence that his brother couldn't control?

"The book." Cyril called them back to business. "You said you found it in the back of a cupboard? Not damp, I hope."

"Not so much a cupboard as a hidey-hole" Rupert indicated the large stone fireplace at the end of the room. The hearth clearly showed where the masonry had been repaired and the paneling beside it restored. "Couldn't find a snugger place." He gave his brother a look of triumph as he pushed one side of the paneling and it turned to reveal a cunningly concealed cupboard, with a bookshelf.

"Very clever," Cyril conceded. "But, recall, Rupert, it's nothing to your credit. If this valuable manuscript hadn't been hidden away it would have been as subject to moth and mold as the rest of your collection. I don't know how many times I've warned you." He started to reach for the book as he continued his diatribe. "You really are a disgrace to the family. How anyone raised with the standards and the heritage—"

To everyone's surprise, the lackadaisical Rupert shot his hand out and seized Cyril's wrist. "That's quite enough, brother. More than enough, I should think." Twisting Cyril's arm behind his back, Rupert shoved his resisting brother across the room, knocking a pile of dusty books off a table in the process. "Now I'll thank you to just calm yourself a mite..."

At first Felicity was shocked at the brothers' behavior—as unalike as they were one might have expected them to have come to terms over the years. Yet she thought of her own brothers roughhousing in their backyard. Perhaps men never outgrew such behavior.

She nudged Antony to clear a place for them at the table already partly cleared by the pile the bickering brothers had dislodged. Since she was doing without her crutch today, she was able to grasp the ancient volume carefully in both hands. She placed it on the table and all but bumped heads with Antony in her agitation to learn the secrets of their find.

Was this what Neville had found? Was there something here that had led him to whatever it was he wanted to show them at St Benet's? Felicity's mind leaped forward. Margery had been an enthusiastic pilgrim. Did she collect icons and tell about it in her book? And knowing that, would they then know why the icons had been stolen and where to look?

Felicity's imagination was ready to take another leap when Antony, who had been scrutinizing the volume, pulled back in disappointment.

Felicity looked at the open page, then turned to Antony with furrowed brow. "Did Margery Kempe write in Latin? No, you said she dictated. So did her son write in Latin? If she was dictating in English…"

Antony nodded. "That's it exactly. Much of Margery's historical significance is that she is credited with writing the first autobiography in English."

"And this is Latin." Felicity sat back with a sigh. She had had such high hopes. Another dead end. "This can't be Margery's." On the other side of the room the brothers were still absorbed in a heated argument. She looked back at the book, open on the table. "And pretty awful Latin, at that." Still, her interest was piqued. Once a classicist, always a classicist. She drew the volume closer. "This has to be what Neville found, doesn't it?"

"It must be. Although he was pretty vague. And then we were interrupted."

"Well then…" Felicity bent over the volume.

Eventually the sibling altercation quieted, and Antony reported their findings. Disappointed, the brothers left the room, Cyril saying he had plans to show Cynthia the local sites. Antony foraged around among the piles on the table to find a pencil and notepad, and offered them to Felicity. "Make any sense of it?"

She raised her head slowly. "Well, I'm not really sure. This doesn't seem to be the whole thing, whatever it is. It just starts in the middle of the story. See," she turned back to the front pages, "there's no title page or introduction or anything."

"No, and not a printed book. A bound manuscript. Any clues to how old it is?"

"I haven't found any dates, but I suppose I might hazard a guess at mid to late fifteenth century based on some of the forms the writer uses. It's pretty hard going. My training was classical Latin, you know, not late medieval."

"Can you tell what it is?"

"I'd say it isn't any sort of a scholarly study. Too informal for that. And it's very personal, immediate. I could be wrong, of course."

"A journal, perhaps?"

"Well, yes, it does have something of that feel, but there are no dates, and it seems more topical than chronological."

"A memoir, then?"

"Ah, yes. That seems just right. A rather rambling one."

"And do you have any idea who the author might have been?"

"Someone acquainted with this area, I would say. He seems to be talking about St Margaret's Church. Here's an interesting bit I was just working on." Felicity glanced back at the page. "He's talking about Margaret of Antioch. Apparently that's the Margaret this church is named for. He refers to legends about her defending her virginity from the lusty Roman prefect who wanted to marry her, but this is the bit I liked the best: 'a dragon, which was really Satan, swallowed Margaret alive and then burst open, with Margaret emerging unhurt. The power of her cross held up to the dragon overcame the power of sin.'"

Felicity looked up and smiled. "Apparently because she emerged unhurt from the 'womb' of the dragon, she is associated with childbirth. Isn't that perfect—Margery Kempe, who had fourteen children, worshipped in a church dedicated to the patron saint of childbirth."

"Yes, and the name Margery is a derivation of Margaret." Antony sat quietly for a time while Felicity returned to her translating. At length he interrupted to muse, "It's really wonderful to think of this book resting here undisturbed, essentially *in situ* all these centuries."

"But it couldn't have been, could it?" Felicity looked up, her finger resting lightly on the page to mark her place. "This house is only Georgian, isn't it?"

"Oh, yes, but when they built the new vicarage they undoubtedly moved the library, lock, stock and barrel from the former parsonage or whatever they had, probably without looking at the individual volumes."

"And sometime later someone thought this book valuable enough to put it in that special cupboard."

Antony smiled. "Fun, isn't it, to think of a scholarly Victorian vicar sorting through his library and recognizing the antiquity of this tome, so putting it in the cupboard closest to the fireplace where it stayed through succeeding incumbencies. I doubt that this was designed as a cache for proscribed reading or anything. It seems to be more in the nature of a drying cupboard."

"Oh, not built for a priest with a collection of pornography, then?" Felicity suggested.

"Well, one does hear about such things, but this looks more like the result of benign neglect than purposeful hoarding."

"I wish whoever wrote this had given some clues to their identity. Do you think it's worth going on with? I'm not sure there's anything very useful here."

"If it was written by a parishioner, or more likely, the priest of St Margaret's, some time late in the fifteenth century, they must have known Margery. Certainly would have known some of her children or grandchildren, at least. And I can't imagine they wouldn't have known stories about her."

Felicity nodded. "Yes, if they were going to bother recounting stories of Margaret of Antioch—did you know her lusty Roman attempted to boil her in a cauldron of oil, but God protected her?—you're thinking that he would also tell tales of the local holy woman?"

"Seems worth a try, if the translating isn't too hard slogging."

"It's rather fun to get my hand back in, but I'm surprised Rupert hasn't done it already. Or Cyril. They both have such scholarly backgrounds."

Antony looked toward the door through which the squabbling brothers had departed. "I expect they would each give some excuse about being too busy or something, but I suspect the truth is closer to the fact that Rupert lacks the focus but refuses to allow Cyril the privilege. Having a third party do it is the perfect answer for them, but it seems taking advantage of you."

"I don't mind at all. It's sort of its own form of sleuthing, icons aside. If only it weren't so cold in here." Her body was shaken with a shiver and she cast a baleful eye at the cold stones of the elegant Adam fireplace. "Do you think Rupert would mind if I take this back to my room to read? At least that tattered duvet on my bed is warm."

"It is uncomfortable here. Tell you what—you finish looking that over in your room, and I'll duck out and rent a car. We can be back in Kirkthorpe this evening."

"What?" Felicity was torn between incredulity and anger at his suggestion. "Go back to the Community empty-handed and tell Father Anselm, 'Sorry, no luck' and leave it to him to figure out what to say to the Patriarch of Moscow and all Russia?"

"Felicity, I want you—"

"You want me what? Safe? You were going to say safe, weren't you? Go tuck up in your bed under the eiderdown and lock your door and then I'll carry you back to the monastery. And what then? You'll go on your way following clues?" She stood and gripped the book to her breast. "Don't even think of it."

The dignity of her exit from the room was somewhat marred by the fact that she was still limping, but Antony's not following her gave evidence that he had received her message. At least, she would have been certain he did if she hadn't looked back over her shoulder and caught his amused grin.

Felicity spent the rest of the afternoon in her room alternately plodding through the often-garbled Latin manuscript and dozing. After the third time she nodded off she gave up fighting and just succumbed to the delicious sensation of letting her body sink.

She awoke to a tapping on her door. "Felicity! Are you

going down to dinner?"

"Oh, sure. Be there in a minute."

It was more like ten minutes, but when she arrived in the dining room she was amazed at the transformation. The heavy, dark oak table and sideboard had been cleared of their clutter, each place set with creamy white stoneware and, most amazing, lighted candles graced the scene. An appetizing aroma rose from the large serving bowl set before Rupert. "I see you've noticed the metamorphosis," he greeted Felicity's openmouthed arrival. "Can't take any credit for it myself, I'm afraid. Simon's home."

Felicity turned to greet the young man he indicated. "Simon? You're—"

"The black sheep," he announced, with a bow. His voice was so like Neville's she almost cried out.

"Neville's cousin," she finished. And he looked just like Neville, the tall, reed-thin form, the pale skin. That is, he *would* have looked like Neville if he hadn't been a skinhead with multiple piercings and copious tattoos, exhibited to their fullest by his sleeveless T-shirt, worn in spite of the cold, which made Felicity hug her thick sweater to herself. She found the contrast between Neville and Simon quite shocking. No wonder this cousin had been so snide about Neville on the phone. Another chalk and cheese relationship.

"That's right." Simon shocked her even further by courteously pulling her chair out for her, and making certain she was comfortable before he took the chair beside her. "Afraid the Irish stew's tinned and the cottage loaves are from the bakery. That's all there was in the larder. But do dig in," he invited.

"So you're the chef?"

"If you call opening a tin—several tins actually—being the chef, then you're welcome to blame me. I did manage to throw in some fresh herbs from father's riotously overgrown garden and it's amazing what adding some red wine will do for the flavor." He even wore gold-rimmed glasses like Neville's and pushed them back up on his nose with a long, white finger that made Felicity shiver at the memory of Neville's hand sticking through the mud. Simon wore no ring, though, just another of his many tattoos.

She would have liked to know more about Simon, but all she could elicit from him was that he had been "away" doing "things" and he visited his father "now and then—when the train schedule suited him."

Before Felicity could query him further Cyril and Cynthia returned from their day out. "Have you had a nice day, darling? We had a delightful time at Castle Acre. We walked all over the castle mound and," Cynthia turned to Antony, "you would have loved the ruined priory."

Felicity found she was very hungry and Simon's tinned stew and bakery bread wasn't at all bad. She was on her second helping when Cyril enquired about her translating.

"Not the lost book of Margery Kempe, I'm afraid. The best I can make out is that it's a memoir. Probably written by a vicar of St Margaret's not too long after Margery's time. He seems to have had a lively interest in all the local doings, but his Latin was atrocious, which makes reading it slow going."

"So nothing about our Margery or her descendants?" Felicity was surprised that it was the tatooed, multi-pierced Simon who asked this, since his interests had seemed to be all culinary.

As her mouth was full of stew, she merely shook her head.

"Brave of you to tackle this for us," Cyril said. "I would enjoy doing the translation myself, but I'm afraid I'm so far away from my schoolboy Latin it would take me too long." He gave his brother a deprecating look. "And Rupert is too dilatory. So you're our only hope of having our great find deciphered in-house, so to speak, my dear." Felicity and Antony exchanged fleeting glances. Antony's surmises about the brothers had been spot on.

"I'm sorry it isn't something more exciting," Felicity said. "Of course, a local historian would undoubtedly be interested in the writer's comments about the market and his account of boiling salt in huge copper pans for export along with wool and grain. Apparently Bishop's Lynn, as it was then, was a hive of trading from Scandinavia. He—whoever 'he' is—mentions trade in timber, pitch, fish and iron."

Cyril laughed. "Well, it does sound as though you've garnered a quite thorough education. We shan't worry about you wasting your time."

Felicity turned to Antony. "Oh, and he mentions building a chapel for pilgrims traveling to Walsingham. Wasn't that one of the places Margery went?"

"Yes, late in life. She made her last pilgrimage to Walsingham and on to northern Europe, when she was sixty and somewhat lame. If I remember correctly, she tricked her daughter-in-law into accompanying her to Walsingham, then set sail on her own."

Felicity applauded. "Oh, I think I'm beginning to like this lady."

The conversation turned to Cynthia and Cyril's sightseeing, and Felicity returned her attention to her dinner. It was Simon's gesture, requesting that she pass the butter, that made his hand tattoo catch her eye. She caught his hand, intercepting his reach for the butter, to have a closer look at the tattoo she had only glimpsed earlier. Yes, it was. The same intricate pattern of cross and intertwined leaves that had been on Neville's ring. "What an interesting pattern. What does that mean?"

"Oh, you like that? Rather nice, isn't it? Sort of a family crest, I guess you might say."

Cyril frowned. "The emblem has been in the family for generations. Although I must say Simon is the first to blazon it in quite such a unique manner." He rose and held Cynthia's chair for her. "Well, thank you for the dinner, Simon. If you'll excuse us now, Cynthia and I will forgo the joys of coffee *en famille* to stroll down to the Lattice House for drinks." At the door he turned back to Felicity. "Good luck with your translating. You will keep us apprised of your progress, won't you?"

When they were gone, Simon brought out a pot of coffee. He poured a large cup and laced it generously with milk and sugar before passing it to his father.

Rupert, who had been almost silent in his brother's presence, drank deeply. "Ahh, Simon, how I've missed you. First decent cup of coffee I've had since Mothering Sunday. You must come around more often, boy." He then became almost garrulous, revealing himself to be a more knowledgeable historian than Felicity had guessed. "Originally this was all part of the manor of the Bishop of Norwich—why it was called Bishop's Lynn, you see. Became royal property when Henry VIII dissolved the monasteries, therefore King's Lynn. Until then all my predecessors had been appointed by the prior of St Margaret's Priory."

"Do you know the names of any of your predecessors?"

"The medieval ones, you mean? No, I'm afraid not. Except for Father Robert Springold, of course. Margery Kempe's confessor, you know."

Felicity blinked. "Wait. You mean the one she dictated her book to?"

"Yes, that's right, Springale, Springall, Spryngald—all the same thing."

"But that's—" Felicity swallowed her words with a quick gulp of coffee. She didn't know why, but for some reason she felt reluctant to reveal her discovery.

Rupert launched into an account of Lynn's most famous son, Captain George Vancouver, and his exploration of North America's Pacific coast, but Antony pushed his chair back, scraping noisily on the wooden floor. "So sorry to interrupt, but I do think it's time you returned to your room, Felicity. You must be tired."

A vehement protest was on the tip of her tongue, but she caught the look in his eye. "Oh, er, yes. I'm still convalescing, you know. Thank you so much for dinner."

Antony followed her into her room and had barely closed the door when she turned. "Now, what was all that about? I'm not the least bit tired."

"I know, but I got a distinct feeling you were about to divulge something interesting from your reading and I thought it best not to make it public."

"Public? But it's Rupert's manuscript. I guess it is, anyway. It's in his library. Or the church's. Anyway, I think he's rather a darling."

Antony smiled. "Nothing much wrong with him a good cleaner couldn't sort out. I suppose with his wife dying when Simon was born, he must have lapsed into bad habits that just sort of escalated over the years. No, it's not Rupert, it's Simon."

"Simon? I agree the shaved head and piercings are a bit much, but his manners are lovely. I suppose he's a bit of an enigma."

"I think he's more than puzzling. I think he's devious."

"Why?"

"I've been thinking. When Angela gave me Neville's contact number and I rang Simon's mobile, he said he hadn't seen Neville since Christmas."

"Well, it was a mobile. He could have been anywhere. Apparently he's 'of no fixed address.'"

"Yes, but Rupert mentioned his being here for Mothering Sunday."

Felicity thought. "Ah, the day Neville disappeared. I suppose it's possible Simon left after dinner and Neville didn't arrive until that evening. Do you think we should tell the police? They could check bus and train schedules and all that. Simon said something about using public transport."

"I'm not sure I'd go that far, but just do be careful what you say in front of him. And Rupert, too, now that I think about it. When I rang Rupert when you were in London, he said Neville wasn't interested in any special manuscript or anything, yet he must have known about this."

"Well, maybe he wasn't; we haven't found anything for sure yet." She indicated the memoir lying beside her bed. "But I did find something interesting I wanted to show you—a name." She opened the book to where she had left off reading and pointed. "I think this translates, 'my predecessor Master Robert Spryngold.' So the writer would be referring to Margery Kempe's confessor, right? Who was apparently vicar of St Margaret's just before our author." A broad smile spread over Antony's face, bringing a light to his eyes as well.

"Do you think it could be important?" Felicity asked.

"It could be what we're looking for."

"What Neville wanted to tell you about?"

Antony lifted his head and put a finger to his lips. "Well, that's hard to say." As he spoke he tiptoed toward the door. "I wouldn't be too sure…" He reached out and flung the door open.

Simon stood there with a hot-water bottle in his hand. "Oh, excuse me. Just thought you might want this. Nights can get pretty cold here."

"Yes, thank you." Felicity took the fleece-covered bag and cradled it in her arms. "That's very thoughtful of you, Simon."

Antony closed the door and they listened to Simon's departing footsteps. "How long do you think he'd been there?" Felicity whispered.

"Hard to tell, depends on whether that creaking floorboard I heard announced his arrival or whether he'd been standing there for a while."

Antony backed toward the door. "Felicity, lock this after me."

He needn't have told her. They could be on the threshold of discovering what Neville had intended to tell them at St Benet's. And she knew all too well what had happened to Neville.

Chapter 29

Wednesday in Passiontide

Felicity was the first at breakfast the next morning, drawn down the stairs by the enticing scent of Simon's sausages sizzling away in the pan. "One egg or two?" he asked.

"Oh, just one, thanks." When he set the platter in front of her she was amazed. "Grilled tomato and fried bread, too! Simon, you're a wonder."

He shrugged his tattooed shoulders. "Not much work to fry bread, as long as you have everything else going."

"But where did this come from? I didn't realize the market was open this early."

Simon looked scornful. "Supermarkets have their place, but there's nothing like knowing a farmer."

"Garden tomatoes in mid-April?"

Now the chef looked smug. "Farmer has a hothouse, doesn't he?"

"Why aren't you a chef somewhere? Or running your own B and B? You have a real knack for this." But when she noticed Simon's dark expression, she was sorry she had asked. Had she insulted him, suggesting he should get a job? Or would cooking for pay be beneath a member of the Mortara family?

Just then Cynthia came in, fresh and fashionable as always. How she managed to stay upright on the cobbled walks and muddy footpaths of rural England in her high heels, Felicity couldn't imagine. And Felicity was the one suffering from a sprained ankle. Life, she decided, wasn't fair.

"Darling, I'm so glad to see you up and about. Pass the toast, will you, please? Did you sleep well? How's your ankle?

Have you had enough of your dusty books? You really must come to Riddlington with us. It's a perfect day for a drive. Cyril is putting our luggage in the Royce right now. We'll be off as soon as he has a cup of coffee."

"I'm fine, Mother." Felicity passed the toast rack to Cynthia. "Riddlington? The Mortara family estate? And I should come with you because—?"

"It's an amazing place. You'll love it. I was there just last week and I can't wait to get back."

"Mmm, yes." *Your naughty weekend*, Felicity almost said out loud. "Actually, I'm going to Walsingham, but perhaps you could drop me there. I haven't looked at a map, but I have an idea it wouldn't be too far out of the way." It couldn't be, could it? Apparently Margery Kempe had walked there when she was sixty-something. Or perhaps she hired a carriage by that age.

They were still discussing the idea, somewhat blindly, since neither of them knew the geography of the county, when Antony came in and, listening to their conversation, interrupted it. "What do you mean you're going to Walsingham? I'm taking you back to Kirkthorpe today."

Felicity jerked around to look him full in the face, ready for the blazing row such peremptory statements of his always evoked. Then her indignation died. They had had that argument countless times before. She didn't want to go there again. Besides, his naturally pale complexion looked pallid and drawn. She tended to forget how much failure to recover this icon would cost him. For her it might be a hide-and-seek game with an edge of risk, but for Antony it could mean a serious blow to a cause he had worked for passionately for years. For a moment she was back in that wet cold perch on the Lindisfarne causeway waiting for the tide to recede when he first, rather shyly, told her about his dream of unity in the church. And they had just one week until the Patriarch would arrive to find…

She smiled and spoke in her softest voice. "Sweet" wasn't

her thing, but she could make an attempt. "Mother Francis Clare at the Priory of Our Lady of Walsingham is expecting me. I called her this morning. I've gotten rather off track from my discernment pilgrimage. And Father Oswin did specifically mention them. Mother said they could take me. It seemed like such a good opportunity. And it will rather complete my Margery Kempe education, since she went there on her last pilgrimage."

Antony burst out laughing as if she had told an exceedingly clever joke. His sense of humor could be completely unaccountable. "All right. I surrender." He held up his hands. "You can stop now. 'The lady doth protest too much.'"

As soon as they were ensconced in the plush comfort of Cyril's car, Felicity turned to Antony. "Finally! I can't wait to tell you. I finished that manuscript. Took me half the night, but I'm so glad I stayed with it. I should have started from the back. He goes into considerable detail about the dedication of that pilgrim's chapel in Bishop's Lynn."

"Red Mount?" Cyril asked over his shoulder. "You should have said something sooner. I could have taken you by there if I'd known you were interested. Very fine listed building, quite newly restored. Unusual—a red-brick octagon—the centerpiece of The Walks, a very fine eighteenth-century park." He glanced at his watch. "Would you like to go back? It's just a step behind St Margaret's. Not a very good day for walking, though." He indicated the rain streaking the windows.

"Oh, no, don't go back. Thanks. It does sound interesting, but the thing is, since it was built after Margery's time it wouldn't be quite on point."

She waited for Cyril to start the music, appropriately Handel's "Water Music," and head down the A148 leaving King's Lynn behind them before she continued to Antony, "The thing is, he mentions, really just in passing, that there were three icons."

Antony's eyebrows shot upwards. "At the chapel?"

"No, if I translated it right that was his complaint. Seems Margery Kempe brought back three with her from the Holy Land. One for St Margaret's, one for Julian's shrine, and one for Our Lady of Walsingham. That must be why she was so determined to get to Walsingham, even in her old age."

Antony nodded. "She wanted to deliver the icon."

They were both quiet for several moments, thinking. Felicity spoke first. "But there aren't any icons at St Margaret's now. Where is it? It can't be the one stolen from the Community of the Transfiguration."

"More likely the one at Rempstone."

"And we know that one was marked. Angela wasn't sure about Julian's, but if they came from the same source…"

"Yes." Antony ran his hand through his hair. "If we can find the one at Walsingham we'll know for sure."

Felicity's brow furrowed in concentration. "So, let me get this straight. We're thinking that Margery, on pilgrimage in the Holy Land, stayed with the Knights Hospitaller—"

"Which was their job, to provide shelter for pilgrims."

"And she bought—or more likely talked them into contributing, she was a very forceful lady, after all—icons for her favorite holy places in England." Felicity thought about what she had said. "I like that, but one thing worries me. Margery was so garrulous. Wouldn't she have included that information in her book?"

"One would think so, unless—" The windshield wipers swished rhythmically as if conducting the swelling music, prodding their thoughts onward.

Felicity gasped. "Antony! You can't be suggesting our favorite holy woman purloined the icons from the knights?"

"Well, it does seem out of character. But whatever she did, she seems to have told her confessor who somehow let at least part of it slip to his successor."

"Who wrote the book I read." Felicity gave a great sigh of satisfaction and leaned back with her arms folded. "That is simply fantastic. We are really getting somewhere."

Antony grinned. "Well, it's certainly interesting. I hope it isn't fantastic in the sense of fantasy. And I'm not sure where it gets us as to recovering them."

They were quiet for some time as the green countryside rolled past them in the rain and the "Water Music" filled the car. A sign alongside the highway caught Felicity's eye. "That said 'National Pilgrimage Route.' Does that mean this is the way Margery would have traveled?"

"And thousands of other pilgrims," Cyril said. "In the Middle Ages, our Little Walsingham was on a par with the grand cathedrals and abbeys as a popular pilgrimage site. We're talking about a major tourist attraction. Actually, Walsingham was second only to Canterbury in pilgrim popularity."

Felicity turned to Antony. "OK, let's have it, then."

"Hm?"

"The Walsingham lecture. Everywhere we go, you reenact the history for the benefit of your poor ignorant student. So let's have it."

Antony chuckled. "I believe you're starting to like it."

Felicity exaggerated a fake yawn. "You've got to be kidding. I just need an excuse for a nap."

Antony's eyes twinkled. "All right, then. Close your eyes." She did and his voice took on the telltale lecture tone. "In 1061, Richeldis de Faverches, the lady of the manor of Walsingham Parva, had a vision in which the Virgin Mary took her to Nazareth and showed her the simple home where the Christ Child grew up. The vision was repeated two more times until Richeldis was convinced that she was to build a replica of the holy house of Nazareth. Which she did, and her son Geoffrey saw to the building of a priory for Augustinian canons to serve as guardians for the Holy House and provide hospitality to the pilgrims.

"Walsingham became known as 'England's Nazareth,' and pilgrims—including many kings—flocked there to experience something of the atmosphere of Jesus' upbringing. The existence of that shrine is one of the reasons England is known as 'Mary's dowry'."

"No wonder this was a highlight for Margery."

"Exactly. With Margery's special devotion to the Christ Child and the great significance she found in relating the everydayness of life to the spiritual, visiting his childhood home would have been just her thing. Which makes it all the odder that she gives us no details of her visit. Of course, Margery had been privileged actually to have visited the Holy Land. The shrine acquired its huge popularity as a place of pilgrimage because people could visit a site closely associated with the life of Jesus when the original was inaccessible due to the danger of the Crusades."

"Which is why the Hospitallers were providing protection."

Antony nodded. "And so it continued for 477 years. A large and wealthy priory grew up around the shrine—wealth which was seized by King Henry VIII in 1538 and the shrine destroyed."

"There's the Slipper Chapel." Cyril pointed.

"Slipper Chapel?" Cynthia had been so quiet Felicity thought perhaps she had been dozing.

Cyril did this bit of the explaining. "Medieval pilgrims left their shoes here before going on into 'Nazareth.'"

"They went barefoot?"

"Yes, correct me if I'm wrong, Father, but one got more points for doing a pilgrimage barefoot. Of course, that was pretty hard going, so the heavenly scorekeepers gave them the same points if they did the last mile or so unshod. Isn't that right?"

"Quite so." Antony picked up the thread of narration. "In

1896 Charlotte Boyd, a devout woman, purchased the Slipper Chapel and saw to its refurbishing. The first pilgrimage in more than 300 years took place the following year—from King's Lynn to the Slipper Chapel."

"Thousands flock there now. Bus-loads every summer. All year long, really," Cyril inserted.

Antony turned to Felicity. "There'll be a group coming from CT in June. You should sign up for it."

"Hmm, I'll keep it in mind. So they've been doing this since Victorian times?" Felicity smiled as the lecture tone returned to Antony's voice. She closed her eyes again as Antony's story poured over her.

Awareness of Walsingham as a historic site grew. In 1921, a young priest, Alfred Hope Patten, was appointed vicar of St Mary's, Walsingham. Patten had heard of the ancient site when he made a cycling tour of Norfolk as a boy, but then forgot about it for many years until the priest under whom he was serving his curacy in London showed him a small carving of the Virgin Mary seated with the Holy Child on her lap and a lily in her hand. "This," his priest said, "is going to Walsingham. There used to be a great Shrine of Our Lady there." And then, seven years later, Alfred Hope Patten was appointed to that very parish.

"As soon as he was settled in his new parish, Father Patten set up a special chapel and invited pilgrims to come for a special day of prayers. Naively, his secretary listed everyone who wrote requesting information as intending to make the pilgrimage, so that Father Patten was told to prepare for forty guests. On the appointed day, a very tall priest and one small woman disembarked at the train station.

"Where are the other thirty-eight?"

"We've seen no one else. As far as we know, we are the pilgrimage.""

Father Patten went around to his parishioners and said, "Forty pilgrims were expected. Food has been provided; it must not be wasted. You must make the pilgrimage." And so the concept of pilgrimage was reborn with the local Walsingham people.

Father Patten then set about securing land on which to build a new replica of the Holy House, as close to the original site next to the ruined priory as he could. By 1931 the Holy House replica was restored, and by 1938 a Shrine Church constructed to enclose the Holy House along with a number of side chapels and altars, and the annual pilgrimages were well established.

A central feature of those early pilgrimages was always a tea party given by Father Patten on the vicarage lawn. Pilgrims were charmed by his sense of humor and enlivened by his sense of mission to bring restoration and renewal.

The Rolls glided through a vast solitude of green fields stretching in every direction until the road was swallowed in shrouding trees and hedgerows. Cyril brought the car to a stop in a graveled parking lot on the edge of small village. "Well, here you are. Hope you have a pleasant stay. Try not to get too wet."

Felicity, always prepared, pulled a rain hat from her backpack. "Not to worry. Thanks for the ride. Bye, Mother." And she was out, breathing deeply of the fresh air. She felt so refreshed. Maybe she had actually dozed off while Antony was talking. She wasn't sure. If so, she hoped he hadn't noticed.

"This way." Antony led down a tiny, winding lane past storybook-charming medieval buildings, most of them of the local brick and flint construction with red tile roofs, interspersed with Tudor black and white, and all with cottage gardens rampant with spring flowers.

Felicity stopped and looked around. "Was that a Rolls-Royce or a time machine we got out of?"

"You could say this is a place time forgot. And what a great favor that was. The fact that the shrine was demolished at the Reformation and the village completely bypassed until its re-founding in the 1920s has done much to preserve it. There was never any need—or money available— to update anything, so today the shrine buildings are the only modern ones in the village. I can't say I'm 100 per cent thrilled with the recent burst of modernization at the pilgrimage center— especially the ultramodern outdoor altar—but then, my tastes are dinosauric."

"You said it, I didn't!" she grinned at him.

They walked past the market square, surrounded by shops, and entered the shrine grounds. Felicity paused to read the plaque by the entrance arch: "The Shrine of Our Lady of Walsingham is a place of pilgrimage which exists to bring people into deeper relationship with God through encounter with Jesus, His Son. Pilgrimage reminds us that our whole lives are a journey with God to the joy of heaven, and at the heart of Walsingham is the Holy House where we celebrate Mary's 'yes' to God. Inspired by her life and prayers, we welcome all people."

Whatever, she thought and started to shrug, then stopped short. This was a beautiful expression of faith, but it painfully highlighted for her what a neophyte she was in such matters. No wonder Father Oswin warned her to go slow.

She smiled as she recalled telling Antony about her casual "Christmas and Easter Only" church upbringing and her rash decision to go to theological college. If Antony hadn't been so accepting and set such a faithful example… Well, she had asked to come here. She would pay attention and get everything out of the visit she could.

They entered the shrine grounds and walked along a curving path through green lawns. At least the rain had let up so Felicity could enjoy the well-sculpted gardens. She looked up to survey the three crosses on a rounded, green hill, when a sharp movement caught her attention. The furtive movement was so out of synch with those of the few other visitors strolling leisurely around the grounds that it made her catch her breath. Had the fleeting figure been familiar? Could her stalker have followed her here? Even so quickly? Surely there had been no one behind them on those country lanes. It didn't seem possible that anyone could know where they were. And that made the specter all the more disturbing.

She thought she had put all that behind her. Surely with Cyril's help Antony would soon find his icon. And the police must be getting near to solving Neville's murder by now. Perhaps already had done. Surely she could just concentrate on her own pilgrimage and let someone else worry about such sordidness.

But she found that once she thought of Neville, she could think of nothing else. She managed to stuff the thought to the back of her mind for a time, but the phantom kept resurfacing. And now, in this place so beloved by so many of her fellow students, memories of her friend flooded her mind, bringing tears to her eyes. She stopped in the middle of the path. "Antony, I can't help thinking of Neville—how much he would enjoy being here. It... it's just so unfair! Why would anyone do that?"

Antony nodded. "Yes, I know. Sin. Injustice. Violence. I suppose we can understand them to some extent in an abstract way—at least realize they exist, if not understand—but it's the specific applications that seem so unbelievable."

She pushed aside his philosophical approach. "But Neville. He was so nice. He would never hurt anybody. He was rich and talented, but always generous. I can't imagine anyone being jealous. I know some of his friends were controversial; unacceptable, even, to some. But would that be a motive for murder?

"And who would have benefited? Or who could have hated him? I've read it's always love or money or hatred—something like that—that's a motive for murder. None of that fits Nev."

"Fear, maybe? Someone feared him because of something he knew? Or saw?"

The question hung in the air as they moved forward on the path, their footsteps slowed by the burden of mounting questions. Felicity returned her focus to her surroundings. The red-brick buildings struck her as looking rather Italiante. She thought it was supposed to be Nazareth. Oh, well. At the red-tiled, white stucco Shrine Church she entered the glass-paned doors and stood on the tile floor, blinking. *What a muddle.* In the dark interior of the building was a confusing array of altars, candles, sanctuary lamps and statues and crosses. How could such a perplexing jumble of medieval religious curiosities possibly represent the childhood of Jesus?

Then she reminded herself sharply that if anyone wanted to hide an icon here, they could hardly find a better place. There must be dozens of icons, shimmering mysteriously in the light of votive candles in the multiple chapels surrounding the church. Finding anything here seemed impossible.

Antony led the way to the center of the building, where they entered the replica of the house where the Holy Family lived in Nazareth. "This tiny room is a symbol of the timeless truth that God in Jesus had a home and family in Nazareth. The Holy House thus represents an earthly home for all who seek to participate in the extension of that family," the placard read.

Felicity sighed. She was feeling more confused by the moment. It was almost certainly due to her lack of experience, but the jumble seemed to overwhelm the mystery. "Yes, OK. I get it. Making the spiritual concrete and all that. It's a beautiful thought. And the sight must have been extremely moving to Margery who burst into tears at the sight of small boys because they reminded her of the Christ Child. But it sure would be a stronger image for me if the house looked like something one might encounter in the Holy Land, rather than something transported from Italy."

She looked around inside the Holy House. "And it would help if the interior really looked like something identifiable as a house." The walls, built from odd pieces of masonry from monasteries destroyed at the Reformation, were lined on each side with hanging sanctuary lamps flickering red and blue. Below them stood banks of votive candles, all making the golden altar at the far end with the figure of Our Lady of Walsingham above it shimmer and glow. Nowhere was anything Jesus would have seen in his boyhood.

Everything was glowing and mysterious, rather like the interior of a magical cave. Felicity felt hopelessly pedestrian to be looking for a table, bed, stools and bowls such as Mary and Joseph would have possessed.

Antony must have sensed her confusion. He attempted an explanation. "All around the church surrounding the Holy House, the small chapels are dedicated to various stages in Christ's early development and the story of his life on earth."

"OK." Felicity knew she should be trying. She beat back her natural instinct to cynicism as they made their way slowly around the room and climbed the stairs at the back. On the balcony they found a quiet spot to sit. Here, above the confusion of lamps, altars and statues, the view was clean and clear, the balanced and precise lines of the overall architecture came into view, and at last she saw it—a stylized version of the little house in its setting, the round window beyond looking like the moon, the rows of arches like trees. It w*as* very Italian-looking, but suddenly Italy didn't seem so very far removed from the Holy Land.

They went back down, toward the door, but Felicity stopped before a bank of candles flickering in a dim corner. "Just a minute." Rather to her own surprise, she lit a candle and knelt. Her thoughts were full of Mary, Margery Kempe, Mother Julian, her own mother...

"Shall we move on to the Holy Well?" Antony asked as

she stood. "Are you all right with all this walking? How's the ankle?"

"I'm fine. Not ready to run any races, but fine enough."

Surprisingly, they didn't go outside to the well. "A natural spring was discovered during the building of the shrine. Father Patten took this for a sign of blessing and incorporated it into his plans so that the well is inside the church," Antony explained.

They processed down a set of narrow stairs. A priest standing by the well offered Felicity a sip of the cool clear water, marked the sign of the cross on her forehead, and poured some water into her cupped hands.

"What was that all about?" she asked as they came up from the water.

"It's a reminder of our baptism and God's ever-flowing grace toward his children. The descent to the well and ascent from it symbolize, like our baptism, going down into the darkness of death and the rising from it to the new life to which Christ calls all people."

"Um, yes." Again Felicity was faced with how little she knew about the life she had chosen so impulsively. Antony never upbraided her for not knowing these things, but she had been an ordinand for almost a year now. She was thinking of becoming a nun... "I think I should get on to the convent. Where is it?"

From the chapel they retraced their steps across the green lawn, climbing upward toward the hill she had noticed earlier topped by three crosses like Golgotha, then on past the abstract angles of the outdoor altar, its white roof looking a bit like a tent an Arab might have pitched in a great hurry. In the far corner of the grounds Antony led the way down a small path to a little white house and rang the doorbell. A plump, round-faced nun in a long, gray habit and black veil opened the door, drew Felicity inside, and closed the door.

Later that evening, Antony returned and entered the same door, walking down the hall to the small chapel where the sisters would be saying Compline. He took a seat in the back corner and was deep in meditation when the door behind him opened. Muffled footsteps on the creaking wooden floor announced the entrance of half a dozen or so sisters who slipped into their individual stalls and immediately bowed in prayer. A further creaking announced their guests—Felicity and Sister Johanna. He was surprised Johanna had left making her Lenten retreat until so late in the season, but even retreat directors found it difficult to make retreats.

Antony tried to concentrate on the brief, reflective service, to bring his thoughts into focus on God's guidance through the day now closing and to find peace for the coming night, but even as he chanted the psalms and followed the prayers, his attention was on Felicity. Merely sitting behind her in the dim light he could sense her vibrant energy. He longed to know what she thought of him—or if she thought of him at all. He wondered if he was even allowed to ask the question when she was considering taking religious vows.

He knew he mustn't interfere, and yet it all seemed so wrong for her—this life of calm and silence, this hiding away behind cloistered walls. He bit his lip in chagrin. What a terrible reaction from him when he himself had so recently thought of taking vows. And now all he could think of were vows of quite another sort. Sometimes it was so hard to know the difference between temptation and guidance. And what did one do while awaiting answers—either human or divine?

"Father, help us to be ready to celebrate the great Paschal mystery. Make our love grow each day as we approach the feast of our salvation." The sisters and their guests sat long in the stillness of the tiny room as the closing prayer winged its way heavenward. At last Mother Francis Clare made her way out, her step so light the boards hardly creaked under her tread. The others followed, some far less silently, leaving Antony in silence, if not in peace.

Finally, with thoughts of Felicity and thoughts of not thinking of Felicity clashing in his mind, he stepped out into the dark stillness of the night, broken only by a slight rustle in the bushes behind him.

And then the dark exploded in a thousand stars in his head, followed by searing pain. He never felt the cobbles of the path as he crumpled forward.

Chapter 30

Thursday in Passiontide

Felicity had been fearful that her sleep might be filled with shadowy figures wearing Maltese crosses lurking around the corners of quaint Italian-style buildings, but instead she had enjoyed one of the best nights of sleep she had known for ages. She sprang out of bed, not even thinking to protect her ankle. And she had felt no lingering twinge, so she guessed she must be fully restored. Great, time to get back to her ballet exercises. She did some bending and stretching warm-ups, then grabbed the back of a straight chair in her tiny cell and did a few *plies* and *relevés*. That would have to be sufficient for the moment.

She had missed breakfast but, thankfully, not her appointment with Mother Francis Clare. She hurried down the hallway, taking time for only the briefest enjoyment of the flower-surrounded fish pond in the tiny, sheltered cloister beyond the window.

The fragile-looking nun with parchment skin and twinkling eyes was waiting for her. "My dear, I do apologize for meeting you in my office, but as we are so few in number I serve on the rota for phone nun with the others and this is my time slot. It is the most efficient arrangement. We can hope we won't be disturbed."

She smiled at Felicity. "I'm more than happy to share anything you want to know about the work of the Society of St Margaret. We were founded in 1855 by the hymn-writer John Mason Neale."

"Oh, yes," Felicity blurted out without thinking. "The order his sister chose not to join when she started her own."

She blushed, realizing that could be taken as a slight.

Mother Francis Clare ignored her outburst. "Our daily life is centered on the Eucharist and the daily office, from which flows our involvement in the ministries of healing and reconciliation."

Felicity must have looked a bit blank because Mother Francis Clare began to speak more slowly and distinctly as she outlined their work, as if talking to a child. "We welcome guests such as yourself here for short periods of rest and retreat, work in education for the shrine, and do volunteer work in nursing homes and provide respite care for those with HIV/AIDS."

"With only six of you? That's wonderful. You must be very busy." Felicity knew she was babbling. This sounded like admirable, important work. And yet she found it impossible to picture herself doing it.

The phone on the desk interrupted with a jangling ring. Mother Francis Clare answered with a quiet "Hello," then became very still, all color draining from her face. "Oh, but that's terrible." Her bright dark eyes sought Felicity's. "Yes, she's with me now."

The Reverend Mother replaced the receiver and looked appraisingly at Felicity as if deciding how to break her news.

Felicity felt the blood drain from her own face. What had happened? Had her mother been involved in an accident? Or… Please, God, not another murder.

Mother Francis Clare leaned toward her. "My dear, that was Father Jonathan West, our Priest Administrator. Your friend, Father Antony, was found by the groundsman early this morning."

"Found?" The room spun crazily. "What do you mean, *found*? Is he…" Felicity's mouth would form no more words.

"He's alive, thanks be to God. He apparently received a violent blow to the head and lay on the path outside the priory most of the night."

Outside the priory? Antony had lain unconscious outside her window all through the long cold hours of the wet night?

"He is badly concussed. They took him to the surgery in Fakenham. It's a very good surgery. One of our sisters is a practice nurse there. Father Jonathan is back now, in the College of Guardians."

To Felicity's ears, Mother Francis Clare was speaking gibberish. Fakenham must be a town. She knew surgery meant something like doctor's office or clinic. But what college? She voiced the question.

"The walled area behind the shrine. It's where the Priest Administrator lives, and the Guardians, like a board of directors, I suppose you might say, meet when they are here," her hostess supplied.

"But he's all right? Antony's all right?"

"I pray so. That's all Father Jonathan…"

Felicity didn't hear the last of her words; she could barely see where she was going as she fled from the office, from the cloister, out into the spring midmorning. She dimly perceived that it was a beautiful day as she ran across the dew-fresh grounds. She had seen the tall flint wall yesterday with the heavy gate marked "Private." Never mind private. Just let them try to keep her out. If they wouldn't open the gate she'd climb the wall.

Fortunately, no such heroics were necessary. Father Jonathan, the bald but youthful Priest Administrator, was waiting for her. Apparently, Mother Francis Clare had warned him.

"I must see him." It was all Felicity could manage between gasps for breath. It had been a dash of some distance, but the main problem was that she had forgotten to breathe.

"Do come in, my dear. May we give you a cup of tea?" He led the way across a cobbled courtyard toward a small cottage.

Father Jonathan was smiling. Tea? *She was supposed to drink tea?* She ducked just in time to keep from hitting her head on the door jamb. "Antony. How is he? I must see him."

"Yes, Of course. I'm sure he'll be back soon. Sister Anne is with him. She'll bring him back as soon as he's released from the clinic. There's no need for alarm, I'm sure." He was still smiling. "Please let us make you comfortable here while you wait."

Since she had missed breakfast, she succumbed to the offer of tea and toast. Father Jonathan brought them quickly, then waited in silent watchfulness as Felicity devoured them. "It may be a while until Sister Anne returns with Father Antony. Perhaps you would like to see around the college?"

Felicity stood. "Thank you. What do you teach?"

The priest blinked at her question, then laughed. "Oh, College of Guardians, you mean? No, no. College as in the oldest meaning of the word: A group with common duties and special privileges; people who are colleagues."

"So what are you guarding?"

"The work of the shrine. Especially by promoting pilgrimages. Our goal is always to honor the incarnation of Christ and to keep the shrine a place of refreshment and healing for all people. There are twenty Guardians, ordained and lay, men and women. If you're here on a ceremonial occasion you'll see them in long blue velvet robes."

He continued talking as he moved down the narrow hallway of the ancient low ceilinged building lit by pale light coming through the small, leaded windows. But Felicity could take in no more. Her anxiety for Antony overflowed into a sense of fear. And in spite of Father Jonathan's sprightly openness, each appraising look he gave her made her suspicions grow. She wanted to cry out, *A place of refreshment and healing? Antony was bludgeoned on your doorstep. Maybe by one of your people. Maybe by you!* Long blue velvet robes? Ornate pomp again. Like the Knights of Malta? Were they in league? Had Father Jonathan stolen their icon?

"The building is seventeenth century—derelict farm laborers' cottages. They knocked them together to make the accommodation. Our refectory is upstairs. It's our best room." He led the way up narrow, dark wood stairs.

Felicity surveyed the chamber. Was this room with its white stucco walls and black beams, heavy refectory table and dark paintings holding a secret?

The Priest Administrator placed a round, flat disc in her hand. She turned it over to reveal the image of a seated Madonna holding the Christ Child on her lap and a stylized lily in her right hand. Felicity nodded as she recognized the image as being the same as the statue she saw in the Holy House yesterday. "The seal of the Augustinian priory that built up around the original shrine. It's been dated as 1538. It's how we know what the original image was like."

Felicity nodded and thrust it back at him. She tried to sound casual. "Do you have any icons?"

"Not here in the college. In the Shrine Church, of course. Many."

"There's a legend that Margery Kempe presented one to the shrine."

Was Father Jonathan faking his surprised look? "Margery Kempe visited the shrine, indeed. In April of 1433, we believe. But there is no record of her making a gift. Of course, everything was destroyed at the Reformation."

"Yes, of course," Felicity mumbled. She really couldn't stay in this enclosure any longer. "I think I'll go for a walk." She ignored her host's startled expression and fled down the stairs, out of the building and right out of the gate in the high wall.

She entered the shrine building quietly and heard the gentle rhythms of a mass being conducted in a side chapel with a brown-robed Franciscan friar and perhaps a dozen pilgrims. Clear pale shafts of mid-morning light fell in streaks through the long, round-arched windows onto the red-tiled floor.

She was determined to make sense of the jumble. She could hardly believe that the attack on Antony was a random occurrence by a passing madman. There must be something here they weren't supposed to find. With Antony unconscious it was up to her. She had a job to do. A crime to solve. Perhaps, even a life to save. Maybe her own.

An echoing foot tread made her spin around. But she saw only apparently casual visitors to the shrine. Still, she must be careful. It would make little difference what her discernment process taught her if she became a victim. Keeping her ears sharply open and with frequent glances over her shoulder, she began walking slowly around the church, noting the name of each side chapel. Antony had said they represented the various events in Christ's earthly life: the Annunciation, the Nativity, the Presentation in the Temple... she went on around... the Death on the Cross, the Resurrection, the Ascension. The walking became a prayer: prayer that Antony would be all right, prayer that they would find the solution to their investigation, prayer that she would know the right way for her life. She stopped and examined each chapel that wasn't in use.

Candles, crucifixes, paintings, vessels, and— yes, icons—she examined them all. Wherever possible she checked the back of each icon, even though none of them looked to her as if it were old enough to have been brought from the Holy Land by Margery Kempe. Was it all extravagant conjecture?

But if they were completely off-base, why would anyone have bothered attacking Antony? She paused and looked around her, then walked swiftly to the Holy House. She stood before the altar. There were so many legends of icons traveling. Were there any of icons speaking? If there was anything to be found in this shrine, the icon would have to speak to her. She stood silent. Listening. Only the murmur from the mass in the side chapel came to her: "The body of Christ."

She turned to go. And there it was. A tiny icon just inside the door. A flickering candle in a blue glass pointing to it like a finger. There was no explanatory plaque beside it, but the subject was clear: The Adoration of the Magi. Three kings knelt at the feet of the Virgin, offering gifts to her holy child. But what made Felicity catch her breath was the fact that Mary was seated, holding the Christ Child on her lap. So similar to the statue that had become the symbol of Walsingham.

Did Margery Kempe bring this icon back from her pilgrimage to the Holy Land? If so, it must have been the source of the image Father Jonathan had shown Felicity a few minutes ago. Surely the Administrator would have been aware of that connection. But he had seemed so vague about icons at the shrine. Could she trust him?

Felicity reached out a trembling hand to see if there was a mark, a telltale Maltese cross, on the back. Then dropped her hand in disappointment. The icon was affixed solidly to the wall. There would be no checking its back. But, untutored as she was, the icon felt old to her. As old as the fifteenth century? She shook her head. Robert Tennant could have told her at a glance. Had he died for that knowledge?

Was he killed because of their visit to him just a few hours previously? And Antony, lying concussed in a doctor's surgery, was it her fault for not mentioning the lurking figure she more sensed than saw yesterday? If only she hadn't dismissed her own perception. Was it through fear that Antony would think her too imaginative? Or that he would be too protective of her and try to send her home again? Would he have been more on his guard if she had spoken?

And why? Why would anyone do that? Did it mean they were closer to finding the stolen icon than they'd thought? Did Father Jonathan know the history of the icon in the Holy House? Would he kill to protect some secret it held? Were they nearer to the truth than they realized? But what good would finding the icon be if Antony weren't there to greet the Patriarch? What if Antony weren't there at all?

Her musings had taken her out of the church and across a

corner of the grounds toward the main gate. And now it began
to rain. Mostly to get out of the rain she ducked into the shrine
shop. The icons on their display shelf called to her straight away.
If this mystery had taught her no other thing, it had certainly
awakened her to the beauty and power of iconography. These
compelling images with their knowing eyes looked straight
into her heart. No wonder Sir Robert had loved them so
passionately. As she surveyed the modern offerings before her,
she confirmed her sense of seeing the difference between one
of modern production and one of antiquity. Plainly none of
those before her were of great monetary value. Even the one on
the top shelf priced at more than £100 didn't approach those
worth thousands she had seen in the Tennant Gallery. Clearly,
the one she had noted in the Holy House was genuine.

She browsed through the offerings in a small basket and
selected a two inch by three inch rectangle, a copy of the icon
in the Holy House. She paid the small price and tucked her
tiny treasure in her bag with a murmured prayer for Antony.

Now that she had located the Walsingham icon, Felicity
felt she had done all she could to keep Antony's investigation on
track, and her mind allowed her heart to dictate the direction
of her steps. So she began to walk swiftly back toward the
College. Surely Antony would be there by now—she had been
gone for ages. And if Father Jonathan was hiding something,
she couldn't leave Antony alone with him. It was all she could
do to keep from breaking into a headlong dash across the wet
grass. She wasn't aware of the quiet in the college grounds until
it was shattered by her near-frantic pounding on the door.

"Have you heard from him yet? Is he back?" she demanded
of Father Jonathan.

"Sister Anne rang a few minutes ago. Father Antony has
regained consciousness, but has a splitting headache. They
are also keeping an eye on him to be sure he doesn't develop
complications from the hypothermia."

Complications? No, she wouldn't think of that. "Can he have visitors? When will he be back?"

"Perhaps tomorrow. He needs complete rest for now. Is there anything we can do to make you more comfortable in the meantime?"

She looked at Father Jonathan's kind, ever-smiling face. Was his concern genuine? "Um, no. Thank you. Well, actually, I'd like to do a bit of research on the Internet. Do you know if Mother Francis Clare has a computer I could borrow?"

"I'm sure she does. But you're most welcome to use mine. I have a group of pilgrims coming in so I'll be out of my office the rest of the afternoon." He indicated a door to the left of the lounge where they stood. "And do feel free to get a bite of lunch in the pilgrim's refectory—upstairs in the new building just at the top of the slope."

Thanking him, she ducked into the office and closed the door behind her. She sat at the administrator's battered mahogany desk, the blank computer screen before her, but she made no movement to get started. Her fingers toyed absently with the curling edge of the green leather desk top that age had begun to peel away. Did she really want this? Could she truly find within herself the courage to do as Antony had, and steadily pursue the search for the missing icon, deeper and deeper into danger? Peril seemed to lurk around every corner. No place felt safe any more. Could she really do this by herself, while he lay helplessly in his hospital bed? Did she care for him enough? Would it not be simpler to slip back into her taster tour of convent life, enjoying the hospitality of community guesthouses in the English countryside?

No. She must do this for Antony now that concussion and hypothermia had incapacitated him—perhaps putting him out of the picture for some time. What if Antony was still in hospital when the Patriarch arrived? Father Anselm had entrusted Antony with preventing disaster. And Antony had turned to her for help.

Still unsure about the answers to her deeper questions, she knew she had to try. So what did she know, or at least suspect, and what did she need to know in order to make any sort of informed deductions? She unzipped her backpack and pulled out the notebook Antony had handed her in the library of St Margaret's rectory. She opened it and shook her head. The pages were mostly empty. Another example of her lack of diligence.

She reviewed the few notes she had scribbled while translating the manuscript: Margery Kempe, three icons brought from her pilgrimage where she stayed with the Knights Hospitaller—St Margaret's: (now at Rempstone?) attempted theft; Julian's shrine: stolen; Walsingham: (in Holy House?) theft intended by Antony's attacker?

She sighed. Conjecture again. Besides, all that was background. The liturgical clock was ticking. This Sunday was Palm Sunday. The Great Three Days, the Triduum, began Thursday. The Patriarch of All Russia would arrive a week from today to pray before his treasured icon in an unprecedented ecumenical effort. Which would be an unprecedented ecumenical debacle if they—if she—failed.

So what was the Russian connection in all this? Could there be someone trying to sabotage the ecumenical effort? Or someone wanting to steal the treasure to take it back to Russia? Surely if that were the case they would wait until the loan had been made.

She turned her attention to the computer, waiting patiently as she brought the blank screen to life. She had a reference to Peter the Great in her notes. Might as well start with a search on him. She scrolled through several articles. At last she sat back.

No doubt about it, there was a link between Peter the Great and the Knights of Malta. In 1698, Peter sent a delegation to Malta to observe the training of the knights and their fleet. Peter was big on fleets; he established the Russian navy.

Peter's envoy also investigated the possibility of future joint ventures between the knights and Russians. From then on, Russian volunteers served on the order's ships, and members of the Russian gentry became Knights of the Order. OK, that could explain a Maltese cross on CT's icon if it was, indeed, brought to England by Peter the Great. If it had the mark.

So Margery's icons had once belonged to the knights, and Peter's icons had once belonged to the knights. Maybe. And now they wanted them back? But why?

For all the time she had spent investigating Knights of Malta sites, her notebook was woefully devoid of notes. She turned again to the computer. St John Ambulance was the first site she looked at. It was hard to imagine a more respectable organization. It had been chartered by Queen Victoria and had a history of doing lifesaving work. Queen Elizabeth II served as Sovereign Head of the Order.

She tried another website, this one purporting to prove Nazi connections to the Knights of Malta. The site had a ranting tone that made her think it was put together by people with too much time on their hands. They could have been better occupied writing novels, she thought.

She selected another site: mostly statistics—a large number of the knights and dames from the aristocracy... Oh, this was interesting: "Worldwide about fifty have taken full religious vows. Others, the Knights of Obedience, have taken lesser vows of obedience to their religious superior. There are also many clergy who serve as Chaplains of the Order..." Were any of them connected with Kirkthorpe or any of the religious orders she had visited?

Kirkthorpe and all the houses she had visited were Anglican. St John Ambulance was ecumenical. But what if these other orders were fanatically Roman? That might be a motive for trying to get their icons back. But surely not for theft and murder?

She added "Anglican" to her search terms and learned that the Grand Master could confer the order *Pro Merito Melitensi* on individuals who rendered outstanding service to the Order of Malta or its works. Unlike knights and dames of the order itself, those in the Order of Merit did not need to profess the Catholic Faith. Right. That widened the field considerably. That was all she needed—more possibilities for suspects.

Hmm... restoring their ancient icons could be construed as outstanding service for someone wanting prestige in this ancient order...

Just before she clicked the close button she saw, almost as a footnote at the bottom of the page, a reference to self-styled orders; unofficial groups that claimed validity. Interesting. A self-styled group could be anxious to gain official recognition.

She turned off the computer just as Father Jonathan returned. He flipped on the light in the office. "Thoughtful of you to be careful about our budget, but no need to work in the dark."

"Oh." She had been so lost in thought she almost jumped off the chair.

"You look pale. Have you had anything to eat today?"

Felicity thought. "Well, there was the tea and toast you gave me this morning."

"I thought as much. To the refectory with you!"

Rather than the noisy pilgrim dining hall, though, she chose to return to St Margaret's, especially since she hoped Sister Anne would have returned and she could question her about Antony.

Mother Francis Clare introduced her to the tall, angular nun with strong features. "Oh, he's gone, my dear."

"Gone?"

"Yes, left just before I went off duty. His brother came for him."

"He doesn't have a brother. Just a sister."

"Perhaps his brother-in-law, then?"

"She isn't married." Felicity's voice rose an octave with each statement.

"I suppose a spiritual brother, then. From the Community. I didn't see him."

Felicity so much wanted to believe this. It must be the explanation. Antony would be back at Kirkthorpe now being cared for by the Brother Infirmarian. Of course he was. Everything was fine.

It had to be.

Chapter 31

Saturday in Passiontide

Felicity awoke with a sense of desperation. She had been dreaming she was trapped in a cage. She had to get out. She had to run. Her heart was in her throat pounding like a jackhammer. She had to get out of Walsingham. Had to get back to Kirkthorpe and see Antony there. Safe. With her own eyes. His image and presence filled her mind and the huge hollow in her chest where her heart should be. Until this moment, she had never been forced to admit to herself how much she cared for him. The realization floored her. She had no idea she could feel so desperate; could care so much.

What was she doing here still? This prison was real. But how did she get away? There was no train service, no place to rent a car. Would the sisters be willing to lend her their car for the day? Was there a bus service? She didn't even know how to find out, and public transport was sure to be slow and clunky. She threw her few belongings into her backpack and headed for the refectory where the nuns would be breaking their fast. Surely Mother Francis Clare could help her. With her present rush of anxiety-fueled adrenaline, Felicity felt as if she could run the distance.

In her blind rush she all but cannoned into Sister Johanna just coming from the refectory. "Felicity, my dear, what is the matter? You look frantic," the nun whispered, as the Greater Silence wouldn't end until after morning mass.

"I have to get back to Kirkthorpe. How can I get out of here?" Felicity's voice rose to full pitch as she spoke. Veiled heads turned in her direction from the refectory.

"Well, then, you're in luck. I'll be driving back to Norwich in a few minutes. You can easily catch a train from there." Sister Johanna's pitch stayed at its soft, serene level. "Have your breakfast and meet me in the car park in twenty minutes." She put her hand briefly on Felicity's shoulder as if in a gesture of benediction.

Felicity managed to swallow a piece of dry toast and gulp two cups of strong, hot tea. The porridge congealed in its bowl in front of her as her mind raced. Sister Johanna had been here two nights ago when Antony was attacked. Sister Johanna had been in London when someone pushed her down the escalator. Sister Johanna had reacted sharply—even guiltily?—when she had mentioned Neville to her. She could still hear Barnaby's sharp yip and the clatter of the teacup as it crashed to the floor. Then she realized she was hearing her own crockery as she set her cup down far too hard.

And St Julian's icon had been the first to be stolen. Who would have had better opportunity? Johanna hadn't been at Kirkthorpe as far as Felicity knew, but she could have an accomplice. If there was any truth to this, could there be a more stupid thing to do than to get in a car with the woman? But then, what better opportunity would she have to question her?

At least she could leave a trail in case she didn't arrive. She let Mother Francis Clare know her arrangements. And rang Antony to let him know she was coming. She had to borrow Johanna's mobile because, even with it switched off, the battery on hers had finally run down. There was no answer, so she left a message: "Antony, I'm coming. I'm with Sister Johanna. I have so much to tell you." She wanted to go on and on, tell him what she'd learned, ask her questions, tell him how worried she was about him. But she would see him soon. It would be better in person. She handed the phone back.

Sister Johanna's little silver Vauxhall slid along between the flat, green spring fields broken by rows of trees sheltering farmhouses with red tile roofs, and through little villages, each one with its own square-towered stone church. And over all, a wide, pale blue canopy with fluffy white clouds. Sister Johanna's hands were steady on the wheel, her face a smooth, calm profile. She seemed so young, not all that much older than Felicity herself—and far more serene. Could this possibly be the face of a thief and assailant? Perhaps a murderer?

Felicity shivered. Well, she had to know. She could think of no subtle approach. And when had she ever done anything but run straight at a problem? "Sister Johanna, that first day at All Hallows you dropped your teacup when I mentioned Neville's name. Why?"

The nun was silent for several moments. Felicity studied her. She didn't look angry or frightened. She looked hurt.

At last she sighed. "So silly of me, I know. All my reading, all the spiritual exercises I do—commitment, obedience, indifference, even. I never did get over him. Odd, how the might-have-beens are the hardest things to commit. I pray he wasn't murdered for my sin. Not that I really think God works that way, but still..."

Felicity boggled. "Sister Johanna, are you saying that you and Neville—but that's impossible. You're a nun. He was going to be a monk. I mean, I always thought he was gay, for Pete's sake!"

For the first time Johanna took her eyes off the road. "What makes you say that?"

"Well, he belonged to a gay rights organization, his family thought..."

Johanna smiled. A very sad smile. "There is a difference between a call to celibacy and homosexual orientation. But no one understands that in today's world. He was probably perfectly happy to let his family think that. They argued with him less about his call to the religious life that way."

Felicity wanted to know more. But how could she phrase her questions? Even she balked at asking outright if they had been lovers. Then her mind took another turn. Had they had a child? Was it hidden somewhere? How long ago would that have been? Neville was an older student. He had achieved success in his art career. Mid to late thirties, perhaps? It was impossible to judge a nun's age. If it had been a teen romance that child could be a teen himself now. The lurking hoodie? "You're probably wondering the extent of our relationship."

"You don't have to—"

Johanna smiled again. "I know. But after all this time, it feels so good to talk about it. We met at uni in Manchester. I was studying sociology, he art, of course. Neither of us had—or at least was aware of—any religious vocation. But there must have been some unrecognized stirring of a call because we were both involved in the chaplaincy program, and even when we were dating—talking of marriage, even—we didn't jump into bed together.

"Then I began to feel consciously drawn to a religious life. Started going on retreats, pilgrimages, weekends working with the poor. I couldn't get enough of it. Neville realized it before I did. He was very understanding, even though his call came years later. He even had the ring he wanted to give me—ornate antique gold engraved with a cross."

"A Maltese cross? With a nine-pointed star behind it?"

"Yes, how did you know? He wanted me to take the ring anyway. To remember him by." She smiled. "As if I would ever forget."

"But you refused."

"Of course, what would a nun do with a piece of jewelry like that? Besides, I think it was an heirloom. I felt it should stay in the family."

"It did. He wore it. Always."

Johanna was quiet for a long time. Then she said softly, "He had such slender fingers."

The spire of Norwich Cathedral was visible before they spoke again. "Do you mind terribly if we stop by All Hallows before I take you to the train station? I want to be sure Barnaby has been seen to."

"Oh, no. That's fine." Felicity was only too happy to be accommodating—any penance for the terrible things she had thought of Sister Johanna.

When they pulled into St Julian's Alley, however, it wasn't Barnaby that greeted them.

"Mother!" Felicity tried to keep the groan out of her voice.

"Darling!" Cynthia pulled Felicity's door open and might have lifted her from the car if her seat belt hadn't been fastened. "Aren't you surprised!"

"Flabbergasted." She grabbed at her backpack in the back seat.

"You didn't think your mother was such a good detective, did you? Of course, if you would keep your cell phone switched on I wouldn't have had to bother that convent place where you were staying in Walsingham, but they told me you had left with Sister Johanna. Hello, Johanna. Lovely to see you again You see, dear, Cyril had to go back to London on some boring business, so I rented a car. We can explore on our own. Just the two of us. Won't that be lovely?" As she spoke she was propelling Felicity toward a car parked across the street from the visitors' centre.

Felicity wrenched herself from her mother's grip long enough to turn back. "Sister Johanna, thank you." She wanted to say so much more, but the chance had been snatched away.

"Do get in, dear." Cynthia flicked the unlock button on her keys. "I simply can't wait to tell you all about Cy and the lovely time I had. Darling, you wouldn't believe that manor house of his. It's vast and ancient and glorious in a crumbly sort of way.

Talk about atmosphere. If you could have seen it when the mist rose off the Broads the other night—just like something out of *The Hound of the Baskervilles.*"

Felicity shivered at the alarming reference, although she was quite certain that story was set in entirely another part of the country. While Felicity sorted through the barrage of words, Cynthia started the car and headed for the ring road. At last Felicity said, "Er—Cy?"

Cynthia laughed. "Oh, yes. Cyril asked me to call him that. Oh, the charm of that man. Just pure charm and class. I've never met anyone like him, I can tell you. Darling, where shall we go first? Would you like to explore a castle or a cathedral? I don't suppose I can lure you on a shopping spree." She briefly took her eyes off the road to assess her daughter's attire. "Although I must say you could certainly use it."

Felicity ignored the slur on her wardrobe. "Mother, I have to get back to CT."

Cynthia sighed and tapped the steering wheel with a perfectly manicured nail. "That dull place?"

"Yes, Mother, that dull place that I call home." *And, Lord, let it be dull.* She had had enough excitement to last a lifetime.

"Well, all right. If you insist." Another sigh. "What a mother endures for her children."

"Mother, I've got to see Antony." Perhaps it was the urgency in Felicity's voice that made Cynthia focus but the car suddenly picked up speed as they left Norwich and headed up the A47. Felicity realized that her mother was putting all her effort into doing as she had asked. Simply because she *had* asked. Cynthia didn't know what had happened or why this was of supreme importance to Felicity. She just knew that it was. And Felicity realized that, whatever their past history may have been, at least this was someone she could trust, someone who would never intentionally try to harm her.

Felicity had been angry because she felt her mother had

shut her out of her life, but now she saw that she had done the same thing. The least she could do was attempt a small breech in that wall. "Mother, someone attacked Antony. He was in hospital and I haven't seen him since he got out. I've been investigating on my own, but all I have are more questions.

"And I've been thinking about Antony..." her explanation petered out.

"And?"

"And all I have are more questions."

"Tell me about them"

And Felicity did. In a lengthy, disjointed, rambling way she told her mother all she and Antony had done together working to solve Father Dominic's murder and about how getting to know Antony had changed her perceptions of life so completely she thought she wanted to be a nun.

Cynthia listened and nodded and drove. All the way across Norfolk, Lincolnshire and Nottinghamshire, the look of grim determination growing on her face with every mile.

"I'll get you there," she said. When they hit the M1 just beyond Nottingham Cynthia put her foot down and they roared up the motorway.

"Maybe not quite so fast, Mother." It felt like the first time Felicity had smiled in days.

More than an hour later Felicity felt herself leaning forward in her seat urging them ahead as they drove through the tiny village of Kirkthorpe on its green Yorkshire hillside toward the Community set in the woods on the top of the hill. Not really such a bad place to call home, Felicity thought as the storybook quaint houses with their tiny gardens passed her window.

"You'll have to direct me to your apartment, darling. You weren't here to show me when I arrived before."

To be fair, Cynthia made it a plain statement, not an accusation, although both of them knew Felicity had been running away from her. Was that only two weeks ago? It felt more like two years. "No, Mother. Take me to the Community. I must see Antony. I imagine he'll still be in the infirmary. Turn right at the next corner, then straight up the hill. You'll see it on your left. Second gate should be open, that takes you to the parking lot."

She had once likened being in the alternate universe of the Community to Hogwarts. Now she decided it was Brigadoon. With the difference that, thankfully, one *could* come back.

Cynthia hadn't quite come to a full stop before Felicity was out of the car and running up the path toward the monastery. Evening prayers should just be ending. Father Superior could take her to Antony.

Her timing was good. She met Father Anselm in the hallway just coming out of the church. "Father Antony? No, I haven't seen him for days. I had so hoped he would have recovered our icon by now. It's most distressing."

"You mean he's not here? But one of the brothers collected him at the surgery in Fakenham. Sister Anne said so."

"Surgery in Fakenham? Was he visiting the sick?"

"No, no. He *was* the sick…" Her knees went weak and she backed against the wall to steady herself as realization flooded her. They had been wrong in their conclusion that "brother" meant a CT brother. Antony, in a dazed, possibly drugged state, must have been checked out of the clinic by someone posing as his brother and taken—she came to an abrupt halt.

What had they done with him? His attacker must have left him for dead outside St Margaret's Priory. Then when he learned Antony was concussed but not dead he came back to finish the job. *Oh, God! No!* That could mean that Antony was—

She lurched forward, caught the startled Father Anselm by the shoulders and almost yelled at him. "Call the police!"

Chapter 32

Palm Sunday

"We'll find him." Inspector Nosterfield's words were the first Felicity heard in her head when she awoke after a few hours of restless sleep. At least the stocky policeman had seemed less like a bull in a china shop than he had on their previous encounter. He had asked sensible questions and made careful notes: Where she had last seen Antony, who was there, what Father Jonathan had said to her... She had made a great effort to be precise and to appear calm while all the time wanting to demand, *Don't you realize, this is Antony! You have to find him. Fast. He's in danger. Maybe...* No. She wouldn't even think that. She made certain the police had all the names she could think of, but it was the names she couldn't give that made her frantic. A shadow ducking behind a cross on a hillside was hardly evidence.

"Right then. You stay here, Miss Howard. Relax." The subtext was clear: *Don't go barging off halfway across the country and get yourself into trouble like you did last time.*

Yes, but last time we did find Father Dominic's murderers, she wanted to respond to the broad, implacable face, but wisely bit her tongue.

Relaxing wasn't an option, but worship was a requirement. She splashed some water on her face and dressed quickly, buttoning her regulation long black cassock over a sweater and pleated skirt. She was trying to decide whether or not to waken Cynthia, who had spent the night on the sofa in her small sitting room, when her mother poked her head into Felicity's room.

"Ready, darling?"

And there she was, complaining about being awakened by the bells, looking crisp and fresh and liturgically correct in a classic red suit with gold jewelry.

"Um, Mother, the procession starts on the lawn. Are you sure you want to wear those shoes?"

Cynthia looked in surprise at her spiky black patent leather heels with their pointed toes. "But they're what I always wear."

Wordlessly, Felicity led the way up the hill and into the Community grounds to where the faithful were gathering on the wide expanse of green lawn behind the college. Felicity and Cynthia joined monks, ordinands and guests in forming a wide circle in front of the borders just beginning to burst into full springtime glory. The cantors, all fellow students, stood on one side of the lawn wearing brilliant red copes, supplied from the Community's vestment chests, over white albs. The clergy beside them were likewise splendid, vested in red. The breeze billowed the vestments, making the morning sun glint off the gold embroidery. Felicity felt a lump in her throat that threatened to choke her. Antony would love this. He should be here.

She was saved from completely breaking down by a server thrusting a tall palm branch into her hand, calling her back to the present. Father Anselm circled the lawn twice, blessing the palms first with holy water, then with incense. "Blessed is the King who comes in the name of the Lord," he proclaimed.

Felicity forced herself to respond with the others, "Peace in heaven and glory in the highest." But she couldn't force herself to focus on the prayers and readings that followed. Everything in her was insisting that she shouldn't be here. She should be in swampy, soggy east Norfolk where Antony disappeared. She should go to that clinic and tear it up one side and down the other until she found someone who could tell her what had happened to Antony. What did anyone know about that po-faced Sister Anne? She could be working for the icon thief.

She could *be* the icon thief. Wearing a habit didn't make one immune from temptation. Maybe she was collecting them for her convent. Maybe...

"Blessed is he who comes in the name of the Lord." Felicity jerked back to the present from her wild surmises.

"Hosanna in the highest." Cynthia, beside her, almost shouted the response, waving her palm as if she thought herself on the street in Jerusalem 2,000 years ago.

Suddenly Felicity shivered, recalling how quickly the shouts of *Hosanna!* that day had turned to *Crucify him!* One was never safe. And she was an idiot to think she was safe here. While she had been lost in overheated conjecture, someone could be stalking her right here in this bright congregation. She looked around the circle, tried to observe each face, but then the cantors began singing "All Glory, Laud and Honor" and the procession started moving, making their way up the green, daffodil-strewn hill with the breeze blowing palm branches and vestments, and birdsong joining their singing.

The procession paused at the church door and the cantors began a Latin hymn which echoed as they processed around the inside of the vast stone church following the cross. On the last circuit of the sanctuary, Felicity slipped into a pew near the back. When Cynthia gave her an impulsive hug, she was so shocked she almost dropped her palm. "Oh, doesn't it just give you shivers? It's so medieval. Just as if we'd stepped backward several hundred years."

Felicity wasn't sure which was more surprising—that her mother hugged her or that Cynthia actually liked this ancient rite.

Felicity was doing her best to focus on *The Passion According to St Matthew* which was being sung by the cantors. Maurice, Neville's plump, redheaded friend was singing the part of Chronista, the narrator. He had a surprisingly strong, reliable voice, and seeing him again for the first time since he had walked away from her on a spring-fresh day talking to Neville brought back to her the gaping sense of loss left by her friend's death—the talent, the kindness, the dedication… she was searching her pockets for a handkerchief when a movement to her left caught her eye. She just glimpsed a cassock-clad figure slipping into the sacristy. Something about the way he moved, the way he carried his head jutted forward, set off alarm bells in her mind. Besides, why would anyone, even the sacristan, be going in there now in the middle of The Passion?

"Stay here," she hissed at Cynthia, and thrust her palm and service folder into her mother's hands.

The door to the sacristy was in the far left corner behind the Resurrection Chapel, still shadowy even on a Sunday morning. Behind her the very stones seemed to hold their breath as Pilate's solo voice called out: *What shall I do then with Jesus which is called Christ?*

And then the angry, thunderous reply, shaking the arches: *Let him be crucified!*

She grasped the cold brass handle of the door and shoved. The creak of the opening door was muffled by the frenzied cry of the worshippers behind her enacting the Gospel story. Felicity looked around the deeply shadowed space. Only one window gave light to this north-facing room—a tall, gothic window of leaded diamond lights. The morning sun dazzled the beveled panes, but did little to penetrate the gloom.

It took the dark figure peering into the silver cupboard a moment to realize he was not alone. And in that moment Felicity recognized him.

She had suspected, but even so the reality was a surprise. All the shadows that had been chasing her for the past two weeks took flesh and stood before her. He had shaved and wasn't wearing glasses but there was no doubt. The pale young man who had attempted to purloin papers from The Knights of Malta museum was now attempting to steal something else.

She let the door behind her close with a slam that must have startled the worshippers and strode forward, coming to a halt alongside a heavy oaken vestment chest. "So it's you again. You've been following me for days, haven't you? What have you done with Antony? If you've hurt him, I'll—"

The figure, no longer shadowy, but made powerful by anger and evil intent, lunged toward her, wielding a hefty candlestick, growling like an animal.

Felicity was so stunned at his alteration she stood rooted for the space of a heartbeat; a split second that could have been her last if the heavy weapon crashing toward her had connected with her skull. At the last instant she flexed her knees, shifted her weight to her toes as years of ballet training had taught her and performed a perfect *jeté en tournant*, throwing one leg to the side and executing a half turn away from her attacker.

Her assailant, already in forward momentum, struck his head on the corner of the vestment chest and fell to the floor.

Momentarily too shocked to move, Felicity remained fixed to the spot exactly where she had landed, the swell of the choral music invading every corner of her consciousness. *And they stripped him and put on him a scarlet robe … and mocked him, saying Hail, King of the Jews! And they spit upon him … and smote him* … She might have stood there, not moving, hardly breathing, until the end of The Passion, had she not been overcome by the shattering thought that she might have killed her attacker.

She knelt on the stone floor, recoiling from touching the still form before her, yet knowing she must. The arm that had been wielding the candlestick was flung out. She pushed up his cassock sleeve, wondering which student he had stolen his disguise from, and felt for a pulse in his wrist. It took her a moment to locate it and in her panic she almost cried out, but then she felt it. Not strong, but steady.

She had just released his hand when she looked closer at the ring he wore. A simple gold band, almost as plain as a wedding ring. But then she looked closer at the engraving. The same pattern of star and leaves scrolling from a Maltese cross.

Felicity was wondering what she should do next when she felt a strange vibration in her knee where she was kneeling on the edge of her assailant's cassock. The vibrations produced a faint, muffled grinding sound on the stone, and it took Felicity several moments to realize it was a mobile set on vibrate.

She reached through the slit in the cassock into his jacket pocket and drew out the still-dancing instrument. When she looked at the caller ID on the screen she was so surprised she almost dropped it. Julian Centre? But it couldn't be. She had been so certain Sister Johanna had been telling the truth.

My God, my God, why have you forsaken me? The strong tenor voice of the cantor singing Christos came to her. The Passion was drawing to a close. Then she could go for help. But first, perhaps she could find out something about her attacker. Would his name be on his mobile? She began clicking buttons.

At first she thought the list that appeared on the screen was recent calls he had received. Then she realized they were photos. She clicked and began looking closely at the miniature pictures: Lovely paintings, crumbling a bit, but such graceful images, The apostles, perhaps, and the archangel Michael? Were these panels from a reredos or rood screen? Ancient, but well restored, she would guess. And a detail of a glowing white rose on an orange-red background. Then an altar frontal and close-ups of the embroidered design: a heron, a frog and a dragonfly among marsh grasses seemed like strange adornments for an altar cloth.

She was just ready to flip the display closed when she saw that the next set of pictures were of quite a different subject: Dark squares, taken where almost no light penetrated, and yet she was certain that she could make out a bound and gagged form in the corner, propped against a rough wooden wall. She scrolled further, peered more intently. Yes, that was Antony. She more felt it than saw him, but she was certain.

Antony, bound, gagged, slumped in a dark corner. His eyes closed. Was he alive? Surely, he must be. There was no point in binding and gagging a corpse, was there? At least Antony had been alive when this picture was taken. To what purpose? Sheer sadism? To prove to a boss that the deed had been done— orders followed? Or was Antony being held for ransom? If so, why hadn't they received a demand yet? But overriding all, the question *where*? Where was Antony at this moment?

The form beside her groaned. She picked up the candlestick, ready to hit him again if necessary, but at that moment the sacristy door creaked open and Father Anselm and Maurice came in. The monk paused to close the door carefully, the wild tumult of music having now given way to the serene rise and fall of quiet voices as the service continued in the church, but Maurice began babbling about being desperate to get to her as he had seen both her and "Ricky" enter the sacristy.

"I knew that Ricky was up to no good." He observed the prone figure stirring at his feet. "I never did like him. Never trusted him. Neville, of course, always thought the best of everyone, wouldn't listen to a word against anyone, but I told him…"

"Wait a minute! *Ricky?* You *know* him?"

Maurice shrugged. "Cousin of Neville's."

Felicity's mind boggled. Simon's brother? Or another branch of the family?

The door creaked open again to a clatter of heels as Cynthia rushed in and grabbed Felicity. "Oh, darling, what's happened? I was so worried when you didn't come back. Then I saw this young man—" She turned to Maurice. "You have a lovely voice, by the way—it was a stunning performance."

"It's not a performance, Mother. It's an act of worship." Felicity unwound her mother's arms from around her.

"Call the police," she said to the Father Superior. "He was

trying to steal your silver." No point in going into it all now, just get him into custody, she thought. She could explain everything when she had found Antony.

"I think an ambulance might be more to the point just at the moment," Father Anselm said.

"Here, Father, use my cell phone." Cynthia held out her Blackberry.

That recalled the photos on Ricky's phone to Felicity's mind. "Maurice, do you recognize these paintings? Do you know where they are?" She held the screen out. "It's important."

"These are apostles. You can tell by their symbols, Peter with his key—"

"Yes, yes." She didn't want to take time for all twelve.

"And this is St George. Oh, no, archangel Michael—he has wings."

"Maurice!" He had no sense of the urgency she felt. "Do you have any idea where those were taken?"

He moved on to the altar frontal with its marsh creatures and then the white rose on its coral background. "Oh, of course. That's the 'Ranworth Rose.' St Helen's Ranworth." He snapped the mobile shut and handed it back to Felicity. "Great shots. When were you there?"

"I wasn't. But I'm going." She paused in her frenzy to look Maurice in the eye. She didn't want him to miss her instruction. "When the police get here, tell them Antony's been kidnapped. He's being held at St Helen's Ranworth. Got that?"

"Sure, but why? I don't get it. What's—"

"Just do it." Felicity slipped the phone in her pocket and grabbed her mother's arm to pull her toward the door. "You better tie him up. He may come around before the authorities get here, and he's dangerous." She noted with satisfaction that Maurice was already pulling a rope cincture off a server's alb.

Still pulling Cynthia, Felicity dashed back into the church and out the side door and headed toward the parking lot. They were halfway across the wide front lawn when an ambulance pulled in at the gate.

"Mother, take your shoes off so you can run. Do you have your car keys with you?"

Cynthia obediently pulled off her high heels and held out her purse containing her keys. "Where are we going?"

"We have to get back to Norfolk. Just pray we aren't too late."

Chapter 33

Monday of Holy Week

"**D**o you think this Ricky person killed Neville?"

"There has to be some connection, but I see him as more of a sneak thief than a murderer." Felicity had to believe that. She couldn't give in to the fear that Antony had fallen into the hands of whoever killed Neville. The idea that even now Antony could be in a shallow grave in some isolated place in the Broads, hidden until the rains washed... "Mother, can't you drive faster?"

They hadn't arrived in Norwich until after midnight last night. First there had been the traffic tie-up on the M1 due to an overturned lorry, then on a deserted strip of the A17 below Holbeach Marsh they had run out of gas and had to walk to the nearest village. Of course the gas station was closed and it had seemed like hours to Felicity before their banging on the door at a nearby cottage roused the surly attendant. At last he had fallen prey to Cynthia's gushing charms—or to the enormous tip she offered him—and had given them a lift back to their car along with a can of gas. Just remembering it now in the early morning sunshine made beads of sweat stand out on Felicity's forehead.

And her desperation had only increased during the brief hours they had spent at All Hallows awaiting the sunrise. All of Felicity's instincts had been to carry straight on in the dark, but she knew they would be lucky to find their way even in daylight. Cynthia had kicked off her shoes and curled up in the lovely soft bed Sister Johanna, roused from her sleep, but smiling, offered them. But Felicity sat by the window, watching for the first rays of sunlight and praying. And keeping guard in case she had been wrong to trust Sister Johanna.

And now, in the grey dawn, she was struggling with the map Johanna had given them. "It's the B1140, Mom. And please hurry."

"I'm doing my best, darling. But I'm sure that cute Maurice—don't you just adore all those masses of red curls?— has got on to the police and they've dealt with the whole thing. Antony is probably back in Kirkthorpe right now, wondering where you are. Shall I give him a call?" Cynthia whipped out her Blackberry.

But the effort was useless. "His phone's switched off. Maybe he's at prayers or something. Or more likely helping the police."

"I hope you're right, Mother." Surely she was.

Then new doubts assailed Felicity. Why hadn't she left Rick's phone with Maurice to give to the police? But Nosterfield would have rung the Norwich Constabulary. They would have it all well in hand. They must. Still, her urgency wouldn't let up. "Is this really as fast as you can go?"

"Where do I turn?" Cynthia's voice had picked up Felicity's ring of anxiety.

"I don't know, Mother. She squinted at the map in her lap. It's one of these little white lines. They don't have numbers." Oh, why hadn't she paid more attention when Antony was driving? There, that must be it. "Here. Turn here!"

Cynthia wrenched the wheel and the car whipped around the corner onto an even narrower lane.

The looming hedgerows closed in on them, adding to Felicity's disorientation by blocking all vistas. They were traveling through a tunnel of branches roofed with a menacingly brooding sky. And Felicity had no idea where the tunnel was leading them.

Mud splashed on their windshield as if the very land were

mocking them.

Cynthia tore along the winding lane. "How much further, darling?"

Felicity bit her lip. If only she knew. Then she saw a thatched roof peeking up over the hedge. The first sign of life in miles. And she remembered seeing it before. "Turn here. Left. Turn left!" Felicity almost shouted.

They zoomed around the corner. And came face to face with a horse rearing in terrified panic. It cost them precious time as the rider struggled to calm his mount and move him to the side of the road.

The equestrian yelled every name under the sun at them as they accelerated away but Felicity's focus was all on what they would find ahead. *Please, Lord, let Detective Inspector Marsham be there.* In her mind she conjured up a picture of two white squad cars parked on the verge beside the church, their blue lights blinking merrily, with Antony shaking hands with D. I. Marsham while Sergeant Caister closed his notebook, still wearing the perplexed frown of a man who was afraid he had misspelled most of the words in his report.

Around one more corner, and Felicity saw the sight she had been yearning toward for endless, nightmare hours. St Helen's solid, square Norman stone tower with the adumbral sky almost touching it greeted them. Bits of Antony's narrative came back to her: "The Cathedral of the Broads," so isolated by flooded marshes that Cromwell's destructors couldn't get to it to smash the art. The very paintings she had seen on Ricky's mobile. Antony, newly freed by D. I. Marsham, could show it all to her now. She would listen with rapt attention to all the minute detail he wanted to lecture her about. If only...

Past a screen of shielding trees the full church sprang into view. Sitting isolated and deserted on an island of wet green, surrounded by a low stone wall, aged tombstones leaning drunkenly across the churchyard. But that was all. There were no flashing police lights. No Marsham. No Antony.

"Pull up over here." She waved toward the green verge. "Anywhere. Just stop." Felicity was halfway out the door before the car had come to a stop.

"Felicity! Shouldn't we wait for the police?"

"I'm sure they'll be along in a minute, Mother. You stay here and watch for them. Better yet, ring them. Tell them where I am. They caught that little creep Ricky, remember, so there's no danger."

She squished her way in long lopes across the sodden grass, praying that the door would be open. The iron latch was cold and stiff, but it gave under her determined twist. The heavy oak door was likewise unwieldy, but moved on the third insistent shove of her shoulder. "Antony!" she cried, as she sprang into the church. She was met only by the cold comfort of an echo.

The sanctuary felt empty. White stucco walls climbed high over her head to the dark-beamed ceiling. Anemic morning light sent a pale nimbus through the tall leaded windows, filling the room with an almost phosphorescent quality. She stood by the crumbling stone font standing prominently on its two-tiered octagonal platform, and surveyed the room. Where could he be? There were no half-hidden side chapels, no niches, no vestry or sacristy doors leading enticingly to side rooms. Antony had been held someplace dark. Unless, of course, the pictures had been taken at night when it would *all* be dark.

Her footsteps falling hollowly on the stone floor, Felicity moved forward, listening intently for any sound. She stopped before the gorgeously painted medieval rood screen. She was definitely in the right place. She recognized some of the apostles from Ricky's pictures. To her left, a barrel-shaped pulpit rose from wooden steps. A bound and gagged person could be stuffed in there. "Antony?" Her voice came out in a choked whisper as she moved forward, praying he wasn't in there. It was too quiet. Too *dead*.

She let her breath out in a rush of relief at the sight of the empty pulpit. That only left the chancel. Could Antony simply be lying trussed on the floor behind the rood screen? She stepped through the arch in the center of the painted barrier. Her scrutiny revealed more painted panels on the back of the screen, but no flesh and blood, breathing figure. Behind the folding seat of a misericord in the choir she spotted the Ranworth Rose. Surely so many clues had to mean she was in the right place. She moved up to the high altar, draped with the marsh-themed frontal Ricky had photographed. Oh, was that the ultimate clue? Had she followed the trail exactly? She plunged forward and all but jerked the fine silk cloth from the altar. Only to be met by bare stone. Solid and unyielding.

She backed away, tears blurring her vision. She recalled their search for St Cuthbert's hidden body in Durham Cathedral. Antony had managed to shove the heavy stone mensa from a side altar. And she had been struck then how like a sarcophagus it was; appropriately reminding worshippers of the entombment of the body of Christ. But at this moment Felicity was not thinking about the burial of an ancient saint or of our Lord. She was terrified that there might, indeed, be a body inside that stone coffin-like altar.

Through the rood screen she turned and ran, with choking sobs, the length of the nave. She stopped at the font, clinging for support, gasping for air. She had to pull herself together. But the pain and terror bubbled up from inside her. She had never truly faced the possibility before that Antony could be gone. Gone from her life forever: his strength, his commitment, his knowledge, his mellow voice, his humor. What would she give to see his lopsided smile just once more, watch him run his hand raggedly through his hair, or listen to one of his interminable lectures on an esoteric point of history.

The anguish burst from her in a great scream to the towering, dark rafters: "Antony!" Once she started she couldn't quit. "Antony! Antony! Antony!"

And then she stopped, her body frozen. Had she heard something? Was it merely the echo of her own voice? Perhaps the call of a marsh bird outside. But it was something. She was sure. "Antony!" This time her call was less hysterical. And again, louder. "Antony! Are you here?"

Definitely a thump. From above. Could something be on the roof? She looked around carefully. And then she saw the small, wooden door in the far corner. Of course! Why hadn't she thought of that before? St Helen's tower was its most distinguishing feature. Of course there would be stairs to the bells. "Antony, I'm coming!" *Oh, thank you, God.* A sob of relief broke from her. They weren't too late. "I'm coming!" she cried again, and wrenched the door open.

She stepped into the shadowy darkness. Yes, just the quality of obfuscation the pictures had shown. She had to suppress her desire to race up the stairs. One false step on one of those narrow, smooth stone wedges spiraling upward would be disastrous.

It seemed as if she had been toiling upward for ages when there came a brightening of the light. As she rounded the next turn of the stairs an iron grille covering a two-foot square opening in the stone walls came into view. As she panted past, one quick glance through the opening revealed a view down past the treetops to the bank of the wide, flat river. The Bure where she and Antony had sailed such a short time ago, thinking they were to be reunited with their missing friend. "I'm coming!" she shouted again as she hurried on, but it only came out as a strangled sob.

Her heart pounded in her ears and dizziness threatened to overwhelm her, but still she lunged forward, pulling herself toward the top with both hands on the railing. She was concentrating so hard on forcing her flagging body upward that she barely noticed the thickening gloom around her. Watching the steps as well as she could in the gathering darkness so as not to miss her footing, she failed to see the ceiling closing in overhead—not until she gasped up a steep step and banged her head hard enough to see stars. Had she not been holding on she would surely have plunged the depth of the tower, breaking her neck on the spiraling downward tumble.

She shook her head to clear it of the image of her own body lying crumpled and broken at the bottom of the stairs. This couldn't be the end. She hadn't found Antony, but he was here, she knew he was. A muffled thudding over her head made her look up. Then she saw the cut in the heavy wooden ceiling. Not a ceiling, actually, but the bottom of the floor above, with a trapdoor at the top of the stairs. Still holding the railing with one hand, she put her other hand flat on the coarse wood and thrust upward with all her strength. The door fell back with a crash.

She bounded forward onto the rough-planked platform. "Ant—" She looked around, peering into the dusty emptiness. Her heart sank. She had been so certain this was where the sound was coming from. She was in the chamber where the bell-ringers tolled. In front of her she saw the pulls, carefully looped up for safety, awaiting the next practice of the ringers. Imagine, climbing all the way up here to ring bells.

Felicity shivered, thankful that the ropes were undisturbed. The image preying on her mind of a corpse dangling from one of those heavy, knotted cords made her stomach churn.

One quick glance around the loft revealed she had not reached the top yet. The iron rungs of a ladder leading upward into yet more gloom beckoned coldly.

The climb took her to a deck narrower and rougher even than the one below. She surveyed the scaffolding above and below, then leaned cautiously over the railing to peer down on the great, iron bells supported on their heavy timbers. She recoiled from the edge, realizing that if crashing onto several ton of cast iron didn't kill a person, the fall to the floor hundreds of feet below certainly would. And again, there was no Antony.

But surely, the pictures on the cell phone came from here? The murky gloom lighting the corner was just what she had seen. Holding her breath, she forced herself the few steps to examine the floor more closely. Then heaved a sigh of relief. No blood spots. Perhaps the dust on the floor had been disturbed. It was hard to tell. But she was certain there was no blood.

She looked around. What next? Another ladder stood in the corner, this one with wooden rails. This one would surely take her to the top. This would lead to Antony. She listened. There were no more sounds. No more thumps calling to her, encouraging her to come to him. Was he too exhausted? Had he used his last thread of strength to summon her, and now lay unconscious?

She grasped the wooden rung and scrambled upward, no longer bothering to call out, afraid Antony could no longer hear her. Daylight shone through the cracks highlighting the door onto the roof of the tower. After so long in the gloom of the tower even the pale, overcast light she stepped into nearly blinded her. She blinked and gazed out over the parapet, allowing her eyes time to adjust.

As far as she could see stretched a liquid green, broken by silver ribbons of water, disappearing in the distant mist. It was almost a shock to see scattered farmhouses. She had felt so isolated. It was a comfort to realize there was humanity around, even though no one could hear her cry or come to her aid.

A slight noise on the far side of the exit chamber made her turn in delight. "Antony!" She flung her arms out as she whirled around, irrationally expecting him to embrace her, forgetting that he would be bound.

She froze mid-whirl. It wasn't Antony. "Simon!" Her startled rebound pushed her against the parapet. Terror clutched her as she thought of the long plunge gaping behind her. Wide-eyed she stared at Neville's cousin, his piercings and tattoos seeming suddenly sinister and malevolent.

"Surprise." He took a menacing step forward.

"You look different." What an inane thing to say. But it was true: a woolly cap covered his shaved head and a heavy, knitted jumper concealed his tattooed shoulders and sinewy muscles as the light glinted off the many rings and studs accenting his features.

"Sorry to disappoint. No hamper of fried bread and grilled mushrooms to offer you, I'm afraid. Great view from up here, though, eh?" His grin was more a leer.

"What's going on? Where's Antony?"

His laugh was mocking. "So sorry, my lovely." He advanced another threatening step. "You didn't really expect us to leave him here for you, did you? When that hopeless git Ricky got arrested it wasn't hard to guess you'd see the pictures on his mobile. We got your friend out just ahead of the erstwhile Norwich Constabulary. Quick off the mark they are, I'll give them that. Then I came back to wait for you. Knew you'd come."

Her heart sank. The police had been here already. She could look for no help from that quarter. "What have you done with Antony?"

Simon raised one pierced eyebrow and curled his be-ringed lip. "Fancy him, do you? Lucky man. Well, let's just say that he's safer than you are at the moment. But I'm sure he would be touched by your concern."

"Ricky rang you?"

"Exercised his precious right for someone to be informed of his arrest by giving them my number. He knows who his friends are."

Felicity snuck a sideways glance toward the open doorway. What were her chances of making a dash for it and getting down before Simon? Pretty slim. Less than slim, actually. "But I don't understand. Why would you attack Antony? What have we done to you?"

He leaned forward so that his leer was inches from her face. She smelled his hot breath. He'd had fish for breakfast. "Maybe it's more a matter of what I'd like to do to you."

She whirled sideways, his fingernail just grazing her cheek as she lunged for the doorway. Grasping each side of the ladder she fairly slid down, her toes barely skimming each rung. Her knees buckled as she hit the platform. She sprang up with a dancer's grace and bounded toward the ladder to the bell chamber.

Simon was so close she could almost feel his long, tensile fingers closing on her. The iron ladder was easier to slide down than the wooden one had been. She landed with a spring and turned toward the trapdoor opening. But Simon was there before her. She realized the heavy thud she had only half-heard a moment before she landed had been Simon simply swinging down the opening. Why didn't she think of gripping the edge of the opening and letting go? She was almost as tall as Simon. Too late now as she backed against the railing beside the bell chamber.

"You wouldn't really, would you? Believe me, I can make the earth move for you in a much more pleasurable way than falling down that shaft would." He gave a loud guffaw. "Simon, you're a punster," he congratulated himself. "'Shaft.' Get it?"

He lunged toward her. She sidestepped. For a split second she thought of grabbing his ankles and tipping him into the chasm. But she had a more realistic idea of her own strength than that. Instead she sprang to the center of the room, arm extended, and grabbed the bell rope. The bell swung with such force it almost pulled her off her feet. As the clanging overhead reverberated in her ears she bent her knees and sprang upwards, then down again, pulling with all her might. The clashing din shook the tower, and for a moment stunned her attacker. He even took a half step backwards as she continued pulling.

And then, as the bell turned upward with a mighty swing, Felicity, clinging to the rope, let her body go upward with it.

With both feet off the floor she swung forward and kicked out, connecting full in Simon's chest. The force wasn't great enough to knock him over, but it was sufficient to send him reeling against the wall.

Felicity let go of the rope as she landed on both feet, already in motion toward the stairs. Simon recovered quickly and was right behind her as she whirled her way down the spiral stairway, round and round, down and down. She could hear his breathing close behind her, imagined she could feel his hot breath on her neck, his hands gripping her shoulders—either pulling her to him or shoving her down the stone spiral. Either one equally abhorrent.

At last she was on the final curve. Solid floor opened before her. She leaped and lunged at the door, bursting into the brilliant whiteness of the church. She spun around to slam the door. Surely there was a lock? Some way to latch it shut?

Simon pushed the door open with such sudden force it threw her onto the floor. He was on her instantly, pulling at her sweater. "Ha! Knew I'd get you on your back sooner or later. You could have saved us both a lot of trouble. But that was rather invigorating, wasn't it?"

He bent closer to put his slobbering lips on hers.

It took only the slightest shift of her head to free her mouth for a scream. She opened her mouth wide. Then closed it. Hard.

It was Simon who emitted the scream. Really more of a roar. "You bit me! You—" His words were muffled by his hand covering his bleeding lip.

With his loosened grip Felicity was able to twist and shove under him, knocking him aside. He made a feeble lunge to recover his position, but at that moment the church door flung open and an irate redhead stepped forward, her hair streaming out like an avenging Boudicca and her green eyes blazing. "Simon! What is this almighty row? Are you trying to summon the whole population of the Broads?" She strode across the floor and yanked him to his feet. "Leave it to you to make a dog's dinner of the simplest task.

"I said *bring her in*. I did not say to rape her. What you get up to on your own time is your business. But this is *my* time and I will not have you screwing it up."

Simon hung his head and muttered something inaudible. Angela turned to Felicity. "Are you all right? He didn't hurt you, did he?"

The words were solicitous. The tone was cold. "I'm fine." Felicity picked herself up and began brushing at her clothing. She longed for a hot shower: boiling and steaming, pounding down on her head. Enough to sterilize. She could easily have given in to hysterics, but she refused to give Simon the pleasure. She turned sharply and walked toward the door. She expected to be stopped at any moment. It was clear that Angela was up to no good—had obviously been behind Ricky and Simon's doings. But why? And what else was she responsible for? Could she be a thief? A murderer?

If so, why was she letting Felicity walk out free? Felicity resisted the urge to run. She expected to feel a knife or a gun at her back at any moment. She was certain that if Angela were wielding the weapon she would make a clean job of it.

She tensed as she reached the door. This would be the moment. She threw the door wide and leaped out into the clean, fresh air, filling her lungs with great gulps. It was raining. Not the hot shower she longed for, but it would do. She raised her face to the blessed cleansing and flung out her hands, letting the drops pool in her palms.

But she mustn't dally. She almost skipped to the car and yanked the door open. "Mother—" Cynthia lay slumped in the back seat, her wrists and ankles bound, a small trickle of blood oozing from her forehead.

Chapter 34

"Sorry about that." Angela indicated Cynthia's limp form with a nod of her head as she started the engine of the hired car. "Your mother's a feisty one, though, isn't she? I see where you get it from. I didn't mean to hit her quite so hard with that rock, but she really wasn't willing to cooperate with me. Don't worry. She'll be all right. Probably a bad headache, but we'll get her some paracetamol."

"Where are you taking us?" Felicity spat from the back seat, straining against the leather thong binding her wrists, in spite of the fact that she knew it was hopeless.

"For a lovely drive. Just sit back and relax. Enjoy the scenery. A bit soggy, I know. I apologize that the rain blocks so much of the view."

"Where's Antony? What have you done with him?"

"He's quite safe. As you will be if you behave."

"But why are you doing this?"

"That's enough." Angela flipped the radio on. "*Afternoon on 3*, my favorite. And I don't like having my listening interrupted." She turned the volume up.

Felicity adjusted her position under the seat belt which Angela had snapped into place as an additional restraint, and reached her bound hands over to grasp Cynthia's. They were icy cold. But not lifeless. She felt a faint stirring as she squeezed her mother's hands.

"It's all right, Mom. Hold on. We'll be all right," she murmured softly under the soaring piano obligato of a concerto—by Bloch, the presenter's voice had informed them.

She didn't know whether or not Cynthia could hear her, but she found her own voice comforting, so she continued, encouraging her mother to consciousness as if Cynthia were a small child and Felicity the mother.

"Please, Mother, come back to me." She tried to rub some warmth into her hands. Not easy with her own hands bound. "It'll be all right. We'll get out of this. Somehow." As she continued her cooing monolog, Felicity gradually became aware of how acutely she meant the whispered phrases. Not with any blithe assurance that everything would, indeed, be all right. But the deeper impulse behind her words, that she desperately, achingly longed for her mother to recover—to be her lively, pushing, overbearing self. She missed her mother. With that realization, hot tears spilled from the corners of Felicity's eyes. She couldn't brush them away without letting go of her mother's hands, and she had no intention of doing that. She held on as if to a lifeline and let the tears trickle down her cheeks.

Felicity was amazed at the relief. She felt like she was ten years old again when she had skinned her knees taking a headlong flyer on her skates. Andrew had heard her shrieks, as much in frustration at having fallen as in pain, and carried her into the house, murmuring to her just as she was now doing to her mother. He had carefully swabbed the grit from her wounds, sterilized and bandaged them, without ever once chiding her for refusing to wear her knee pads.

That simple memory of the kindness and security of those days overwhelmed her. Days now so long gone: her father lost to her in another woman's arms, her mother alienated by her own rebellious stubbornness. Would she ever be able to tell them? And Antony, whom she had callously ignored, had been abducted and was being held—where? For what purpose? All this, after the alarms of the day, was too much. The slow trickle became a raging river and her body shook as she gave in to uncontrollable sobs.

The storm of tears passed quickly. Fortunately, it lasted no longer than the forte crescendo of the piano concerto filling the car. Stretching her seat belt to the limit, Felicity put her head on her mother's shoulder, turning her face to dry her tears. A few broken hiccups jerked her body before her breathing steadied.

"Darling, what's wrong? Are you hurt? Ow! I've got a blazing headache."

"Mother! You're awake!" Felicity tried to compel her voice to stay under the crashings of BBC3 which had now turned to the vigor of Mendelssohn's "Scottish Symphony."

"Yes, darling." She frowned at the redheaded woman in the driver's seat. "Why is Angela driving my car? What happened?"

Felicity whispered. "I'm not sure what's happening. Angela hit you. She's holding Antony prisoner."

"Was that why you were crying? It was you crying, wasn't it?" She paused for a moment. "You know, I don't believe I ever heard you cry since you were an infant. And then it was more of a screech than a cry. You didn't like being hungry. And wet diapers offended you. I must say, it made you easy to potty train."

"Mother…" In spite of their dire circumstances, Felicity had to suppress a nervous giggle. Imagine discussing potty training at a time like this. "You're concussed."

"Am I? It's true anyway."

Felicity felt herself blushing. She had never thought about it before. This exasperating woman beside her had changed her diapers, suckled her…

"Mother, was I breastfed?"

"Well, of course, dear. And a bit ahead of my time, I was, too. Happiest time of my life. What a strange question. Ow! I can't turn my head."

Felicity was silent for miles, trying to sort out the pictures in her head, discard those formed by prejudice, replace them with these revelations. She gradually became aware of the surroundings outside the windows. She had been under the impression they were heading for Norwich, but now they had turned north again, skirting the city. Still holding Cynthia's hands, but with less urgency, she sat up and looked out the window. Maybe if she could gain some idea of where they were going she could think of something to do about their circumstances.

Rackheath, a sign pointing south read. Belaugh, a few miles later on. Then Neatishead. It was hopeless. She had never heard of any of them. They could be anywhere in this wild, marshy county. Abruptly Angela swung the car off the main road onto a narrow, tree-lined track like so many others that confusingly criss-crossed the Broads. Angela switched on the headlights as the black clouds overhead loomed even lower, all but touching the hedgerows. Felicity now became aware of another vehicle following them. Undoubtedly the odious Simon driving the vehicle that had taken him and Angela to Ranworth. Felicity shivered. *Please, God, don't let Simon touch me again.*

The radio presenter was introducing the Estonian Philharmonic Orchestra when another turning brought them to a rutted, single-lane path, barely passable by the large car Cynthia had rented. Now Simon's headlights glared in through the back window and Felicity could hear his engine roar over the strains of the music. If she hadn't been bound she might have tried to fling herself from the car, so acute was her flight impulse.

Perhaps a mile up the track the wheels ground on a gravel drive. Angela swung around a curve and before them stood a vast red-brick and limestone manor house, railing-topped bow windows, smaller, traceried windows, and multiple gables lining the front, a turret complete with cupola finishing each end. "Riddlington!" Cynthia gasped.

"Got it in one," Angela said in her derisive voice. "Actually, I thought you might notice."

"But it looks different," Cynthia persisted.

"Back side, isn't it? You don't think Uncle Cyril would give front door keys to the lower orders, do you?"

"*Uncle* Cyril?" Felicity and Cynthia said together.

"Oh, yes. My mother was one of the much-vaunted Mortaras. Married beneath herself, of course. Never mind that my father actually has a bean or two, it's the name that matters, you know. Some very good St Claire's of course, but my father was from the wrong branch. Pity. Still, blood's thicker than water and all that. And what Uncle Cyril doesn't know won't hurt him."

"Won't the staff report to him?"

"Oh, he took the faithful Bicknell to London with him. He would rat, of course, but Mrs Simmons is quite easily bought off. Especially since Simon does all the cooking and she can stay cozy with her feet up reading her Mills and Boons. I brought her a truckload of Barbara Cartland this week. She'll be far too busy galloping over the moors on the back of a white horse by moonlight to have a clue what's going on upstairs." Angela's laughter contained a note of pure pleasure at the idea.

"But there were other servants. Cyril had a large staff," Cynthia protested.

"Locals. Don't live in. Only come when the lord and master is in residence." Angela snatched up her purse and got out of the car. "Come on, now." She yanked the back door open, unbound Cynthia's feet and snapped her seat belt free, then walked to the other side of the car and performed the same service for Felicity, leaving only the prisoners' hands bound. "Out you get. Mind your head."

Felicity was quite willing to obey when she saw that Simon had swept on around them and was heading toward one of the outbuildings. Probably used the former stable block for a garage, she assumed. They crunched across the gravel toward the house. Felicity gaped when a timbered bridge led to the door. "A moat! I don't believe it."

"It's quite true." Angela seemed delighted to have impressed her captive. "But, sadly, no alligators, I'm afraid."

Angela produced a key and ushered them in the massive side door under an arch inscribed 1607. Heavy draperies were pulled across every window, rendering the rooms as dark as St Helen's tower had been. Darker, Felicity realized, as she barely avoided bumping into a table placed in the center of the room. "Careful," Angela barked. "Everything here is priceless. Or a reasonable imitation." Built in the days before hallways were invented, each room opened onto the next. "Here." Angela led into the great hall where she flicked on a dim electric light. A heavily carved black oak stairway branched before them. Huge, dark portraits, undoubtedly of Mortara ancestors, lined the stairwell and the gallery above it. Angela all but prodded them up the right-hand flight.

At the top, Cynthia spoke. "Oh, this was my bedroom."

"Ah, the Chinese room. Cozy, isn't it? The wallpaper's original seventeenth century, you know." Angela looked to the far end of the hall. "I am surprised Uncle put you here, given that his room is down the hall and around the corner." She gave a meaningful pause. "Next to the Peter the Great room."

Felicity almost choked. "Peter the Great room. Peter the Great stayed here?"

"That's the story. Although, as a professional researcher I'm honor bound to say it can't be authenticated. Still, one of our ancestors," she paused and eyed the row of portraits. "That one—fourth on the right—was an attaché to the Ambassador to Russia, so it's just possible." She pushed them along another dark corridor. "Sorry I can't offer you quite such sumptuous accommodation this time. Up you go."

This stairway, unlike the grand Jacobean showpiece of the entrance staircase, was dark and narrow with shallow steps; obviously designed to be trodden only by servants. And the next one was even narrower and the ceiling lower, obliging Felicity to stoop to keep from banging her head. Angela took them to a small room with two iron beds, a small, bare table, and a single straight-backed chair. "Not the Chinese room, I know. But it's quite clean and almost warm. And I'm sure Simon will be only too happy to bring you a pot of tea and one of his excellent steak and kidney pies."

"No!" Felicity almost shouted. "Tell him not to bother."

Cynthia was more practical. "Frankly, darling, I'm starving."

Angela laughed. "Don't worry, I'll give him what-for. The plan was for a simple abduction. His little sideshow was pure entrepreneurism. Or showmanship, I suppose—he feels he has to prove something to uphold the family honor."

"But—" Felicity began, then bit her tongue.

Suddenly Angela turned toward her, brandishing the knife she pulled from her purse. Felicity jumped back, almost knocking Cynthia over. Angela gave another peel of laughter. "Oh, don't be so melodramatic." She reached out, grabbed Felicity's bound hands and cut the thongs, then did the same for Cynthia. "I really don't think these are necessary any longer, and you are our guests."

"But why? What do you want with us? We haven't done anything. We don't know anything," protested Felicity.

Angela stood in front of the door, her hands on her hips, surveying them. "No, you're quite right, aren't you? You're really quite useless. Such a shame you had to stick your nose in. But then, I suppose that's all just as well. You're such a waste of space you won't be missed."

"Just wait until Cyril—" Cynthia began.

"Oh, yes, I was forgetting my esteemed Uncle Cyril. So wrapped up in his power and his secret order. So proud of his precious art collection. Just wait until he sees mine. Then we'll see who's in line..." She stopped herself, then continued with a little shake as if to recall the words. "Oh, well, what Uncle

Cyril doesn't know won't hurt him. Although it's quite likely to hurt *you*. You're worthless, but we have excellent value in your Father Antony. I'm certain Rempstone and Walsingham will be quite happy to exchange their precious icons for the life of such a beloved priest. Since my cousins were so cack-handed at their attempts at burglary I'm sure my more direct approach will succeed."

"Antony would never agree to such a thing!" Felicity advanced a step forward. "Especially not if you hurt us."

"Oh, I don't think he'll have much to say about it. And if he did he would agree to anything that would get him out and about—free to save his lady love."

"What?" Felicity grabbed the back of the single chair next to her for support. "Love? I'm not..."

Angela gave another shout of her explosive, mocking laughter. "You can't be that stupid. Even when he was heavily concussed you were all he could talk about."

Felicity only heard one thing. "*Was*. You said *was* concussed. He's OK now?"

"Oh, fully recovered, my dear, have no worries. Quite well enough to make some most heart-wrenching phone calls for us. I'm sure he'll be back at his monastery in plenty of time for whatever Easter hocus-pocus he wants to perform with his bearded Russian friend. Without *my* icon, of course, but I'm sure they'll make do." There was a footstep on the floor behind her. "Well, I'd love to stay and chat, but here's your supper tray, right on schedule. Just see what good service we manage here."

Angela stepped aside to admit Simon bearing a heavily laden tray from which rich smells of meat, garlic, and thyme emitted. He put the tray on the table and paused for a lengthy, undressing leer at Felicity. He licked his lips, then threw his head back and laughed. "Only teasing. Wouldn't want to put you off your dinner."

Her hand on the door, Angela turned back, waving a heavy,

antique key. "Remember, you are four storeys up with a moat below. Not even a vine to climb down, so don't be tempted. Just make yourselves comfortable. Oh, yes, there are chamber pots under the beds. We offer every convenience." She had almost shut the door when she stuck her head in one more time. "Oh, and you can keep your mobiles. They don't work out here. No reception for miles around." At last she closed the door. Felicity and Cynthia stood rooted, listening to the key turn in the lock and the footsteps retreat down the creaking wooden stairs.

Then they fell on the steaming, flaky meat pie, full of chunks of tender, juicy steak and delicate mushrooms in a golden, buttery puff pastry. "I don't even care if the repugnant Simon put poison in it. Better to die of that than of starvation," Felicity said between mouthfuls. Besides, she thought, Simon was too proud of his cooking to spoil it with poison.

When the last drops of gravy were gone from their plates, Cynthia picked up the satiny brown box Simon had placed beside the tray. "Belgian chocolate." She slid the brown silk bow off. "Mmm. Nehaus. The best." She lifted the lid and an intoxicating rich bouquet filled the air. "Oh, bless Cyril. What stores he keeps. I wonder how Simon managed to purloin the key." She bit into a dark chocolate triangle filled with smooth vanilla cream wrapped in a crunchy nougantine. "Oh, heaven." She pushed the box across the table to Felicity.

Sometime later, replete with rich food and sumptuous chocolate, both women lay, propped on pillows, on their squeaking iron beds. In spite of the danger of their situation and Antony's—or perhaps because of the danger—Felicity knew there would never be a better time for what she had to say. There might not be any more time, period. "Uh, Mom, I want you to know. I've forgiven you for abandoning me."

Cynthia gasped and rolled to her side to stare at her daughter. "You what? Abandoned? I was always there."

Felicity pushed herself to a more upright position. "Always.

'There' being your office. Your office at the firm all day. Your office at home all night. I can't imagine how my brothers and I got conceived. Dad must have made love to you while you read a casebook."

To Felicity's amazement, her mother's voice choked. "You don't know anything about it."

"I know you abandoned your family emotionally. Why have us if you didn't want to be involved?"

Cynthia was quiet so long Felicity thought she wasn't going to answer. Then, "I was so determined our family wouldn't be dysfunctional. And I failed so miserably. More with you than with Jeff or Charlie. Most of all, I wanted to spare my daughter from a childhood like mine. And it was good when you were tiny. But then—"

"What do you mean, a childhood like yours? Your childhood was perfect. I remember all the stories: the family farm where you grew up, your uncle teaching you to milk cows and squirt milk to the cats; the apple orchard with the tree house your grandfather built for you where you went to read; the old shack at the foot of the pasture under the hill where—"

"Where I would run to hide when my father took to one of his rages." Felicity was shocked by the bitterness in her mother's voice. "He never actually beat me. Only Billy—who joined the army on his eighteenth birthday and was killed in Vietnam. But I was never sure he wouldn't. I wasn't taking any chances. So I always ran at the first outburst."

She pulled up her sleeve revealing the jagged silver scar on her wrist. "You asked about this when you were little. I told you I tangled with a barbed wire fence. I didn't tell you I did it running from my father."

"But why? Why did he do it?"

"Why was he a rageaholic? I never understood as a child, of course. But I studied it later, almost majored in psychology in college. Like any obsessive-compulsive disorder—alcoholism, kleptomania, compulsive overeating—the psychologists would say he was responding to trauma or pain in his own childhood. Textbook. I expect his father beat him before he was killed in Germany. These things go on generation after generation. I was determined it would stop with me. Our family wouldn't be like that.

"All those years of counseling. And it seemed to have paid off until Billy was killed."

"Your brother."

"No, yours. Named for my brother." The silence throbbed in the room. Felicity was too amazed even to gasp. Cynthia covered her face. Eventually the words came, slowly as if in a dream, muffled by her hands. "Our first child. He had the bluest eyes you've ever seen. And the sweetest smile.

"It was all my fault. We were going for a walk. I had stopped to chat to a friend. I was just pregnant with Charlie and she wanted to hear about my morning sickness. Billy got restless and chased a kitten into the street.

"He was killed right before my eyes. Just ready for kindergarten. A golden, precious child. And I killed him."

Felicity slipped from her bed and nestled close to Cynthia, holding her shaking body. There were no tears; no sobs. Just the convulsions wracking her body. "No, Mom. It was an accident. It wasn't your fault." And like earlier to the unconscious Cynthia, Felicity continued to murmur, to soothe.

At last the shuddering calmed to a slight tremble. "Mother, that was so horrible for you. I understand you would never really get over it. Or want to talk about it. But you had Charlie and Jeff."

"Yes. And then I had you—the icing on the cake. I always wanted a daughter."

"Then why—"

"Why wasn't I a better mother? Even after more children, even with the counseling, I was haunted by that moment. I kept hearing the sounds in my sleep. Not dreams, really. Just the sounds. The squealing tires. The thud of his little body.

"There was only one thing that made the sounds go away. Work. I had to have absolute control of everything in my life. Work harder. Be better organized. I didn't dare let my guard down for one minute or the sounds would return." She clapped her hands over her ears and shook her head.

Felicity sank back on the pillows, exhausted with the pain of hearing her mother's story and the realization that flooded her. All the times she thought she despised her mother—now she saw that she didn't despise her. Really never had. Misunderstood her, yes. Had been hurt by being shut out, yes. But she had never truly hated her mother.

The release was so great she could have jumped from the bed and danced around the room. Only the overwhelming comprehension kept her immobile. The understanding of how much she wanted to be a real daughter to her mother. But was it too late?

Chapter 35

Tuesday in Holy Week

At some point in that long night Felicity slipped from the narrow bed beside her mother's warm, sleeping body and slid under the cool covers of her own to fall finally into an exhausted sleep. And that was when Mother Julian came to her. She walked right into the little locked room as naturally as if it were her own sunny cell, and sat on the bare, straight chair, her hands folded serenely in her lap, her smooth oval face framed in a soft grey veil. She smiled at Felicity. Julian, who had encountered such a shining vision of God as our Mother, smiled at Felicity who had taken her own mother into her heart. And then she spoke: *On one occasion the good Lord said, 'Everything is going to be all right.' On another, 'You will see for yourself that every sort of thing will be all right.' … This is his meaning: 'Everything will be all right.' We are to know that the least thing will not be forgotten.*

"*All shall be well, and all shall be well, and all manner of thing shall be well.*"

The figure faded to become Mary, holding her Son on her lap, pointing to him with a long, slender finger as she did in so many icons. And then it seemed that the hand was beckoning to Felicity, urging her to something.

Felicity woke slowly, sweetly with a sense of well-being. And then she opened her eyes and remembered where she was. She padded across the room on bare feet to pull the curtain back from the small leaded window. Rays of pink and gold streaked the sky. A chill shook her body. She hurried back to bed. She was sitting snugly tucked up when she saw it. On the wall across from her bed, above the chair where her dream visitors had sat, a small icon hung. She blinked to be sure. Had that been there last night? It was possible that she had missed it, but she was so certain the walls had been bare. She remembered Sir Robert recounting the stories of icons miraculously showing up in a village. But those were ancient Russian tales. She had simply overlooked it in the dim light last night, surely. Still, its presence was comforting.

As was the presence of her mother sleeping soundly so near her. Felicity was thankful for such tranquility as they teetered on the precipice of she knew not what. But she didn't want to think about the chasm that yawned before her. She thought instead about the fact that this was Tuesday in Holy Week. Back at the Community of the Transfiguration all would be in peaceful order with the full round of the daily office punctuated by long periods of silence, and meals, of course. The food was almost as important as the prayers. It would have started yesterday at sunrise: Matins, mass, breakfast—Felicity could taste the porridge with golden syrup—then Father Clement's Holy Week lecture, midmorning tea, midday office... her mind carried on in the soothing pattern: Lunch—vegetarian, of course—then private reading or strolling in the garden before afternoon tea, then another lecture, followed by evening prayers, dinner and Compline bringing to a close its serenely ordered day.

She glanced at the golden streaks hitting the panes of her window. Matins would be over now, mass just beginning. Her daydream had planted her so firmly in the incense-filled church back at the Community that at first she thought the simple chime of a bell over her head was part of her imagining. Then it came again. More clearly this time. She held her breath and waited. One more. As she knew there would be. Automatically she crossed herself and bowed her head.

She held her breath, waiting, the familiar words running in her mind: *Likewise, after supper he took the cup ... Do this ... .in remembrance of me.* And then again: The bell for the genuflection. The bell for the elevation of the chalice. Felicity crossed herself. The bell for the genuflection. She bowed again. Someone was celebrating mass. Right above her head. Someone had consecrated the body and blood of Christ exactly as it was done unfailingly at the Community of the Transfiguration. And at the exact time it would be done there.

Felicity knew only one priest who was that precise. "Antony!" she cried. Last night's water jug sat empty on the table. She grabbed it, jumped back up on her bed and thumped on the ceiling.

"What on earth are you doing?" Cynthia yawned and stretched.

"I'm signaling Antony. He's there, Mother! Right over us."

"Nonsense, darling. there's nothing above us. We're at the top of the stairs."

Three dull thuds answered Felicity's knocking, although they seemed less directly overhead than she had thought the bells to be. Still, he had answered. "See, what did I tell you? There must be an attic room. An old house like this would very likely have a priest's hole or something. I'll bet the Mortaras were recusants in Jacobean days. I bet there's a hidden chapel up there." She thought for a moment. "Yes, there has to be, if Antony had consecration bells."

She pulled on jeans and a shirt, not bothering with shoes, ran to the window and wrenched it open. There was just room for her to wedge her shoulders out as she leaned far to one side and then the other. They were, indeed, at the very top of a sheer brick wall, as Angela had said. If she could just spot a window to tell her where Antony was … She stretched farther and twisted, gazing upward to survey the roof beyond the ornamented gable over her head. "Careful!" Cynthia cried and grabbed Felicity's ankles.

Felicity reached an arm up. If she could grasp the edge of

the parapet she could swing herself onto the roof. If she could only see where to go from there. If no window, surely an air vent. There must be an aperture of some sort. But the roof line was unbroken.

And then she knew. She ducked back into the room. "Mother, I know where Antony is. I'm going to him."

"Don't be crazy. You don't know that was Antony. It could have been anybody, or anything. Birds hopping on a roof can make an amazing thumping."

"Mother, that wasn't a bird. It was Antony. Signaling me."

"You told me how Simon attacked you, darling. How do you know it wasn't him, egging you on to finish what he started yesterday?"

"It was Antony. I know." She wasn't sure that she could have explained how she knew, and anyway, there was no time to explain. But she did know. She was sure. "You hold one foot to steady me. I can balance on the windowsill then swing one leg over the parapet to get on the roof. He has to be in the turret. An attic room hidden under the cupola."

"But how will you get to him? He'll be locked in."

Felicity had thought of the same thing herself, but she wasn't going to be this close to Antony and not make an attempt. "I'll find a way."

"What if Angela or Simon come up with a breakfast tray?"

Good point. Felicity thought. She thrust the water jug into Cynthia's hands. "Stand behind the door and bean them."

A mischievous grin spread over Cynthia's face. "With pleasure."

Getting her body out the window and balancing on the sill from the cramped position of exiting through such a narrow window was more difficult than she had bargained for. As Felicity reached upward, groping for a purchase for her fingers—anything to hold onto to pull herself upward—she realized it couldn't be done without being in grave danger of simply propelling herself out to a sheer drop. *Don't look down,* she told herself.

Inevitably, she looked down. And there was the answer. The decorative railing topping the three-storey high bay window below her would be an easy drop. From there she could straighten herself, hold to the window casing, stretch one leg back up to the sill and swing the other over the parapet. Not much more of a stretch than working at the high barre. Not for the first time she blessed the Providence that had provided her with long legs.

She ducked back into the room to put her new exit strategy into operation. "Pray," she said to her mother. Face down, feet first, she slithered like a backward earthworm over the sill with Cynthia clutching her wrists. The sill cut into her stomach, her feet kicked the empty air. Now she was hanging, clinging to the sill with both hands. "OK, Mom, let go."

It was a second before Cynthia released her grasp.

Felicity hung for a moment like a trapeze artist, her bare toes probing frantically for the railing. Had she miscalculated the length of the drop? She knew she didn't have a very good sense of distance, but surely she couldn't be that far off. If only she dared to crane her neck and look down. Then she felt her grip slipping. She could look or drop in blind faith.

She looked. She had only miscalculated by inches. The railing was actually higher than she had thought. And to her left. Her foot found a purchase, taking the weight of her body, and she was able to relax her straining arms. Then, twisting slightly, she brought her right foot over to the railing and she could straighten up.

And stretch. One foot on the railing. One foot back on the window, one hand gripping the window, the other reaching up, up, up to the edge of the parapet. The brick was rough, cool and slightly damp under her fingers. Even if she looked up she couldn't get an angle to see how much further she needed to go. Her face was flat against the brick wall. It felt far rougher to her cheek than to her fingers. At last, the top of her fingers brushed the stone facing on the parapet. Progress, but not good enough. She had to get her fingers over the top. Far enough over for a solid grip.

She needed another three or four inches. She rose onto the ball of her foot. That gave her the four inches at least. But once again she had miscalculated. She could feel the top, but not grip it. Did she dare transfer all her weight to her right foot on the windowsill and lunge upwards with only one hand having a firm hold? She was gathering her energy, focusing her concentration, when she heard something that sent chills down her spine.

A crunching on the gravel walk below her. Someone in the house was up and about. And they could look upward at any moment. She could assume they were walking away from the house at this second, but they could turn in the next heartbeat. And then she heard the distant roar of a motor approaching. A car was coming up the drive. She had no choice.

She flexed her knees and shot her body upward. Her right hand caught a firm hold, her left hand next, followed by her left leg. And there she stuck, kicking her right leg into thin air with nothing to give her that last ounce of momentum to pull herself over. She was flopping like a beached fish.

Then she felt strong hands gripping her, hauling her over the last inches. She lay on the roof behind the parapet gasping for air, her overstretched muscles shrieking with cramp. "What do you think you're doing? I can't believe even you could be so insane!" a melodic tenor voice growled in her ear.

She rolled over onto her back, looking up into Antony's face with nothing but blue sky behind him. "I'm rescuing you. And a lot of thanks I get for my trouble."

"I'm not sure how this is rescuing me. The view is great,

but all exits are very thoroughly locked. Still," he grinned that lopsided grin she had missed so much, "I'm glad you're here."

"You're glad to see me?" She couldn't help smiling.

"That, too, but I want you to see this. You'll think it worth the climb, I believe."

"Keep down. There's someone down there."

"Probably Mrs Simmons going to meet the postman." He started crawling toward the turret on his hands and knees. "Around this way. I started prying at the vent cover when I got your signal. I foolishly thought you wanted me to come to you."

"You knew it was me?"

"Well, it seemed logical. Why would Angela or Simon be bashing the walls when they have my head available for batting practice?"

"It wasn't Simon that hit you. It was Ricky."

"Who?"

"I'll explain later." They had reached the back side of the tower. An aperture that couldn't be much more than a foot square gazed like an empty eye socket a few feet up. "You got through *that*?"

"Your head first, then scrunch your shoulders. Insert one side at a time."

Felicity was doubtful, but amazingly, it worked. And with Antony pushing from behind she was inside in a moment. She sprang to her feet and stood gaping at the amazing sight before her.

"Um, how about giving a hand?"

Her astonishment had kept her momentarily rooted to the spot. At Antony's voice she whirled hastily to help him. His head and shoulders through, he was stuck at the waist. One good tug and he rolled into the tiny turret attic. Then he was standing before her. Gaunt and rumpled, but alive. She threw her arms around him. "Oh, Antony! I was afraid you were dead!" She bit her lip. There was no time for tears.

"No, no. Far from it. Battered, but nothing broken."

"I'm so thankful." She pulled away and surveyed him at arms' length for several moments before turning back to the room. "What *is* this place?"

"Fantastic, isn't it?" Felicity looked around with her mouth open. This tiny, dark room was perhaps the most elaborate chapel she had ever seen. Candles flickered on walls hung with gold-threaded tapestries and gilt-leafed icons; magnificent paraments adorned altar, pulpit and lectern; the engraved golden chalice on the altar seemed to glow as if it held not wine, but fire. And in her mind she saw what she had only heard before with the ringing of the bells: Antony, robed in a heavily embroidered chasuble, bowing before the altar. Alone in that sumptuous room, faithfully performing the task that was life and breath to him. The fiery images before her wavered as tears filled her eyes.

As the vision cleared she hastily wiped her eyes and turned back to the real Antony who stood at her side, unwashed, unshaven and disheveled, his shirt crumpled, but infinitely more dear than any vision.

She started to reach out to him, but he redirected her gaze. "Look," he pointed to the reredos, where an icon displayed on the shelf behind the altar held pride of place.

"Our Lady of the Transfiguration," she gasped. Then she looked again. All the objects in the room were marked with Maltese crosses. Even the chasuble and stole Antony had hastily hung over the altar rail were embroidered with the emblem of the Knights of Malta embellished with a nine-pointed star and trailing vines.

Her gaze came back to the uncovered elements on the altar. "Oh, but I interrupted mass," she said.

"Just ready for the distribution," he said.

Antony turned, slipped on the abandoned vestments and

approached the altar. Felicity knelt at the rail and opened her mouth. "The body of Christ." He placed the broken piece of bread on her tongue.

When the mass was ended, Antony replaced chasuble and stole in the chest where he had found them. "Is this a working chapel?" Felicity asked in wonder.

"Long ago. I think Angela locked me in here as a sort of taunt."

"But you had communion elements."

"Roll and wine, saved from my dinner."

She looked at the flickering candles. "And matches?"

Antony opened a small cupboard and produced a black rock and piece of metal. "Flint and steel. An indication of how long ago this chapel was used for its proper purpose." He stepped to the wall and flicked the switch which turned on the single electric bulb. "Angela used more conventional means for viewing her collection."

Felicity's wonder increased as she gazed at the multitude of witnesses around her. She knew icons existed of every saint and hero of the faith, but these were all on one theme. All were representations of holy motherhood. The Mother of God showing in every gesture love for her Son, who in turn offered love to the world. Suddenly she wanted to say thank you to each likeness. Thank you for her own mother. Thank you that she had been able to open herself to her own mother's love. And to return it.

Antony sat beside her on the bench that served as a miniature pew in the crowded room. "How did you wind up here?"

"I heard the bells."

"No, I mean at Riddlington."

"Oh," She pulled Ricky's camera phone from her pocket and showed him the pictures. Seeing them again brought back the terror of all that had brought her to this moment. She put a hand tentatively on Antony's arm and fought for control. "Maurice recognized St Helen's. Angela and Simon caught us there." She could tell him the rest later. She slipped the phone back in her pocket and looked around. "What is this place? It looks like a miniature of the chapel at the Hospital of St John."

"Exactly. An attempt at a replica of their chapel at the fort of Sant' Angelo on Malta, I would guess."

"But hidden away up here in the dark?"

"This place was built right after the Gunpowder Plot—"

"Um, Gunpowder Plot," she interrupted. "Guy Fawkes, 1605."

"'Remember, remember the fifth of November,' well done. When it became known that Fawkes and four other Catholic dissenters attempted to blow up the Houses of Parliament it was rechristened *the Catholic Gunpowder Plot* and King James I harshly enforced the oppression of nonconforming English Catholics. Even harsher than Queen Elizabeth I's strictures."

"And so recusant Catholics started building their own chapels and hiding priests?"

"Exactly."

"But that was..." she stopped to count the centuries, "400 years ago."

"Yes, this collection is the product of a quite different conflict, I would say."

"Looks like the work of a truly compulsive mind. Angela's, at a guess. She said something that made me think she was in competition with Cyril over his art collection."

Antony looked around them. "So you think Angela has been stealing icons to one-up Sir Cyril? And hiding them in a secret room his *his* house? Why would she do that?"

"Did you know he's her uncle? That would make her Neville's cousin. That family pops up everywhere. No wonder a vine is part of their symbol." She grabbed Antony's arm. "Do you think Neville found out about Angela's collecting and she killed him to keep him quiet?"

"I think she would be capable. A real Lady Macbeth."

"Poor Cyril. He's so proud of his family. This will be a terrible blow to him. But at least we've recovered the icon. And in time to get it back before the Triduum."

"Well, we've located it. Recovered might be a premature assessment."

"Oh, yeah." She had been so relieved and happy to be with Antony she had let the fact that they were still prisoners slip out of focus. "Er—what do we do now?"

"What about Ricky's mobile?"

"Angela only let me keep it because there's no reception out here." Even as she said it, she flipped the phone open and pushed the green key. It lit up and showed less than a bar of reception. "See."

Antony was gazing at the metal cupola roof over their heads when Felicity stopped breathing. Steps coming up the turret. She looked around wildly for a place to hide.

But Antony was quicker. He thrust her toward the still-open ventilation hole. She was halfway out when she heard the key scraping in the lock. Antony shoved. She hit the roof with a thud and Antony had the cover replaced before she looked up.

What was going on below in the room where her mother waited? Would Cynthia be served next? Or had a tray-bearer already been there and received a surprise welcome? If Angela had served Cynthia while Simon delivered Antony's breakfast, it would only be moments before her antics were discovered. And then Angela's ban against violence would surely be lifted.

What could she do? It would be far too difficult to return to either room. If Simon caught her out here, flinging her from the parapet would be all too easy. And if Angela did complain he could say she had slipped.

She looked around desperately for a hiding place. And then she glanced up. Just over her head the turret roof rose to a new height, with a metal flagpole extending high above. If she could get up there, would that increase her phone reception enough? Felicity, who knew nothing at all about the mysteries of electronics, entertained a wild hope that the flagpole might somehow act as an antenna.

The cupola roof was rounded metal, but it had wide eaves. After her earlier clamber over the parapet this would be a cakewalk. Of course she would be thoroughly exposed, but she would only need a few seconds. If it worked.

She gripped the eave of the cupola, threw one leg up, pushed with the other foot and she was up, clinging to a six-inch wide rim. She stretched out full length, her body curving to the lines of the roof, grasped the pole with both hands, and pulled. A moment later she was perched on the pinnacle, both legs and one arm wrapped around the pole as she hit 999 on her would be assailant's mobile phone.

Chapter 36

Wednesday of Holy Week

A ntony sat in the back seat of the rental car as it rolled across Norfolk, Lincolnshire, Nottinghamshire and into Yorkshire en route to Kirkthorpe. The ease with which Cynthia had taken to driving on the "wrong" side of the road was truly admirable. But more to be rejoiced over was the feeling of comradeship between the two women in the front seat. He smiled as he watched Felicity's curtain of silky blonde hair, worn loose today, the way he liked it best, turn toward Cynthia's stylish coif of exactly the same golden shade as they shared another family anecdote that in their new aura of understanding suddenly took on the glow of a happy memory.

Antony was more than willing to sit back and let the talk flow over him as he relived the crises of the past days. He explored the back of his head with tentative fingers. Still sore, but the lump was definitely going down—enough to save him from jokes about having a "swollen head".

He still needed to sort out what had happened. Apparently, judging from the somewhat garbled statements he had heard Angela and Simon making to D. I. Marsham yesterday— between castigating each other with every synonym for "fool" in the OED and quite a few which weren't—his abduction had been a quickly cobbled together Plan B to hold him hostage for the desired icons as ransom. Since the plan had failed and Our Lady of the Transfiguration now rested on the seat beside him, he could count a sore head as a small price to pay. Especially when he considered what the ultimate outcome of that nefarious caper would have been, since they could hardly have let him go when it was over.

Certainly Felicity had been the heroine of the hour. Hanging on to that flagpole in the dewy chill until Marsham and his team made it all the way out from Norwich seemed nothing short of superhuman, not to mention her feat of getting up there in the first place.

"Not at all," she had insisted when he said something of that nature to her. "I was loving the view. And the dawn chorus was incredible." Then she had grinned rather shamefacedly and admitted, "Well, to be honest, I was frozen stiff. Not with cold. With fear. Once the adrenaline rush left me I couldn't have moved to save my life. Especially after I made the mistake of looking down and realized how high I really was. Nothing to do but hang on. If Sergeant Caister hadn't risked his neck climbing up there to bring me down with a harness, I'd still be there."

Hours of bureaucratic paper-shuffling and taking of statements had followed back at the police station. Cyril, tied up in meetings in London, had been astonished to find out what had been going on in his home during his absence. Hearing that members of his own family were responsible for the shenanigans nearly sent him into orbit. It took quite a while before he calmed down enough to pay attention to the request for permission to remove the icon.

"Of course I knew the chapel existed," Cyril insisted. "I know all the history of the manor. In detail. But no one has been up there for years." Antony had cleared his throat meaningfully over the speaker phone. "Or so I thought," a subdued Sir Cyril had added. Then he had asked to speak to Cynthia privately, a conversation that had apparently consisted mainly in apologies from his end and assurances that she was unhurt from hers, but had gone on for some time, ending with his promise that he would be with her for Easter.

Back in the cozy parlor of All Hallows, Antony had fussed over Felicity as much as he dared, adjusting the footstool and tucking an Afghan around her as they continued to talk things through.

"So Simon killed Neville? Or did Angela? I'm not clear on what happened." Felicity asked.

"Nor am I. I expect there will be a round of each of them blaming the other and the police will have to sort it out. My money would have been on Lady Macbeth if the body had turned up at King's Lynn. As it is, I suspect Simon followed Neville to St Benet's."

"He was cutting it awfully close. Assuming Simon was the one in the boat that almost crashed into us." Felicity took a long drink of tea. "So how did Neville get to St Benet's? There weren't any stray vehicles parked there, were there?"

Antony shook his head. "I didn't see any. Maybe Simon took him there in the boat. Something else for the police to deal with."

"Yes, but why? Why kill Neville—whoever did it?"

"I think it's pretty clear that it was either Simon or Ricky that Neville caught trying to steal the icon at Rempstone." He said it slowly, willing the pieces to fit together.

"At Angela's behest."

"Right. Then Neville went to King's Lynn and he challenged his cousins and told them he was on to them and it had to stop."

"And they killed him." Felicity shivered and was silent for a moment. Then a wide yawn forced its way out. "Oh, I'm so glad I don't have to worry about any of that any more. I just want to sleep and sleep and sleep."

Antony had been equally thankful that they could put all thoughts of murder behind them. Today he still felt, as he had last night, that he didn't have all the answers, but it was no longer his problem. And Felicity was safe. He didn't have to worry about her any more, either.

A trill of laughter from the front seat confirmed his sense of gratification. He would freely admit to a degree of satisfaction, even triumph. They were returning with the icon in plenty of time to restore it to its place of honor before Patriarch Kirill and his retinue arrived this evening. The ecumenical process had been preserved. The reputation of the Community remained unsullied. Father Anselm had been incoherent with gratitude when Antony rang him from the police station yesterday.

By inadvertently solving the mystery of Neville's murder they could offer the comfort of closure to Cyril and Rupert, even if the answer brought unimaginable grief to the remaining family. And left plenty of questions unanswered.

Marsham had been completely satisfied, even elated, as he charged Angela and Simon—over their protests of innocence. Now all that was left for Marsham was the paperwork, and he could take Easter week off to spend with his family. All the ends nicely tied up.

A happy ending all around, surely.

So what was the source of Antony's niggling unease— the shadow threatening the brightness? Felicity laughed at something her mother said, filling the car with a sensation of the sun coming out from behind dark clouds. And Antony knew.

He and Felicity had managed to snatch only those few moments alone at All Hallows last night. Precious moments of quiet when he could ask her about the success of her discernment undertaking amid all the alarms of the investigation he had pushed her into.

She had turned to him with glowing eyes. "Oh, it was wonderful!" Then she had placed her hand on his arm. He looked at his sleeve now as if the very memory had burned a hole there. "Don't worry. I really think all the disturbance and excitement—not to mention moments of absolute terror—helped me focus more sharply on my decision. That's so important, isn't it? You understand how important it is that I'm absolutely clear on this." He nodded, unable to give words to more questions.

But then, he didn't need to, did he? Her answer shone quite clearly in her countenance, in the assurance of her voice. The contrast between the peace of the cloister and the turmoil of the world couldn't have been made plainer to her. She had made her choice. Felicity had found her calling. He would have to rejoice with her. No matter the pain it cost him.

Then Sister Johanna had joined them bearing a tray of steaming beakers of cocoa and bars of freshly baked flapjack. How was it possible that cocoa and flapjack could have tasted as bitter as gall?

Chapter 37

Maundy Thursday

The next day Felicity awoke slowly. She felt as if she had slept for a week. She turned her head lazily to look at the clock on her bedside table. After two o'clock! It wasn't dark outside, so it had to be two o'clock in the afternoon. The afternoon of Maundy Thursday. Had she really slept for eighteen hours? She had been wrong again. This was neither Hogwarts nor Brigadoon. It was Sleepy Hollow.

Cynthia barely bothered knocking before breezing in with tea and toast. "Oh, darling, I'm so glad you're awake. I hated to disturb you, but I was beginning to worry. You look perfectly bright, though. Wonderful, isn't it, how sleep 'knits up the raveled sleeve of care.'" As she talked she plumped Felicity's pillows, placed the tray on her lap, poured out the tea and plopped herself on the foot on the bed.

"Has Antony been over?" Felicity asked, after a reviving first gulp of tea.

"No, there. hasn't been a peep from anyone today. Very thoughtful to give you some peace and quiet."

Felicity hid her disappointment behind a healthy bite of marmalade-spread toast. "Mmm. And, of course, all the Community is in the Greater Silence now." As they would be until the Easter Proclamation at sunrise Sunday morning. But still, she was surprised Antony hadn't been to see her. Of course, he had the meetings with Patriarch Kirill and his ecumenical entourage who had arrived last night not long after they had returned with the icon. Not to mention the fact that this was the beginning of the Triduum—the Great Three Days of Holy

Week—the high point of the Christian year, where the liturgy would reenact as closely as possible the way Christians had been celebrating Easter since the first century. There were prayers and rehearsals and… well, she could go on making excuses all day, but a hot shower would do her far more good.

If liturgical matters were more important to Antony than she was then that was just fine. After all, she'd been looking forward to this incredible experience through all the forty days of Lent. She had no intention of missing out on a minute of it.

By the time she entered the hushed church a few hours later, Felicity had entirely convinced herself that all the unanswered questions of Antony's feelings toward her and the tangled affairs of the Mortara family and even the unsatisfactory answer to Neville's murder were mundane matters that she could very well put behind her for the rest of her life.

When the Mass of the Lord's Supper began with the cantors in the organ loft singing Duruflé's *Messe cum Jubilo* and the "Kyrie" washed over her, she felt so lifted out of herself she believed her own determination.

The foot washing came as a shock to her. Weeks ago she had been selected as one of the twelve to have their feet washed in an enactment of Christ washing his disciples' feet on that long-ago night when he instituted the Last Supper. Most of the others had taken their place on the long bench between altar and choir before she remembered. She pulled off her shoes and socks and slipped forward as unobtrusively as possible, taking her place on the end of the bench. Sitting there with her head bowed, though, she realized she hadn't been completely unobserved. The young, black-robed, bearded member of the Russian delegation sitting to her right looked at her with eyes that could have burned holes.

She wanted to say to him, *Look, I wasn't that late. And besides, if it weren't for me your precious icon wouldn't be hanging over there under her veil.* Then Father Anselm, an apron tied around his rotund form, knelt on the stone floor before her. She extended her leg and the Father Superior meticulously washed, wiped, and then kissed each offered bare foot.

She had no idea it would be such a powerful experience. As chills shook her and she fought back tears she wanted to cry out, *No, I'm not worthy.* But then Father Anselm picked up his basin and towel and, as the cantors sang the final, echoing strains of "Ubi Caritas"—Where true charity and love are, there is God—she made her barefoot way back toward her seat over the cold stones of the side aisle.

The ecstasy of the moment faded and she shivered. Surely it wasn't just the chill of the granite. She paused in the shadow of a massive pillar and turned quickly. Ah, it wasn't just her imagination that she was being followed, but the reason could hardly have been more innocent. The Russian priest or deacon or whatever he was who had been beside her for the foot washing stood gazing up at the veiled outline of Our Lady of the Transfiguration. It was hard to read his expression beneath his beard, but Felicity imagined he was anticipating the veneration which would take place at the Easter Vigil.

Back in her seat beside her mother, she looked around for Antony. She knew he would be participating in the service, but she hadn't spotted him yet. The hymn "O Thou Who at Thy Eucharist Didst Pray" had begun when she caught his eye, standing with the other gold and white vested priests who would concelebrate. Even though it was unlikely he could have seen it the length of the nave, she tried to send him an encouraging smile, because she remembered his telling her how hard it was for him to sing this hymn "That all thy church might be forever one" since the goal was so far from being fulfilled. Perhaps he did see her, though. Or was it only her imagination that his face softened?

"On the night he was betrayed—which is tonight..." the Eucharistic Prayer commenced.

After all had communed, the procession began. Servers draped a long, gold humeral veil over Father Anselm's shoulders and, with the ends covering his hands, he lifted the ciborium filled with the reserved host. Two thurifers, their thuribles wafting clouds of incense, and eight priests followed. Lights were extinguished as they processed in stately, measured tread down the choir. The faithful followed, all singing in dirge-like tones:

> *Of the glorious body telling, O my tongue, its mysteries*
> *sing,*
> *And the blood, all price excelling, which the world's*
> *eternal King,*
> *In a spotless womb once dwelling, shed for this world's*
> *ransoming …*

In increasing darkness, Felicity followed with the others down the curving stairs at the back of the nave to the crypt where they knelt before the Altar of Repose, especially prepared for this moment. It was ablaze with candles and banked with white and gold flowers. And then Felicity wasn't in the crypt at Kirkthorpe, but in a side chapel at Durham Cathedral where this same observance would be occurring at this moment, and where Antony had first told her about this ancient rite. And where she had been so convinced St Cuthbert had been entombed. Chagrin washed over her. Was she destined always to be so wrong? Was she equally wrong-headed about her determinations now?

She made her way slowly back upstairs. In a darkened, nearly bare church, a lone voice read Psalm 22: "My God, my God, why have you forsaken me …" as the altar and the entire church was stripped of all its paraments, candles, crosses, holy pictures and sacred vessels. Even the carpets were rolled up and carried away. The lights were extinguished one by one and all departed in darkness and silence. The tomb was prepared.

Felicity couldn't believe it when her alarm went off at 3 a.m. *What a dumb mistake*, she thought. Then she remembered. It wasn't a mistake. It was her turn. She had signed up to watch with Christ in the Garden. "Can't you watch with me one hour?" He had chided his sleeping disciples that night in the Garden of Gethsemane.

Felicity felt considerable sympathy for the disciples as she pulled on jeans and sweatshirt and and went out into the cold night air to make her familiar way up the hill to the community grounds. She groped through the stygian silence of the church. Even her sneaker-shod footsteps seemed to reverberate in the thick stillness. Groping the wall for support, she descended the winding stairs to the Altar of Repose. Her first reaction was disappointment. All the way through the black grounds and building she had held firmly in her mind the glorious blaze of candles that would greet her in the crypt as she had last seen it. But now only two candles burned, shedding barely enough light for her to find her way to a small kneeler on the carpet. The glory had departed.

Two fellow ordinands were kneeling, making vague, rounded humps in the shadow of the tomb. Felicity tried to discipline herself. Shouldn't she be meditating on the meaning of the moment? Or praying for the poor and hungry? Or waiting in openness for a divine revelation or something? Instead her mind kept going back to the dark cavern of the ruined mill at St Benet's Abbey with a very mortal body, trying to make sense of the unsatisfyng, tangled tale. She still had trouble seeing Angela and Simon as cold-blooded, calculated killers. And yet, who else was there?

Her companions completed their watch and departed soundlessly. Alone now, surely she could focus her mind on prayer. But how did Angela manage—she sighed with exasperation. She obviously wasn't very good at this business of keeping watch.

At last her time was up and those taking the next watch entered. Felicity rose stiffly, and stretched her cramped legs. So much for stories of ancient monks and nuns praying, keeling on bare stones, through the night. What a wimp she was.

She was halfway down the aisle of the church when she caught her breath. Did that pillar move? Impossible. She was dreaming. But she did walk more quickly through the denuded church. She was halfway across the monastery grounds, headed for the high iron gate, when she was sure she heard a twig snap behind her. She whirled. Nothing there. It had to be her imagination. All the miscreants were behind bars. Still, she broke into a run.

Chapter 38

Good Friday

No matter how much she insisted to herself that all was well, Felicity kept looking over her shoulder the next morning as she and Cynthia made their way up to the silent college refectory for breakfast. They could have managed with toast and cereal in Felicity's apartment, but the CT hot cross buns were legendary and Felicity didn't want to miss out. Besides, she wanted to get another look at her fellow students. If someone was following her last night she certainly wanted to know who and why.

The spicy, currant-studded, honey-glazed rolls lived up to their reputation. Felicity couldn't help approving of the Community of the Transfiguration's definition of fasting: Hot cross buns for breakfast, boiled eggs with bread and butter after the midday service, and something light for supper. Eating her third bun marked with a white cross, Felicity surveyed the silent room of long, well-scrubbed tables, the narrow benches filled with cassock-clad ordinands and their guests. Several ate quickly because the watch lasted until the midday liturgy and they must each take their turn. Others seemed relaxed, sipping their tea. Some brought reading with them to make the silent meal more comfortable. No one looked guilty or furtive. When she did catch someone's eye they smiled or nodded. It had all been her imagination. The suspense was over.

But not for Cynthia. As soon as they were outside the monastery grounds returning to Felicity's flat, she took in a great gulp of air and almost shouted. "Oh, how can you take that silence? My head is absolutely ringing with it. I can't tell you how *caged* I feel."

"Well, Mom, you don't have to stay. Go to London. Have a fling at that shopping you've been wanting to do. There's no need for you to take part in all this liturgy if you don't enjoy it."

"No, no. I don't mean that. Silent meals are a chore. I hate being able to hear people swallowing. But the liturgy is really rather fun, isn't it? Great theater, actually."

Felicity laughed. "I've heard it said some of the churches in London outdo the West End for production quality. And you're quite right, a lot of it grew out of the early church's desire to reenact the events in Christ's life—"

"Never mind that," Cynthia cut her off. "I'm worried about Cyril."

"Oh." Felicity was so surprised she stood, blinking, in the middle of the pavement.

"He told me he'd be here yesterday for this trillium thing."

"Triduum, Mother. Three days, but all one service. Breaks for eating and sleeping, but no—"

Cynthia didn't even notice the interruption. "The college memorial service for Neville isn't until Saturday. But Cyril said he would be here early. I looked for him all evening. I kept expecting him to show up, thought he might have got caught in traffic or something. I keep thinking he'll call me." She pulled her cell phone out of her pocket and stared at the blank screen, shook her head, and stuck it back in.

"You could ring him, Mother."

Cynthia ducked her head. "Well, I know. But…"

Felicity gave a hoot of laughter, then remembered the Silence and clapped a hand over her mouth. "Mother, you're shy! Are you really that far gone on him?"

"I'm not 'gone' at all. But he is a lovely gentleman who is punctilious about keeping his appointments. And with all the turmoil in his family…"

"Exactly, Mother." Felicity began walking toward her apartment again. "He might have been called on to comfort Rupert, or to give a statement to the authorities in Norfolk, or—"

"Or the police have it wrong and whoever murdered Neville and that art expert in London have done him in, too. We aren't next of kin. We wouldn't have been notified." Cynthia was very near to tears. Felicity had never seen her mother in such a state.

"Mother, you're being silly. Of course the police have it right. I'm sure Cyril is fine," she finished lamely.

But Cyril still hadn't made an appearance by noon when the three-hour Good Friday service began with the Preaching of the Passion: A series of three short sermons, interspersed with a period of silence, prayer, and a hymn: "O Come and Mourn with Me Awhile." Then more silence. Followed by the bare bones of a pared down midday office. Felicity couldn't help admiring how still Cynthia managed to remain, sitting beside her. But she was aware at each break in the service of her mother craning her neck and scanning the nearly full church. None of the lights that had been extinguished the night before had been re-lit. Even in the afternoon the church retained the feeling of a tomb.

A few people moved about in the side aisles. With each one Cynthia's head jerked their direction, her eyes wide. Then Felicity would feel her mother's tense body slumping beside her. The Solemn Liturgy continued with readings, psalms and prayers. All stood for the singing of the Passion according to St John by the cantors. At the line "… He gave up his spirit" all genuflected and paused in silence. Cynthia was right. The silence was shouting. The universe shrieking and raging for all who died unfairly, untimely. For all the victims of sin and injustice. A clap of thunder made Felicity jump as if she had been shot. As Sir Robert had been shot.

Felicity was still on her knees while the rest of the congregation was standing, singing, "When I Survey the Wondrous Cross."

A rough, wooden crucifix was carried in for the next part of the service: the Veneration of the Cross. Cantors sang, "Behold the wood of the Cross, whereon was hung the Saviour of the world. O come let us worship," as the medieval ritual of "creeping to the cross" began. Felicity forced her mind back to the present. She really wanted to participate fully in this. She was determined not to let thieves, murders and criminals rob her of the experience.

Walking barefoot on the cold stone floor beside her mother, she made her way forward through the rood screen arch to genuflect in the middle of the choir. She had read the pattern: *Kneel before the cross, kiss the feet of Jesus, then return to seat.* Kneeling at the foot of the cross, though, she was so overcome she found it almost impossible to rise to her feet. Cynthia put her hand under Felicity's arm and lifted her gently.

The priest brought forward the reserved sacrament from the Altar of Repose, "Behold the Lamb of God that takes away the sin of the world."

"Lord, I am not worthy to receive you, but only say the word and I shall be healed." Felicity returned to the altar to receive the reserved host, then departed in silence. The silence of thunder and gunshots.

Chapter 39

Saturday of Holy Week

Felicity awoke with her head ringing. The icons had come to her again last night. Pleading. But for what? Protection? Justice? If only she could remember; but the impression was so vague. Just a compelling sense that there was something she must do.

With that conclusion she jumped out of bed. "Liturgically speaking, Holy Saturday is a non-day," she remembered Father Clement saying once. The only services were to be the daily office, reduced to the barest essentials, and Neville's memorial service. The schedule was for church cleaning. Real work, yet part of the liturgy, as preparing a body for the tomb. Or a tomb for a body. It all seemed to jumble a bit. Anyway, spring cleaning was a time-honored tradition whatever the symbolism. Good hard work. What was there to feel uneasy about?

Then she remembered. The icons in her dream. They had been urging her to action. To take care of their sister. The idea of visions or talking icons was still new to Felicity, but she knew something about the working of the subconscious mind. And she trusted hers. If there was still someone out there with villainous intent—if there had been anything more than an overactive imagination to her alarms since she returned— what better chance to steal the icon than under the guise of cleaning?

Felicity entered the church with some trepidation. She had missed morning prayers. Maybe she was already too late. The dismantled church was empty as a tomb—except today the tomb wasn't empty. Felicity felt leaden with the overwhelming sorrow of it. It must have been like this for the disciples—the bare essentials would be all they could handle. More than they could handle.

Felicity could hardly move. And yet all around her was a hive of activity. Dusters flicked, mops swished, brushes scrubbed. The Greater Silence was broken by a strange cacophony of hissing spray bottles, clinking pails and humming vacuums as priests, including a briefly glimpsed Antony, monks and ordinands went about their duties. Felicity knew she should be in the sacristy polishing silver candlesticks or brass crosses or gold chalices. But she couldn't let the icon out of her sight. That is, the shrouded shape that had been re-hung and veiled by a grateful Father Anselm when they returned.

Then a terrible thought sent a new chill down Felicity's spine. Who was to say what was under that heavy purple veil? It could be a bare block of wood for all anyone would know. She couldn't just walk up and lift the veil. Could she? She didn't really know the rules, but best to be careful. She spotted a pile of dust cloths on the steps up to the high altar. She picked one up and began an industrious dusting of the pillar on which the icon hung, working her way around to the front. Then, rising gradually, she rubbed her way up to the bottom of the veil.

Switching the cloth to her left hand, she flicked the bottom of the veil with her right, lifting it maybe three inches.

"Ahem." She jumped at the sound of someone clearing their throat a few inches behind her ear. It was the young Russian she had sat next to at the foot washing. Again, she felt his eyes bore into her.

Felicity forced a wavery smile, probably making herself look even guiltier. "Er, welcome," she managed. "Um, *dasvatania.*" Did that mean hello in Russian? It sounded vaguely right to her.

"*Zdravstvuite,*" he snapped, and bobbed his head in a sort of bow to her. "Sergeus."

How did he do that without taking his eyes off me? Was that his name? she wondered as she fled to the next stone column and began scrubbing industriously without taking her own eyes completely off the icon. She had seen enough to let her know it wasn't just a block of wood there. She had caught a gleam of gold leaf and a border of the deep red madder that edged Our Lady of the Transfiguration. Surely all was well. She was just being silly.

Silly or not, she kept the icon in view as she worked. Her Russian friend stood for a long time as if rooted to the floor, then at last seemed to drift away as if he rode a cloud of incense.

Eventually, Felicity had to abandon her pretence of assiduous attention to the cleanliness of the ledges and corners of every pillar and pew near the precious icon. She ran home and slipped on a black dress. It was time to join Antony and others in the small college oratory for the memorial service for Neville. Nothing, not even the safety of the icon, took priority over that. Now that the murder had been solved, the police had released his body to the family and there would undoubtedly be a full requiem mass at King's Lynn later. But in this more private, intimate setting his friends would bid him farewell in the place that he loved much as if it had really been his home.

Pale light fell through the leaded windows, making watery pools on the bare floorboards. It was still Lent for a few more hours, so there were no flowers, but the starkness was a powerful statement of the vacuum left by the loss of an active life.

Father Clement, Principal of the College, was conducting the service and Father Antony was assisting. Felicity had barely seen him since their return and her heart caught at the sight of his pale, drawn features. She tried to catch his eye to give him an encouraging smile, but he looked steadily ahead.

Felicity almost jumped off her chair when an elbow poked her in the ribs. "Look who's here, darling." Cynthia, stunning in her simple black dress, whispered in Felicity's ear.

Felicity didn't have to look. No one else could have made Cynthia look so radiant. Felicity nodded to Cyril and turned her attention back to the service. After several brief readings and prayers, Father Clement spoke on how appropriate it was that they were remembering their departed friend on that day because the liturgy for the dead was an Easter liturgy, finding its meaning in the resurrection. Felicity gave a vague assent to his words, but she found it hard to concentrate.

When at last Father Clement prayed, "May the souls of the faithful departed, through the mercy of God, rest in peace," her "Amen" was as heartfelt as any in the room, but it was more of a plea than an affirmation. She simply couldn't feel confident that Neville was resting in peace.

Outside the oratory she shook Cyril's extended hand and muttered her condolences. It came out in a garbled statement of regret for Neville, for Angela, Simon, Ricky… What could one say, really? *Sorry that your family turned out to be such a bad lot?*

Cyril, however, wasn't at all put off, but faced the facts straight on. "Simply appalling, isn't it? And, of course, I bear so much of the blame."

Felicity started to dispute. "Oh, no—"

"No, no. You're very kind, but I know my responsibility. I trained Angela. Took her as if she had been my own daughter rather than my sister's. Taught her art history, nurtured her love of beauty, encouraged her pride in art collecting. I even entered gently into her idea of competing with me. Who would have thought she would take it to such extremes?" And here he choked, undoubtedly realizing, thought Felicity, that rabid collecting, even to the point of stealing, was still a far cry from murder.

Felicity saw that courtesy did not require her to linger, once she had greeted Cyril and offered her condolences. He and Cynthia, who had been holding hands all through the memorial service, had eyes only for each other. With a sense of relief, she murmured a farewell and moved out into the rain-washed day. The storm had cleansed the air as fully as the church had been purified, and the rain still fell.

Then she stopped, looking this way and that, having no idea where she should go, what she should do. Even the church was barred to her. After the cleaning it would have been fully reassembled—every space adorned with flowers, masses of extra candles lined along every ledge, every altar and lectern draped with white satin and cloth of gold. The church was ready—adorned like a bride for her bridegroom. Locked up securely to protect her virginity. Felicity felt entirely helpless. And isolated. There was no one she could even talk to about her misgivings, and nothing definite she could say.

She stood there, letting the rain soak her head and shoulders until the drops ran down her sleeves and dripped off her fingertips. She was the woman of action. But there was nothing to do. Assaulted by a thug, she had outmaneuvered him. Faced with a rapist, she had outrun him. Sealed in by an abductor, she had scaled a parapet. But beset by insubstantial fears and doubts, she felt paralyzed.

Easter was coming. Even now she could sense something akin to a spirit of hilarity about to break out of the silence. The waiting was almost over—the rejoicing about to erupt.

But to Felicity it felt like the tremors of an earthquake rumbling toward her.

Chapter 40

The Great Easter Vigil

They met in total darkness on the wide gravel path in front of the church, not far off four a.m. by Felicity's guess. A lone bird on an overhead branch proclaimed its faith in the approaching dawn, but the sky showed not a streak of promise. At least it had quit raining, but the pre-dawn damp was no less chill.

The circle of gathered faithful, each holding an unlit candle, drew closer as Father Anselm approached the mound of kindling that in a few moments would flame forth as the new Paschal fire. Felicity looked around, trying to guess how many had assembled at this unearthly hour, but the darkness swallowed the outer reaches of the circle. A server knelt to strike a match as Father Anselm proclaimed, "Dear friends in Christ; On this most holy night in which our Lord Jesus passed over from death to life ... we share in his victory over death."

At first Felicity thought the movement she sensed at the church porch no more than a shadow from the flames leaping to the top of the dry kindling. Or even smoke wafting from the pyre. But then her ears detected the familiar slight creak of the hinges beneath the crackle and hiss of the fire, as the "shadow" stole surreptitiously into the newly unlocked church.

Behind her, the ceremony of igniting the Paschal candle from the freshly kindled fire, then lighting all the candles held by the worshippers began as Felicity dashed for the church. The totality of the blackness inside the church made the darkness outside seem like noonday by comparison. Stepping into such a complete absence of light was disorienting. Even though her mind told her the floor was solid stone, Felicity stood motionless, straining to see something—anything—to lessen the sensation of stepping into a complete void.

Which way should she go? She listened, not even breathing, for a sound from her quarry. Then she more felt than saw a movement. By the front right pillar. Where Our Lady of the Transfiguration hung.

In this moment, Felicity found her night vision. Her eyes adjusted to the deep gloom enough to let her creep forward, making what haste she could in the darkness. If that bearded Russian with the burning eyes thought he could undo all they had fought for in order to promote some hidden agenda of his…

Straining her eyes to see, she glimpsed the shadow of gathered darkness, huddled as though it carried something, slipping stealthily across the chancel. She changed tack to cut the intruder off in the north aisle, and had almost closed in on him when the procession entered through the south porch door. "The light of Christ," sang Father Anselm, elevating the Paschal candle he carried. Behind him more than a hundred candle-bearing processors answered as one, "Thanks be to God." The procession snaked forward along the south aisle, bringing the Light into a darkened world.

Felicity had paused only momentarily, but it had been enough to allow her object of pursuit to reach the sacristy door. She flung herself at the door, thrusting her foot over the threshold just as it would have slammed shut.

"The light of Christ."

"Thanks be to God." The procession was drawing nearer.

The door she had jammed open wrenched back. A hand grabbed her roughly and yanked her into the sacristy. Before she had time to recover her balance she heard the sacristy door shut behind her. "Might as well make ourselves comfortable, my dear." He reached out and flicked on the light. "It's a beastly long service."

"Cyril!"

The motion he made with a long-bladed knife for her to sit down was entirely unnecessary. She was too shocked to stand.

"Has it been you all along?"

"Who else would you suggest has the brains for this operation? Surely you wouldn't nominate my feeble niece and her sad minions?"

"But Angela is accused of murder. Surely she isn't willing to take the rap for you?"

"Of course not. But what she doesn't know won't hurt me. I simply played on all her natural instincts of acquisitiveness and competitiveness and let her work, thinking she was outsmarting poor old Uncle Cyril. Delusions of grandeur, of course. Her idea of becoming the first Grand Master of the True Branch of the Knights of Malta was completely unrealistic. But it was easy enough to plant the seed and let sheer human greed and lust for power do the rest."

"So her secret chapel—"

He chuckled unpleasantly. In the church beyond the closed door, the cantor had begun the Exultet: "This is the night…" The recitation of the saving acts of God had begun. The church would still be lit by only two pairs of candles at the reading desk, but cantors and readers would provide sufficient cover for any noise in the sacristy.

"Very nice job she did, didn't she? Even I was impressed. Of course, it was hardly secret. I even managed to plant suggestions for her collection by telling her of artifacts I had discovered that I hoped to acquire one day, and let her do the legwork."

"But why?"

"To revive the family honor, of course. To take my rightful place, as head of the Mortara family, as head of the English

Langue of the Knights of Malta."

"I simply don't understand." Felicity knew the service would go on for ages yet, but just maybe, if she could keep him talking long enough, help would come. Or not. She looked at the dangerous glint on the sharp blade he held.

"Let me enlighten you with a little history lesson, my dear. From the very beginning of the Knights Hospitaller there were Mortaras. Mortaras served in that first hospital in Jerusalem. A Mortara rode in the conquest of Jerusalem beside Brother Gerard in 1099. Mortara was there when the Hospitallers retreated to Cyprus after the fall of Acre in 1291. And when the Order of St John conquered Rhodes in 1309, it was a Mortara who discovered Our Lady of Philermo in her shrine. And who do you think carried Our Lady of Philermo in procession when Emperor Charles V gave the Hospitallers possession of the island of Malta in 1530?"

Felicity's head was spinning with dates and battles. She had made no attempt to follow his boastful tale. But she knew the right answer. Like a child in Sunday school who knows "Jesus" will be the right answer to any question, she said, "Mortara?"

A sneer of disdain curled his lip. "And so it ran through all the centuries until Napoleon ousted the knights from Malta and sent Our Lady to Tsar Paul of Russia who had been illegally elected Grand Master by a group of rebel knights.

"The true French knights formed a Council of the English Langue in 1832, investing the executive power in—"

"Mortara," she ventured to interrupt him

Her following his theme did not appear to displease her captor. "Count Alexander Mortara, to be exact. Who established his headquarters at St John's Gate in Clerkenwell."

"Ah, where Ricky was trying to steal documents."

Now the sneer was not approving. "One cannot 'steal' one's own property."

"So why aren't you Grand Master now?" Felicity risked touching the sore spot.

"By rights I am. But I am not acknowledged—yet—because a rival faction in the English Langue falsely accused Count Alexander of selling knighthoods and expelled him. A smirch on our family name I have vowed to right. The Mortara family crest shall be restored to all its rightful glory—on the unknown effigy at the Temple Church, on the gatehouse at St Benet's Abbey, on—"

"Wait." At the mention of St Benet's Felicity could no longer hold back the accusation that only the threatening steel weapon had kept her from blurting out long ago. "Neville. You killed your own nephew!"

"And gave him the honor of burial with his ancestors. Until that cack-handed policeman dug up Count Alexander, that is."

Felicity would have loved to know how he had known where Alexander had been buried, but she was far more concerned with Neville.

"But why? Why on earth would you kill Nev? He was the best of the lot." And as she said it, she realized she had answered her own question.

"He saw Ricky trying to reclaim *our* icon at Rempstone. When Neville stopped him, Ricky ran off at the mouth and Neville, too clever for his own good by half, saw through my plan. He summoned *me* up to King's Lynn from London. Can you imagine the nerve? He rang me and demanded *I* come to him. I was sure I could make him see sense if I talked to him in person, so I acceded to his demands. Of course, he was too self-righteous to cooperate. He said our own manuscript—which you so kindly deciphered for me—proved the icons weren't ours. He put his own vaunted ideas of right and wrong ahead of family loyalty and honor. So he left me no alternative. He had even found out about Count Alexander."

"But that didn't have anything to do with you." Felicity

struggled to recall the date he had mentioned. "Er—Victorian times."

"All family honor has to do with me. I'll not have my great-grandfather's name dragged through the mud. Some idiot in the popular press would just use it as an argument that I shouldn't be Grand Master when we are the true knights. All this is our rightful property. Our heritage. The matter is indisputabe. It bears our mark." Still holding the knife in one hand he picked up the icon from the table he had laid it on and held it up to exhibit the back.

Felicity gasped. "It did have the insignia. We had guessed…"

"So, you see I had to acquire it before these Russians take it entirely out of reach."

Felicity shook her head. She felt like she'd stumbled into a Borgia family reunion. "Some Victorian ancestor of yours killed some other ancestor and Neville found out about it—I suppose from something else in Rupert's library. So you killed him."

"And buried him with his ancestor. Poetic, don't you think?"

"So that's why Nev wanted us to meet him there? To dig up the evidence or something? Why didn't he just call the police?"

"You are gullible, aren't you, my dear? You and that priest friend of yours make a fine pair. Pity I'll have to break this up in a minute" Behind Cyril the diamonds of the sacristy window shimmered with a rosy glow that heralded the approach of the Easter sunrise. But Felicity's immediate attention was on the knife blade he twitched closer toward her. Cyril's exit would be hers, too.

"Poor Father Antony, so gullible he didn't notice the change in voice after that unfortunate disruption of service. Of course, that's the problem with modern technology. Mobiles can be so unreliable. And I'll admit he was set up to hear his friend's voice when I called back right after our dear Nev was, uh, indisposed. And, of course, I do fancy myself as a rather good mimic."

"You killed Neville in the middle of a telephone conversation, and then rang Antony back?" It was beyond believing.

"Not quite, although I do rather like your scenario. Only a tad less dramatic. I simply took the phone from him and disconnected while I did the deed, then rang back to make arrangements."

"But why have us meet you at St Benet's?"

"You were a bonus, my dear. But I couldn't take a chance with Antony. I didn't know how much Neville had told him. There would have been such symmetry, having them share the same grave. And then those Girl Guides arrived and I'm afraid I had to make a rather shabby job of finishing the burial before my hasty exit. A shame. It was a lovely plan, really, but then, 'the best laid plans of mice and men' and all that."

"And you shot Sir Robert?"

"Pity, that. He really was most highly educated. Of course, that was the problem. Knew too much. Then when your most charming mother told him about the mark on the stolen icon— and he asked me to meet him at the gallery after hours…" He shrugged his shoulders inside his well-tailored suit jacket. "Well, it was really more like suicide than murder. I can't be responsible for other people knowing more than is good for them.

"Like you, my dear." He raised the knife.

The first rays of dawn flamed in the beveled pains of leaded glass to her right. From the room to her left Father Anselm proclaimed loudly, "Alleluia! Christ is risen."

What a moment to die, Felicity thought. Cyril lunged. She dropped to the floor and rolled. The knife just grazed her ear. He would not miss the next thrust.

"He is risen, indeed. Alleluia!" A fanfare of trumpets followed the triumphant shout, then the rejoicing erupted with the cantors singing "Gloria in Excelsis," and the congregation blowing noise makers and the bells pealing forth.

The jubilation echoed around her as Felicity tensed to evade the next attack.

Cyril launched a flying spring. Felicity rolled. But there was no impact of steel.

Instead the room seemed to explode in a cacophony over her head: the wooden door banging open, footsteps pounding, steel clattering on stone, a crash of breaking glass, and in the church, the clanging bells and rejoicing continuing.

Felicity sat up, dazed. Incredibly, Cyril lay at her feet in a pool of splintered glass.

As Felicity shook her head to clear it Detective Inspector Nosterfield jerked Cyril to his feet. "What happened?" she managed to choke out.

Nosterfield snapped handcuffs on Cyril before he spoke. "This one thought he could bash his way out through yon window."

The policeman addressed his prisoner. "Didn't realize how impenetrable a leaded window is, did you?" He addressed Cyril's coldly defiant stare. "The solder joining all that lead caming is strong enough to hold up for hundreds of years."

Nosterfield turned back to Felicity, a slow grin spreading over his face. "Pity you missed the show. Once he broke the glass out by slamming into it the lead stretched like a net and just bounced him back to us."

Nosterfield led his prisoner out the door where two sturdy policemen were assuring worshippers all was under control. Through the open doorway, Felicity could see the church flare into golden beauty as the flowers, altar cloths, gleaming crosses were all illumined by the light of hundreds of candles being lit by ordinands. As Felicity stumbled to her feet she realized the sacristy was now full of fearsome-looking black-robed Russians. Sergeus detached himself from the group and approached her.

"You are all right?"

"Er, yeah, thanks. You called the police?"

He gave a jerky nod. "I keep watch. I see the man remove Our Lady. I report to holy father."

Felicity turned to the Patriarch of all Russia. Should she bow? Curtsey? Kiss his ring? In the end she settled for nodding her head. "Thank you, Father."

"My honor. It seems I protected two ladies." He turned to the table where Cyril had placed Our Lady of the Transfiguration. Elevating her high above his head, he processed back into the church, his attendants following him. They paused at the stand where one of the priests took up the smoking thurible and the procession continued to the pillar where Father Kirill replaced the Mother of God, then made a thorough job of censing her.

Behind them the exultation of the Easter proclamation had quieted and a lone voice prayed, "O God, who made this most holy night to shine with the glory of the Lord's resurrection: Stir up in your Church that Spirit of unity which is given to us through your Spirit..."

It wasn't until Felicity realized that it was Antony praying that her knees gave out.

Chapter 41

Easter Morning

Easter breakfast at the College of the Transfiguration was legendary, but Felicity was still feeling a bit like the survivor of an earthquake, and she wasn't at all certain her stomach was stable enough for the bacon, eggs, and sausage piled on her plate. She reached instead for a piece of dry toast and turned her attention back to her mother, whose appetite apparently hadn't been the least bit subdued by recent revelations.

"Mother, I can't believe you've already managed to book a ticket—for tomorrow, even."

"Well, you know me, darling. Once I've made up my mind I've never seen any reason to let the grass grow."

"So you've decided on the Los Angeles office?"

Cynthia set her coffee cup down slowly. "Well, I suppose it may come to that. I certainly realize now how much to blame I am."

"Mother, what are you saying?"

"I don't know if Andrew will even want to talk. He may be far too happy with his new, er—arrangement. I don't know. But I have to try. I must say that one good thing to come from the debacle with that rat Cyril was that it did help me appreciate Andrew's understated qualities."

Cynthia sighed, then continued, "I don't know whether or not he'll be able to forgive me, but I have to be able to forgive myself." She was quiet for a long time, the boisterous chatter of the hall swirling around them. Finally she looked up. "And, darling, I have to ask. Can you—"

"Oh, Mom, you needn't ask. Of course I forgive you. I just hope you can forgive me for misjudging you so."

Cynthia held up her orange juice glass in a salute. "Cheers, darling."

Felicity clinked hers against the rim. "And also with you, Mom."

The eggs and sausage were long gone by the time Antony entered the crowded refectory. He turned his back on the lone piece of bacon left on the serving tray. Black coffee. Strong. That was what he needed.

He spotted Felicity sitting across from her mother at a table by the window. She sketched him an airy wave and scooted over to make room for him on the end of the bench. He took a deep breath and crossed the teeming room of jubilant people, his own heart so heavy it was an effort to get one foot in front of another.

Once seated, he couldn't have been more thankful for Cynthia's rattling monolog which relieved him of any need to converse. "… of course, I feel terrible about that lovely Sir Robert. If I hadn't told him about that cross emblem… And poor Rupert. I feel so sorry for him. Poor, doddering fool. I suppose he's left as head of the family now. But imagine his own son involved in all this evil, sordid mess! And I just can't get over Angela being such a snake. I do believe she truly loved the art, before it became an obsession for her—egged on by Cyril, of course. Now there's the real snake. He said he did it for his family, but all he really cared about was the power." She paused for a bite of well-mustarded sausage.

Antony took the opportunity to turn to Felicity. He couldn't put it off any longer. "Well, have you decided?"

She blinked, then stared blankly. "Huh? Decided what?"

"Rempstone, Ham Common, St Margaret's? Your calling."

Felicity smiled, then looked down at her plate, almost shyly.

"Oh, that. Yes. Definitely called, I think."

He waited for the blow. Whatever it was, he had to be glad for her.

She looked up into his eyes, grinning broadly. "I definitely want to take the veil. Fingertip net, I think. Over my face, too. With an orange blossom halo."

He blinked. Did he dare trust what he was hearing? "You mean—"

"I think I quite fancy being a vicar's wife. That could be considered a calling, don't you agree?"

He didn't realize until he heard the applause that he had kissed her in the middle of the crowded refectory.

Felicity and Antony will return in

An Unholy Communion

Chapter 1

The black figure plummeted over the edge of the tower and hurtled toward the earth. Then, as the skirt of his cassock flared like a parachute, the scene changed to even more horrifying slow motion. Falling, falling, falling…

Would he never reach the ground? Felicity screamed. But still the figure fell. She screamed again. And woke up.

"Oh, no!"

She grasped her alarm clock and groaned. How could she have overslept this morning of all mornings? She had looked forward to Ascension so much. She had been in Oxford on May morning, and it had been such fun to gather below Magdalen's Great Tower to listen to the college choir singing up the sun. Ascension Day at the College of the Transfiguration was going to be just like that, only better, because she would be up on the tower with her fellow ordinands singing "God has gone up on high" and all the wonderful Ascension hymns she got to sing only once a year.

But now it was all wrong. And the phantom of her nightmare hanging over her like an incubus was the least of it. She had so carefully set her alarm last night. Then failed to switch it on. If her scream hadn't wakened her… Sunrise at 4:49, BBC Weather had said. That gave her 20 minutes.

She thrust off her tangled duvet, splashed water on her face and pulled on her jeans. Still clumsy with sleep, her fingers tangled as she struggled to do up all 39 buttons of her long, black cassock—a task which it never paid to rush. How could she have been so stupid? What was the point of all this scramble if she was late? Her frenzy increased as she searched under her bed for her second shoe.

The moment she flung open her door, however, she found herself engulfed by the fresh, cool air of an early June dawn. She was captivated once again by the spirit of the day that had seemed so far fled. The sky was beginning to brighten and an exultant dawn chorus rang in her ears as she raced up the hill toward the tallest building on the grounds.

She would surely have made it on time if the slick-damp stones under her feet hadn't brought her to disaster in a border of lady's mantle, Canterbury bells and freesia. She picked herself up, brushed impatiently at the stains on her cassock and raced on.

As she started up the steep green mound that led to the tower a triumphant shout and enthusiastic clanging of handbells told her she was too late. Her fellow ordinands had already ascended the tower of Pusey Hall to sing in Ascension morn, celebrating the fortieth day after Easter by hymning Christ upward as he ascended to heaven. Felicity would be relegated to observing from the ground rather than singing from the top of the tower herself.

Putting her frustration aside and determining to make the best of the experience, even though she was by nature a doer rather than a watcher, Felicity sought a reasonably secure footing on the precipitous side of the embankment. At least her fellows would be happy to have an earthly audience as well as the heavenly one. With one more burst of tintinnabulation they began the hymn "Hail thee, festival day". Felicity stood alone in the peaceful garden, gazing upward just as that band of disciples must have done on the hill outside Jerusalem on the first Ascension morning. Trying to picture what that long-ago morn would have been like, Felicity's mind scrolled through the artists' interpretations she had seen—all the way from full-length paintings of a ghostly, white-draped Christ floating in the air, to a silver-gilt plastic cloud with just the nail-pierced soles of Jesus' feet poking through. Her favorite depiction of all, though, was one she had seen once in some cathedral of a fully ascended Christ, looking back through the clouds, with his hand raised in blessing, appearing for all the world as if he were waving just to her.

Felicity wasn't sure whether she was gesturing to the ascended Christ or to her fellow ordinands as she flung her arm upward. "Blessed day to be hallowed forever;/Day when our risen Lord/Rose in the heavens to reign." At the end of the song the exultant singers leant over the parapet shouting and ringing their bells until Felicity wanted to yell at them to be careful—a warning that she herself needed to heed as her vigorous waving almost caused her to lose her footing on the steep hillside covered with wet grass.

> *See, the Conqueror mounts in triumph; see the King in royal state,*
> *Riding on the clouds, His chariot, to His heavenly palace gate.*
> *Hark! the choirs of angel voices joyful alleluias sing,*
> *And the portals high are lifted to receive their heavenly King.*

The next hymn was as much shouted as sung but the words were almost drowned out by the crashing of bells, as the choristers made a determined attempt to rouse any of their fellows who might have been so daft as to think they could sleep in this morning. The sunrise exuberance continued with a shouted versicle from the tower: "The Lord has gone up on high, Alleluia."

Felicity cupped her hands around her mouth to shout the response: "And has led captivity captive, Alleluia."

The tower-top choir began, "Hail the day that sees Him rise, ...Christ, awhile to mortals given, Alleluia!/Reascends His native heaven, Alle—"

The final Alleluia never reached Felicity. It was extinguished by a much nearer shriek. The scream reverberating in Felicity's ears tore a second time from her throat as she saw, in horrifying slow motion, a cassock-clad figure from the back of the choir catapult across the parapet and arc over the side of the tower.

The singing must have continued, as no one on the tower appeared to have seen what was happening. But Felicity heard no music, only the shuddering thud as the body hit the earth. Then, appallingly, rolled down the steep hill to come to rest at her feet.

Too shocked to scream or to run, Felicity stood frozen, staring with unbelieving eyes. This wasn't real. It was her morning's dream replaying in her subconscious. She squeezed her eyes shut so hard they hurt. The ghastly specter would be gone when she opened them.

But it wasn't. This was no dream. Somehow the earlier chimera had translated itself into flesh and blood—a slow trickle of blood, oozing from blue lips and trickling into a matted black beard.

Felicity pulled her mesmerized gaze away from the staring black eyes and followed the line of the out-flung arm to the hand that was almost touching her foot. She jerked her foot away, then moaned as she realized she had kicked the white hand. It opened to release a folded scrap of paper.

Felicity bent to pick it up with fingers so stiff they could hardly grasp the fragment. Shaking, she unfolded it and glanced at the strange emblem drawn there. Then shrieked again, and flung it from her as the paper burst into flame.

About the Author

Donna Fletcher Crow is a former English teacher, a lifelong Anglophile and history buff. She has written more than thirty books, most of them dealing with the history of British Christianity, including *Glastonbury: The Novel of Christian England* and a six-book series, *The Cambridge Chronicles. A Very Private Grave,* Book 1 in *The Monastery Murders* series, was published in 2010.

She and her husband live in Boise, Idaho. They are the parents of four adult children and have ten grandchildren. When not writing or working in her English cottage garden, Donna is kept busy visiting their sons and families who live from coast to coast in the US, and their daughter in Canada who is married to an Anglican priest. Donna is a Companion of the Community of the Resurrection in Mirfield, Yorkshire, England, and a member of The Guild of Our Lady of Walsingham.

You can visit Donna at www.DonnaFletcherCrow.com to learn more about *The Monastery Murders* and her other books.